Romantic Suspense

Danger. Passion. Drama.

Yukon Wilderness Evidence
Darlene L. Turner

Hidden In The Canyon
Jodie Bailey

MILLS & BOON

YUKON WILDERNESS EVIDENCE
© 2024 by Darlene L. Turner
Philippine Copyright 2024
Australian Copyright 2024
New Zealand Copyright 2024

First Published 2023
First Australian Paperback Edition 2023
ISBN 978 1 038 90771 4

HIDDEN IN THE CANYON
© 2024 by Jodie Bailey
Philippine Copyright 2024
Australian Copyright 2024
New Zealand Copyright 2024

First Published 2024
First Australian Paperback Edition 2024
ISBN 978 1 038 90771 4

MIX
Paper | Supporting
responsible forestry
FSC® C001695

Published by
Harlequin Mills & Boon
An imprint of Harlequin Enterprises (Australia) Pty Limited
(ABN 47 001 180 918), a subsidiary of HarperCollins
Publishers Australia Pty Limited
(ABN 36 009 913 517)
Level 19, 201 Elizabeth Street
SYDNEY NSW 2000 AUSTRALIA

Cover art used by arrangement with Harlequin Books S.A.. All rights reserved.

Printed and bound in Australia by McPherson's Printing Group

Yukon Wilderness Evidence

Darlene L. Turner

MILLS & BOON

Darlene L. Turner is an award-winning author who lives with her husband, Jeff, in Ontario, Canada. Her love of suspense began when she read her first Nancy Drew book. She's turned that passion into her writing and believes readers will be captured by her plots, inspired by her strong characters and moved by her inspirational message. Visit Darlene at www.darlenelturner.com, where there's suspense beyond borders.

Visit the Author Profile page
at millsandboon.com.au.

To him which led his people through the wilderness:
for his mercy endureth for ever.
—*Psalms* 136:16

DEDICATION

Susan Snodgrass and Caron Tweet
You are missed, my sweet reader friends

ACKNOWLEDGMENTS

My Lord and Savior, thank You for walking with us through life's wilderness. Knowing You're right beside us brings comfort.

Jeff, your continual support and encouragement make me smile every day. I think it's time for you to retire and become my full-time PR guy. LOL. I love you.

My agent, Tamela Hancock Murray. You're amazing. Thank you for everything you do for me.

My editor, Tina James. I appreciate you! Thanks for believing in me and my stories.

Darlene's Border Patrol, we've had a rough year and lost friends. Please know how much I love and appreciate all of you. xo

My readers, I'm grateful for your support. Thank you for reading my books.

Chapter One

Being alone in a creepy forest wasn't how Dr. Keeley Ash expected to start the late-spring day. Normally, she'd be just finishing her botany class at Carimoose Bay Community Campus, but not today. She had called Professor Audrey Todd to take her place. The older woman knew enough about the Yukon's plant life that she could sub in for Keeley at a moment's notice.

It was now almost noon, and Keeley once again squatted in front of a pair of skeletons, studying the plant and tree life pushing through the remains at the base of the aspen in Yukon's Elimac Forest. She'd been tasked to help determine how long they had been buried. Botany was an underutilized form of forensic science in North America, but thankfully she'd proved her skills after she helped solve a case four years ago. The pollen found on the victim's body had also been discovered on a suspect's boot. This, along with other evidence, helped seal the case and convict the killer. Since then, she'd consulted on cases across the Yukon.

Carimoose Bay's forensic department had called Keeley to use her botany specialization to help date the trees growing among the bones. Investigator Cameron Spokene had allowed her to come along to photograph the scene and surrounding areas before they took plant life samples, including a large portion of the tree. They carefully placed all specimens into cardboard boxes, labeling each appropriately. After measuring and pruning the roots surrounding the bones, she took in-depth pictures of the tree and plants to examine when she returned to her lab. Dr. Everson, the anthropologist, had given Keeley permission to investigate the vegetation, as he had to drive from Whitehorse, which was five hours from her present location. He would arrive soon to extract the bones.

She tucked her trowel into her bag and checked her watch. Thirty minutes had passed since she'd last seen or heard from either Cameron or Constable Hopkins—the officer assigned to secure the scene. They had left to load the evidence in their forensics van and also recheck the crime scene perimeter. Neither had returned.

A prickle skittered over her arms, and she shivered. Where were they?

Keeley rose to her feet and unclipped her radio—a necessary tool for the backcountry—from her belt. She pressed the button. "Cameron, need your help at the scene."

Silence answered.

She tried again. "Where are you?" She paused. "Constable Hopkins?"

Nothing.

Movement rustled the pine branches to her right.

Angst bristled the hairs at the back of her neck and cemented her muscles. She extracted the trowel, held it in a vise grip as a weapon and waited. However, nothing appeared.

Keeley adjusted her camera around her neck and strapped her bag across her body. She headed in the direction Cameron and Constable Hopkins had taken. The relentless fog won the battle with the sun and continued to blanket the region, obstructing her view through the trees.

She glanced over her shoulder to get her bearings, but the scene she'd left minutes ago disappeared behind the foggy wall. How was that even possible so quickly? Great. Getting lost in the wilderness was all she needed.

Ignoring the trepidation warning her to run, she continued deeper into the forest. She required the investigator's help before she signed off and released the chain of custody so his forensics unit could transport the evidence to her lab. There, her trainee, Beth Bower, would begin the process of their examination of the plants. Keeley planned on using this case to help the woman develop her botany skills.

A shadow passed among the trees.

Keeley stopped and listened, her heart pounding. What was that? Animal or human? She held her breath and waited, but the forest stilled.

She pressed her radio button once again. "Cameron, where are you?"

Her voice sounded nearby like an echo. How? She turned in the direction her words had traveled.

She spoke again. Seconds later, she heard herself ask the same question.

Cameron was close, but why wasn't he responding? And where was Constable Hopkins?

Keeley crept through the thick bush and moved branches. She ducked under them and stepped into a small grove. She spoke into her radio again, turning toward her slightly delayed voice.

And drew in a ragged breath.

Cameron lay among the trees, multiple stab wounds on his chest and abdomen.

"No!" Keeley raced toward him and dropped to her knees by his side. She placed both her index and middle fingers on his neck, praying for life. *Please, Lord.*

But the forensic investigator was gone.

A moan filtered through the bush to her right.

She hopped to her feet and glimpsed uniformed legs. "Constable Hopkins!" Keeley rushed to his side and checked his vitals. Weak pulse. Also stab wounds.

He required medical attention—and fast.

She lifted the constable's radio and pressed the button, grasping for words to get paramedics here quickly. "Dispatch, Dr. Keeley Ash requesting medical assistance approximately half a kilometer northeast of the reported remains in the Elimac Forest." She noted the puncture wound in the constable's stomach and pressed her free hand on the injury. She had to slow down the blood loss. "Knife wound in Constable Hopkins's abdominal area."

She waited.

"Dr. Ash, where's Spokene?" Dispatch asked.

Keeley sighed. "I'm afraid he didn't make it. Multiple stab wounds."

"Sending paramedics. Are you safe, Dr. Ash?"

Was she? She checked all directions of the grove. Nothing. "I think so."

"Dr. Ash, this is Constable Layke Jackson. I'm en route from Beaver Creek to your location." His deep voice and a siren thundered through the radio. "Do you have any type of weapon to defend yourself?"

She checked Constable Hopkins's duty belt, but his gun was missing. Not that she wanted to think of discharging a gun. She had taken both self-defense and weaponry classes but prayed she'd never have to use the skills she'd learned. "No," she whispered.

"Stay secluded," Constable Jackson said. "I'm about ten minutes out. Paramedics will be there soon, too."

"Understood." Keeley breathed in deep and exhaled. Great. Alone in the woods with a killer and no weapon. Not a good combination. *God will keep you safe. He's got you.* She prayed that was true.

She studied the scene as she kept a heavy hand on the constable's wound. Keeley noted a trail of trampled brush leading to where Cameron's body lay. Multiple footprints surrounded him. More traveled to where she now knelt. Some of those were her own, and she regretted contaminating the scene, but she had to get to the men quickly. She'd forgotten all protocol. *Stupid, Keeley.*

An idea formed. She could take pictures of the scene while she waited. With her right hand, she lifted the camera hanging around her neck and shot numerous photos, turning the lens in different directions while keeping her left hand on the constable's wound. After help arrived, she'd take samples of the flowers and other plant life. Maybe pollen or seeds had been embedded in the suspect's shoes. This could link them to the scene.

After she took photos for ten minutes, movement sounded behind her. She startled and turned.

Two paramedics and a police constable holding his gun darted to her side.

"What's the situation?"

Keeley's jaw dropped as recognition dawned on her. She stared up at the male paramedic, a man she hadn't seen in five years.

The father to her child.

"Mickey?"

His eyes widened.

The female paramedic stepped forward. "Brett, who's Mickey?"

"Mickey was the nickname my buddies called me back in college." Brett knelt. "Keeley Ash? Wow. It's been years. How are you?"

Keeley swallowed to contain her emotions and gestured toward the fallen officer. "Been better. He's bleeding heavily."

Brett nodded and inched closer, grabbing gauze. "Okay, remove your hand."

She obeyed.

He pressed the gauze on the wound. "Tina, we need to stabilize him and get him to the hospital." The pair attended to the constable.

Keeley had so many questions for Mickey—Brett—but they'd have to wait. She turned to the constable. "Are we safe?"

He holstered his weapon. "I'm Constable Layke Jackson. I checked the area and didn't see any suspects. Can you tell me what happened?"

"I was examining the scene north of here, gathering samples. Cameron and Constable Hopkins went to load the evidence into the forensics van. When they didn't return after thirty minutes, I came looking for them. Found this scene." She shot to her feet. "I need to take plant samples."

"I've read about the cases you've helped with throughout the Yukon. Your botany experience is valuable."

"I wish everyone felt the same as you, Constable Jackson." She peeled off her bloody gloves and removed her bag to grab another pair. "Unfortunately, people forget there's valuable evidence hidden in the plants at a crime scene." She put on her gloves.

"What are you going to do now?"

"Take samples of the plants around Cameron and Constable Hopkins." She gestured toward the forensic investigator. "They also may have pollen under their nails or on their bodies."

Constable Jackson addressed the paramedics. "You both okay? I just want to do another sweep of the area."

They nodded.

Keeley moved carefully to Cameron's body. Her gut told her the suspects still lingered nearby, and she wouldn't let this valuable evidence be destroyed if they returned. She had to act fast. For now, she'd ignore the father to her son, who had just stumbled back into her life. The question was—how long would he stay?

Keeley went into her botany zone and did what she did best—examining the plant life and collecting samples. She inserted them into a small cardboard box from her bag.

Ten minutes later, a noise rustled nearby in the forest. She jumped up and turned around, dread hardening her stomach.

A man dressed in full hunting gear—his hat low on his face and eyes hidden behind dark glasses—stood behind the paramedic, holding a rifle.

He'd entered the area in stealth mode, with none of them hearing him.

Strong arms seized her from behind.

Her knees buckled. *Lord, bring help. Now!*

"Bro, we have a purdy one here," the whispered voice said close to her ear.

His foul breath told Keeley he'd already been drinking.

She recoiled from the rotten combined smell of cigarette smoke and whiskey.

"Isn't she the one we were told to take?" the other asked.

What?

The man behind her lifted a lock of her hair. "Yup. Redhead. She's the one."

Lord, help me!

"Who are you, and how do you know me?" Her question could barely be heard over the man's deep breathing behind her.

Brett stood. "Let her go."

A cool blade pressed against her neck as her heartbeat escalated.

She was going to die, and she'd never see her son again.

Paramedic Brett Ryerson's pulse pounded in his head, not only from the dangerous situation in the forest but also from the woman being held at knifepoint. A woman he let slip through his fingers. "Keels, stay still. I'm here."

A twisted, confused expression flashed over the redhead's face, and Brett remembered. He'd given her the nickname on their first date. He had met the beautiful Keeley at a party in Whitehorse. Brett had just finished his courses when he'd trained to be a police officer. They had dated for a few weeks, and their powerful connection hit him hard, but once he graduated, a constable position he couldn't refuse became available in Ontario. Plus, he wouldn't do a long-distance relationship. He'd seen what it had done to his parents when his mother lived abroad with Doctors in Foreign Lands for months at a time. His parents' marriage suffered from it.

Shortly after moving to Ontario, everything fell apart for Brett. During the first couple of months, he learned quickly that policing wasn't his calling because of his mistake that cost his partner's life. Since he had also studied in the medical field, he resigned to become a paramedic. Thankfully, he had taken the proper science courses in high school and college, so the career fit nicely with his plans to switch occupations. It was the best decision he'd ever made, but the reason he left the force still haunted him today.

A similar situation to what lay in front of him right now. A hostage at knifepoint. Would it end in more deaths, like years ago?

Determination squared his shoulders. Not if he could help it.

Brett took a step forward. "Let Keeley go."

"Is this a reunion?" The hunter with the straggly shoulder-length hair pressed the knife harder into Keeley's neck. A thin line of blood trickled from where the tip punctured her skin.

A tear rolled down her cheek as fear contorted her face.

"Please, you're hurting her. Take me instead." Brett lifted his hands in surrender.

"How touching." The other hunter raised his shotgun. "Well, we have an interesting situation on our hands here."

"What do we do? We were only told to bring her." Long Hair adjusted the bandanna across his face. Dark glasses hid his eyes.

"Shut up, little bro. Let me think." The bearded man tapped his chin.

The constable groaned and shifted his position, bringing Brett back to the situation.

He eyed the wounded constable. Where had Jackson gone to? Ugh! It was up to Brett to save Keeley and the others from whatever plan these two hunters had cooked up.

He raised his hands and gestured toward the bleeding constable. "Listen, this officer needs medical assistance. You have one death on your hands. Do you want to add more? How about you let us all go so we can help him? We won't pursue you. I promise."

Tina moved forward.

Brett hauled her back. "Stay behind me," he whispered. His former police training resurfaced as takedown scenarios ran through his mind.

But no successful ideas formed without someone either getting stabbed or shot. *God, if You're there like Dad says You are, show me what to do.* A month ago, Brett had returned to his hometown after getting a panicked call from his aunt, stating his father's cancer had progressed, and he required full-time care. Brett had immediately put in for a transfer, hoping a position opened up. He hated to leave Ontario so quickly, but his father came first.

The hunter kicked at a stick in his path. "You think we're dumb?"

Brett noted a figure lurking in the trees out of the suspects' sights. Constable Jackson had returned. Brett had met this officer on a recent call. Layke Jackson's wife was a border patrol officer at Beaver Creek and was pregnant after doctors told her she probably would never birth a child. *God protect us. This man is about to become a father.*

Jackson pointed his index finger toward Keeley.

What was he trying to say? Save Keeley?

Brett concentrated on her. How could he overpower the man with the knife and keep both women safe? He must try. He turned back to Jackson and nodded.

First, he had to distract the men. "I never implied you were dumb. Far from it."

The man sneered, revealing a silver-capped tooth. "You got that right, bucko."

"Why did you hurt these men?" Brett shifted his gaze back to Jackson, moving slightly to get closer to Keeley, but not enough to catch the hunter's attention.

Jackson raised three fingers.

In three.

Once again, Brett dipped his head in acknowledgment. He looked back at Keeley and captured her attention. He inched his elbow in an upright position and thrust it backward, hoping she'd catch his drift.

Her eyes widened, but he caught her slight head tilt.

"I ain't telling you anything." The hunter shifted his rifle.

Brett turned his attention back to the hunter and Jackson.

He raised two fingers.

Brett fisted his hands at his sides and prayed Tina wouldn't react to what he was about to do. He took another baby step toward Keeley.

Two.

Lord, give both Jackson and me strength to over-power this duo of hunters.

Another step.

One.

"Now!" Jackson advanced through the trees, pointing his gun. "Police! Let her go!"

"Tina, down!" Brett barreled toward the other man.

Keeley screamed and elbowed her captor in the stomach.

He grunted and shifted backward but kept his grip on the knife. "Why, you little—"

Brett slammed into the suspect, cutting off the man's words. The pair stumbled to the side, but not before the blade sliced into Keeley's arm.

She cried and clutched the wound.

A shot rang out.

Brett regained his footing from the scrummage and pivoted to face the other hunter.

The man thrust his rifle's butt into Jackson. The constable slumped.

"Nice try." The man bounded forward and hit Keeley in the head, rendering her unconscious.

"No!" Brett stepped toward Keeley.

"Stay back." The older suspect aimed the shotgun directly at Brett. "We don't want you."

"Why do you want Keeley?" He noted the slightly hidden cardboard box sitting close to the deceased man. Had Keeley uncovered some evidence these men wanted to keep hidden?

"That's our secret. None of your concern."

Sirens sounded in the distance. Other constables had arrived.

"Bro, carry the woman. We're leaving. Now!" He directed the gun toward Tina and addressed Brett. "Don't try anything else, Mr. Paramedic, or we'll shoot your partner. You want her death on your shoulders?" He paused. "Don't think the approaching cops will get far. We're not the only ones in the forest."

There were more hunters?

The man lifted Keeley over his shoulder as blood dripped from her forearm.

Brett's attempt to save her life had failed.

And now he risked losing track of her...again.

"Go, bro. I've got this." The older man planted his stance, pointing the shotgun at Tina. "Don't follow us."

Tina whimpered beside Brett, revealing her frantic state.

Brett raised his hands in surrender. He couldn't risk his partner's life.

Gunfire erupted in the distance.

"See, told ya we weren't alone." The man sneered before he backed out of the grove and dashed after the younger hunter carrying Keeley.

Assured they were gone, Brett turned to Tina. "You okay?"

She bit her lip and shook her head.

Brett clutched her shoulders, getting into her personal space. "Listen, I know you're scared, but we have to tend to these officers. Can you do that?"

She inhaled and exhaled. "Yes."

He gestured toward the fallen constables. "Let's check them, and then I need to go."

"What are you going to do?"

"I'm going after Keeley. I can't leave her alone with those men."

Tina scrunched up her face. "The boss won't like that. You're new here, remember?"

"I'll explain everything to him. Keeley is hurt and needs my help."

Brett spoke into his radio. "Paramedic Ryerson requesting additional officers and an ambulance at my known location. Be aware of armed hunters."

The radio crackled. "Officer Len Antoine here. We're en route. Encountered resistance, but two shooters took off. Other officers are in pursuit. Heading your way."

Jackson mumbled and opened his eyes. His hand flew to his head.

"Ryerson, I've deployed another ambulance," Dispatch said.

Brett turned to Jackson. "Let's get you stabilized."

After that, Brett would find Keeley.

Not only did she need medical attention but help staying alive from the dangerous hunters who commandeered the Elimac Forest.

Chapter Two

Water splashed onto Keeley's face, jarring her awake. Pain seared her arm as she attempted to identify her surroundings.

"Wake up, princess," a sinister voice whispered in her ear.

His foul breath brought the memories of the attack back into focus.

She wiped away the water and cowered from his closeness. "Get away from me!" She rubbed her throbbing forehead. A goose egg had formed from the abductor's previous assault. Keeley jumped upright, but the room spun and she plopped back down. Her fingers grazed a crudely applied bandage around her arm where the blade had penetrated. Why treat her wound when they were probably going to kill her anyway?

The earlier events plagued her with questions. *Mickey!* Was he okay? And why did the other paramedic call him Brett? She'd met Mickey at a party and they'd instantly bonded. Keeley had dated other men throughout her university years but never fallen for someone after one dinner. Their connection grew after their brief relationship, but then out of the blue, Mickey broke it off, stating the police force in Ontario had offered him a position. He wouldn't do a long-distance relationship.

"Best break off whatever we have now before we both get hurt," Mickey had said. "Besides, I have lots of baggage."

She realized then she'd fallen for him harder than he had for her. She'd brushed off the sting and threw herself back into finishing her doctorate in botany.

A month after he left, she discovered she was pregnant. She tried to find a Mickey Ryerson in Ontario but failed. Checked all social media platforms. Nothing. Now she understood why. Mickey wasn't his real name. Why lie? Five years had gone by without MJ knowing his father. Their brief relationship had all happened before God tugged at her heartstrings and transformed her life. Even though she realized her mistakes, one blessing emerged.

Michael Joshua—MJ—was the love of her

life and brought her joy. Being a single parent had been challenging, but with her mother's help, Keeley finished her schooling and got her doctorate in botany. Ironically, Keeley and her mother, Chief Justice Olivia Ash, always had a shaky relationship. Keeley never knew her father. He died from a heart attack when she was one. God had failed to save her father and robbed her of knowing him, so she rejected God.

When she gave birth to MJ and gazed into her child's eyes, she no longer doubted God's existence. She decided at that moment to go back to church, surrendering her life to Him. She'd hated that she couldn't find MJ's father, but she raised him as a single mother.

And now, Mickey—Brett—had reappeared. It had shocked her to see him earlier, and she was even more stunned to realize he'd become a paramedic. He'd left to join the police force in Ontario.

What was his story?

"Princess, are you in there somewhere?" The man adjusted the bandanna wrapped on his chin before pushing the dark glasses farther up his nose. He had fastened his shoulder-length hair into a ponytail.

His look reminded Keeley of a character from an old Western movie. Who exactly were these men?

He shook her shoulders before slapping her face. "Get with it. We need ya to concentrate."

She winced, and her hand flew to her cheek, the sting burning. "What do you want from me?"

"The evidence you took back there by them bones."

She flinched. What did this hunter know about these victims? Did he have something to do with their deaths? *Play innocent and get more information.*

"What are you talking about? What bones?" The team had loaded the evidence from the skeleton remains into the forensics van, and she'd signed the chain of custody over to the investigators to transport. *Please, Lord, help them to have made it to Beth at the lab.*

Keeley had left the other cardboard box of the latest samples by Cameron's body. She clenched her fists as remorse over the investigator's senseless death threatened to bring tears. *Stay focused. There's time for mourning later.*

As the man carried Keeley over his shoulders, the jostling had woken her briefly, and she had removed the camera, dropping it next to a group of pine trees. She didn't want to lose the valuable pictures she'd taken, and her gut was telling her they were important. Turned out, her instincts were correct. She'd obviously uncovered something these men wanted to remain hidden.

"Our leader sent us to nab you and get what yous collected."

"Your leader? You mean the other hunter?"

He chuckled. "*Pfft.* Naw. He just thinks he is."

Definitely a rivalry going on between the two. She could use that to her advantage. Play them against each other. "Exactly who are you guys?"

"I ain't sayin' nothin' more." He walked to a table and took a swig of soda.

She scanned her surroundings. The hunters had taken her to a run-down cabin somewhere deep in the forest. At least, that was her guess. Multiple antlers lined one wall, while trophies were displayed proudly on top of the fireplace mantel.

A chill scampered down her body as a thought emerged. "I'm freezing. Can you start a fire? Please." She exaggerated rubbing her arms. Perhaps the smoke would lead someone to their location.

At least, she prayed that would be the case.

"Fine." Her captor lifted matches from the mantel and lit one, throwing it into the pre-made tepee of logs. The fire ignited, and soon the scent of smoke permeated the small cabin.

Keeley glanced at the window to determine the time of day, but the attached cardboard blocked the outdoors. Heat rose and flushed her cheeks as panic silenced every muscle in her body, immobilizing her. *Lord, please help someone find me, and help Brett be okay.*

"Come on. Tell me where it is." The younger hunter withdrew his knife and traced the tip along her chin. "Or I will mess up your purdy face."

She raised her hands. "Did you find anything on me? I don't have it."

"You was playing in the flowers, Miss Botonist."

Her jaw dropped. "How do you know so much about me?"

"We's got our ways."

"Who's 'we's'?" She must keep him talking to determine anything to use against them, or to help identify them if she ever escaped her captivity. "Where's your partner?"

"Ya think I'm stupid, don't ya?" He stood and walked to the hearth, poking at the logs. "I might not have graduated from high school, but I ain't dumb."

"I never said you were. Tell me your name." Something told her this guy was the weaker link between the two. She peeked at the door. Could she make a run for it? Perhaps distract him first? *Think, Keeley.* She had to get back to her son. The thought of leaving him alone in this world, if something ever happened to her, broke her heart.

And now…she had the strong desire to tell MJ she'd found his daddy.

"I ain't sayin' squat." He paced the room.

Wait—the other hunter had called him *bro.* "Are you and the other guy brothers?"

The man turned. "Maybe."

So they were.

"Is it just the two of you?"

The door burst open, and the older hunter appeared, shotgun in hand. "Don't tell her anything. She won't like it."

She?

"I didn't." The younger brother raised his hand. "I promise."

"Did you find out where she hid it?"

"Nope."

"Do I have to do everything?" He approached his brother and cuffed him on the side of the head.

The older brother definitely was the leader—and more dangerous.

Keeley slowly rose to her feet. "Listen, I know nothing and won't say anything. Please, just let me go."

Voices mumbled from a machine on a nearby desk.

The older brother raised his hand. "Shhh... listen." He turned up the volume.

"Suspects last seen heading north from the scene. Rising smoke spotted in the distance. Pursuing on foot. Paramedics are transporting victims to the hospital."

The older brother snatched his water bottle and sprayed it on the flames. They sizzled from the sudden action. "How could you be so stupid, little bro? Now we need to leave."

"She said she was cold."

"So, your soft spot for a purdy lady won out again, huh? Just like that hiker."

Keeley stiffened. She remembered something in the news about missing hikers from a year ago. The case had grown cold. Could that be who these brothers referred to? They killed them, and it was the hikers' bones the police discovered?

"Approaching the cabin now," a voice said over the scanner.

"Bro, grab your gun. We're gonna have to fight our way out." The older brother pulled a walkie-talkie from his cargo pants pocket. "I and D need assistance at the huntin' cabin. Stat."

There were more of these brothers? A shudder snaked down Keeley's spine.

"Roger dodger, bro," another voice said.

"How far out are ya?"

"Ten minutes. Were settin' traps for those coppers. Then we'll—"

"We know you're in there," a voice boomed from outside. "Come out with your hands on your heads."

"Keeley!" Brett shouted.

She jumped to her feet. "Mickey! Help!"

"Shut your trap." The older brother backhanded her hard across the face.

Keeley fell onto the couch.

The hunter ripped the cardboard from the window and stuck his shotgun through a hole in the bottom right of the glass, firing a shot. "We's got a hostage. Stay back or we kill the lovely Dr. Keeley Ash."

How did this band of brothers know so much about her?

Lord, save me. Keep Mickey—Brett safe so I can tell him about his son.

Brett leaned against a tree, studying the small cabin hidden deep in the Elimac Forest. After he had mentioned his former police training and need to treat Keeley's wound, Constable Jackson agreed to let Brett tag along since the other constables were farther out. Brett's leader threatened to fire him when he explained he was helping to rescue Keeley. He argued paramedics didn't engage in confrontation—that was the constable's job. However, Brett couldn't wait. Keeley's life was at stake.

As Brett waited for Jackson to update him on the other constables' progress into the woods, visions of Brett's first shoot-out that had ended his policing career flashed through his mind. Similar to today's events, suspects had taken a hostage at knifepoint—Brett's partner. They had stabbed her before shooting the witness they'd been protecting. Brett had tried to save both, but failed. He didn't have the tools at the scene to bring her back to life. That catalyst had thrust him into becoming a paramedic.

He wanted to save lives and never feel helpless again.

But now a different woman lay beyond the cabin's walls at their mercy. Could he and Constable Jackson save Keeley?

She had stolen his heart over six years ago—too quickly for his liking. They'd bonded fast in their short dating stint. Would he get a second chance with the beautiful redhead to explore the idea?

Or would God take that from him, too?

First, his mother had been killed, and now his father was on his deathbed. The cancer had progressed quickly, and the doctors had suggested to Brett yesterday he get Harold Ryerson's affairs in order. He probably had less than three weeks to live.

And the possibility of losing his father crushed his heart. His dad was his best friend. When Brett lived in Ontario, they'd spent hours over video chat talking about their favorite hockey players. Just last week they'd watched a Rangers versus Leafs game.

How could his dad have deteriorated so fast?

Jackson darted to a tree closer to Brett. "I realize you have a former police background, but we need to wait for backup before breaching the premises. Constable Antoine is close."

"Something tells me Keeley doesn't have that long. These hunters are reckless and dangerous. I saw that firsthand."

"Agreed. They've already killed our forensic investigator and injured Hopkins." Worry crinkled the man's brow.

"He's in excellent hands. We stabilized him before my partner and the other paramedics transported him to the hospital."

"Thank the good Lord."

Constable Jackson's radio squawked.

"Say again, Antoine."

"I'm approaching from your rear. The other constables aren't far behind."

"Copy that."

Brett's muscles locked as alarm traveled through his body. *Hurry!* Keeley needed him.

Seconds later, Constable Antoine emerged from the tree line and approached. "What's the play?"

Jackson studied the cabin before speaking. "Okay, I'm gonna circle around to the rear and see if there's a back entrance."

"Let me do that," Antoine said. "You stay here and cover the front in case the other constables come."

Brett gestured toward the building. "I'm coming, too. I need to tend to Keeley's wound. I'll wave to you if I find a door."

Jackson puffed out a breath. "I don't like you being so close to the danger, so stay behind Antoine. He's armed. You're not. I'll distract them by trying to get their attention. Brett, if Keeley is able, get her far away from the cabin and tend to her wound. We'll cover you."

"The others are close." Antoine motioned toward the side of the cabin. "Let's go!"

Brett and Antoine scooted behind another aspen tree to the right. Slowly, they crouch-walked as they made their way to the cabin's rear.

Brett followed standard police procedures. Funny how they came back to him when necessary. Muscle memory or God?

His father would say God, but Brett had a hard time believing that. God wasn't listening to Brett's pleas to heal his dad, so why would He listen now?

Brett suppressed thoughts of God and skulked from tree to tree, following Antoine and making his way through the woods. Finding a perfect position for spying, they peered around the tree trunk and observed the cabin's rear. The two windows at the back were obstructed, but he noted a door. Perfect.

He shifted to a spot where he had a line of vision to Constable Jackson, then waved.

The constable cupped his hands around his mouth to act as a bullhorn. "We just want to talk. Tell us what you want in exchange for Dr. Ash."

"We's don't negotiate," a voice yelled.

"Please. No one else needs to die today."

Brett veered to the side of the cabin after Antoine, keeping himself low. With their backs against the log wall, they inched closer, one on each side of the door.

Antoine peeked inside the small door's window, then motioned for Brett to do the same.

Brett complied. The dusty glass obstructed his view, and he carefully wiped to clear a corner before looking through.

Keeley sat on a couch facing him. Across

the room, one hunter leaned into the window with his shotgun raised. The other stood beside Keeley, his hand resting on her shoulder.

Fury coursed through Brett at the thought of this man touching her. His former attraction to the woman returned, and he pried his gaze away, resting the back of his head against the cabin. He breathed in and out, trying to slow his heart rate. *Stay calm, Brett.* If he was going to help Keeley escape, he had to keep his emotions in check.

He let out a slow, elongated breath and once again looked through the glass.

This time, she spotted him.

Her eyes widened.

He raised his index finger to his lips, indicating for her to keep silent.

She dipped her head slightly, her eyes averting to the hunter standing with the shotgun by the window.

"Give it up, man. You're surrounded." Constable Jackson's voice rose a notch.

An indication of deception. Brett knew the signs and also realized the constables still hadn't arrived. Jackson was attempting to buy time.

It was up to the three of them to save Keeley.

Brett raised his index finger again to show her to wait for a second.

Once again, she tipped her head, acknowledging his instructions.

"You get ready to breach. I'll signal Jackson." Brett returned to the side of the cabin, caught Constable Jackson's attention, then raised five fingers before switching his grip to appear as a fake gun.

Five seconds.

Then shoot.

Jackson nodded and hurried to another tree closer to the cabin, positioning himself to enter.

Brett returned to his spot opposite Antoine. "I'll motion to Keeley we're breaching in five seconds. You ready?"

Antoine lifted his nine millimeter and nodded.

Brett once again stared into the cabin.

Keeley's eyes remained on him.

He elevated his five fingers and then made a pushing motion to instruct her to nudge into the man beside her.

She nodded.

He slowly counted to five, depressing each finger one at a time.

On one, he waited for Jackson.

A shot echoed through the forest.

Antoine thrust open the door. "Police! Hold it there!"

Brett inched into the cabin at the same time Keeley plowed into the man beside her.

The hunter at the window turned at Brett and Antoine's appearance, pointing at them. "Bro, get these guys. I'm busy. There are more coppers here."

The man beside Keeley raised his gun toward Antoine, his finger twitching on the trigger.

Antoine fired.

The young man dropped his weapon and clutched his opposite hand, yelling in pain.

The other hunter turned. "Little bro!"

It was enough of a distraction for them to act and Antoine motioned toward the door. "Get Keeley out of here."

Brett nudged her forward. "Keeley, run to the trees!"

She bolted through the rear exit.

He followed, glancing over his shoulder to ensure they weren't being pursued.

Shouts from out front revealed other constables had arrived to help. Thankfully. They would protect Jackson and Antoine. Brett had to get away from the cabin as fast as he could and protect the woman in front of him.

Was that possible with a band of hunters on their tail?

Chapter Three

Pain burned Keeley's arm as blood seeped through the bandage. Wrenching free from the younger brother's hold had reopened the knife wound. Adrenaline pumped through her veins, giving her strength to run despite the throbbing in her arm and head. However, would the rush of energy be enough to outrun these brothers while more lurked somewhere in the forest?

Gunfire erupted behind them, and she prayed for safety. *Lord, thank You for bringing Brett to me, and keep the constables alive. Stop these men.*

The sudden appearance of Brett shocked her but filled her with relief. He'd risked his life to come after her. Something she wouldn't forget easily.

More gunfire sounded, interrupting her thoughts. She skidded to a stop. "We need to help the constables."

Brett halted. "Backup arrived just as we escaped the cabin. Constable Jackson told me to get you to safety." He gestured her forward. "We need to distance ourselves. Then I want to look at your arm. You okay to keep going?"

She nodded.

So much she wanted to say.

So much she wanted to ask.

But for now, she'd press on.

Fifteen minutes later, Keeley stumbled on a root, but she clutched a branch to prevent her fall. Her legs wouldn't allow her to proceed. "Need. To. Stop." Her breathless words came out like a child whining after a few hours of travel. However, her previous adrenaline had waned, zapping her strength. She leaned against the tree, inhaling and exhaling.

Brett pointed. "Let's take a break and hide behind those bushes. We're too out in the open here. I'll help you."

He wrapped his arm around her waist, and together they trudged into the secluded bushes.

Keeley looked left, then right. "Where are we? I have a terrible sense of direction."

"We're north of the cabin. These woods have grown since I was a kid, so I have no idea."

Keeley nestled between branches, sitting on

the ground. "Why did the other paramedic call you Brett?"

"Let me see your arm first, and then I'll explain."

She held out her bloodied, bandaged arm.

He gingerly unwrapped it and pushed on the wound.

She winced.

"Sorry, just trying to get a better look. It's not deep but requires stitches. Looks like the bleeding has stopped. For now." He brought out gauze from his pocket and placed it on top before adding a bandage. "This will have to do until we can get to a hospital. I only stuffed a few things in my pockets before I followed the constable to rescue you. The others were otherwise engaged, and I needed to help find you to treat your injury."

"Tell me your real name."

His gaze snapped to hers. "Brett Michael Ryerson."

Her eyes locked with his, and her heartbeat ratcheted up a notch at his nearness. She remembered how she'd fallen for his baby blues.

Keeley couldn't fall again. Not for her sake— or MJ's. The last man she thought she loved had left them both brokenhearted and confused. She promised herself she wouldn't put MJ through the pain of loss. MJ had taken to Preston fast, just like Keeley.

She wrenched her arm away, averting her stare to the ground. "Tell me why you lied and said your name was Mickey."

He changed his position and leaned his back against a log. "Not entirely a lie. I was young and foolish back then, Keeley." He harrumphed. "Even though it was only six years ago. My college buddies started calling me Mickey instead of Brett. They said it would go over with the girls, so we all made up nicknames for each other. It stuck until I moved to Ontario."

She observed the man before her. How could he have grown even more handsome? Now wasn't the time to ponder their past relationship. *Focus, Keeley.*

He rubbed the bridge of his nose. "I'm sorry I never told you my given name. Like I said, I was foolish and let peer pressure govern my actions back then. I've grown up in the past six years."

A shadow passed over his face before he fixed his attention to peeling the bark off the log.

Something had happened to him, and she desperately wanted to uncover his story. Did it have to do with why he switched vocations? *Keeley, not now.* "When did you move back to the Yukon?"

"A month ago." He let out a ragged sigh. "My dad has cancer. I came back to help take care of him. He doesn't have long."

"I'm so sorry." She read the sorrow in his saddened eyes.

"Why are you here? Didn't you live farther north?"

"Yes, but my mother was offered a prestigious position—Chief Justice Olivia Ash."

Brett whistled. "Wow, the Supreme Court. Impressive."

"Yup, and she found a job for me teaching botany at a campus here in the area. So, I moved my…"

Could she tell him about his son now? Here when they were on the run? She fingered her collar and remembered something from earlier. She popped to her feet.

She had to retrieve her camera before the brothers did.

Brett rose. "What is it?"

She gripped his arm. "We have to go back. When the brothers were carrying me, I woke for a minute and removed my camera. Something told me to hide it, so I dropped it near pine trees close to the cabin."

"You want to go back into the line of fire? You can find the camera later."

"You don't understand. The younger brother let something slip that makes me believe he knew we had uncovered bones. He kept asking me about the evidence I had and said, 'She's the one,' like they knew exactly who I was and what I did." She brushed weeds from her pants.

"How is that possible?"

A question she'd been asking herself ever since her conversation with the duo. "No idea. He also mentioned hikers."

"Hikers?"

"A man and woman vanished over a year ago, but the case went cold after all the clues to their whereabouts had diminished. I'm guessing these brothers know exactly who those bones belong to, and they wanted to stop me from proving it."

"Wait—these hunters are brothers?"

"They kept calling each other *bro*, and the younger one didn't deny it when I asked." She dug her nails into his arm as the urgency of the situation plagued her. "Plus, there are at least two others, and he also referred to a woman.

Not sure in what capacity. If the police can catch the younger one, we can use him against the others. He feels like the weak link. We have to go back." She lifted her sleeve and checked her smartwatch. Midafternoon. She also had to pick up her son—his son.

He peeled her fingers away and unhooked his radio. "Let me see if I can get in touch with anyone. Check out the situation first. I don't want us to walk back into a raging fire—so to speak."

She squeezed his shoulder. "Wait—switch your channel. The brothers had a scanner and are listening."

Brett obeyed.

After discovering the brothers had escaped, Constable Jackson assured Brett through the radio that the hunters had fled. They created a diversion, and when the constables stormed the premises, they were gone. An area sweep had proved useless. It was like the hunters had disappeared.

Somehow Keeley doubted that. These brothers appeared to own the forest. They were somewhere close. Her gut was screaming at her to stay away from the creepy cabin.

But the evidence on her camera warranted their return to the lion's den.

Brett positioned himself in front of Keeley twenty minutes later, as they approached the grove near the cabin. The one place he didn't want to revisit, but the one place Keeley had to return to. "Get behind that tree. I want to study the area before we rush back there."

Keeley tugged a band off her wrist and fastened her red hair into a ponytail as she situated herself behind the aspen. "Still have some cop left in you?"

"Always."

"Why did you become a paramedic?"

"Later." But would there be a later? Would they go their separate ways once they retrieved the camera and he safely escorted her out of the forest? For all he knew, she was married or had a boyfriend.

He checked her wedding ring finger. It was bare.

That still meant nothing.

And why did he care suddenly? It wasn't like he'd been thinking about dating again.

He restrained the exhalation wanting to escape. Her presence today had refueled the electricity between them he remembered from six years ago. How was that possible?

His buddies Zac and Mitchell had labeled him a player when they first met. Zac had even challenged his dating life and lack of commitment. The jolt made Brett change his casual ways. His actions would horrify his Christian father, and that, too, drove him to become a better man. Sure, he still dated, but after a woman claimed he'd fathered her child when he hadn't and another betrayed him, his faith in women faltered.

So, why even think about a *later* with Keeley when his trust factor was at the bottom of the barrel? *You know why.*

He shifted his position and ignored her penetrating stare. Her hazel eyes had always been his undoing. *Stop.*

Time to focus on the scene before him. He analyzed every hiding spot in the area, but thankfully, the forest was silent.

All except for the constables scouring the cabin's perimeter. Brett radioed to Constable Jackson, confirming their approach.

The man gave them the green light.

Brett tucked the radio back on his belt. "Okay, let's go. Where did you drop the camera?"

The duo emerged from their hiding spots and advanced toward the cabin. Multiple constables surrounded the area, on guard for further threats.

"Well, I was in and out of consciousness, but I remember seeing a group of pines before the cabin. That's when I unsnapped the strap and gently threw it. I coughed to cover up the sound and then slumped, pretending to be unconscious. After a surge of pain, I really passed out again and didn't wake until the younger brother threw water on my face." Keeley circled the small area, checking the trees, then stopped. "Over there."

She dashed toward a cluster of pines that reminded Brett of a Christmas tree lot. He'd loved searching for the perfect tree with his father as a boy.

Keeley squatted in front of the shorter pine, reaching between the branches. She pulled out a camera held by a strap and a cell phone attached. "Got it!" She unhooked the phone and swiped the screen, then grimaced.

"What is it?"

"My mother's numerous texts from earlier. Seems like she's wanting to get in touch with me."

"Still trying to run your life?" Brett remembered Keeley complaining of her judge mother's ruling thumb. It had extended from the courtroom into her daughter's life.

She scrolled, then froze. "No."

"What?"

"Something's wrong. I need to call my mother." She clicked on her phone. "No service. Great. Not sure what she wanted. Time to get out of here. I also need to ensure all the evidence made it to my lab." Keeley stuffed the phone into her pocket.

"Let's check in with the constables quickly before we leave." Brett strode over to Constable Jackson. "Any updates on the other constable? Did the paramedics make it out of the forest okay?"

"They did. Constable Hopkins is still in critical condition." Jackson addressed Keeley. "You okay?"

"Tired but fine. Did Forensics send the evidence to the lab?"

"Yes. Your employee, Beth Bower, signed for it all." He pointed at the cabin. "Tell me about the men who took you."

Keeley recounted everything she had told Brett. "Did you find anything in the cabin to uncover their identities?"

"Nothing yet, but constables reported two assailants at the entrance earlier, so that makes four. This sounds like the Diglo brothers to me."

"The who?" Brett asked.

"A notorious gang suspected of many crimes in the area, but nothing we've been able to prove." Jackson fished out his notebook and flipped through his pages. "Here it is. Reports of a couple of armed robberies and assaults. No one has ascertained their names or any witnesses. Seems everyone fears these brothers and isn't talking."

"I can see why. The older one is especially scary and dominates the younger. I believe they have something to do with the skeletons found earlier today. Maybe the evidence links them, and you can finally convict them."

"Yes, and solve the missing hiker cold case. The female was the mayor's daughter. He was not happy when we told him we had no leads."

"Hopefully, the coroner can identify the victims after Dr. Everson finishes with the bones. Is there anything else you need from me? I have to make a call and get to my lab."

"First, Keeley, I'm taking you to the hospital." Brett held out his hand to the constable. "Good to see you again."

"You too." Jackson shook both of their hands. "Thanks for your help. Stay safe. I'll get an officer to escort you."

A constable bounded from the cabin waving an item. "Jackson, look—"

Movement rustled in the trees to their right.

"Fire in the hole!" a voice shouted seconds before a rocket launched from the tree line.

"Get down!" Jackson commanded, unleashing his gun.

Brett knocked Keeley to the ground, covering her body. His pulse spiraled out of control.

The rocket-propelled grenade blasted toward the cabin and exploded into a fireball, the boom deafening anyone in the area. Debris sailed in all directions.

Brett lifted his head just as a chunk of wood whacked Jackson's arm. The constable's weapon flew out of his hand, landing beside Brett.

Gunfire erupted from his left. The younger brother stood with his weapon aimed at Keeley, his intent clear.

Brett scrambled upward and snatched the nine millimeter at his feet, firing multiple shots.

The younger hunter dropped.

"No!" the other brother screamed before glaring at Brett. He pointed at him. "You're a dead man!" He retreated into the forest.

Brett waited for further shots but none came. A question arose. Where were the other two brothers?

"Constables, secure the area," Jackson hollered as he moved to a crouched position and spoke into his radio for emergency services.

Brett handed Jackson his weapon. "Sorry, my instinct took over when I saw the shooter."

"Good shot. That happened so fast. I'm going after the rocket launcher. Brett, check to see if the suspect and constables need medical attention. These brothers won't get away with attacking our own. Not on my watch." His angry tone revealed his elevated emotions. He sprinted after the suspect.

"Constable, you okay?" Keeley yelled as she rose to her feet.

"Stay low." Brett observed the cabin.

The blaze would quickly spread if firefighters didn't get there fast.

Constable Antoine sat up. "I'm good."

Keeley hurried over to the younger brother.

"Wait!" Brett ran after her. "He could still be dangerous."

Keeley knelt beside the man and lifted the bandanna from his face. She sucked in a breath. "I've seen him before."

"Where?"

She paused as if searching her memory. "I don't remember."

Brett placed his fingers on the man's neck. "He's gone." He searched his pockets for some type of identification but only found a picture.

He gazed at it intently. A young redheaded boy wearing a backpack, leaving a school with a woman. He handed the photo to Keeley. "Do you know this boy?"

She looked at the picture and blasted upright. "No!"

He pushed himself to his feet, grazing her arm. "Keels, who is it?"

Her eyes widened before softening. "My— your son."

What?

He had a son?

And now the boy was in danger.

Chapter Four

Keeley caught Brett's contorted expression as he raked his fingers through his short dirty-blond hair and stepped to a cluster of trees, obviously distancing himself from her presence. What was the emotion overtaking him?

Confusion? Doubt?

You don't believe me. Not that she blamed him. It was a lot to take in after just reuniting with an old flame. Perhaps that was all she had been. For her, it was more. She had fallen deeply for him. Maybe even loved him. Was that possible after only a few dates? Many of her friends had believed in love at first sight. Not her mother. Chief Justice Olivia Ash's analytical mind could never comprehend something so rash. So illogical.

However, Keeley's broken heart had disagreed with her mother's thinking. She *had* strong feelings for MJ's father.

Keeley strode to where he stood and placed her hand on his shoulder. "Mick—Brett, it's true. MJ is your son, and right now, he's in danger from these men. We have to get back and contact my mom."

He turned, his expression shifted to one of contempt. "How can I believe you?" His words held both sarcasm and anger.

She stumbled backward, away from the sudden rush of disdain permeating from him. "I wouldn't lie about something like this."

"No? Other women would."

What did that mean? She fisted her hands, curbing the anger from overflowing. "Well, I'm not other women. Trust me. MJ is yours, Brett. You can take a DNA test if you want."

"Maybe I will."

Keeley studied his handsome face. Another emotion replaced his previously caring expression, and she didn't like it. Perhaps he wasn't the man she'd thought. She positioned the camera case strap across her body. "Well, obviously something has happened to you over the past few years, because this isn't the Mickey I knew. Then again, you lied to me about your name. Maybe you've never been truthful to me about anything during our short dating time. I need to—"

Constable Jackson jogged to their sides. "You guys okay?"

"Fine." Keeley pursed her lips as she glanced at Brett. "Any signs of the other brother?"

"None. It's like he vanished. I'm guessing the hunters are familiar with these parts of Elimac Forest and know where to hide. I've called in firefighters. They should be here anytime." The constable squeezed Brett's shoulder. "You okay? You're ghastly white."

Brett shifted his gaze to hers, then back to the constable. "I'll be fine. Listen, I need to check on the other constables and then get Keeley back in town. She needs stitches. We okay to leave?"

Jackson turned to Keeley. "We have to take your statement on today's events."

Keeley had to get to her mother's and check on MJ. She didn't have time for statements. "I have to attend to a family emergency. Can I come to your station later?"

"Of course."

Twenty minutes after Brett ensured the other constables on the scene were okay, Keeley followed him through the forest and back to her vehicle. The fog had finally cleared, but the woods still held an eerie silence within its grip.

Or could that perhaps be the tension between them?

Keeley reached into her camera bag and dug out her key fob. "I can take you back to your paramedic station."

"Keels, you need stitches." His softened expression replaced his earlier hardened one.

"No, I need to get to my mother's home. I'll go to the hospital later. Our—*my* son needs me. Don't you need to get back to work?" Not that she expected Brett to take the news of his son lightly, but his reaction had upset her. She never gave him any deceitful signs. She'd always been that proverbial open book.

Maybe that was her downfall. Too trusting. Her track record had proved it, and her son had paid the price. She remembered his tortured little face when she had told him Preston wouldn't be coming around any longer. He'd been heartbroken, perhaps more than Keeley.

She wouldn't let another man hurt her son again. Perhaps introducing MJ to his father wasn't such a great idea.

However, she refused to withhold from her

son the opportunity of knowing his father. But would Brett leave again?

"I'm sorry for my earlier reaction. Let's just say… I have trust issues with women."

There was a story behind his words. "I never lied to you before. Why would I start now?"

He hung his head. "I know. It's not you. It's me."

Clearly. Keeley hit the button to open her SUV. "Where do you want me to drop you off?"

He lifted his gaze to hers, studying her. "I'm coming with you."

"Thought you didn't believe me." She opened her door and climbed into the driver's seat.

He jumped in beside her. "I'm not saying I do, but I have to know. If MJ is my son, I will not let him down."

"Understood. I need to call my mom." Keeley hit the Bluetooth and speed-dialed Olivia Ash.

"'Bout time you called. I've been frantic. Didn't you get my messages?"

Keeley gritted her teeth. She didn't need her mother's attitude right now. "Mom, I will explain everything when I get to your place. Let me talk to MJ. Now." She started the engine, then drove out of the park's entrance and onto the highway, which would take her back into town.

"I can't. They. Took. Him." Her mother's broken words came in between sobs.

Terror seized Keeley at her mother's erratic state. Her hand flew to her chest, willing her sudden rapid heart palpitations to slow. "What? Who?" The picture in her coat pocket of her son at the school told her the answer to her question.

Somehow the Diglo brothers had gotten to MJ. A haunting question arose.

Why had they targeted Keeley and MJ?

Lord, please don't take my son. Please.

Brett squeezed her shoulder. "We need to call the police."

"No! Don't know who they are, but they said no police, or they'd kill MJ. Who's with you, Keeley?"

How could Keeley explain what had transpired in such a short period of time when she herself didn't truly comprehend everything? "I'll tell you when I get there, Mom. See you in ten minutes." She punched off the call and accelerated, gripping the steering wheel like it was a lifeline to a drowning victim. *Lord, that's how I'm feeling. In over my head. Help me get above these deadly waters.*

Brett withdrew his cell phone. "I'm going to touch base with my supervisor on the way. He'll be wanting an update." He tapped the screen. "And I need to tell him I'm taking a personal day." He dialed his supervisor and explained the situation.

Ten minutes later, Keeley yanked open her mother's front oak door and scurried inside the five-bedroom luxurious estate. "Mom, where are you?"

"Living room." Her mother's weakened voice stopped Keeley in her tracks. The normally stoic woman had been reduced to tears. Keeley couldn't remember a time when she'd seen her mother cry. Nothing fazed the woman.

Keeley bounded into the room and fell in front of her mother, sitting in her favorite rocker. "Where's MJ?"

Fresh tears tumbled down Olivia Ash's forlorn face as she raised her cell phone with a shaky hand. "They have him."

Keeley viewed a picture of her gagged son with a caption below it:

Tell your daughter to stay out of the forest or her beloved son dies. Chief Justice, pay up or he also dies. No police or he dies. We're watching.

Keeley gasped and burst upright.

She felt Brett's presence behind her. "We'll find him," he whispered.

Her mother sprang out of the rocker. "Who are you? Wait. You!" She charged into his personal space and poked him in the chest. "I recognize your face from a picture my daughter showed me. Where have you been for the past five years?"

Keeley slid in between her mother and Brett, creating elbow room between them. "Mom, let me explain."

Her mother stumbled backward. "If he'd been here, maybe MJ wouldn't have been taken."

"What? Mom, this isn't Brett's fault."

Her glaring eyes shifted toward Brett. "Isn't his name Mickey?"

"Long story, which we don't have time for. Is this the only message you received from the kidnappers?" Brett shoved his hands into his pockets.

"So far, yes." The fifty-five-year-old judge positioned herself in front of the bay window overlooking her enormous front yard.

"Mom, tell me what happened." Keeley's pulse intensified at the thought of her son at the mercy of the deadly brothers. She dropped into a nearby chair and buried her face in her hands. "I can't lose him."

Brett squatted in front of her. "I'm here. I can help."

Keeley lifted her head and examined his face. Could she trust him to stay and help after his previous angered response to the news of his son?

Her mother turned from the window. "How can you help?"

"Mom, don't—"

The house landline rang, the shrill noise echoing through the still room.

Her mother snatched the cordless phone from the coffee table and hit the speaker button. "Olivia Ash here."

"Good. We know you're all together, as we've been watching," the distorted voice said. "You can't hide from us. Let's get down to business, shall we?"

Keeley ran to her mother's side. "Where is my son?" She failed to suppress the anger burning inside.

"Patience, Dr. Ash. Patience."

"What do you want from us?"

"Simple. Judge, we want five hundred thousand dollars wired to our account in the next three hours."

Her mother grimaced. "I can't get that kind of money so quickly."

"Of course you can," the caller said. "You're a judge, after all."

Keeley leaned closer to the phone, attempting to focus in on the voice. Even though they had used some sort of distortion app, the tone and words the caller used were familiar. "Who are you? Do I know you?"

"No more questions. Dr. Ash, you stay out of our forest and you'll see your son again. If not, he dies. Easy peasy."

Keeley's knees buckled, and she stumbled but held on to a nearby chair. "I want proof he's still alive. Now!"

Brett wrapped a protective arm around her waist.

A commotion sailed through the phone. "Mama?"

"MJ! Are you okay?" Keeley leaned into Brett's supportive hold.

"I'm okay. God's with me, Mama. But I'm hungry and just want to come home."

Keeley's heart hitched. "Soon, baby. Soon. I'll—"

"Okay, that's enough. You have your proof. We'll text the ransom instructions. You have three hours. Remember, no police." The resounding click followed by a dial tone blasted into the spacious living room.

Keeley dropped onto the couch and sobbed, unable to hold her emotions in check any longer. MJ was her entire world.

Would she see her precious son again?

Brett hesitated, not knowing how to respond to Keeley's breakdown. He looked at her mother—the Honorable Chief Justice Olivia Ash. She, too, seemed cemented in place. Wouldn't a mother know how to console her only daughter? Had their relationship deteriorated even more since Brett and Keeley dated?

After another sob, Brett couldn't take it any longer and rushed to Keeley's side, bringing her into an embrace. "Shhh. We'll get MJ back. I promise."

Keeley recoiled from his hug and popped to her feet. "How can you say that? You don't even believe he's yours." She walked to the window.

"Why would my daughter lie?" Olivia's harsh tone revealed her anger.

Brett struggled to suppress his temper. "That's

a long story, and we don't have time to get into it."

The judge's cell phone dinged, and she swiped the screen. "Instructions from the kidnapper."

Keeley raced back to her mother's side and plopped onto the couch. "What does it say?"

"'Wire five hundred thousand into the account below. Don't try tracing it. Then Keeley must come to the park across from MJ's kindergarten at exactly six p.m. and sit on the bench on the northeast side. You'll then get instructions on where to find MJ. Any deviation from this plan and he dies.'" Olivia's voice quivered on the last words. "Who are these people?"

"Why the charade of having to go to the park? I don't like it. It puts you in danger, Keels." Brett rubbed his chin stubble.

She shrugged. "Not sure, but I have to follow their instructions to the letter, or I won't see MJ again." She bit her lip.

"Do you think it's the Diglo brothers?" Brett rubbed his tightened neck muscles. "You were with them longer."

Olivia bolted to her feet. "No! Not them. Word in the criminal justice realm says they're extremely dangerous. And smart. They've evaded capture, and no one has been able to identify any of them."

Keeley's jaw dropped. "And Brett killed the younger brother."

"What?" Olivia latched on to her daughter's hand. "Why didn't you say that before?"

"I haven't really had the chance, Mom." Keeley gave her mother the abridged version of their day. "Brett, do you think this is payback for you killing one of them?"

"The timeline doesn't add up. You said your mother had been texting you all day. Olivia, when did you get the picture of MJ?"

The woman checked her phone. "Eleven this morning."

"Our altercation happened after that. Besides, I'm not on their radar. I haven't been back in town that long." Brett wanted to add that they wouldn't know he was MJ's father—if he was indeed. No sense in adding heat to an already blazing situation.

Why can't you believe?

A question his father had asked many times. Harold Ryerson had been referring to God, but in this case, Brett couldn't believe he had a son.

He needed proof.

However, he also wouldn't leave Keeley alone to deal with MJ's abduction.

"Mom, give me your phone. I want to read the instructions again, and you need to make arrangements to get the money." Keeley held out her hand.

Olivia passed it to her. "I'll go call my banker. I have to move some funds around." She left the room.

Keeley removed the elastic from her ponytail and twirled a red lock of hair. Over and over.

A habit he had noticed on their dates. She was nervous.

Brett sat beside her. "What are you thinking?"

She raised the phone. "The sentence structure. It's too perfect. The brothers I met today didn't talk like this. They used 'we's' and other slang. It's not them."

"Could it be the woman they referenced?"

"Perhaps." She tossed the phone on the coffee table and wrung her hands together. "I need my son back."

"We'll get him."

She tilted her head. "Why won't you believe he's yours?"

He stood and paced. "I've made many mistakes in the dating game."

She drew in an audible breath. "You think I was a mistake?"

He turned.

Her widened eyes flashed annoyance.

"I don't mean you, Keels." He returned to the couch and sat, taking her hands in his. "You never lied to me."

"Exactly. So why would I now?"

"Let's just say others have." He hung his head. "I need proof."

"You're a doubting Thomas."

He jerked his head up and stared into her hazel eyes. "A what?"

"You know. Thomas wouldn't believe Jesus was who He'd claimed. He needed to touch Jesus's scars first." She grazed her fingers along his stubble. "MJ is yours, Brett."

A tremor slivered down his spine from her simple gesture. *Don't do this to me.* His gaze traveled to the text message still showing on Olivia's phone.

He jolted upright as he remembered the earlier conversation with the kidnappers.

"Keels, the caller said they're watching us."

His alert senses escalated, and he darted to the window, studying the perimeter.

Movement in the bushes caught his attention. Someone was indeed out there...watching.

Stress thundered in Keeley's head at Brett's proclamation of someone watching. She placed her hand over her heart, willing the storm forming inside to slow. *Lord, protect us. Protect MJ. Calm the waters.* She gathered strength and shuffled to Brett's side. "Do you really think someone is out there?"

"I do. At least, that's what my gut is telling me." He pointed to the bushes by her mother's gate. "I saw movement a second ago. I think we should call Constable Jackson."

She caught hold of his arm. "No! They said no police. Besides, you have training. You can defend us."

An emotion passed over his handsome face before she could label it. Fear? Anger?

He shook his head. "I have no weapon."

Keeley studied the bushes. "I don't see anything. Maybe it was an animal."

"Perhaps."

"Brett, why did you stop being a police

officer? You were so excited about it when we dated."

"That's a story—"

Her mother stormed into the room, interrupting their conversation. "Okay, it will take a bit, but everything is in place. How do we know they'll hand MJ over? What if I transfer the money and it's all for nothing?" She sank down on the couch.

Keeley eyed her mother. The woman had become unraveled at the thought of losing her grandson. Her mother had the same faith, but lately she'd stopped going to church. Why, Keeley didn't know. Her mother wouldn't say when she had asked.

"Mom, it's gonna be okay. We need to trust God." She sat beside her on the couch. "He's in control."

Her mother swatted the escaped tear away with her manicured nail. "Is He? Where was He when they abducted MJ, and why are you so calm? You're his mother!"

Keeley sprang to her feet. "Did I look calm a little while ago? I'm struggling, too, Mom, but I have to trust that God is in the middle of this storm. He's the only thing that's keeping me from falling apart. If I don't have my faith, I don't have anything."

Did she really mean those words? Lately, she'd been wrestling with doubts about God's presence and His direction over her path in life. What was this circumstance telling her? *Lord, show me.* Guilt punched her in the stomach. Why couldn't she have the same faith like MJ? Faith without questions. *Help my unbelief.*

She moved to the window and folded her arms, gazing at the blossoming spring foliage.

Brett cleared his throat.

She turned.

He picked up a poker from the fireplace stand. "A weapon. I'm going to walk the perimeter while we wait. I want to confirm no one is out there."

Her mother rose to her feet. "The gate to the property is secure. No one can get in."

"I just want to be sure. Stay in the house, okay?" Brett left.

Keeley watched from the window as Brett walked around the front yard, looking behind the bushes and other foliage. Then he disappeared around the side of the house. After five minutes of searching, he returned to the living room and gave them the all clear.

Three hours later, after her mother trans-ferred the money into the kidnappers' bank ac-count, Keeley sat on the allotted bench. Her knee bounced in anticipation, and she checked her watch: 6:05 p.m. Five minutes had passed since the last time she looked. *Is that all?* Where were they?

Brett positioned himself at the other side of the park behind the playground. Waiting and out of sight. She'd text him when she got word of MJ's whereabouts. Her mother waited in the luxury of her home. Their home. Keeley longed to get out from under her mother's wings, but being a single parent made leaving difficult. Perhaps one day. Soon.

A young woman pushed two small boys on the swings. The higher they went, the louder they screamed.

Keeley chuckled despite the angst reinvading her previously calm demeanor. Her pendulum of emotions matched the boys swaying on their swings. Her earlier words to her mother tum-bled into her mind. *I'm a hypocrite.* She tight-ened her fingers around her cell phone as if that would bring a text. She keyed in a mes-sage to Brett.

They're late. I don't like it.

She waited.

Only a few minutes. Hang tight.

She replied with a sad-face emoji and viewed the spot where she knew he sat. The top of his head towered over the playground equipment.

Keeley tugged on her jacket and shifted her position. If only they'd gotten reacquainted under more cheerful circumstances. Would they have dated again?

Doubtful. Not with his obvious trust issues.

Plus, she couldn't risk him leaving again, not with MJ's little heart at stake.

A ding announced a text.

You passed. You'll find MJ around the corner in the park's favorite tree. But hurry. Sometimes old tree branches break.

No! She vaulted off the bench and raced toward Brett. "Brett, quick."

He jogged toward her. "Did you hear from them?"

She raised her phone in his direction. "We need to find the tree they're referring to."

His eyes widened before his gaze shifted to each tree in the area. "Which one?"

"I have an idea." She approached the two young boys who had vacated the swings. "Hey, guys, can you tell me what tree is your most favorite in this park?"

The older one pointed toward the edge of the path. "That one. It's huge, and my friends love climbing it."

"Thank you." Keeley dashed toward it with Brett close behind. "MJ! Where are you?"

Silence.

"MJ!"

Mumbles sounded from above.

Keeley reached the tree and looked up.

And gasped.

They had gagged and tied her son to a high, partly broken branch. If Keeley and Brett didn't hurry, the limb would break, and MJ would plummet to his death.

She sucked in a breath.

Crack!

The branch snapped, and MJ slipped.

"No!" Keeley lunged forward, extending her arms to catch her boy.

Lord, save my son!

Chapter Five

Brett ignored the panic coursing through his veins and made his way up the tree, praying the broken branch would hold long enough for him to reach MJ. *Lord, I know we haven't spoken in a really long time, but please hear my plea. Don't let MJ fall. Give me swiftness. Guide my steps.* Brett reached for the next branch and scaled higher.

"Hurry, Brett! You're almost there."

Keeley's cry from below urged him forward. Gave him strength. Or was his sudden rush of adrenaline from God? Perhaps muscle memory from his younger years? His friends had labeled him king of the jungle since he was always hiding in trees, climbing the highest of any of his buddies, to his mother and father's detriment.

Kind of ironic that his first meeting with his son—if MJ *was* his son—would be in a tree. Brett had done his best thinking at higher altitudes. He'd often sought solitude and refuge in the trees.

The boy whimpered, bringing Brett back to the task at hand.

Saving a five-year-old.

Brett had to reassure him and give him hope. "I'm coming, MJ. Hang on. You've got this." Brett lunged for the next branch and lifted himself higher. *Almost there.*

Within moments, Brett reached MJ and removed his gag. "I'm here, bud."

The boy looked up at him, tears glistening in his crystal blue eyes.

Shock stole Brett's breath as he viewed a mirror image of himself, minus the red hair. Could MJ be his son?

Son or not, Brett had to save him. "Wrap your arms around my neck, okay? Nice and tight."

The boy whimpered as his lip quivered. "Are you a bad guy?"

The branch dropped another inch.

MJ screamed.

"What's happening?" Keeley hollered from below. "Save him, Brett!"

They only had seconds before the branch would break from the boy's weight. Brett was shocked it held this long. He focused on MJ. "No. I'm a friend of your mommy's, and I'm here to get you to safety." Brett would properly introduce himself once they were safely on the ground. "Don't be afraid. I'm used to climbing trees and getting back down."

MJ nodded and hung on to Brett's neck.

Brett untied the rope fastening the boy to the broken branch and pulled him away from its deadly grip. "Okay, now wrap your legs around my waist."

MJ obeyed.

"Got him, Keels."

"Thank you, Brett. Mama's here, baby boy." Keeley's voice trembled.

"I'm not a baby," MJ replied.

Brett chuckled. "Of course you aren't. We'll remind your mother of that later. Here we come, Keels."

Now for the hard part. Getting MJ back down the tree. Brett grabbed the rope and tethered himself to the five-year-old, praying the knot would hold. If they fell, Brett would break MJ's fall. "Keep hugging me. Tight as you can."

MJ squeezed harder.

"Good boy. Okay, we're going to make our way down branch by branch."

A gust of wind swept through the tree, causing the limbs to sway.

No! Not now. Brett held tighter to the boy and the trunk, willing the sudden spring wind to remain at bay.

"I'm scared." MJ sniffed.

Brett breathed in. Out. In. Out. He had to cool his own nerves in order to keep MJ calm. "I know, bud. Your mama is praying for us right now." At least, Brett assumed that to be the case. "We're going to inch back down. Ready?"

MJ nodded.

Brett placed his foot on a lower branch and hugged the tree with his free hand, slowly descending limb by limb until they reached the bottom.

Brett untied MJ and tousled his red hair. "You did good, sport."

"You're a good climber, mister."

"MJ!" Keeley squatted and hugged her son. "I'm so glad you're safe."

"Mama! Too tight."

Brett plucked a leaf from MJ's hair. "Keels, he's a brave boy."

She glanced at Brett, tears welling. "Thank you for saving him." Keeley released MJ and held him out at arm's length. "Did they hurt you?"

MJ shook his head before reaching up and wiping away his mother's tears. "I okay, Mama."

Brett knelt in front of him. "MJ, I'm a paramedic."

The boy scrunched his nose. "A what?"

"I look after people who are hurt. Can I check on you just to be sure?"

"'Kay."

"You tell me if any of this hurts." Brett gently squeezed each of MJ's limbs, but the boy didn't respond. "He seems fine, but we need to get him checked at the hospital. Plus, you still need stitches, remember?"

Keeley rubbed her arm. "I know." She turned back to MJ. "This is Mr. Brett."

MJ held out his hand. "Thank you, Mr. Brett, for saving me."

The boy's simple act and words softened Brett's heart. Brett cupped MJ's little hands into his own. "You're very welcome." He addressed Keeley. "Let's go."

"Mama, wait." MJ fished out a note from his pocket and handed it to Keeley. "The man told me to give you this."

She unfolded the paper.

Brett stiffened and didn't miss Keeley's soft inhalation. "What is it, Keels?"

Brett inched closer and peered over her shoulder at the crudely written message.

Dr. Ash, stop your investigation or we'll get to your sweet red-haired boy. Again.

"No!" Her legs buckled.

Brett caught her before she collapsed.

Anger flushed his face and snaked throughout his body at the thought of someone hurting this child.

His protective nature took over, and he steeled his shoulders.

You'll have to get through me first.

No matter what, Brett would pay with his life to protect this boy.

Keeley clung to Brett and snuggled against his chest, her heartbeat mingling with his rapid pulse. If she let go, she was positive her weary legs would buckle. Questions flooded her mind. Who were these people? How did they know so much about the Ash family?

"Mama?" MJ rubbed the backs of her legs. "Don't cry. I okay."

Keeley tensed in Brett's embrace, then pulled back and wiped her tears before turning to her son. "Mama's just so happy to see you again, slugger." She dropped to her knees and caressed his face.

"Slugger? MJ, do you like the Blue Jays?"

MJ jumped up and down. "Yes, Mr. Brett!"

Nothing like her son's love of baseball to lighten their heavy moods. Keeley pushed herself upright. "Shall we head to the hospital?" She had to remain strong and put up a brave front for her son—*their son*.

Keeley examined the playground. She wanted to tell MJ she'd found his father, but right now she was concerned they were still being watched. Later.

First, she had to ensure Brett would stick around. She refused to tell her son about his father if the man was moving away again.

Two hours later, after getting checked by a doctor and discharged, Keeley closed her son's Bible storybook. MJ had fallen asleep after only one page. Tonight, he wanted to hear all about David and Goliath. He said today he'd faced a giant and won. When Keeley and Brett had inquired about his captors, MJ clammed up, not wanting to talk about it.

Keeley hadn't pressed him, but hopefully tomorrow MJ would give them information that could help shed some light on his captors.

Since Keeley wouldn't call in the police, Brett had begged her mother to let him stay with them for protection. Surprisingly, she agreed.

Keeley kissed her son's forehead and turned off the lamp near his bed, leaving only his superhero night-light to illuminate his room.

She backed out and eased the door shut.

Brett's muffled voice drew her toward the living room. She scuffled down the hallway and stopped at the entrance, not wanting to intrude on his conversation.

"Dad, remember to do everything the nurse tells you, okay?" A pause. "I'll be back tomorrow. I have some news to share." Another pause. "Night, Dad. Love you very much." Brett shoved his phone into his jeans and sighed.

Keeley wrapped her buffalo-plaid housecoat tighter around her body and entered the room. "Your dad okay?"

He turned, his eyes glistening from unshed tears. "Not really." He plunked down in the nearby rocker and wiped his eyes. "I'm not sure how to say goodbye. My dad is my best friend."

Keeley sat beside him on the sofa, placing her hand on his knee. "I'm so sorry. Do you know how long he has?"

"Doctors are saying only a few weeks. I'm in

the medical industry and feel so useless. I can't even help my own father."

She didn't miss the waver in his voice. "It's hard to lose a parent. I never knew my dad. He died when I was one."

"I can't imagine not knowing my father."

Keeley removed her hand and leaned back. "Life without my dad wasn't easy, and my mother struggled raising me."

"Has she always been this stern with you?"

"For the most part, yes." Keeley envisioned the day their relationship took an abrupt turn. She pictured it vividly. "When I was six, my mom yelled at me for stepping into her rose garden. I had been playing with a friend and tried to hide. I ruined one bush, so I decided to find some wildflowers to make it up to her."

"So, you've always liked plants?"

She grinned. "Yes. Anyway, to make a long story short, I went into the woods and got lost. I had wandered too far and couldn't find my way back. I got scared and had my first panic attack."

Brett rose and positioned himself by the stone mantel. "Oh my. How long were you in the forest?"

"Until around nine o'clock that night. It's

why I have a fear of getting lost." She puffed out a breath. "I'll never forget the harsh treatment from my mother when they finally found me." She raised her wrist, showing a smartwatch. "Now I'm GPS connected all the time. It also has SOS on it."

Brett picked up a picture.

Her favorite photo of her son—their son—on Santa's knee. MJ had howled, and the photographer snapped the shot at the right moment. "He was three when that was taken."

Brett laughed. "Too funny."

"Trust me, he got over his Santa fear quickly, especially after his grandmother spoiled him with lots of presents."

He placed the picture back. "I was the same way at that age. My mother told me I refused to sit on Santa's knee. She had to bribe me with treats."

"Like father, like son."

"I wish I would've known about MJ." He leaned against the fireplace. "I'm sorry."

Keeley stuffed her phone back into her housecoat pocket and fiddled with the belt. She prayed he wouldn't blame her for not knowing his son for five years. "I honestly tried everything to find you. Even called around different Ontario police departments. No one knew you."

"Not your fault. I should have been honest with you from the beginning." He moved back to the rocking chair. "I was young and stupid, thinking I was this macho police officer." He shook his head. "Boy, was I wrong on that one."

She examined his handsome face as past feelings toward him resurfaced. "Why did you change your vocation?"

"I just realized it wasn't for me." He averted his gaze toward the front window, squeezing his lips into a flat line.

Keeley tensed. He held something back. What haunted his time with the police department? Clearly, he still didn't trust her enough to share.

Time to change the subject. "Brett, do you think the Diglo brothers are responsible for MJ's kidnapping? Something is telling me it wasn't all for the money."

He turned back to her. "You mean like a ruse to get under your skin?"

"Or get close to our family. Maybe this is all about Mom. She's made some pretty powerful enemies in the criminal justice system."

"Do you think MJ will tell us anything about his abductors tomorrow?"

"I'm hoping so." Keeley fiddled with the belt on her housecoat. "If the Diglo brothers are behind this, they've underestimated the Ash family. We don't quit that easily. I collected valuable plant evidence, and I'm determined to figure out exactly what it's telling me."

"Then you won't mind if I talk to the police department and request protection for all of you."

"I'm good with that." She bit her lip. "My mother, on the other hand, may not be. She's more stubborn than I am and likes her privacy."

"I noticed. However, in this case, that's a good thing." Brett returned to his seat. "I'm surprised you still live with her with your strained relationship."

"Well, I'm saving up to buy a house. It's tough being a single parent."

Brett reached over and placed his hand on hers. "I'm here to help. Are you going to tell MJ about me?"

She yanked her hand back. "That depends. Are you planning on sticking around here in Carimoose Bay?"

He exhaled. "Not sure yet. I'm gonna be

honest with you. My supervisor in Ontario left my spot open in case I wanted to return. He even hinted at a promotion, but—"

She shot to her feet. "Until you know, we don't tell MJ. I can't break his heart again."

"Again? What do you mean by that?" He stood and reached for her hand, but she retreated.

"You have your secrets. I have mine. I'm heading to bed. See you in the morning." Keeley hurried from the room. She hated her abrupt change in mood, but when it came to her son, Mama Bear took over.

She would do anything to protect MJ.

Even from his own father.

Chapter Six

The pitter-patter of little feet outside Brett's door woke him, but he didn't mind. The sweet boy's charm was hard to resist, and Brett wanted to get to know him better. Especially if he was his son. What would Keeley tell MJ? He had noted her shift in demeanor when he asked last night. Brett couldn't answer her point-blank question on whether he planned on staying in the Yukon. His former supervisor in Ontario had left it open for him to return once his father passed away and even hinted at a promotion—a position he wanted badly. However, could Brett now leave behind a possible son…for a job? He understood Keeley's hesitation. She was only protecting the boy from getting hurt.

Was MJ really his son? He clenched his fists and pounded the bed. His trust issues plagued his mind and prevented him from fully believing. Even though the resemblance to his son was undeniable, he wondered if he should still get a DNA test to be sure. Keeley would never forgive him if he insisted on it. But the last woman who told him he'd fathered a child had lied. He met Paula at a party back in his way-ward days. That night was foggy, as he'd had too much to drink, but he was positive he went home by himself. She'd insisted her son was his, but the test proved she'd lied. After that expe-rience, Brett vowed to stay out of the dating game and clean up his life.

Brett checked the time on his cell phone: 8:00 a.m. He'd missed the numerous texts from his current supervisor. *Ugh!* Why hadn't his alarm sounded? He punched in Fred Swift's number and waited.

"Where have you been, Ryerson? I've been trying to get in touch with you." The man's angry voice sailed through the phone.

Fred's paramedics often said his rough de-meanor reminded them of nails on a chalk-board. Irritating and they wanted to run in the opposite direction. But the man had been fair to Brett in the short time he'd been back in the Yukon.

"Sorry, sir. Yesterday was a tough day after the attack."

"Tina didn't give me all the details. Did they catch those responsible?"

"Not yet. Keeley is still in danger, and now her son has been targeted." Brett got out of bed and pulled a T-shirt from the bag he'd packed quickly. "Sir, I hate to ask this, being so new and everything, but are you okay if I take another day? I need to handle getting them protection."

"Why you? How do you know Dr. Ash?"

Brett cringed. How could he explain without revealing all? "I met her a few years ago, and she was in the wilderness when the attack happened." He held his breathing as he waited for Fred's response.

"Ahh...a Good Samaritan."

Brett silently exhaled. "Something like that."

"Fine, Ryerson. You're walking on thin ice, but I know Chief Justice Ash, and I don't want to get on her bad side." He chuckled. "One more day, then I need you back on shift."

The man hung up before Brett could thank him.

The smell of bacon enticed Brett's stomach into hurrying. He tossed his phone on the bed and dressed as he planned in his head how to approach Constable Jackson for additional protection without putting Keeley and MJ in more danger. Just how close were the Diglo brothers watching?

Several loud knocks interrupted his thoughts. "Mr. Brett. Brekky! It's bacon, eggs and pancakes."

Brett smiled and opened the door. "Morning, MJ. Well, that sounds like a delicious breakfast. Did you make it?"

MJ scrunched up his face. "No. Mommy did." He caught his hand. "Let's go."

Brett let the boy lead him into the Victorian-style dining room furnished with an antique mahogany table, chairs and china cabinet.

Olivia sat at the head of the table, sipping from a mug and reading the paper.

Keeley looked up from her position beside her mother and smiled. Her red curls flowed over her shoulders and sparkled from the sun shining in the bright room. The green blazer she wore took his breath away. He'd always loved the color on her.

Brett fought to suppress his attraction and moved farther into the dining room. "Morning, ladies."

Keeley pointed to the coffeepot sitting on a side serving table. "Hey there. Coffee?"

"Yes. I need an extra kick this morning."

Olivia closed her paper. "You're finally up. Keeley insisted we wait."

"Sorry, I slept in." He lifted a mug and poured. "My alarm didn't go off."

MJ scrambled onto a chair and stole a piece of bacon, stuffing it into his mouth.

Keeley's jaw dropped. "MJ! You know better than that. We have to bless the food first."

"Sorry, Mama," he replied in between chews.

Brett restrained the laughter threatening to surface and sat beside MJ.

"Okay, time for grace." Keeley bowed her head and prayed a blessing over the food.

"Amen!" MJ yelled before grabbing more bacon.

"Michael Joshua, simmer down." Keeley's tone revealed her lighthearted mood.

Michael Joshua. "So that's what *MJ* stands for." Brett smiled inwardly. Had Keeley named him partly after Brett?

"Yup. Joshua was my grandpa. Michael is after my papa." His lip quivered. "I just wish I knew him. Mama doesn't know where he is."

Brett gripped his knife and fork tighter, curbing the sudden rush of emotion from MJ's innocent statement. He observed Keeley.

Her eyes widened.

Olivia cleared her throat. "MJ, can you tell us what happened yesterday? How did the bad people get to you?"

Leave it to the judge to address the proverbial elephant in the room.

"Mom, I wasn't going to ask him until after breakfast." Keeley added scrambled eggs onto her plate.

"Well, we need to know." The woman sipped her coffee.

MJ dropped his fork. The clang echoed in the room, silencing them. "I okay, Mama. The arc name-sess-es snatched me."

"The who?"

"Duh, Mama. The bad guy in superhero movies." MJ twisted up his nose.

Brett covered his mouth to hide his grin. He could tell the boy was serious, and Brett didn't want to make fun of him.

"An archnemesis?" Keeley scooped eggs onto her fork.

"Yeah, that's it."

"Do you mean he wore a mask?" Brett glanced at Keeley and raised a brow.

MJ nodded. "Yeah, they wear masks. Those bad guys."

"How did he get you at school, honey? Where were your teachers?" Olivia added fruit onto her plate.

"I had to go to the bathroom, and my teacher's phone rang. The bad guy poked me, and I fell asleep."

Olivia bolted to her feet. "I'm calling that school. They need to be held accountable."

MJ whimpered.

"Mom, stop. You're scaring him." Keeley turned to MJ. "How did you get up in that tree?"

"They made me climb a ladder, then tied me."

Keeley moved closer to her son and wrapped her arm around his shoulders. "Did they hurt you?"

"No. One played checkers with me after they came back with some food."

"They left you alone?" Fire burned in Brett's gut at the thought of these men abandoning the boy.

"Yes, when I was sleeping."

"How many were there?"

The boy counted on his fingers, then raised four. "And their mama, Mr. Brett."

The woman Keeley had referred to earlier.

Keeley jolted forward, her knife clattering to the floor. "Their mama was there, too?"

"Yup. She was nice."

"Did you see what she looked like, or did she wear a mask, too?" Brett took a bite of his bagel.

"Sunglasses. Scarf. On. Face." MJ mumbled between bites.

Keeley huffed and leaned back in her chair, crossing her arms. "I don't believe this." She shifted toward Brett. "What type of mother would kidnap a child?"

He inched closer and didn't miss her lilac scent. "Do you think she's connected to the Diglo brothers?"

"Possibly."

"I need to report this to the police and get you more protection," he whispered.

"Mama, you told me no whispering. Rude."

Keeley bounced back into her position. "You're right, MJ. I'm sorry. Let's finish our breakfast so we can get you ready for school."

"Yay! I'm gonna play with Liam." He turned to Brett. "He's my bestest friend."

Emotion clogged Brett's throat as he thought of his own best friend—his father.

MJ gobbled down the rest of his food. "Done.

Mama, can I be ex-cus-ed?" He staggered over the word.

She smiled. "Yes, you're excused."

MJ hopped up and skipped out of the room.

A buzzer sounded.

Olivia walked to a panel on the wall and pushed some buttons. An image of the front gate displayed on a screen, revealing an SUV at the entrance. "Good. They're here."

"Who?"

"Terry and Vic—the bodyguards I called in to protect my grandson." Her eyes flashed at Keeley. "Since you insist on going into work, even after MJ's life was threatened. He needs someone with him at all times."

Keeley stood quickly, her chair scraping on the hardwood floor. "Mom, I can take care of my son."

"Clearly, you can't." Olivia pushed a button, opening the gate. She brushed by them, her heavy perfume lingering in the room. She turned from the entrance, gesturing at Brett while her gaze remained on Keeley. "Now that he's here, perhaps you can quit your job and raise your son. Stop playing in the weeds." She pivoted and continued down the corridor, her heels clicking on the hardwood floor.

Wow. Chief Justice Olivia Ash's claws had emerged, ready to sink into any prey.

Even her own daughter.

Brett had the sudden urge to strike back, protecting Keeley and MJ.

Keeley's shoulders slumped as she walked into her lab at Carimoose Bay Community Campus, her mother's harsh words continuing to haunt her mind. Keeley realized Olivia Ash only wanted to protect her grandson, but she didn't have to criticize and deflate Keeley in the process. *Mom, I can't deal with you right now. God, please calm my spirit. I have a job to do.* Hearing about the people who'd abducted MJ increased her determination to examine the evidence. The Diglo brothers wanted something to remain hidden, but Keeley would find it.

If it was the last thing she did.

She opened the lab door, turning back to Brett. "You didn't have to come. I'm in a secure building." She subconsciously rubbed the healing wound the Diglo brother had inflicted as determination to do her job emerged.

"My supervisor agreed to give me today off, too. Besides, I'd love to see your lab." He grazed her hand. "I know what you do is important, even if your mother doesn't agree."

"I can't do anything right in her eyes." Keeley twirled a curl. "It's especially times like these I wish Dad was still alive. A father would know how to bring the Honorable Olivia Ash down a peg or two." She entered her lab. "Speaking of fathers, how's yours doing?"

"I spoke with the nurse this morning, and he's holding on for now. She's shocked he hasn't passed. It's like he's waiting for something." He followed her. "I just wish I knew what it was."

She studied his profile. How could he be even more handsome than when she'd first met him six years ago? She ignored the sudden rush of attraction. "Do you have any family members he's waiting to say goodbye to?"

"I only have my aunt, and she's been to see him multiple times. My mother is deceased, and Dad's brother passed three years ago."

"Well, maybe—"

"Dr. Ash, you're here." Her coworker shuffled toward them and embraced Keeley. "I'm so glad you're okay, darlin'. Beth told me what happened."

The woman in her late fifties rubbed Keeley's

back in comfort. She always knew when Keeley required a mother's touch.

Unlike Keeley's own. "Thanks, Audrey. I'm doing okay. MJ is safe with my mother's bodyguards."

The woman released her. "Bodyguards?" She rolled her eyes. "That woman."

"Right?" Even her colleagues had seen the judge's ruling demeanor. "Although, MJ loves having them around. When we dropped him at school, he bragged to all his friends that he's under the protection of superheroes."

Audrey chortled and threw her head back. "That's just like MJ." She clasped Brett's hand in hers. "And who's this handsome gentleman?"

"Brett Ryerson, meet Professor Audrey Todd." Keeley gestured to her other colleague. "Brett, these are my coworkers. This is Audrey, and that's Beth Bower."

He waved. "Nice to meet you both."

Keeley leaned in toward Audrey. "This is Mickey."

Her jaw dropped. "*The* Mickey?"

Keeley nodded.

Audrey looked him up and down, whistling. "You failed to tell me how handsome he was."

"Shucks, you're too kind."

She turned back to Keeley. "I'd keep him." Audrey picked up her briefcase from a nearby chair. "Well, I'm off to teach. Got your classes covered today, as I figured you had lots to get done."

"You're a lifesaver. Both of you. Don't know what I'd do without you ladies." Keeley placed her camera bag and briefcase on a table. "Have a good day, Audrey."

"You too, darlin'." She flicked her hand in dismissal. "Ta-ta." She glided out of the room.

Brett folded his arms. "Well, isn't she just something now?"

"And then some." Beth rolled her eyes.

"She certainly keeps us on our toes. She has a heart as big as the ocean, though." Keeley withdrew her camera and handed it to her assistant. "Beth, can you load these into our system? I want to review them up on the screen."

"Sure can." She gestured toward tables on the other side of the room. "The evidence is all set up and waiting for you."

The middle-aged Beth Bower added another blessing in Keeley's work and personal life. She'd recently been widowed and wanted to try something new, so she went back to school to take botany. She now trained with Keeley, and the two made a great team.

"You're the best. Thank you." Keeley took her lab coat off a wall hook. "Brett, you don't have to stay. Go see your father. He needs you."

"I will soon." Brett's cell phone chimed, and he fished it from his pocket. "Constable Jackson is asking when you're coming to their station to give them your statement."

"Shoot. I forgot about that. Tell him later this afternoon. I have to start examining this evidence. Stat."

"Understood. I'm calling him because I want to get some officers watching your campus and MJ's kindergarten."

Beth sucked in a breath. "You don't think we're safe here?"

"I'm sure you're fine, but I'm not risking it. What can I say? You can't take the policeman out of me." He tapped on his phone and placed it against his ear. "Not after what happened yesterday." He positioned himself by a window that faced Carimoose Bay's favorite turquoise lake as he spoke on his phone.

Keeley's office was on that side of the building and where she did her best thinking. There was just something about staring at the gorgeous glistening water that sparked her mind and creativity. *Thank You, God, for Your creation.*

Speaking of thinking...

Time to work.

Keeley spent the next several hours examining the evidence she had collected and doing a thorough analysis on plant taxonomy. She identified each type of vegetation, pollen and seeds. Spring was in full bloom in the Yukon, and the forest sprang with new life.

At Keeley's insistence, Brett had left to visit his father. She couldn't work with someone hovering, and although she appreciated Brett's concern for her safety, she had to practically kick him out of her lab. He contacted the campus's security team and asked them to watch Keeley's lab closely. They promised to report any suspicious activity to the police. Brett would return later in the day to take her to the police station after he'd made arrangements with Constable Jackson.

She analyzed the tree samples she'd taken of the roots growing from the skeletal remains. She also examined the photographs she'd taken, magnifying each for a detailed look to determine how much the roots had grown.

Her tummy growled, reminding her she'd

skipped lunch. Beth had often reprimanded her for getting so immersed in her work that she failed to take care of herself. However, right now, her concern was to study the seasonal rings on the tree and roots. She guided her magnifying glass closer to the vegetation and gasped.

"What is it?"

"I want your opinion, Beth. Come and look at this. These are the thick roots that had grown into the remains. Plus, a section of the tree." She handed the magnifying glass to Beth. "What do you see?"

Beth viewed Keeley's findings. "The light-colored rings suggest growth in the spring and summer. The dark ones later in the year."

"What does that tell us?" Keeley tested her student.

"The remains had probably only been buried close to the tree twelve to eighteen months ago."

"Very good." Keeley flipped to another photo. "Check these plants. What do they tell us?"

Beth inched closer to the screen. "They haven't been there for long."

"Correct. Often when someone buries a body, they disturb the plant life, and other vegetation sprouts up." She pointed. "Now, it is spring, so plants have been dormant for the winter, but study this cluster. Even though they haven't fully blossomed yet, they're taller. That tells us they weren't disturbed." She traced her index finger in a circular motion. "This is the area we need to concentrate our efforts on. I want you to study each sample closely, okay?"

Beth stumbled backward. "Me? Are you sure?"

Keeley clutched onto both of her arms. "Yes. You've got this."

"What are you going to do?"

Keeley checked her watch. "Order us some lunch. Then I'm going to examine the plant life I collected near Cameron's body." She bit her lip. "That reminds me… I need to find out from Constable Jackson who I contact in their forensic department to consult with and share my findings."

"I'm sorry about Cameron. He was such a nice man."

Keeley gripped the sides of the table. "His death was senseless. I need to finish with the evidence and help bring those responsible to justice." Her screen flickered several times. "What's going on?"

Beth wiggled the mouse. "Don't tell me the system is on the fritz again."

The monitor flashed, then went dark.

Keeley froze, her stomach knotting. What—

An explosion rocked the building, imploding her lab's windows. Glass, plaster and other debris hurled toward the pair.

Keeley shoved Beth and dived behind a counter with a thought pummeling through her mind.

She was getting too close.

Chapter Seven

Brett tucked the blanket closer to his father's neck, checking his pulse at the same time. Weak. Tears threatened to torpedo Brett if he didn't hold his emotions intact. His best friend didn't have much longer in this world. At least hospice had provided a caring nursing staff to attend to Harold Ryerson in his own home. The nurse assigned to him today stood in the corner getting meds ready.

"Don't look at me like that." His father's whisper could barely be heard over the beeping heart machine. "I'm not gone yet, but my Savior is waiting. It will be soon." He drew in a ragged breath.

The nurse darted to the bedside and increased the morphine drip. "That should help with the pain, Mr. Ryerson." She returned to counting meds.

Brett cupped his father's hands in his own,

pondering how to word his next question. *Spit it out and don't hold back.* A saying Brett's father often repeated to him when he determined something was on his son's mind. "Dad, what are you waiting for? I'm here. Yes, it's hard to say goodbye, but I don't like seeing you suffer."

His father's gaze shifted to the nurse. "Nancy, can you leave for a few moments? I need to talk to my son alone."

Nancy dipped her chin in acknowledgment and silently left the room, closing the door.

Only the annoying beeping remained.

Brett hated the silence.

Always had, ever since he was a boy. He had told his dad that white noise was his friend. He either had music playing in the background or the television blaring in the next room. At night, he used a sound machine to lull him to sleep.

"Son, I'm waiting for you."

Brett snapped his attention to his dying father. "Dad, I'm here."

"That's not what I mean. Come back to God. He's waiting." He patted Brett's hand. "It's time to surrender to Him."

Brett stood. "How, Dad? God has taken so much from me. First Gideon and then Mom.

How can I surrender to Someone who continually fails me?"

"Gideon's death wasn't your fault. It was mine."

Brett's muscles tightened as anger flushed his face. The day his younger brother, Gideon, died slammed into his mind. The annoying twelve-year-old had been interrupting Brett's time with his friends, and Brett finally had had enough. He yelled at him and then took off with his friends, leaving Gideon home alone. Their father was working, and their mother was away on another of her doctor missions.

The fire consumed their home quickly, and Gideon died in the inferno. The fire department had found evidence of several Molotov cocktails, and the police determined a gang was out to take revenge on their father—Constable Harold Ryerson.

"But, Dad, if I'd been home, I could have saved Gideon." Brett closed his fingers into fists.

"If you had been home, I may have lost two sons. That gang was after me and out for revenge. I was supposed to be off work that day but took another shift."

"But why didn't God stop it? Why didn't God also stop the serial killer who took Mom's life?"

Another wave of pain twisted his father's face.

But Brett guessed it was emotional pain, not physical. Even though their parents had had a rocky marriage with her being away so much, they had held a deep love. Her death not only sparked Brett's journey into law enforcement but ended his father's career. He retired shortly after the killer was caught.

His father reached for Brett. "I need to tell you something about God."

Brett returned and grasped his best friend's outstretched hand, holding on tightly. "What is it, Dad?"

"Sometimes God allows us to enter the wilderness to shape us. Mold us. Then use us. He is in every detail, even life's rough ones." He inhaled a rattled breath. "Let Him in."

"It's so hard." Brett hung his head and dropped into the chair.

"Son, look at me and come closer."

Brett obeyed.

His father reached for his Bible on the nightstand and passed it to Brett. "Read Exodus. God prepared His people in the wilderness. He will do the same for you. Just trust Him."

Brett took his dad's Bible in his hands and traced his finger along the worn leather. "Thanks, Dad. I'll do that."

"Promise?"

"I promise." It was the least he could do for the man who had raised him. "Dad, I don't know how to say goodbye."

"That's easy, son."

Brett's mouth hung open. "How can you say that?"

His father smiled. "We say, 'Catch you later,' because we'll see each other again one day."

Brett's breath hitched at his father's peaceful expression. His smile reminded Brett of MJ's excitement over his new superhero bodyguards. "Dad, I need to tell you something." He fiddled with the buttons on his shirt, pondering how to tell his father the news of MJ. "I think I have a son."

His father's eyes brightened. "What?"

"His name is MJ—Michael Joshua."

"Why do you only *think* he's your son?"

Once again, Brett stood and paced. "Dad, I've had another woman tell me I fathered a child when I didn't. I just don't know if I can believe Keeley."

"Has she ever lied to you before?"

"No, but I really don't know her that well. We only dated a few times six years ago." Brett eased the drapes open, letting a ray of light into the darkened room.

The symbolism wasn't lost on Brett. Was MJ a ray of light in his pain? He turned back to his father. "But you should see him. He has bright red hair and looks exactly like I did at five."

"I want to meet my grandson. Now, before it's too late."

Another promise to fulfill.

But how could he, with Keeley's overprotective nature holding MJ back?

Brett squared his shoulders. He would convince her to give his father this last dying wish.

"I will, Dad. I promise." Brett returned to his father's side. "You will love him. He's such a good kid."

Harold Ryerson's lips curved upward before his eyelids fluttered.

Brett patted his father's hand. "Rest, Dad. You're tired."

"Remember, God is in the details." The sixty-nine-year-old closed his heavy eyes.

A question plagued Brett. Was his father right? Was God in every detail?

His cell phone buzzed, and Brett fished it from his back pocket, swiping the screen. Constable Jackson.

Explosion at Carimoose Bay Community Campus. Thought you'd want to know.

Brett failed to quash his sharp intake of breath. Keeley needed him.

Questions about God would have to wait.

Muffled voices sounded in the distance, bringing Keeley back to consciousness. How long had she been out? Her erratic pulse held her in a dark grip. Warmth trickled down her face. She brought her hand to her pulsating temple. A drop of blood greeted her and raised her panicked state. She inhaled, held her breath, then exhaled slowly. Repeating the process calmed her nerves. She shifted her position and winced. Glass slivers bit into her hand.

Pounding steps and shouts nearby pushed through her foggy brain. Help was approaching.

Or could it be someone wanting to finish the job?

Keeley eased up on her elbows and scanned the room for Beth.

She lay still within inches of Keeley's position.

"Beth!" Keeley ignored the spots flickering in her vision and scrambled toward her coworker. *Lord, please help her be okay.*

Keeley placed two fingers on Beth's neck. Steady. *Thank You, Lord.* She gently shook her friend. "Beth, wake up."

The woman stirred and blinked her eyes open. "What. Happened? Pain. Hurts." She struggled to move.

"Explosion. Where does it hurt?" Keeley ran her hands over Beth's legs.

Beth winced. "There. Hit my knee when you pulled me down."

"Sorry. We had to escape the flying glass. I didn't mean to hurt you in the process." Causing pain for this amazing older woman was the last thing on Keeley's mind. But she had to protect her from harm.

"Dr. Ash!" Constable Jackson pounded on the door. "Are you in there?"

Keeley pushed herself upright and staggered to the entrance, unlocking the door. "I'm glad to see you, Constable Jackson."

He entered the room with other officers and paramedics.

"Call me Layke." He glanced around the room. "Are you both okay?"

"I have minor cuts, but Beth whacked her knee."

"I'll check her over." Tina rushed to Beth's side and squatted.

Keeley followed. "Tina, you were in the forest with Brett yesterday. Sorry we have to keep meeting like this."

"I know, right? Haven't seen you in a few weeks, and now you're on every call." She smiled and opened her medical bag. "Wow, you've been attacked twice in just over twenty-four hours? Someone sure doesn't like you."

The male paramedic approached. "I'm Otto. Let me look at your forehead."

Keeley puffed out a breath and let the man examine her head. "Layke, was anyone else hurt?"

"No, it appears the blast was isolated to the room next to yours. We're examining the scene with local firefighters, but my gut is telling me it was deliberate."

So, once again, Keeley was targeted, and this time Beth was put in the crosshairs. She gritted her teeth. *Lord, these people have to be stopped.*

Layke withdrew a notepad. "Can you tell me what happened?"

Keeley winced from the paramedic's pressure. "We were examining evidence, and our screens began flickering, then went dark. Moments later, the explosion ripped out a wall and shattered the windows."

"Your computers were affected?" Layke asked.

Keeley pushed Otto's hand away. "Yes. I need to check the system. I can't lose valuable evidence I've logged."

Otto scowled. "Wait. I need to examine you."

"I'm fine." She returned to her computer and hit several keys, but nothing appeared on the screen. "No!" She pounded the table. "This can't be happening."

"What is it, Dr. Ash?" Layke moved beside Keeley.

She choked in a breath and placed her hands on the table to steady her shaky muscles. "Our computers were in the room next door. Someone wiped them out."

"Backup servers will protect the evidence."

"Only if I saved everything, Beth." She racked her brain trying to remember if she had. She normally did it like muscle memory, but had that memory failed in her weary and shaken state of mind after everything that had happened with MJ?

MJ! She had to check on her son. *Ugh!* She had left her purse in her office with the phone number for the bodyguards. She fumbled for her cell phone and hit her mother's number. *Come on, Mom. Pick up.*

"Keeley, I'm about to head into the court-room. Not a good time." Her mother sounded out of breath.

"Mom, check with your bodyguards. I need to know if MJ is safe." Keeley failed to subdue her panicked state.

"Why? What's happened?"

"Bomb here on campus."

"Keeley, I told you not to go to work." Her mother's harsh tone revealed her anger.

Keeley gripped her phone tighter. "Mom, I don't have time for this. Just check with them. Please!"

"Fine. I'll call you right back."

Keeley hit End and stuck her phone into her pocket.

Running footsteps echoed outside their door moments before Brett darted through the entrance and to her side. "Keeley! Are you okay?"

"Fine. Just a scrape."

"No, you're not. You're bleeding." He addressed Otto. "She needs her wound cleaned."

The paramedic threw his hands in the air. "I was trying, but she wouldn't let me finish."

Brett crossed his arms, tilting his head. "Keels, let him help you. Why are you so stubborn?"

"My evidence is at risk, and I have to protect

it now." Warmth flushed her cheeks. "I can't let them get away. They need to be brought to justice." She turned to Layke. "I hate to ask this so soon, but who's taking Cameron's place as forensic lead?"

"Virginia Volk. She's on her way."

"No, she's here." A thirtysomething brunette entered the room and approached Keeley, holding out her hand. "Call me Ginger. I'm here to examine the scene next door once firefighters have contained any lingering flames from the blast. I understand you were working with Cameron on yesterday's crime scene?"

The constable lifted his hands to get everyone's attention. "Okay, we need to clear the area before discussing this any further." He addressed Otto and Tina. "Do these ladies need to be transported to the hospital?"

"I'm fine."

Brett moved closer and grazed Keeley's forehead. "Thankfully, it's a tiny cut."

"Beth needs to get her knee x-rayed. It's swollen." Tina addressed Otto. "You finish bandaging Keeley's wound, then we'll take Beth to the hospital."

Fifteen minutes later, the paramedics left with Beth, even though she'd claimed she was okay.

But Keeley knew better. She read the pain on her face. Beth had only been trying to put up a brave front.

Like Keeley.

Ginger pointed to Brett. "What about him? He's not law enforcement."

"He saved my life, and I want him here." Something told Keeley she'd need him beside her.

Layke nodded. "Agreed. He also has a police background and could prove helpful."

Keeley's shoulders relaxed. "I haven't finished studying all the evidence, but I came to one conclusion today."

Ginger folded her arms, tilting her head. "Okay, I'm not sure that plants will reveal anything in this case, but what did you find?"

Great—she didn't acknowledge how botany could help solve cases. Keeley would miss Cameron's cooperative attitude. He knew the value of what she had to offer. "The tree roots growing with the remains reveal they'd been there anywhere between twelve to eighteen months." Pain shot through her temple. She waited for the sensation to pass. "Has Dr. Everson given you any information on the bones?"

Ginger extracted a notebook from her vest

pocket and flipped the page. "Two remains. One female. One male."

Just as Keeley had suspected. She addressed Layke. "When did you say those hikers went missing?"

"Thirteen months ago." His jaw dropped. "Could this be them?"

Keeley shrugged. "Possibly. Contact the mayor since one of the missing hikers was his daughter."

"Layke, did you identify the deceased man at the cabin?"

"Not yet. No hits on his fingerprints. Either the man was squeaky-clean before this or someone erased any records we may have had on him."

Ginger closed her notebook. "Is he one of those Diglo brothers?"

"Well, since we don't know exactly who they are, we can't say for sure." Layke's radio crackled. "Go ahead, Constable."

"Building has been cleared," the female said. "No further bombs."

"Copy." Layke turned to Keeley. "Dr. Ash, is there somewhere we can go to take your statement from yesterday? I want Ginger to examine the lab and the computer room, so we need to clear out."

"Please call me Keeley. Yes, there's a lunch-room down the hall. Ginger, please preserve my evidence. I still have work to do." Keeley hated to bark orders, but this woman had already re-vealed her dislike for forensic botany. Keeley wouldn't let anything happen to her samples.

Ginger's lips pursed. "Even if I don't totally buy into forensic botany, I'm a professional. I wouldn't tamper with evidence."

Rein it in, Keeley. "Of course. Sorry, I'm just a little testy with yesterday's and today's attacks." Her cell phone chimed, and she checked the screen before hitting Answer. "Mom, is MJ okay?"

"He's fine. Stop scaring me like that and quit messing around with this investigation. You're putting your son at risk." The woman hung up.

Keeley viewed the blank screen. "And good-bye to you, too, Mom." She crammed the phone back into her pocket. *Wow, you are crusty today.*

Brett grabbed her hand, tugging her off to one side. "What is it? MJ okay?"

"Yes, but my mother is trying to get me to stop investigating, too. Brett, I can't. I have to help solve this case. We need justice for Cam-eron and for the other two victims." She stared at the cardboard boxes containing the vegetation and pollen samples she'd collected around the investigator's body. She still had to examine those, and something told her time was running out. Wait—

She scurried back to where Layke and Ginger were talking. "Layke, has the clothing been removed from the assailant's body?"

Ginger stepped forward. "I can answer that. Yes, it's bagged and being examined right now."

Layke's radio squawked.

"Constable Jackson, I have news for you," the female constable said. "Sergeant wanted me to tell you the coroner has reported the suspect's body has gone missing."

A collective gasp filled the room.

Layke pressed his radio button. "What do you mean 'missing'? Someone stole it?"

"Affirmative."

Keeley clenched her jaw. How was that possible? Someone desperately wanted to hide the man's identity.

A thought arose, and she snagged Layke's arm. "I need the suspect's boots. They may have valuable evidence on them."

If they couldn't identify the man, maybe

the vegetation would at least link him to the crime scene.

Perhaps giving them something to go on and help finding the other brothers.

Whoever they were.

Chapter Eight

Brett paced outside his father's bedroom as he waited for Keeley to arrive with MJ. She had agreed to let him visit, but Brett could only introduce Harold as his father—not MJ's grandfather. At least, not until Brett committed to staying in the Yukon. She was adamant about not taking the risk of breaking her son's heart. However, Brett knew his father was on borrowed time and wanted to introduce him to MJ before he passed. He could at least fulfill this promise.

Coming back to God would have to wait for now. Brett wasn't ready to put his complete trust in Him until he had proof God really loved His children.

Constable Jackson had finally taken Keeley's statement and had promised to have the suspect's boots delivered to her lab tomorrow once Ginger had finished her investigation. Thankfully, the damage from the bomb was mostly isolated to the computer room. Keeley had determined that she had backed up the files, and they were safe and sound.

But would the perps keep trying to destroy the evidence?

The bell rang, and Brett opened the door.

"Hey, sport." Brett raised his hand, palm out. MJ high-fived him.

Brett noted the two bodyguards behind MJ and Keeley. Seemed Olivia wasn't letting her grandson go anywhere without protection. "Hey, everyone. Come on in."

Keeley's half smile told him she wasn't happy about something.

Brett pointed toward the living room. "Guys, you can wait in here while MJ, Keeley and I visit with my dad."

The pair remained silent but didn't move.

"We'll be fine. Please give us some time alone."

They nodded at Keeley and left the foyer.

Brett leaned into Keeley. "You okay?"

She huffed out a breath. "Just frustrated with my mother's attitude. We had a huge argument when I told her MJ was coming to meet your dad."

"She doesn't like me, does she?"

"Right now, she doesn't like anyone. She also said you don't need to stay at her house since she now has superhero bodyguards." Keeley rolled her eyes.

MJ tugged on his mother's hand. "But, Mama, I want Mr. Brett to stay with us. Can he?"

Keeley shrugged. "Okay with me. I will tell your grandmother it was your idea. You good with that, Brett?"

"Of course."

"Yay!" MJ hopped up and down. "Who lives here, Mr. Brett?"

Brett squatted in front of the boy. "Someone very special to me. Wanna meet him?"

"Yes!"

Keeley took her son's hand. "Slugger, we have to be on our best behavior, okay? Be nice and quiet."

"Why?"

"Because the man is very sick."

MJ's bottom lip quivered, tears welling. "Is he gonna be okay?"

Shivers tickled Brett's arms. The boy's eyes were filled with compassion for someone he hadn't even met yet. *You're a sweet boy. I really hope you're my son.* "Only God knows, sport."

What? Where did that come from? Maybe Brett's view of God was changing.

He held out his hand. "Let's go."

MJ released his mother's grip and held tightly to Brett, skipping as they made their way toward his father's room.

"Remember, no running around. Can you do that?"

"Yes, Mama."

Brett eased the door open. "We're here. Safe to enter?" He glanced at Nurse Nancy.

She nodded.

Brett opened the door wider and gestured to MJ. "This way."

The boy gawked around the room, his eyes widening when he noticed the nurse. "Is this a hospital?"

"Kind of." Brett led MJ to his father's bed. "MJ, I would like you to meet Mr. Harold. Dad, this is MJ."

His father lifted a limp hand. "Nancy, raise my bed. I want a good look at Brett's friend."

MJ hesitated.

Keeley nudged her son forward. "Go on, honey. It's okay to say hi."

Brett placed a step stool by the bed. "You can stand on this."

MJ obeyed and held out his hand. "Hello, Mr. Harold. I'm Michael Joshua, but you can call me MJ."

"Nice to meet you, MJ." Brett's dad took the boy's hand, and then his gaze landed on Keeley. "This has to be your mother. You have the same beautiful red hair."

"Yes, sir, and freckles." MJ pointed to the spots on his face. "I hate freckles."

Brett's father chuckled. "Oh, but, son, freckles are a sign of beauty."

MJ scrunched up his nose. "I'm a boy!"

The group laughed.

Keeley stepped forward, holding a book. "I'm Keeley. Nice to meet you."

"You too." His dad pointed to the hardback. "What do you have there?"

Keeley held up a Bible storybook. "MJ wanted us to read you a story. Would you like to hear it?"

"Sure would." He patted the bed. "MJ, crawl up here beside me."

MJ looked at Brett. "Is that okay, Mr. Brett?"

Brett struggled to keep his emotions intact. This polite boy was stealing his heart. "Sure is."

MJ climbed onto the bed and stretched out beside Brett's father. "Ready."

Brett pulled a chair closer to the duo. "Sit here, Keels."

She shook her head, handing Brett the book. "MJ wants you to read it." She patted the back of the chair. "Sit."

Brett hesitated. Could he do this?

"Come on, Mr. Brett. Read. Now." MJ snuggled closer to Harold.

His father wrapped his arm around the boy. "Yes, son. Hurry."

Outnumbered.

Brett sat and opened the book. "Which one?"

"How about Noah?" MJ clapped.

"Okay." Brett flipped the pages until he found the story.

Keeley leaned over his shoulder. "MJ likes it when I put on a different voice for each character."

"Are you kidding?" Brett whispered, trepidation sneaking up on him at the thought of entertaining a child.

"Nope. You've got this." Her eyes glistened as a smile danced on her lips.

And caused Brett's heart to hitch. *Don't do that to me.*

He focused back on the page and read the story of Noah and the ark, inserting different voices and animal sounds.

His father's and MJ's laughter warmed his heart, and Brett wrestled with his rising feelings but concentrated on reading.

The group cheered when Brett finished.

His father yawned.

Brett hated for the evening to end, but his father required rest. "Sport, it's time to go. My dad needs to sleep now."

"Not yet. Mama and I always pray before sleep time." He sat upright and folded his little hands. "Can I do it?"

Brett didn't miss the tears in his father's eyes. "Of course, MJ. Go ahead."

"God, Mr. Harold has to go to sleep now. Can You help him to get better? I like him. Amen." MJ cleared his throat. "Oh wait, and can you tell Mr. Brett to stay? I like him, too. Amen."

Brett focused on Keeley's face.

Her twisted expression revealed her surprise at her son's prayer, too. She composed herself and held out her hand. "Time to go, MJ."

MJ leaned forward and kissed Brett's father's cheek. "Night."

His father reached up and patted his grandson's face. "Please come back and see me soon."

"I will! Bye." He scampered off the bed and waved. "Mama, can we go in Mr. Brett's car?"

"Sure." She turned to Brett. "I'll tell the bodyguards that we're going with you. That okay?"

"Sounds good."

"We'll grab the booster seat. You almost don't need it any longer." She ruffled MJ's hair. "You're a big boy now, right? Tallest in your kindergarten class."

"Yes!" MJ stood on his tippy-toes as if proving it to the group.

"Excellent. Just want to say good-night to Dad. I'll be there in a minute." Brett held the door open, letting the duo go ahead of him.

"Son," his father whispered.

Brett turned. "Yeah, Dad."

Tears tumbled down his father's face. "Stop being a doubting Thomas. You don't need more proof. That *is* your boy. He not only looks and sounds like you when you were his age, but his movements are identical. No doubt in my mind."

His father's soft words bull-rushed into Brett, and he stumbled backward.

Could his father be right?

After all, the decorated police officer was

known for his sixth sense in all matters of justice—and the heart.

Keeley ensured MJ was buckled into his seat before jumping into the passenger side. "Ready." She checked her watch. "Good, just enough time to see MJ's favorite television show before bedtime."

MJ raised his hands. "Yippee! Let's go, Mr. Brett."

"Yes, sir." Brett chuckled as he shifted the Jeep into Reverse. "ETA fifteen minutes."

Keeley loved how Brett and MJ were getting along. The interaction soothed her soul, and she was touched at how Harold had reacted to his grandson. She could tell that he already adored him. *At least he seems to believe me.* She drew in a deep breath, catching Brett's woodsy cologne, and rested her head against the seat. Feelings for this man were coming back at full force. Already. She had to rein them in. *He's probably not staying, Keels.* Keels. The nickname he'd given her on their second date. No one else called her that, and she liked it. But now? It brought back too much pain and regret.

Brett turned left out of his father's driveway. She checked the side mirror and noted the bodyguards' vehicle follow, cutting off another car. The driver honked and shook his fist. Their "superheroes" weren't letting them out of their sight. They knew that if they lost the judge's grandson, they'd never hear the end of it from the Honorable Olivia Ash.

And neither would Keeley.

She recalled their earlier conversation when she explained the theory of the skeletal remains being the mayor's daughter. Her mother had yelled at her for breaking the kidnappers' demand of not getting involved. Keeley had tried to explain her commitment to providing any information that would help reopen the cold case and get justice. However, her mother wouldn't hear of it—said she was putting her grandson's life in danger.

Keeley had suspected something else was behind her mother's objections. Normally, the woman was committed to bringing criminals to justice, so what was really behind her anger? Keeley had asked, but her mother bit her lip before storming out of the room—a habit Keeley had come to recognize over the years as the judge withholding information.

Did her mother have a secret of her own?

A car horn brought Keeley back into the present. A white sedan cut in front of them.

Brett braked to avoid a collision. "Whoa, buddy!"

The sedan sped up, but their wheels caught on the gravel shoulder, edging them toward the embankment. They swerved back and forth before losing control, careening into the ditch on the other side of the road before plowing into a tree.

MJ screamed. "Mama! Accident."

"Oh dear. I gotta stop. They may be hurt." Brett put his four-ways on and pulled over. He hit the Bluetooth button and called 911, requesting emergency services at their location.

A man staggered onto the road, holding his head as blood trickled down his face. He raised his other hand and beckoned them to come.

Brett cut the engine. "Stay here."

The bodyguards parked behind them, and one hopped out, racing toward Keeley's side. He tapped on the glass.

Keeley hit the button to open the window.

"You guys okay?" The bald, muscular man leaned into the car to check out MJ in the back seat.

"We're fine." Keeley unfastened her seat belt.

"Brett, I'm coming, too. MJ, go with Terry. Mama has to help."

Terry tilted his head. "Are you sure that's wise?"

"MJ has both of you. We'll be fine. I'm sure I saw two people in that vehicle."

Brett clasped his door handle. "I agree with your superhero on this one, Keels."

She scrunched her nose. "Don't take his side. I'm going."

"Fine, but your mother won't like it."

"Does she need to know every move we make?"

"According to her, yes." Terry opened MJ's door and leaned in, unbuckling his seat belt. "Let's go, little man."

MJ crossed his arms. "I told you I'm not little. I'm the tallest in my class."

Keeley smirked and opened her door, stepping onto the shoulder. *Good for you, slugger.*

"We'll be close in case you need us." Terry patted the gun Keeley knew was hidden under his suit jacket. "Your mother would also not want us to leave you."

Keeley nodded.

Brett hurried to the back and returned with

an emergency first aid kit in his hands. "Come on—hurry. We have to ensure they're okay."

After confirming her son was safe and sound with Terry and Vic, Keeley followed Brett over to the injured man.

"Help me, please." He pointed toward the wrecked car. "This way."

Keeley studied the man's face. Something about his expression niggled at her. Where had she seen him before?

"I'm a paramedic," Brett said. "Where are you hurt?"

"Doesn't matter. My friend is unconscious, and I can't wake him. Help!" The man hobbled toward the crashed car.

Brett took Keeley's arm and guided her down the embankment. "Stay close."

They approached the vehicle.

Brett pointed to the leaking gas tank. "That's not good. We need to get him out."

Gas dripped onto the weeds beside the demolished vehicle. Brett rushed forward and stuck his head through the open driver's door.

Keeley stood back and observed Brett checking the man's vitals. "Is he okay?"

"His pulse is steady. Can you help me get him out of the vehicle?"

They each grasped the man under his arms, tugging backward until they were able to remove him from the car.

Brett gestured to a bunch of rocks farther down the ditch. "Quick, get him over there."

They beelined toward the area Brett had pointed out. The injured man followed.

"Keels, open the kit and hand me the smelling salts. I want to revive him."

She obeyed.

Brett waved them under his nose, and within seconds, the man's eyes flew open. He tried to sit.

Brett held him down. "Whoa, buddy. Relax. You were just in a car accident. Tell me where you hurt."

The man groaned and pointed to a deep cut on his right leg. "There." Once again, he squirmed and tried to sit.

"Coz, stay still and let him help." The other man fell to the ground and leaned forward, exposing a gun tucked into the back of his waistline.

Keeley sucked in a breath and eyed the other man.

They both turned to face her.

Two mug shots, pictured side by side, flashed

into her mind. That was where she'd seen them.
Their pictures were in the paper a few days ago.
They were wanted fugitives—two cousins who
had escaped custody after attacking and killing
a young woman a few towns over.

And Keeley and Brett had just stopped to
help them.

She drew in a long breath to slow her rapid
heartbeat. *Stay calm.* She scooped up some gauze
from his kit and fumbled with it. "Brett, can I
speak with you for a minute? I need help unraveling this."

Brett raised an eyebrow.

She dipped her chin in the one man's direction, attempting to give Brett a clue.

"Sure." He stood and took her by the elbow,
steering her away from the two men. "What's
up?"

She held out the gauze and leaned closer,
keeping up her ruse. "I've seen these guys in
the news. They're the cousins who killed that
young girl a few towns over. They escaped custody."

Sirens sounded in the distance.

"Good. The police can help," Brett whispered. "I'll have—"

"Seems we have us a situation here."

They turned.

The first man held his gun and gestured toward the other. "Help my cousin or I'll kill you."

Keeley glanced over her shoulder and spotted the top of her mother's bodyguards' black roof. Could she somehow signal that they needed help? They were trained professionals.

"Don't even think of it, Dr. Ash."

Keeley's gaze snapped back to the deadly fugitive.

He nodded. "That's right. We know exactly who you are."

"How?" she asked.

"The brothers told us. We was following you and wanted to toy with your minds, but little coz here went all race-car-driver crazy on me. Ended up in the ditch." He kicked his cousin's foot. "Stupid, coz. Now you've put us in a pickle."

Keeley balled her hands into fists. "Do you mean the Diglo brothers?"

"Keeley, let's just treat these men and go." Brett took the gauze from her and bandaged up the man on the ground.

Keeley knew she shouldn't press them for information, but when would she have an opportunity like this? The police would be here any minute. Plus, she could easily tap SOS on her smartwatch. Her mother had made her add the bodyguards to her emergency contact list.

The cousin with the gun snorted. "You think we're going to give away their valuable services?"

"What are you referring to? Where do these brothers operate out of? Elimac Forest?"

"How did you know that?"

Bingo.

"Petey, zip it. You've already said too much." The other cousin swatted Brett's hand away. "Never mind. Don't need your help." He sat up, then pushed himself to his feet. He limped over to his cousin and snatched the gun.

The sirens blared. Closer. Help was almost here.

"You might as well give up and tell us what operation the Diglo brothers are into." Brett waved in the direction of the sirens. "Police are here."

Petey squinted. "Wait a minute. You're the doofus who killed Eddie. You better watch your back. Horrible things are fixin' to happen. Roy's got your number."

"Who's Roy?" Keeley had to probe the men. They were holding back information.

The cousin slapped Petey on the back of the head. "You're a fool, coz. You just put a target on our backs. Now they'll never get us out of the country."

Wait—what?

Keeley swallowed to soothe her parched throat. "Do you mean that they're helping fugitives escape across the border into Alaska?"

"Now look who's gone and done it." Petey snatched the gun back, waving it in Keeley's direction. "Let's silence this redhead, shall we?"

Brett stepped in front of Keeley, raising his hands. "You better think this through. Do you really want to hurt the daughter of a Supreme Court judge?"

"Are you her boyfriend, mister?" Petey snickered.

It was time for intervention. Keeley tapped the SOS button on her smartwatch, praying that Terry or Vic would get the message.

"Look, we helped you get out of your crashed car." Brett dangled his key fob. "Take mine. Go. We won't tell anyone you were here."

"You think we're stupid?" Petey lifted the gun higher.

Thudding sounded on the pavement.

The cousins whirled around.

Terry stood with his gun raised. "Give it up! Police are coming now. You have nowhere to run."

Petey aimed the gun toward Terry.

Brett bulldozed into him, knocking him to the ground. The gun fell into the weeds.

Terry scrambled down the embankment and hauled Petey to his feet. "Nice dive, Brett."

Brett nodded and clasped onto the other cousin just as a police cruiser arrived. "Good. Your ride is here. Now you can tell the police everything about the Diglo brothers."

Thoughts of her son so close to danger plummeted into Keeley's head. She had to get him to safety. Now. She took a step up the embankment, but movement rustling in the tall weeds behind them stopped her in her tracks.

Keeley pivoted and caught sight of two masked men dressed in camouflage gear emerging from the tree line beyond the ditch. She recognized the older brother's body type and movements from when they were in the cabin.

Before Keeley could open her mouth, the duo raised their bows, and two arrows flew in unison, hitting each of the fugitives in their chests in a perfect bull's-eye.

The cousins dropped, simultaneously.

The two men darted back into the trees.

The Diglo brothers had silenced the only witnesses Keeley had who could reveal to authorities whatever operation they hid in the forest.

Chapter Nine

Brett threw himself at Keeley, drawing her to the ground out of harm's way. "Stay down." He covered her body with his. Shouts sounded around him as Constable Jackson and another officer pursued the shooters into the woods. If there was ever a time to pray, it would be now, but Brett's stubbornness held him captive. Why couldn't he believe? He really was a doubting Thomas. *God, please help my unbelief. Why can't I trust like Keeley? Like Dad?*

Keeley pushed on his shoulders. "Can't breathe."

Brett studied the tree line to ensure the perps were gone before he rolled off Keeley. He wouldn't put her in the line of fire. Not for her sake or for MJ's.

"I need to check on MJ!" Keeley hopped up.

Terry appeared by her side, extending his hand. "Come with me, Dr. Ash."

Brett stood. "I can help her to the vehicle."

Additional sirens grew louder.

"I think you've done enough," the bodyguard barked. "You should never have stopped. You put her life and MJ's at risk. The judge won't be happy about this."

Keeley's eyes widened. "Terry! That's not true. He's a paramedic. He has an obligation to tend to the wounded." She addressed Brett. "I'll go with Terry to see MJ. You check on the cousins here. They could still be alive."

Brett highly doubted it but knew she was right.

Terry wrapped his arm around her waist as he raised his weapon. "Stay low."

They hustled up the embankment.

Something about the man's action needled Brett. Jealousy? He wanted to be the one to protect Keeley and MJ. Not some hired supposed superhero.

Brett ignored the green-eyed monster rising and dropped beside Petey, pressing two fingers on his neck.

Weak. He was still alive.

He raced to the cousin's side and checked his pulse, but the other fugitive was gone.

An ambulance stopped on the side of the road. Tina and Otto exited the vehicle.

Brett stood and waved. "Over here. This male is still alive."

The duo staggered down the ditch and ran to Brett's side.

"What's the situation?" Tina dropped her medical bag and knelt.

"Two males with arrows to the chest," Brett said. "One deceased. Petey has a weak pulse."

Otto whistled. "Arrows? That's not something you hear of every day."

"Trust me, I'm realizing these Diglo brothers are from a different breed." He faced Tina. "You met two of them yesterday."

Her mouth hung open. "Not them again. Who are they?"

Brett lifted his hands, palms up. "No idea. No one seems to know. How these brothers have managed to stay under the radar is beyond me. I'm guessing that Diglo isn't their real name."

"Identifying them will keep the police busy." Tina began her assessment of Petey's condition.

Otto radioed ahead to the coroner's office to request one to the scene.

Constable Jackson and his fellow officer

emerged from the woods, approaching the group. "I've radioed for additional constables to scour the area, but the shooters are gone. It's like they vanished into a wormhole in the vast Elimac Forest." Jackson rubbed his brow. "It's a mystery with these guys."

"I was just telling Tina and Otto here that no one seems to know their identity. Have you had any updates on the missing body?" Brett eyeballed the black SUV.

Terry stood leaning on the driver's side, studying the scene below with his arms folded over his chest.

Something in his stance and glare didn't sit right with Brett. His police training sent his tingling senses into overdrive. Was the man simply checking out the situation or was there another reason he intently watched the group?

"That's another mystery. The coroner has no idea how the body disappeared, and there's no sign of it anywhere." Jackson paused. "Video surveillance went dark for an hour on their feed, so that didn't help the investigation. Obviously someone who knew computers was involved."

Jackson's words silenced Brett's thoughts on the bodyguard's motives, and Brett returned his gaze to the constable. "So, a hacker?"

"Possibly." Jackson fished out his notebook. "Okay, can you tell me exactly what happened here?"

"Sure." Brett explained the sequence of events leading up to the crash and how they stopped to intervene, then recognized the fugitive cousins. He relayed the conversation they had regarding some sort of operation the Diglo brothers had in getting wanted criminals across the border.

Jackson slammed his notebook shut. "There have been reports of other fugitives seen in our area. This explains why. Not good." He unhooked his radio. "I need to call this in and get in touch with Hannah. Border patrol needs to be advised of the situation."

"Good plan."

Jackson moved closer to Petey. "What's his condition?"

Tina turned. "Stable. For now. I've dressed the wound. We're ready to transport him."

"Good," Jackson said. "I'll follow, as I want to chat with him at the hospital and get more information."

"Are we okay to leave the scene? Does Keeley need to talk to you? I'd like to get MJ back home."

"You can leave, Brett. I'll call if I need anything additional from either of you." Jackson sauntered toward the other constable, talking into his radio.

Brett faced Tina. "You good, or do you and Otto need my help?"

Otto marched toward them. "You're not on shift, so not your job."

Brett raised his hands. This paramedic did not like him. He was always sharp with him. Brett didn't understand why. "Okay, I'm leaving. Chat later."

He trudged up the incline and approached Terry. "We can leave now. I gave the constable a brief statement."

Terry pushed away from the door. "Good. You follow us. I don't want them riding with you. I've already placed MJ in his booster seat." The bodyguard didn't wait for a response and climbed into the driver's side.

Brett bit down hard on his lip to squelch the anger rising. Why did everyone seem to be against him suddenly? He just couldn't win. He grimaced and jogged to his vehicle.

Ten minutes later, he followed Keeley and MJ through the front oak doors of Olivia's estate.

"About time you got home." Olivia reached

for her grandson's hand. "Time to get your teeth brushed and ready for bed, young man." She focused on Brett, wagging her finger in his face. "I will speak to you soon."

Great. Another person who wanted to ream him out.

"Mom, this wasn't his fault. He was only doing his duty of tending to the injured."

"What's your excuse? You should have told him to keep driving." Her eyes flashed. "He put you and MJ at risk."

Keeley placed her hands on her hips, standing her ground. "He did no such thing."

MJ tugged on Olivia's hand. "Gramma, I want Mr. Brett to read a story to me."

The judge's face softened. "I was going to do that tonight, love."

"No. I want him to. He read one to Mr. Harold, and his voices are funny." He scrunched his nose. "Yours aren't."

Brett covered his mouth, hiding the grin from the stoic woman as he imagined her character voices. A saying passed through Brett's head: *Out of the mouths of babes.*

Leave it to his son to speak the blatant truth.

Wait. Did he just refer to MJ as his son?

Was he admitting to himself that his father's assessment of the five-year-old was correct?

Perhaps he didn't need that DNA test after all.

His cell phone buzzed in his pocket. He removed it and checked the screen. Tina.

Why was she calling?

He raised the device. "I gotta take this. I'll read to you in a minute, MJ."

"Yay!" The boy practically bounced down the hallway.

Brett relocated to the large living room and hit Answer. "Hey, Tina. What's up?"

"Just wanted to tell you Petey didn't make it. He went into cardiac arrest, and we couldn't revive him."

No! His legs turned to jelly as his knees buckled and he plunked himself into a chair. "He was stable. What happened?"

"Not sure."

Wait—she normally didn't call him to report on their patients. "Why are you calling me?"

"Because he told me to."

What? "Why would he do that?"

"Before he went into cardiac arrest, he said to give you a message to watch your back. The Diglo brothers are coming for you. They have means everywhere to get to you. They're just waiting to lay the brother you killed to rest. Then you die. His words, not mine."

Brett drew in a sharp, audible breath. Could this day get any worse?

Now he had a target on his back.

Keeley logged her final conclusions eight days later, after scrutinizing every photograph, plant and pollen, then hit Send. She had found a specific pollen on the suspect's boots that matched the sample she'd collected near Cameron Spokene's body, linking the man to the crime scene. However, the missing suspect's body was never found, so the police could not make a positive identification, and the murder weapon still hadn't been located. Thankfully, Keeley and MJ remained safe, even though Keeley had continued on with her investigation. Her mother's bodyguards were good at what they did, and a couple of men were arrested when someone was found stalking her son's kindergarten and watching outside Keeley's college campus. Layke was unable to obtain any information from them. Their lips were shut like an uncooked clam. Someone had paid them well for their silence. They stated they were only in both areas making deliveries. Unfortunately, Layke had nothing to hold them on.

The police department suspected it was the Diglo brothers claiming their sibling's body, and after Brett revealed his conversation with Tina, they knew that to be a fact. Had the brothers taken his body to give him a proper burial, or were they trying to hide some sort of evidence? Their existence eluded everyone. Even after a full search of the woods near the cabin and the accident scene, they'd found no trace of anyone living in the area. Questions haunted Keeley's mind. Where were these brothers hiding? And why had they remained somewhat silent when they had threatened her and MJ? Brett went back to work with Layke on standby.

Brett had visited MJ on several occasions. Watching the two together warmed her heart. They were so similar. It was like looking into a mirror image in their movements and actions. Why couldn't Brett see that? He'd shared what his father said, but he still had lingering doubts. Something from his past held him back, but what?

Audrey entered the lab and plunked her briefcase on the table. "I sure hope you're ready to return to your classes. Those students are sucking the life out of me." She plopped into a chair. "How do you do it?"

Beth approached Keeley and set a coffee in front of her. "Your fave. Fuel for your upcoming class." She winked.

"Thanks." Keeley was amazed at how Beth could almost read her mind. The long hours she'd spent studying the evidence over the past week, along with being on edge that someone was watching them, had drained her energy. She required strength and alertness. Even if it came from caffeine, she'd take it.

She sipped the hazelnut coffee and addressed Audrey. "You just have to know how to handle their antics. Were they continually playing with their phones?"

"Yup."

"Didn't you make them put them in the basket on the front desk?"

She threw her hands into the air. "Now you tell me." She gestured toward Keeley's laptop. "You finish?"

"Yes. Just sent everything off to the forensics team." She held her hand toward Beth, palm facing her assistant. "Couldn't have done it without you."

They high-fived. "Teamwork. You hear anything else about the case?"

"Nothing, Beth, but I'm guessing something is brewing. The suspects have been too quiet." How much should she share with these two? "I'm concerned about Brett's safety. That threat has us all on edge. I can even sense that MJ is worried."

"Seems like he's taken a liking to Mr. Brett." Audrey put air quotes around *Mr. Brett.* "Have you told MJ yet that Brett is his father?"

"Nope. Not until Brett can commit to staying in the Yukon." She sipped again. "MJ moped for days after Preston dropped the bomb that he was breaking up with me and moving. I can't do that to my son again."

"Poor little guy." Audrey gathered her belongings and pushed off her chair. "Don't forget to back up all your evidence. You don't want it to go missing."

Keeley bristled. "Why would you say that?"

"Just because of what happened a few days ago, remember?" She pulled a list from her briefcase and tossed it on the counter. "I gotta run. You okay to teach your afternoon class? Here's the roster and where I left off."

Keeley ignored Audrey's earlier suspicious

comment and brought the older woman into a hug. "Yes. Thank you for everything. I also couldn't have done this without you, either." She swallowed the thickening in her throat and willed the tears to stay away.

Audrey rubbed her back. "Love, anything for you."

The lab's landline rang, and Beth scooped up the receiver.

Keeley broke their embrace. "I better get ready for those rambunctious students. Have a great day, Audrey."

"You too, darlin'." Audrey left the room.

"Yes, she's right here." Beth held up the phone. "For you. It's the coroner. I'll go get your class set up." She handed Keeley the phone before heading out of the lab.

She took another quick sip and set down her mug. "Mrs. Faris, how are you?"

"Keeley, how many times have I told you to call me Pat?" Patricia Faris was near retirement but confessed to Keeley recently she planned to work until she reached seventy. She was married to her job.

Keeley smiled as she pictured the stout grandmother of three. "Sorry, Pat. How are you?"

"The usual. Working hard." Silence stilled the conversation. "I have news."

Something in the woman's tone told Keeley whatever she was about to say wasn't good. "Tell me." She held her breath. *Lord, give me strength.*

"You didn't hear this from me, and I'm only telling you because I know your mother is friends with the mayor and his wife. I tried to get ahold of Olivia, but she's in session right now."

"Okay."

"I've identified the skeletal remains. It's the mayor's daughter and her boyfriend."

Keeley closed her eyes, gripping the phone tighter. *Lord, no. This will break Mom's heart.* Olivia had doted on the mayor's daughter, Zoe, after she took the young woman under her wing when Zoe had shared that she wanted to become a lawyer. Something her own daughter had failed her on. "I appreciate you telling me. I'll let Mom know before the news breaks."

"Also attempting to do a DNA test just to complete the process, but the forensic artist and anthropologist did a three-dimensional reconstruction of both skulls. The mayor confirmed it's them." She clucked her tongue. "Such a shame. Zoe had a promising future as a lawyer. That girl was smart."

Keeley twirled a curl. Her mother had confirmed time and time again how smart Zoe was, to the point Keeley had become jealous of the younger woman. "Definitely a shame. I appreciate the heads-up."

"No prob. See you and your mom this Sunday at church? I missed you both last week."

Keeley loved their tight-knit community. Most of the time. Some days she wished she lived in a larger city so she could hide from prying eyes, but the community banded together when they knew one of their own required help. "Hopefully. Have a good day, Pat."

"You too. And, Keeley? Watch your back. You never know who you can trust. These hikers were murdered."

Keeley tensed. "I'm being protected, but I'll be careful."

"Good." The woman hung up.

Keeley drank more of her coffee before dialing her mother's office number. Hopefully she was out of session now, because Keeley didn't want to give her the message over a text. She tapped her thumb on the desk as she waited for her mother to pick up. *Lord, be with the mayor and his wife, Sofia.* The Coateses were a close family and did everything together. While this news gave them closure, they always had hoped Zoe would return unharmed. Somehow.

"Just getting out of court, Keeley." Her mother's breathless voice revealed her hastened movements. "What's up?"

Sweat beaded on Keeley's forehead as a rush of warmth blanketed her body. Did someone turn up the heat? She ignored the sensation and concentrated on the call. "Mom, I would rather do this in person, but I have bad news."

"Is MJ okay?"

"He's fine." Keeley inhaled. "I'm sorry to tell you the female skeleton we found was Zoe, Mom."

"No!" Grief filled her mother's one-word reply.

A wave of nausea attacked Keeley, and she swayed. *I need rest.* Her body screamed at her to take a break. "I'm so sorry, Mom. I wanted to tell you before it hit the news. I knew how close you were to Zoe."

"Yannick and Sofia will be devastated. I need to call them. See you at home." She clicked off without saying goodbye.

Figured. Her mother seemed to have more

love for Zoe than her own daughter. *Harsh, Keeley. Lord, forgive me. I know what Zoe meant to Mom. Give her and the Coateses strength and comfort during this difficult time.*

Once again, dizziness plagued Keeley as sharp pains jabbed her stomach. She gripped the sides of the table to allow it to pass. What was happening?

Approaching movement sounded, and then her lab door opened.

Brett entered.

Her knees buckled as spots blocked her vision, and another pain attacked her abdomen. Words became stuck in her throat. His voice registered in her foggy mind. She extended her hand, silently begging for help.

Brett yelled her name moments before darkness ushered her into its embrace.

Chapter Ten

Brett barreled to Keeley's side and wrapped his arms around her waist, catching her before she fell. "Keeley!" *Lord, please don't take her, too.* He gently laid her on the floor and checked her pulse, then her breathing. Both weak. He took out his cell phone and dialed 911, requesting an ambulance. He had wanted to check in on her before his night shift. Good thing he did. Was his intuition to do so from God? What had caused her fainting spell?

Her assistant ran into the room. "Keeley, where—" She halted. "No!" She fell beside her boss. "What happened?"

"No idea. I just entered the room, and she passed out. I caught her before she fell and called for an ambulance." Brett felt her forehead. "She has a fever. Not good."

"What do you think is wrong?"

"Not sure." He examined her limbs. Nothing stood out. "Has she had anything to eat or drink?"

"She had a muffin, and I brought her a coffee a bit ago." Concern shone in Beth's eyes. "Do you think it's from exhaustion? She has been working way too hard these past few days."

"Is that new for her, though? Does she normally not eat well when under deadlines?"

"Happens all the time. I've scolded her often about not looking out for herself." She clucked her tongue. "After all, she has a child to consider."

Brett racked his brain, trying to figure out the cause. "Has she fainted before?"

"No."

Brett eyed her complexion. Pale. An idea formed. "Where did the muffin come from?"

"She brought them in from home. Said she made them herself." She clutched his arm. "Wait—you think she was poisoned?"

"Possibly." Once again, he took out his phone and hit Constable Jackson's number. "Where did the coffee come from?"

"I made it." Her jaw dropped. "You don't think I poisoned her, do you?"

"I'm not saying that."

The call clicked in. "Jackson here."

"It's Brett. I'm at Keeley's lab, and I believe she's been poisoned. An ambulance is on the way." *Please save her, God. Don't let MJ lose his mama.*

Jackson barked orders in the background. "On my way with a team." He punched off.

Brett addressed Beth. "Can you find a pillow or something to cushion her head?"

She nodded and left the room.

Now for the hard call. He dialed Olivia's number and waited.

"Olivia Ash. Who's this?"

"It's Brett, Olivia."

"What do you want?" Her harsh tone seeped through the phone.

And sidelined him. Why was this woman so miserable toward him? He ignored his question and took a breath to calm his racing heartbeat. "I'm here with Keeley at her lab. She's fainted. Ambulance is—"

"What? Aren't you a paramedic? Help her!" she demanded.

Approaching sirens sounded near the campus property.

Beth returned and handed him a pillow.

Brett eased Keeley's head up and positioned the cushion underneath.

"I've examined her, and the ambulance is here now. They'll take her to Carimoose Bay Regional, if you want to meet us there. Can you get MJ, or should I pick him up?"

"No. I'm his kin. I'll get him." She disconnected.

Brett whistled and tucked his cell phone back into his pocket. "Wow, she really doesn't like me."

Beth harrumphed. "Join the crowd. She doesn't like me, either. No idea why."

"Did anyone else drink the coffee?" Brett changed the subject.

"No, it was from a coffee pod. Single serving."

Odd. How could someone have tampered with the pod? "Did you throw it out? The police will need it and her coffee mug."

"I'll get it from the garbage."

Brett hauled her back. "Wait. Let Forensics do it. They'll want to take your prints."

"You think I somehow injected a poison into her coffee pod?" Beth placed her hands on her hips.

He shook his head. "Again, I'm not saying that. The police will just want to rule out your prints because you touched the pod and her mug."

Rushed footsteps sounded in the hallway moments before Otto and another paramedic appeared.

Brett explained the situation. He then backed away, allowing them to do their job.

Constable Jackson and the forensic woman hustled into the room moments later.

"Brett, tell us what happened," Jackson said.

Brett gave them all the details, including his idea of her being poisoned. They quickly went to work bagging the evidence, dusting for prints and questioning Beth. They'd take her downtown to obtain her prints to rule her out.

The paramedics loaded Keeley onto the gurney.

"Layke, you okay if I leave with Keeley? I want to go with her to the hospital."

"Of course, Brett. We'll let you know what we find here. Ginger will check for poisons and consult with the hospital after they take a blood sample."

An hour later, Brett paced outside Keeley's hospital room. The doctor admitted her and ran a gamut of tests. Brett had called Tina to tell her he'd probably be a bit late. The older paramedic wasn't happy with him, but it couldn't be helped. Thankfully, he'd arrived at Keeley's lab hours before his shift started, or he would have had to ask for another day off.

Terry, the bodyguard, held his position beside the entrance. Feet apart, arms crossed and eyes in constant movement, scouring the area for threats. Vic lingered down the hall, watching the exits. No one was getting by these two.

The doctor emerged from Keeley's room.

Brett stepped forward. "I'm one of the paramedics on-site. Can you tell me her condition?"

He tilted his head. "You should know I can't reveal anything. You're not family."

Brett knew that but had to find out how she was doing. "Can I at least go in?"

He gestured toward the door. "You'd have to ask the almighty judge in there that question. Apparently, she's calling the shots in this hospital now. If it wasn't for her grandson, I'd have security throw her out. No one talks to me like that." He marched down the hall.

Leave it to Olivia to take over.

Brett tapped on the door and edged it open. "Okay to enter?"

MJ turned from his position at Keeley's side and raced toward him. "Yes, Mr. Brett. Come see Mama. She's sick." He took Brett's hand and dragged him into the room.

Olivia didn't have a say in the matter. Her grandson had spoken. She sat on the opposite side of the bed, barking at someone on her phone.

Brett approached Keeley with MJ at his side. "Your mama is gonna be okay." He kept his voice low.

"I know, Mr. Brett. Jesus is on our side."

Oh, to have the faith of a child. A faith without doubts.

You once did.

Where did that thought come from?

It was true. He had committed his life to Christ at a young age, but after tragedy struck when he was fifteen, Brett gave up on his childhood faith.

Let Him in.

His father's words from a few days ago returned. Was it time for him to come back to God and shake off his doubts?

Olivia bolted upright. "Well, you tell him if he doesn't put a rush on it, then I'll sue the entire police department." She mumbled before stuffing her phone into her purse, then turned her fiery eyes in his direction. "Who let you in?"

"I did, Gramma." MJ trotted over and tugged

on the hem of her blouse. "I'm hungry. Can I have a snack?"

"I didn't bring anything."

MJ pointed to the door. "I saw chocolate bars in a case down the hall."

"I can take him there if you want, or I can stay with Keeley." Brett shifted his stance, preparing for a fight but praying she wouldn't argue in front of her grandson.

She snatched her purse. "You stay here. I need a coffee anyway." She held out her hand. "Let's go, slugger."

Brett waited until they left the room before bringing the chair closer to Keeley's side. He took her hand in his and stared at her ashen face.

A lump formed in his throat at the prospect of losing this woman—again. How had he left her so easily six years ago? His feelings for her returned, punching him in the gut. Dare he admit he had cared for her back then? They had barely known each other, but he now realized their attraction had gone deep.

What about now?

He caressed her cool face. Good—her temperature had dropped. "Come back to us, Keels. I promise I won't leave you again."

Even if he was offered the promotion in Ontario, he couldn't take it. Not now. Not when he had a family here.

He owed that to both Keeley—and his son.

His heart hitched.

Brett straightened, pressing his shoulders back as determination emerged.

He leaned forward and kissed her forehead. He would do anything to protect Keeley and MJ. Even give his own life.

Lord, catch those responsible and bring them to justice. I need my family to be safe.

Keeley labored to open her heavy eyelids. Fog crowded her mind as she scrambled to determine where she was and what had happened. She moaned and licked her sandpaper-like lips.

"Keels, can you hear me?"

Someone rubbed her hand.

Her heart hammered in her heavy chest. Why did she feel like a bulldozer had taken her out?

"Keeley, it's Brett. Can you open your eyes?" The voice grew louder.

She opened her eyes, but her cloudy vision blocked her view. She fluttered her eyelids until the room cleared.

The handsome man from her past hovered over her. "Keels. I'm here."

"Brett?" Her voice squeaked out his name. She tried to clear her throat, but it felt like she'd swallowed slivers of glass. She pointed to her neck. "Dry."

"Here, drink." He held a bent straw to her lips.

She sipped and winced as the liquid slid down her parched throat. "What…happened?"

"We think you were poisoned. I got there just as you fainted." Brett's voice shook. "Do you remember anything?"

She drank more water, allowing it to cool the fire. "I remember talking to Mom, then falling. Where was the poison?"

"We believe in the coffee. Ginger is examining the mug and the pod. The hospital has taken lots of your blood." He rubbed her arm.

"How long have I been out?"

"It's now six in the evening, so almost seven hours."

Keeley drank more water. "Where's MJ?"

"Your mom took him to get a chocolate bar from the vending machine." He chuckled. "Rather, it was MJ who took her."

Keeley tried to smile, but her lips hurt too much. "He loves chocolate."

"I gathered that." Brett caressed her face. "How are you feeling?"

"Tired. Am I dying? Is that why I feel like an elephant is sitting on my chest?" She coughed.

Brett pushed the call button. "I'm going to get the doctor in here, but they believe we got to you in time." He pointed to the IV drip. "They flushed your system and treated you."

Seconds later, the door burst open, and the medical staff entered. A man approached her bed. "Dr. Ash, I'm Dr. Garrison. How are you feeling?" He placed his fingers on her wrist.

The nurse checked the machines.

"Chest is heavy. Tired. Am I dying?" She repeated her earlier question to Brett.

Dr. Garrison patted her arm. "All indications are showing improvement, so we believe you're going to be fine. Someone was looking out for you, young lady."

"Have they determined the poison used?"

Dr. Garrison turned toward Brett. "Wait. I remember now where I know you from. You're the newer paramedic."

"Brett Ryerson. Friend of Keeley's." He extended his hand.

The doctor returned the gesture. "Nice to meet you, but I still can't discuss her condition."

"Doc, it's okay. Brett was the one who found me. If it wasn't for him, I'd probably be dead." She drank more water before continuing. "Please tell us."

"Well, we won't know exactly until our lab speaks with the police." He chortled. "However, if your mother has anything to do with it, we should know soon. I've heard she's putting on the pressure."

"Yeah, she tends to do that. Sorry." In this case, Keeley didn't mind her mother's interference.

The doctor finished his assessment. "Your vitals are improving. That makes me happy."

"Her color is returning, too." Brett smiled at her. "That's also a good sign."

Keeley absentmindedly reached to smooth her hair. "I'm sure I look a fright."

"You're as gorgeous as ever, Keels." Brett kissed her forehead, then backed away quickly. "Sorry."

"You don't—"

The door opened, and MJ bounded toward the bed. "Mama!"

Her mother ended her phone call and approached. "How are you feeling?"

How many times would she be asked that today? "I'm tired."

MJ stood on the bed railing, drawing himself upward.

The doctor held him back. "Just a minute, young man. Your mother still needs rest."

"It's okay, Doc." Keeley patted a spot beside her. "He's all the medicine I need right now."

MJ crawled onto the bed and nestled himself close to Keeley.

"Okay, but they will have to leave soon." He gestured toward the nurse. "We'll leave you alone now. I'll check on you a bit later, okay?"

"Thanks, Doc."

The doctor and nurse left the room.

Keeley wrapped her arm around MJ and kissed his cheek. "Love you, slugger."

"Wuf you, too, Mama." MJ rested his head on Keeley's chest.

A knock sounded moments before the door opened and Layke stuck in his head. "Can we come in?"

Keeley wasn't sure how much longer she'd be able to keep her eyes open, but she waved him in. "Of course."

Layke entered, followed by Ginger.

"We have news and thought you'd want to know."

Keeley's mother stood from where she'd been sitting. "Have you completed your tests yet?"

MJ squirmed in Keeley's arms.

She winced at her mother's use of her judge voice when she'd asked the question. "Mom."

Ginger raised her hand. "It's okay. She's already proved how far her gavel and wallet reach."

"Mom, please take MJ for a walk." She didn't want her son to hear what the police were about to say. "Go with Gramma, slugger."

He pouted. "I want to stay here."

That sad face is hard to resist. Keeley suppressed a grin. "It will only be for a few minutes. How about you get Mama some chips, okay?"

His eyes sparkled. "Me too?"

"No. You can have some of mine." Not that Keeley wanted anything to eat right now, but her son didn't need to know that. She grazed her lips on his forehead. "How does that sound?"

"Good!" He hopped down from the bed. "Let's go, Gramma."

Her mother scowled but took MJ's hand before exiting.

"Go ahead, Ginger. Tell me what you found."

Keeley gripped her hospital bedsheets tighter, bracing for the forensic investigator's news.

Ginger took out her notebook and read from it. "The poison wasn't in the coffee but on the rim of your mug."

Brett whistled. "Wow, that's a new one. What poison?"

"Highly concentrated privet."

"What?" Was it a coincidence that Keeley was poisoned by a plant? Was someone sending her a message? "That plant isn't found in the Yukon."

"I'm thinking that whoever did this was only trying to scare you. This plant doesn't normally kill." Ginger tucked her notebook back into her pocket. "We tested all the mugs in your lab, and yours was the only one with privet on it."

"Did you always drink from the same cup?"

She pictured the World's Greatest Mama mug. "Yes, Layke, mostly. MJ gave it to me for Mother's Day last year."

Layke withdrew his notepad and handed it to her. "I'm gonna need the names of everyone in your department who'd have access to your lab and lunchroom."

"Do you really think it was someone I work

with? Lots of folks come and go in my lab." Her fingers shook as she took the pen. The thought of having to name all her precious colleagues tore at her heart. It felt like a betrayal. A tear slipped down her cheek.

Brett grazed her arm. "It's okay. It may not be one of them."

Her gaze snapped to his, her heart lodging in her ribs from his gentleness. How did he know her thoughts?

His cell phone buzzed, and he looked at his screen. "Tina again. I gotta get to work." He pocketed his phone and focused on her. "You rest. I'm on the night shift. I'll be back early in the morning."

She nodded, words wedged in her throat.

"Constable, I realize Olivia has bodyguards outside the door, but they'll probably leave when MJ does, as they're tasked to protect him. Can you have someone keep watch over Keeley?"

"Of course, Brett."

"I'm concerned that when whoever did this realizes Keeley didn't die, they'll try again in some other form."

Keeley didn't miss Brett's tone. Her stomach fluttered at the thought of him caring, but she also realized the danger wasn't over. The question was—when and where would this person try again?

"Sorry again for being late earlier." Brett jumped into the back of the ambulance he shared with Tina, his thoughts still on Keeley. Constable Jackson had promised to protect her, but Brett wanted badly to stay by her side. He wasn't a police officer any longer, but he still felt responsible for keeping her safe. He and Tina had been dispatched multiple times throughout the night. Brett was ready for this busy shift to be over.

"You already apologized." Tina refilled the cabinets with supplies, getting ready for their next call. "It's clear you care for the woman."

Was he that obvious, and when had his feelings leapfrogged into something more than friendship? *Face it, you're smitten.* "Yeah, I guess I do."

"Her son is a cutie."

He reached for the cabinet door, but his hand stopped in midair. Where had she seen MJ? Suspicion crawled up his spine. "Have you met MJ somewhere?"

She looked down, concentrating her efforts

on restocking supplies. "I saw him at that accident you helped with."

How could she have? He was in the back seat of the bodyguards' tinted SUV. "But how—"

The buzzer blared throughout the garage moments before 911 dispatched their ambulance to a woman in labor on the bridge over Elimac Lake.

Their conversation and Brett's suspicions would have to wait. For now. "Let's go." He hopped from the back and darted around to the driver's side.

Nine minutes later, Brett drove onto the bridge separating Carimoose Bay and the nearest town.

A car sat at the top, the driver's door open. Streetlights illuminated the area and revealed a man waving his hands, beckoning to them.

Brett parked behind the red vehicle and jumped out, leaving the lights fixed on the car.

Trucks barreled onto the opposite end, parking nose to nose, blocking anyone from either exiting or coming onto the bridge.

Tina caught his arm. "What's going on?"

Two more trucks pulled onto the other end, parking in the same position.

Trapped with nowhere to run.

The man beside the car shoved a balaclava down over his face and pointed a rifle in their direction. "Time for you to pay, Mr. Paramedic."

Men on both sides of the bridge leaped from their trucks. All masked and dressed in hunting gear, rifles attached to their shoulders.

One approached. "Mama says our mourning time is over. Time for you to pay for killing our little brother." He turned to the others.

Bile burned the back of Brett's throat as terror seized every muscle in his body. He dropped his medical bag.

"Brett, they're gonna kill us." Tina's forced words revealed her apprehension.

Lord, what do I do?

Brett stepped in front of his partner. "It's me you want. Let her go."

"Sorry, she's collateral damage. Don't worry—Keeley and MJ are next. This time we'll succeed. Don't think those bodyguards or her judge mother can keep them safe at that hospital."

Brett's legs weakened, and he stumbled but caught himself. *Lord, protect my family!*

The hunter peeked over his shoulder. "Time to do this."

One man stood guard with his rifle trained on Brett and Tina while the other members climbed onto their truck's cargo bed, then removed dirt bikes.

They sped off the bridge, but one driver stopped and dismounted.

It was then Brett noted multiple bags close to where they left their abandoned vehicle.

No! They were going to blow up the bridge with Brett and Tina on it.

The man held up a device. "Fire in the hole!"

"Jump!" Brett grabbed his partner's hand and charged to the other side of the bridge, catapulting over the railing.

He plunged into the dark water feetfirst and prayed Tina had done the same thing.

Their lives depended on it.

Chapter Eleven

Brett emerged from the icy waters and gulped in a breath, struggling to see in the darkness. He treaded water, circling to find his partner. "Tina!" he yelled as water gushed into his mouth. He spit it out, inhaled and submerged again with his eyes open, searching for her. The murky waters inhibited his hunt for Tina, so he broke to the surface again. He finally spotted her a few feet away. Brett swam quickly to her location and towed her face up to the river's edge and onto the rocky shore.

Brett checked her vitals.

She wasn't breathing.

"No!" Brett cleared her airway and gave her rescue breaths, then compressions. Without his equipment, he had to administer CPR the old-fashioned way.

He repeated the process. "Come on, Tina! Talk to me."

She coughed, spewing out water.

Brett rolled her onto her side, allowing the rest to expel. "Thank God. I thought I lost you." He helped her to sit up. "You okay?"

"I will be." She breathed in and out multiple times.

Brett pushed himself upright and scanned the area to ensure the Diglo brothers had left the vicinity.

All was quiet. For now.

"Can you walk? We need to get through those woods and onto the highway to flag someone down."

She nodded, holding out her hand.

He helped her stand, wrapping his arm around her waist. Any earlier suspicions about Tina dissipated. She wouldn't have put her own life on the line if she was one of them.

Would she? Or was she good at deception?

Together, they stumbled through the dark woods to the side of the highway. Brett gestured toward a boulder. "Lean on that. I hear some traffic, and I'm going to check it out."

She sat. "Make sure it's not them!"

Brett hid behind a tree and listened for dirt bikes. When no rumbles sounded, he stole a glimpse at the road. Headlights approached from around the bend. Without daylight, he couldn't make out the vehicle, but he had to take a risk. He stepped out and waved his hands, praying the driver was a friend, not a foe.

The van stopped, and a woman rolled her window down, eyeing his soaked clothing. "Are you all right?"

"Yes. Do you have a cell phone? I need to call 911. Accident ahead and the bridge—out." He realized his garbled words probably didn't make sense. *Calm down, Brett.* But he had to get to Keeley and MJ. Their lives were in danger.

Her head turned, and she pointed.

He followed her line of vision.

Smoke billowed upward toward the starry sky, confirming his statement regarding the bridge.

The woman fished in her purse and passed him the phone. "Here. Let me pull to the side."

"Thank you for being a Good Samaritan." He dialed 911 and requested emergency services at his location.

Forty minutes later, after getting checked and cleared by Otto, a constable agreed to take him to the hospital once he explained the situation. They followed the ambulance as Otto rushed Tina to be checked by doctors.

Brett hopped from the cruiser as soon as the constable parked. He sprinted through the double doors toward the stairs, taking the steps two at a time to get to Keeley's room in the ICU. He couldn't wait for the constable or the elevators.

Reaching her floor, he ran down the corridor and stumbled into her room.

Only to find it empty. They had changed the bedsheets. No sign of Keeley.

Where was she? Brett wiped his sweaty palms on his pants, then raced toward the nurses' station. He slapped his hand on the counter.

The nurse glanced up from her screen. "Calm down, sir." Her eyes traveled over his dirty, wet uniform. "You're a paramedic. You should know better. Now, how can I help?"

Brett, relax. He inhaled. "Where's the patient in room 204?"

"Are you family?"

"No, but I was just with her last evening." He realized he was breaking protocol, but he had to find her.

The doctor from earlier walked around the corner. "Brett, you're back. Keeley has improved, and we needed the bed in ICU, so we moved her to the fourth floor."

"Thank you. What room?"

"Jill? Tell him. The patient would want him to know." He snickered. "Trust me, you don't want the judge's wrath. She just arrived with her grandson."

Already? It's still early. Clearly, Olivia had made quite the reputation in under twenty-four hours.

The nurse tapped the computer keys. "Room 408."

"Thank you." Brett turned to the doctor, a plan forming in his mind. "Is she stable enough to be discharged into my care this morning? As you know, I'm a paramedic."

"Well, she's stronger, but I wouldn't recommend it." He tilted his head. "What's this about?"

Brett leaned in and lowered his voice. "Her life has been threatened, and she's too accessible here."

"Even with her buffed bodyguards?" He laced his words with sarcasm.

"I just barely escaped from the men who are after her. I need to get her to a secure location." Brett's police lingo returned in a flash.

"Well, you would need her authorization." He hesitated. "And probably the judge's."

"Okay, we'll be in touch." Brett raced to the

exit, pushed the door open and bounded up the stairs two more floors. He skidded to a stop after entering the corridor and spied the body-guards. He headed toward them.

They eyed his crumbled, damp uniform and stood side by side, blocking the entrance.

"What happened to you?" Terry crossed his arms in his normal protective stance.

"Long story. Listen, Keeley and MJ are in danger." Brett had to tell her the plan. "I need to see her right away."

They looked at each other.

"Come on, guys. I wouldn't harm either of them." Brett raked his fingers through his dirty hair.

Terry opened the door. "We're watching." He sniffed. "Take a shower, man."

Brett ignored them and hurried into the room. "Keels, we have to leave."

Her eyes widened, and she sat straighter in bed. "What happened?"

Olivia rose to her feet, took one look at Brett and grabbed MJ's hand. "Slugger, let's go for a walk."

Brett motioned toward the door. "Be sure to take either Terry or Vic with you. Leave one at the door."

Olivia pursed her lips and nodded at Brett before exiting with her grandson.

"We need to get you discharged and back behind your mother's guarded estate." Brett hated the distress coming out in his breathless words.

"Tell me what's going on." She reached for him.

He took her hands in his. "Tina and I were targeted on the Elimac Bridge. The Diglo brothers told me I had to pay for killing their little brother, and he said you and MJ were next." He explained how they blew up the bridge moments before he and Tina launched into the water.

Her eyes widened. "Are you okay?"

"Bruised from hitting the water, but Tina almost didn't make it." He rubbed his brow. "I had to resuscitate her."

Keeley's mouth formed an O.

"How are you feeling? Did you get a good rest?" Her regular peachy skin tones encouraged Brett.

"Much better but tired." She raised her arm. "They still have me hooked up to an IV."

"I spoke to the doctor. He said you were improving. I realize I'm not a doctor, but I'm trained, so he may discharge you to my care. If you and your mother agree, of course." Brett resisted the urge to roll his eyes.

"Yeah, she yelled at him earlier." Keeley swung her legs over the edge. "I'm feeling stronger, but do you think it's wise for me to leave so soon?"

"We need to get you out of the hospital. The Diglo brothers know you're here. They've targeted you, MJ and me." Brett wasn't sure how she'd take the next news, but he had to be honest. "Keels, we all need protection, and the safest place right now is in your mother's gated community. We have to lie low for a while, including your mother."

Panic twisted Keeley's facial muscles. "But what about your father?"

Brett's shoulders slumped. *Good question.* How could he protect them and spend time with his father? *Lord, I need to do both.* "I will check with Nancy to see how he's doing. It should only be for a few days. Hopefully."

"My mother won't like it, but at least we have her bodyguards."

Brett recalled his earlier suspicions of Terry's behavior. "Do you trust Terry and Vic?"

"I don't have any reason not to. Why?"

"Just a vibe I get from Terry." He tapped his

chin. "Nothing I can put my finger on at the moment. Your mother should take a leave of absence from the courts, too. Stay out of the limelight."

Keeley grasped Brett's arm. "You don't think they'll come after her, do you?"

"We can't take any risks. Will she agree? I know she doesn't like me."

"She'll have to." Keeley rang the call bell. "I'm going to get the doctor here so they can start my discharge."

"I'll make some calls once I get a new phone." Brett walked to the large window and peered into the parking lot. Dark clouds had blanketed the sky and blocked the rising sun, ushering an eeriness into the region. "When are you going to tell your mom?"

The door opened. "Tell me what?" Olivia and MJ returned.

Keeley stepped into slippers by her bed and approached. "Mom, Brett thinks we all need to sequester ourselves in your gated home." A pause. "Including you. No court appearances. Nothing."

"Really? Yay!" MJ bounced on his tippy-toes.

At least one of them was excited.

Olivia placed her hands on her hips and

turned to Brett, eyes glaring. "You come back into her life, and you think you can just take over? My daughter and grandson are my responsibility, not yours. How dare—"

"Mom. Stop." Keeley's tone halted the conversation. "Brett is only trying to help. We're doing this."

Olivia positioned herself in Brett's personal space and waggled her finger at him. "If her condition worsens, I will hold you personally responsible. You hear me?"

Loud and clear.

There was no denying the judge's hammer would come down hard if Brett put her family in danger. He didn't know which was worse—facing the Diglo brothers or the wrath of Chief Justice Olivia Ash.

Keeley shuffled into the kitchen early the next morning, willing strength into her weary body. She was happy to be in her own bed but still perplexed on who would use plants to poison her. The Diglo brothers seemed to be more of the hunting type. They used knives, rifles and arrows for their kills. Not weeds. She also wanted to do more research on the Yukon's plant life. The doctor thought Keeley had only ingested a small portion of the poisonous weed, and that was why she didn't die. *Thank You, God. Tell me, who would do this?* She refused to think any of her coworkers would betray her. No, it had to be someone else. Many had passed through her labs for tours—law enforcement, coroners, students, doctors, to name a few.

Keeley reached into the cupboard for a mug but hesitated. Could someone have gotten into her mother's kitchen? Surely not. Her mother had the best security at her residence. However, Keeley wasn't taking any chances, so she vigorously washed all the mugs before grinding beans and brewing a large pot of hazelnut coffee.

She took her mug and nestled into her favorite chair in the sunroom to catch the sunrise. She loved watching the colors change as the sun peeked over the mountains. Yesterday's dark clouds had produced strong winds, hail and rain, but had passed quickly. Keeley pictured MJ snuggled in Brett's lap last night to take shelter from the sound of hail pinging on the windows. MJ hated storms.

She smiled as she placed her lips on the rim of her coffee cup. *Lord, I could get used to picturing that sweet sight of MJ being rocked by his father.*

A sunray bounced off the mountainside,

sending a line of illumination on the treetops. Perhaps a sign of things to come? She prayed it would happen. Her feelings for Brett had sneaked up on her, and she found herself dreaming of a life together with MJ and Brett—one happy family.

Was that possible?

Not if her mother had any say in Keeley's love life. Her mom hated that they made her postpone all her court proceedings, but Brett had told them about his conversation with the older brother on Elimac Bridge. He was coming for all of them. Brett had negotiated a week off from his job and would check in on his father every day. Vic would escort him there and back.

The arrangement was perfect.

At least, she prayed it was.

"You're up early." Brett approached from the opposite door.

She flinched and placed her hand on her chest. "You scared me."

"Sorry. How are you feeling?"

"Coming along. Felt good to sleep in my own bed." She took a sip of coffee before raising her cup. "Don't worry—I scrubbed all the mugs. They're safe. Grab some and join me."

"Will do. I have news from Constable Jackson." He left and returned within two minutes, sitting in the chair next to her. "Magnificent view."

"The best. I love God's handiwork. Look at those colors." She stole a peek at his profile.

His tightened jaw revealed his angst.

She remembered he didn't like to talk about God. "Why do you find it hard to trust God?"

His gaze tore from the sunrise to her within seconds. "Because He took too much from me."

She reached over and settled her hand on his arm. "Tell me."

His previously peaceful face morphed into a haunted, tortured expression. He rested his head back. "Well, for one thing, an escaped convict murdered my mother. God could have stopped it but chose not to."

Her jaw dropped. "I'm so sorry. I didn't know that."

"I just don't understand why He allows His children to go through so much pain. It's like stumbling through the wilderness, not knowing which direction to go sometimes."

"So, you made a commitment at one point?"

"Yes, as a boy. And then..." He took a sip.

"Then what?" She hated to probe but, at the

same time, knew if he talked it out, perhaps it would help.

"I'd rather not say."

Secrets. She had enough of those with her tight-lipped mother.

He fished out his cell phone from his jeans pocket. "We're going to have a meeting today."

Misdirection. Obviously that was the end of their God talk. "What type of meeting?"

"Constable Jackson texted me. They've been looking into the growing number of fugitives spotted in the area. He's bringing his wife, Hannah, to talk to us about it."

"It will be good to see her again. But why us? We're not law enforcement." Keeley finished her coffee and set her mug on the glass end table in between their chairs.

"Well, Layke knows my background and wanted to report on what they found regarding the two fugitives we talked to at the accident. Thought maybe something would stand out to us." Brett leaned toward her. "Are you up for a visit?"

"Of course. What time?"

He checked his watch. "Nine. Is that okay? I can make it later if you want." He set his phone beside her discarded cup.

She hopped to her feet. "That's fine. I just need to go make myself more presentable."

"You look great so soon after being poisoned." He winked. "In fact, *gorgeous* would be the word I'd use."

She huffed. "Hardly. I also want to check my emails." She pointed to the kitchen. "There's lots to eat."

"What about MJ?"

"We're keeping him away from kindergarten, too. I should get him up, though."

Brett pushed himself upright. "Can I do it? I love spending time with him."

"Of course." She crossed her arms, tilting her head. "Do you believe me that he's your son now?"

"I'm getting there, but it's hard when…"

Once again, he let his sentence drop.

More secrets?

His phone flashed as a text appeared on the screen.

Keeley caught the note before it disappeared.

The promotion is yours, if you want it. Come back to Ontario.

Keeley stiffened every muscle in her weary body. *He's leaving.* What was the point in even trying to get close to him again? No, she couldn't let him back into their lives. "Never mind. I'll get my son ready." She marched down the hall and up the stairs to MJ's room. She hated to act like a two-year-old going through a tantrum, but she couldn't help it.

Just when she thought they'd made a breakthrough, the imaginary wall became impenetrable.

And she wouldn't let her son get hurt again.

Even though she realized it was probably already too late.

Chapter Twelve

Brett studied the text from his former supervisor in Ontario. Had Keeley's sudden shift in mood been because she'd seen the message regarding the promotion? *She thinks you're leaving. Tell her. Tell her you're staying.*

Could he? The question was…did she *want* him to stay? He wrestled with his internal thoughts, bouncing back and forth like a Ping-Pong ball. But he knew in his heart he wouldn't leave when he wanted to be involved in MJ's life—even if that meant Keeley didn't want to further a relationship with him.

The front gate buzzed on Olivia's security monitor system, interrupting his fluctuating thoughts.

Vic appeared around the corner and clicked a button. "You know these folks?" He pointed to the screen.

Brett stood and walked over, leaning in to

get a better look. "Yes, that's Constable Layke Jackson and his wife, Hannah. They're here to see Keeley and me. Please let them in."

Vic shook his head. "They're not on the list."

"List? What list?" Brett scrunched up his nose.

"Judge Ash's. No one gets in unless approved by her."

Shuffling feet sounded behind them, and Brett pivoted.

Keeley appeared dressed in a green-and-navy plaid tailored shirt and jeans. "Since when does my mother have this supposed list?"

"Since you made us sequester ourselves in her home." He held up his tablet. "If they're not on the list, they're not allowed in."

"That's absurd. These people are here to help with the case so we can all get on with our lives." Keeley pushed Vic aside and hit the button to open the gate.

Brett held in a chuckle. Seemed Keeley found the strength to get by the bodyguard. *Good on you, Keels.*

Vic scowled. "Fine, you can answer to your mother. Not me. I'm adding that in my notes." He keyed on his tablet before marching down the hall.

"Wow. Your mother does rule the roost." Brett squeezed her shoulder. "Listen, I wanted to tell you—"

The doorbell chimed.

"I gotta get that." She hurried down the hardwood corridor.

A couple of minutes later, after they greeted the guests, the group sat at the dining room table.

Brett's knee bounced in anticipation of what news Layke and Hannah had to share. His childhood nervous habit of shaking his leg had followed him into adulthood, and he hated it. Brett placed his hand on his knee to settle his nerves.

"Hannah, how are you feeling? You must be due soon."

Hannah rubbed her protruding belly. "Three weeks, but this baby has been kicking up a storm, Keeley. I think he or she is trying to break free of my womb."

Keeley laughed. "How's Gabe?"

"Excited to meet his baby sister or brother." She squeezed Jackson's hand. "Daddy is, too."

"Sure am." Jackson cleared his throat. "Let's get down to it. I spoke to Hannah regarding the conversation you had with the fugitives."

"Did you find out their names?" Brett asked.

"Yes. Peter and Tom Lees. They were both convicted of murder and escaped custody during prison transport." Jackson opened a file folder he'd brought. "Also, the arrow tips were laced with privet."

Keeley gasped. "So, my attack and this one are connected. Do you think it's the Diglo brothers?"

"That's our conclusion." Jackson turned to Hannah. "Tell them what you discovered."

"Yesterday, we caught a fugitive trying to cross the border. He was driving erratically toward US customs, so we stopped him before he could get there. His behavior was suspicious, even though his documentation didn't raise a red flag, so we went through his car." Hannah dragged Jackson's folder closer. "The man's real name is Willy Carson, but that's not what his passport said. When he changed his car registration, he forgot to change his insurance."

"Obviously, a convict not firing on all cylinders," Jackson said. "After an intense interrogation with both Hannah's border patrol officers and us, he finally confessed to the Diglo brothers helping him. He said they were extremely dangerous and scared even him."

Brett leaned back. "That's why you're telling us this. Since they're targeting us."

Jackson shifted in his chair. "Yes. We don't normally share information with civilians, but I know your background, and we want you to be very cautious. We're doing everything we can to find the Diglos."

"Did they tell you who these brothers are?"

Hannah lifted her index finger. "I can answer that, Keeley. I was in the interrogation. Willy said he didn't know their real identities. Apparently, they only referred to each other using initials in front of him. They blindfolded him so he didn't know where their operation was located, only that he could hear lots of nature around him." She made air quotes with the word *nature*.

"Probably the forest." Keeley twirled a curl.

Hannah nodded. "That's my guess, too. He also said they provided all his new documentation."

"Keeley, was there anything that stood out in your time with them?" Layke steepled his fingers and placed his elbows on the table.

"Well, I only met two of them, and the older brother definitely seemed to be the one in charge. They referred to a woman as well. Could that be the leader of the organization?"

"Possibly." Jackson pointed to the paper in the file. "Tell them what else you found, Hannah."

"Okay, your coffee mug and the arrows were laced with privet, and that doesn't grow in the Yukon. So they're importing it somehow." Hannah flipped a page in the folder. "One of our officers stopped a van the other day and found privet seeds hidden among other plant life. The driver confessed he was only delivering them to a certain warehouse, but when we looked into it further, the location was bogus."

Brett leaned forward. "You have no idea where it was actually going?"

"Correct."

"So, if we find where the privet is being grown, we find those responsible." Brett rubbed his tense neck muscles.

"Agree," Jackson said. "We have teams searching surrounding forests. So far, nothing has surfaced."

"I appreciate you sharing this information." Keeley slumped in her chair.

Hannah shifted positions, and her hand flew

to her abdomen. "Baby's kicking." She turned to Brett. "One more thing before we go. Mr. Carson also said something that stood out to me. He said that he was in the room when the brothers were making plans to retarget a paramedic since they had failed to kill him on the bridge."

"They know you're still alive, Brett. You both need to watch your back." Jackson closed the folder. "We're increasing patrols in this area to help. Don't leave the house for now."

Once again, Brett's knee bounced, his blood pressure rising. "I need to check on my father. I'm not sure how much longer he has."

"I understand. Be sure to take a bodyguard with you." Jackson stood. "Rest assured, we're doing everything we can to find these men. We'll brief you with anything new."

Brett rose and extended his hand. "Thanks so much."

After the group left, Brett called Nancy to get an update on his father. She'd reported that he had rallied and was now eating again. That news brought joy to his heart. Perhaps God was finally listening.

Maybe.

Brett pocketed his phone before joining

Keeley and MJ in the kitchen. He leaned on the door frame and observed MJ making himself a peanut-butter-and-jam sandwich. Keeley had her back to him as she reached for something in the fridge. MJ loaded the knife with jam, and it plopped onto the floor.

"Rats." He dropped the knife, and his hand flew to his mouth.

Keeley turned. "Michael Joshua, what did I tell you about using that word?"

"Sorry, Mama." His puppy-dog eyes caught Brett's gaze and widened as if silently pleading for help.

Brett subdued the laughter bubbling inside and entered the room. "Here, let me help." He snatched up the dishcloth and wiped the jam from the floor. "I'll show you how I used to make PB&J sandwiches."

"Okay." MJ stood on his tippy-toes.

"First, take some peanut butter." Brett put some on the knife. "Then slather one piece of bread."

"Slather?"

Keeley chuckled. "He's five, Brett. That's a big word."

"How about *spread*?"

"Oh." MJ dipped his finger into the jam jar and stuck it in his mouth.

"Son, you know Gramma's rules." Keeley's lips curved slightly upward.

Brett guessed she was trying to contain the same laughter as him. He grabbed a spoon and dipped it into the jar. "Okay, now add a little jam to a spoon, because you should never mix the two."

MJ tilted his tiny head. "Why?"

"That's just a rule in every kitchen, right, Keels?"

"Especially this one." She folded her arms. "Gramma hates that. Believe me, I learned the hard way."

"What's next, Mr. Brett?"

He placed the other piece of bread to the left of the one containing the peanut butter. "Add the jam here." He held up his index finger. "Never put one on top of the other. It's a Ryerson household rule." He added the jam.

"But why?"

Brett's gaze shifted to Keeley. "You know, I'm not sure." He set the spoon down and picked up the two slices. "Now you put them together, and voilà—the best PB&J sandwich you'll ever have." He handed it to MJ, winking at Keeley.

She giggled like a schoolgirl.

A sound he loved.

MJ took his sandwich, sat at the table and bowed his head. "Thank You, God, for this food. Amen." He stuffed the bread into his mouth.

Brett's jaw dropped. The way MJ had folded his hands reminded him of when he was a kid. Brett would position both index fingers into a steeple and bring his hands together.

Just like MJ.

Keeley's phone dinged. She withdrew it from her jeans pocket and swiped the screen. "That's odd."

He turned back to her. "What is it?"

"The coroner just sent me an email to my personal account. She doesn't have that address." She tapped on her phone and read. "What? Impossible."

Keeley swayed and dropped into a chair.

Brett moved beside her. "What does the email say?"

She glanced at MJ and then back to Brett, turning the phone in his direction. "Read this." She kept her voice soft.

Brett leaned closer for a better view.

Olivia,
Hey, friend. Tried to reach you by phone but couldn't. I'm sure Keeley would have given you the news of your daughter by now. My deepest condolences for the passing of Zoe. Please let me know if there's anything you need. See you at our next function.
Pat

Brett scrolled and continued to read. "Zoe was your mother's daughter? That means—"

Keeley straightened, her eyes hardening. "Zoe was my half sister, and my mother has been lying to me all my life."

Not the way Brett thought this day would go.

Keeley closed her hands into impregnable fists as her pulse zinged. *How could you keep this a secret, Mom?* She inhaled a long breath, exhaling slowly. She must calm down before she approached her mother.

Zoe was my sister? Mom, there's no coming back from this one.

"Wait. She said Olivia." Brett handed her phone back. "Did she email you by mistake?"

"Looks that way. When I was a teenager,

Mom and I thought it would be cute to have matching emails, except using different numbers. I picked ashtree17. Mom picked ashtree19. They're close, so an easy mistake." Keeley tucked her phone away. "I thought she got rid of that email address. I only use mine when I don't want anything to go to my work email."

MJ approached, interrupting their quiet conversation. "Mr. Brett, that PB&J sandwich was delicious." MJ took his plate to the sink.

"See, I told you, sport. Only way to make one."

"What did I tell you about eating fast, young man?" Keeley pushed herself up to a standing position. "Brett, can you keep him occupied? I need to go have a little chat with my mother."

He nodded. "Sure, but maybe you should wait until you've calmed a bit."

"Yeah, I thought so, too, but I'm afraid that would take too long." Keeley marched from the room and crossed the wide corridor, making her way to Chief Justice Olivia Ash's home office.

She tapped on the door before pushing it open. "Mom, we need to talk."

Her mother turned from her position by the window and wiped a tear away. She rolled her shoulders as if composing herself. "Listen, Sofia, I need to go," she said into her cell phone. "Seems that my daughter has something to say. Chat later."

She strode over to her desk and tossed her phone on top. "What did I tell you about not entering my office before I gave you permission?"

Keeley gripped her phone tighter and strode up to her mother. "Tell me something. Why didn't you let me know I had a sister?"

Her mother's blue eyes widened as she dropped into her desk chair. "What—how?"

The normally well-versed judge stumbled over her words.

Keeley placed her cell phone on her mother's desk. "Seems an email from Pat offering her condolences on the passing of your daughter Zoe came to me by mistake. Were you ever going to tell me?" She refrained from subduing the anger in her voice. She just couldn't help it.

Her mother read the email before slouching back in her high-back desk chair. "I'm sorry."

Heat coiled around Keeley's spine, raising her temperature. "You're sorry? Sorry you were caught? Mom, you had an affair with the mayor, and now you're best friends with his wife?" She placed her hands flat on her mother's desk and leaned forward. "After all the times you've chastised me. How could you?"

Her mother's lips trembled. "It was a mistake that happened when you were one." She pointed to the chair across from her desk. "Sit. It's time you knew."

You think? Man, she had to curb her foul mood. She plopped into the chair, crossing her arms and legs. "I'm listening."

Her mother poured herself a glass of water from the pitcher at the side of her desk. "Yannick and Sofia were close friends of your father's and mine. Yannick suggested I go to a seminar in Vancouver. He was going and thought it would be beneficial to my career."

Keeley guessed where her mother's story was heading.

"Your father didn't want me to go. Joshua said you wouldn't do well without me. You were a—"

"I know—a very colicky baby. You've thrown that in my face many times."

"Please let me finish. Joshua and I had a huge fight when I told him I had to go. My career depended on it. He disagreed." She drank her water. "If he'd had his way, I would've been a stay-at-home mom. Not that there's anything wrong with that. It just wasn't for me." Another sip. "We hadn't been getting along very well, so I went anyway. Yannick was right. The conference was a career changer. We spent long hours in sessions during the day, and in the evenings, we went out together for dinners. We both were having marital struggles. You can guess what happened. One night. One mistake."

"That's how it can happen." Who was Keeley to judge? However, she hadn't been married. "What did you do when you found out you were pregnant?"

"I confessed. Everything." She exhaled loudly. "Your father was livid and—"

Keeley uncrossed her legs and leaned forward, elbows to knees. "That's when he had his heart attack, wasn't it?"

Sadness passed over her mother's normally stoic face. "Yes," she whispered.

Fury scorched Keeley's cheeks. Her mother had contributed to her father's death. *Unforgivable.* "You caused his heart attack? Mom, how could you? You stole my father from me." Keeley gripped the armchair until her fingers went numb.

Her mother waggled her finger in Keeley's direction. "I did no such thing. I found out later your father had a heart condition we didn't know about and that his heart attack was only a matter of time."

Keeley huffed and slumped back in the chair. "But, Mom, why wouldn't you keep Zoe? I don't understand."

Her mother got up and meandered to the window. "I was an instant single mother, stressed and striving to become a Supreme Court judge. I had a reputation to uphold."

"So, you placed your precious career over your unborn child? What did you tell Yannick?"

Her mother fiddled with the blind cords. "That I would somehow hide the pregnancy and put the baby up for adoption."

"But he wouldn't let you, right?"

"No. He confessed everything to Sofia. Needless to say, she was angry, but over the next few weeks, she told Yannick she wanted to raise the child." She turned from the window. "Sofia couldn't get pregnant, and she said even though she hated the fact we had an affair, she felt Zoe was a gift to her, kind of like Hagar's son in the Bible."

Wow. Keeley's respect meter for Sofia increased. For this woman to take in a child who was the result of an affair was amazing. The hurt must have been unimaginable.

"But, Mom, how have you and Sofia remained such good friends?"

Her mother approached Keeley and knelt in front of her, taking Keeley's hands in hers. "Because she chose to forgive us, like God forgives. I'm sorry I kept this from you. Truly, I am. Can you forgive me?"

Keeley stared into her mother's eyes. Could she? She knew God commanded forgiveness, but right now, she struggled with her mother's betrayal.

"I don't know if I can, Mom. You robbed me of the gift of knowing I had a sister all these years. That's hard to come back from." She yanked her hands away and shot to her feet. "Plus, you've treated me harshly ever since MJ was born. Isn't that hypocritical?"

Keeley bounded from the room, distancing herself from the woman's deception.

If only she could escape out of Olivia Ash's fortified estate as easily.

But her son's protection was more important than her own pain.

* * *

Keeley's fan stopped, jerking her awake from a restless sleep. She moaned and peered around her room. Darkness extinguished the normal red light on her computer charging station. What had caused the power to go out? She listened for any storms in the area, but silence greeted her. She realized her mother's generator would kick in, so she closed her eyes, exhaustion sending her back into dream world.

"Now!" a whispered voice said.

Was she dreaming again?

She fluttered her eyes open and found a masked man leaning forward with a pillow in his hands, ready to smother her. A Diglo brother had come for revenge.

Keeley's heartbeat exploded, sending horror throughout her body. How could she fight in her still-weakened state? *Please, Lord.* She mustered strength and pushed her hands upward to block the killer. "No! Help!" She tugged upward on his mask, exposing a barbed-wire choker tattoo on his neck. She thrashed on the bed to free herself from the hunter's grip and extended her hand to hit the panic button her mother had installed.

"Don't bother. We's disabled all security. Your bodyguards ain't coming. My brother is killing your beloved paramedic right now. You both have to pay for Eddie's death." He placed one knee on her shoulder as he stood at the side of her bed, pinning her down. "Then we'll eliminate your mother and take your boy. Mama wants him. He'll love growing up with us boys. We'll teach him to hunt. Kill." He inched closer with the pillow. "G'night, Dr. Ash."

No! Lord, help me fight this brother. Protect MJ, Brett and Mom!

Adrenaline fueled Keeley's feeble body, and she brought both knees upward, knocking her attacker off balance. She grabbed a wad of his hair as he stumbled backward, muttering a spew of curses.

She rolled off the opposite side of the bed and knocked the light in the process, crashing it on the hardwood floor. Keeley had to make noise. Surely, Terry and Vic would hear the ruckus and come.

She swallowed to clear her parched throat. "Help! Help!"

"Davey, abort," a hushed voice said through

the hunter's radio. "Paramedic slugged me, but I got away."

"Keeley!" Pounding footfalls followed Brett's cry.

Relief washed over Keeley's tensed shoulders. *Brett is safe.*

"Dimwits. Do I have to do everything?" another voice barked. "Get back here. Now that we know how to get around their defenses, we'll attack again."

The brother dashed out of Keeley's room, knocking into Brett in the process.

Brett regained his footing and flew over to Keeley, bringing her into his arms. "Are you okay?"

Words caught in Keeley's throat.

A shotgun blast echoed throughout the house.

Keeley pushed out of Brett's hold, still clasping the wad of hair she'd torn from her attacker. "MJ!"

They raced out of her room into the shadowy hallway.

Keeley tripped over something blocking the corridor. She grasped Brett's arm, breaking her fall. She returned her focus to the object in question. Dim lighting from the kitchen shone a thin beam onto the floor.

Vic lay motionless, crimson spreading on his white shirt.

"No!" Keeley buried her face in Brett's chest.

The Diglos had gotten dangerously close to their family.

Again.

Chapter Thirteen

Brett rubbed his neck where his assailant had gripped after Brett knocked the pillow from his hands. He guessed it would soon show redness and bruises. Thankfully, Brett had been able to punch the brother, then kicked him away before the man fled out of the room. Brett had regained his breath and headed to Keeley's room just as her attacker escaped.

Keeley and Brett had checked on MJ only to find him still fast asleep—even with all the noise.

Thank You, God, for that gift.

Keeley had placed the brother's hair in a plastic bag to give to the constables.

Olivia had come running soon after Brett and Keeley had discovered Vic's body. However, only the shotgun blast woke Terry. He'd claimed to be a deep sleeper and stressed that he wasn't supposed to be on duty anyway. He hadn't heard anything else. Odd. Wouldn't a bodyguard be more alert to his surroundings?

The group now all sat around the dining room table, waiting for Constables Jackson and Antoine to return from their perimeter sweep. The duo responded to Brett's 911 call, along with paramedics. After ensuring everyone was okay, Tina and Otto left while the constables continued their search for the brothers on the property.

Olivia fixated her eyes on something across the room as she fiddled with a place mat on the table. Clearly, the attack had left the normally authoritative judge on edge, but who could blame her? Her fortress had crumbled at the hands of the brother army. Somehow.

Brett observed Terry's expression. The man sat with his weapon resting on his knee, void of expression. Why hadn't Vic's death affected him emotionally? Yes, the tough bodyguard rarely revealed his feelings, but seeing Vic's lifeless eyes should have caused some type of reaction. But no emotion passed over the man's face.

Suspicion spiraled around Brett's spine like a corkscrew. Could he have helped the Diglo brothers enter the home? Had he turned off the power? If not, how did they get through the gate? Multiple questions filled Brett's mind, but one thing rose to the top.

They weren't safe in Olivia Ash's home any longer.

The brothers knew where she lived and how to bypass her security.

Steps pounded in the hallway.

Terry sprang to his feet, weapon raised.

The constables entered and stopped.

Jackson raised his hands. "Whoa, put it down, Terry. It's only us."

The man obeyed. "You should have knocked. Good way to get yourselves killed."

Antoine moved closer to the bodyguard. "You have a permit for that?"

"Of course. I'm a professional." Terry holstered the Glock and took his seat. "What did you find? How did these men get by our defenses?"

Jackson pulled out a chair and sat beside Brett. "You tell us. We couldn't find any trace of cut wires. Someone messed with the fuse box, which knocked out the power."

Questions filled Brett's mind. "But wouldn't that have cut the security?"

Olivia's eyes snapped back to the group. "I have state-of-the-art security. Only a code can disarm it, and I've been changing it daily the last few days."

"Well, someone leaked the code." Antoine took a notebook from his vest pocket. "Who has access to it?"

"Myself, Keeley, Terry and…" Her sentence trailed off.

"Vic." Keeley reached for her mother's hand but pulled back.

Brett knew the mother and daughter had exchanged words after Keeley discovered Zoe was her half sister—a secret her mother had kept. Their strained relationship deepened, and the two had barely spoken at the dinner table or looked at each other.

He massaged his tense neck muscles before checking the time. Two in the morning. No wonder Brett was exhausted. The lack of sleep and fighting off an assailant had depleted his energy.

"So, someone in this room gave them the code." Jackson extracted his notebook and scribbled on it.

Terry slammed his hand on the table. "I would not do that."

Jackson focused on Terry. "Not even for a price?"

The bodyguard flew to his feet, knocking his chair onto the floor.

The noise echoed.

"Quiet!" Keeley's whispered command spoke volumes. "You're gonna wake MJ. I don't want him knowing what happened."

Olivia threw up her hands. "Everyone, calm down. This is my house, and I won't tolerate unfounded accusations." The judge had reverted back into her authoritative mode.

The case that had ended Brett's policing career entered his mind. "There's another possibility. They hacked your system remotely and disarmed your security that way." That was how the black-hat hacker had entered their secured premises where Brett was guarding a witness.

"That has to be it. I trust my bodyguards and Keeley explicitly." Her eyes glared at Jackson. "They wouldn't betray me. They know better than to cross a judge."

Keeley toyed with the strings on her sweatshirt. "Is there some way to check if someone got into the system?"

"We'll get Digital Forensics to look into it." Jackson addressed Brett and Keeley. "Can either of you tell me anything about your attackers? What they looked like? Did they say anything? That sort of thing."

"Mine wore a mask and full hunting gear,"

Brett said. "When I fought him off, he swore and ran."

Keeley raised her index finger. "Wait. My attacker said we had to pay for killing Eddie. I'm guessing that was the younger brother. Then another called my attacker Davey. Back when we stopped to help those fugitives, they mentioned the name Eddie, too, and someone named Roy."

Jackson scribbled in his notebook. "So, a Davey, a Roy and an Eddie. I'm guessing their real name isn't Diglo. However, that's more than what we had." He flipped a page. "I should also tell you we found the knife they used to stab Spokene and Hopkins. We're checking it now, but I doubt we'll find prints on it."

"Wait!" Brett went to the counter and picked up the plastic bag. "Keeley was smart enough to pull out some hair. Perhaps you can get DNA from this." He handed it to Jackson.

The constable smiled. "Good work. I'll take it to Ginger." He placed it in his vest pocket. "Anything else?"

Keeley twirled a curl before her sad eyes brightened. "Oh, I almost forgot. I caught a glimpse of a strange tattoo on his neck."

"Can you describe it, Keeley?" Jackson poised his pen.

"It appeared to be barbed-wire links, but they weren't joined and looked like a choker."

"We'll check with local tattoo artists." Jackson jotted down a note in his book.

Brett rubbed his neck again, warding off the pain still lingering from the brother's tight grip. "Hopefully you'll get a break with that information. Can you keep us updated? With what you can, of course."

"I will. There's a lot at stake here." Jackson's expression softened. "I hate to tell you all this, but we're gonna need you to vacate the premises. This is now a crime scene, and they have to do a thorough investigation inside and out of your property."

Olivia burst upright. "What? I refuse to leave my home."

Keeley latched on to her hand, tugging her back into the chair. "Mom, you have to."

"I recommend you separate as well." Antoine tapped his pen on the table. "Judge Ash, do you have someone you could stay with? Take Terry."

Her jaw dropped as her gaze traveled to Keeley. "I can't leave my daughter and grandson."

"Constables and Terry, could you leave the

room for a minute? I need to talk to my mother and Brett alone."

Jackson looked at Keeley as he stood. "Of course. We'll be in the living room calling our forensics team."

The trio left.

Keeley took her mother's hands in hers. "Mom, I know you don't want to hear this, but I think separating is a good idea."

"Well, then perhaps Brett could go back to his father's!"

"I'm not leaving Keeley and my son." Brett tightened his jaw.

Keeley eyed him, a smile tugging at her lips. "You believe me now?"

"I do."

Keeley turned back to Olivia. "Maybe you could stay with the Coates family. The mayor can add more security."

Olivia's eyes narrowed. "Are you punishing me because I didn't tell you about Zoe?"

"Not punishing, just distancing myself. I'm sorry, but I need a break from you right now." She expelled a long breath. "It will be good for us. Don't worry. We'll keep in touch—for MJ's sake."

"I don't like it." Olivia's words spewed anger.

"Mom, you, of all people, should know there are consequences to our actions."

The woman leaned back in the chair, folding her arms.

Brett squirmed, not knowing how to react to the tension between mother and daughter. However, he needed to break the sudden silence.

A plan formed, and he grazed Keeley's arm. "Keels, we need to get out of Carimoose Bay. It's not safe here any longer. It's obvious the brothers can find us." Brett wasn't sure how she'd take the next news, but he had to be honest. "We need to go into hiding. No one—" he looked at Olivia "—and I mean no one can know where we are. It's for all our sakes."

"Is that really necessary?"

"Trust me. I know I'm not a police officer any longer, but my training is still here." He tapped on his temple.

Olivia placed her hands on the table and rose slowly. "I'm tired of hearing that."

"Mom. Settle down." Keeley's voice conveyed her anger. "We have to find a location the Diglo brothers don't know about. They seem to be able to find us wherever we go, and you're a public figure. They know you're my mother."

Olivia marched out of the room without saying a word.

"Sorry about that. Her ego has been taken down a notch, and she doesn't like it." She rubbed his arm. "I'm so glad you finally believe MJ is yours."

"Me too."

She twirled a curl. "But where should we hide?"

"My father has a cabin just outside Carimoose Bay, deep in the Elimac Forest. As you know, that section of woods extends for miles. We could go there."

She let go of her hair. "Does it have internet and cell reception? I want to stay connected to the case—and Mom."

"It's spotty, but it works. I'm going to talk to Layke. He'll get us supplies for protection. I'll find out what he suggests. Pack quickly."

Keeley stood. "What about your dad? Should we bring him?"

"I can't risk moving him, and I can't leave you alone." Caught between two families. But Brett knew what his father would want.

To protect his only grandson.

Keeley shifted her son in her arms and followed Brett into a rustic cabin three hours later. Layke had agreed to Brett's plan and provided them with two sat phones as well as flashlights.

He promised he'd arrange for regular patrols in the cabin's vicinity. He also warned them about telling anyone their whereabouts. Hiding was their highest form of protection. Since they didn't know who they could trust, they had to sever communication with their colleagues and any other friends at this point. Keeley hated that it had come to this but realized its necessity. She sent a vague email to her coworkers explaining she required time off and wouldn't be available. Keeley requested Beth cancel her classes for the next couple of weeks. She didn't want to give Audrey the burden of juggling everything. The students could wait.

Brett had also contacted his partner Tina to let her know he'd be unavailable for the next few days. Brett said she tried to get more information from him and didn't like that he wouldn't tell her.

Keeley hugged her mother before they left her estate and promised to stay in touch. She had kissed her cheek and told her she loved her, despite her indiscretion. Keeley couldn't leave her mother without expressing her love, even if she was still furious with her.

Brett flicked on the light in the cabin, revealing an open kitchen and living area with three bedrooms in the rear. A stone fireplace displayed photos on the mantel.

"I'll turn up the heat and get the groceries from the Jeep." He adjusted the dial on the wall box. "It's not Olivia's estate, but it's cozy." Brett reached for MJ. "I can put him in the middle bedroom. You take the one on the right."

Keeley handed her son to his father. "I can't sleep. Okay if I sit here for a bit? I need to unwind before trying to go back to bed."

"Sure." He lifted MJ and tipped his chin in the kitchen's direction. "Put on some tea. I'd love one."

"Good idea."

Ten minutes later, Brett returned from tucking MJ into bed and putting the groceries in the fridge.

"Your tea is ready." Keeley sat curled up on the couch with the plaid blanket wrapped around her, sipping her tea. "You were gone longer than I expected."

"I wanted to make sure he didn't wake up and get scared being in a strange place." He grabbed the mug and plunked himself in the rocking chair across from her. "Do you want me to make a fire to help take the chill off?"

"I'm good."

"I'm not sure I believe you. It's been a tough few hours." He grimaced. "Well, longer than that. We've been through a lot in a short period."

"Sure have. We've been targeted multiple times, and I found out I had a half sister I didn't know about." She took another sip of the passionflower tea. "My mother has lied to me all my life."

"I'm so sorry. That must be tough to digest."

"More than tough. She not only kept this secret, but her affair was the catalyst that brought my father's heart attack on."

Brett jolted forward, spilling his tea. "What?"

"Well, not exactly. Apparently my dad had a heart condition they didn't know about. After he discovered Mom's affair with Yannick, his anger put him into cardiac arrest." She bit her lip, fighting the pending tears. "I barely remember my father."

"That must have been hard. Growing up without a father and with a—"

"Domineering mother? Yup. Sure was, and I did everything to please her but never seemed to be able to."

"Why do you think that was? You've become

a successful career woman. Shouldn't that account for something?" He drank his tea.

"You'd think, but no. From the time I was a teenager, my mother impressed upon me to become something more than those around me."

"Let me guess. She wanted you to go into law."

"Good guess."

Brett rubbed his finger around the rim of his mug. "How long did she practice law before she became a judge?"

"About twenty years. Becoming a judge is highly competitive, but she knew people and was connected within the Yukon."

"And I'm sure the mayor helped."

"Well, he wasn't the mayor at the time of their affair, but yes, eventually. I watched her through her years in law, and I didn't like the woman she'd become." Keeley set her tea down and inched the blanket closer to her neck. "She worked long hours and barely had time for me. However, she always made time for Zoe." Jealousy over her deceased half sister rose. *Lord, forgive me.*

"Why would she do that?"

"At first I thought it was because she was excited that Sofia finally had a child and she wanted to share in her happiness, but as Zoe grew into a teenager, she expressed an interest in becoming a lawyer. So, of course, Mom loved that. Someone other than her own daughter wanted to walk in her footsteps. The irony of that statement isn't lost on me now." Keeley got up and walked to the mantel, studying the pictures of Brett as a child, his mom and dad, and another young boy. A brother or a childhood friend? He'd never mentioned a sibling.

"So, that angered you?"

She turned and sighed. "I'm ashamed to admit that. Zoe and I were friends, but not close." Her lip quivered. "I regret that now. My mother robbed me of the knowledge of having a sister. I'm not sure I can forgive her."

"I'm sorry. Seems like I'm saying that a lot tonight."

"Not your fault." Keeley stepped to the window and peered into the darkness. Only a single beam of moonlight filtered through the trees. "It's peaceful here. I can see why you chose it. Secluded and out in God's nature. Great combination. How did your father take the news of us leaving?"

"He totally understood and said if I hadn't left, he would have ordered me to."

She smiled at the thought of the sweet older man demanding anything of his son. "How's he doing?"

"Still eating. That's promising, but I know what's coming." He finished his tea and returned to the kitchen. "I hate being apart from him, but I need to look after my family."

His family. Keeley loved the sound of that, but was he still going to take that promotion? Time to change the subject. "Did you come here a lot as a boy?"

Brett smiled. "Yes, whenever we could. Dad was busy on the police force, so we took every opportunity to head here. He called the cabin his oasis from crime."

Keeley walked around the main room, studying the decor. "I can see why. Did your mom come, too? You said she was away a lot."

"She came when she was home from her medical missions." Brett chuckled. "She loved to fry up the fish we caught in the creek. I can almost taste it now. So good."

Keeley returned to the mantel and picked up another photo. Brett stood, raising a fish in one hand as his other rested on the younger boy's shoulder. She tapped on the boy's face. "Who's this?"

Brett's eyes saddened. "My brother, Gideon."

"I didn't realize you had a brother. Where is he?"

Pain contorted Brett's handsome face. "He passed years ago." Brett held his mug over the sink.

"I'm so sorry. How did he die?"

Brett fumbled with his mug, and it slipped from his fingers, crashing to the floor.

Keeley hurried to his side and squatted, picking up the shattered pieces.

"I'd rather not talk about Gideon. I'm heading to bed." He left the room, not bothering to help her with his mess.

What just happened? What about his brother's death haunted Brett?

Something told her it wasn't good.

Chapter Fourteen

Brett slipped out of his bed and tiptoed into the kitchen. The hour was still early, and sleep evaded him. He had tossed and turned but couldn't settle after such a horrifying experience. Images of his attacker and his conversation with Keeley flooded his head, keeping his overactive mind from shutting off. He prayed Keeley had been able to rest.

The broom leaning against the wall reminded Brett of his clumsy accident, and he grimaced. Why had he reacted the way he did last night? His brother had been gone for years, but her question about Gideon's death had transported him back to that terrifying day. The day he left his little brother alone in the house. Why didn't he share it with Keeley instead of making a fool of himself? *You know why.*

He still carried the guilt over his brother's death. His shame subconsciously made him stuff the memories of that day into a box and slam the lid shut. Her question brought it all tumbling back.

Sometimes God allows us to enter the wilderness to shape us. Mold us.

His father's earlier words drifted into Brett's mind. Was he correct? *Does God take us into the wilderness to shape us?*

Let Him in.

Could he do as his father said and surrender to God?

Brett ignored his silent question and took coffee from a cupboard. Since he couldn't sleep, he required caffeine to give him a kick start to the day. He wanted to take MJ to Brett's favorite fishing spot and show him all the places he'd loved as a kid.

Excitement fueled his energy. *I still can't believe I have a son.*

One positive thing in his otherwise-messed-up world.

Brett filled the water reservoir, added the grinds to the basket and hit the power button.

Shuffling footsteps sounded behind him, and he whirled around.

Keeley wiped her eyes and dropped into a

chair at the kitchen table. "Good—you're making coffee. I could use a huge cup."

"Didn't sleep?"

She shook her head. "Not much. Not that the bed wasn't comfortable, just not my own."

"I understand." Brett opened the fridge door. "Bacon and eggs for breakfast?"

"Sounds great. I'm shocked MJ didn't wake up screaming. He can be unsettled in new places."

Brett withdrew the food and set it on the countertop. "Well, this cabin is peaceful, so maybe that helped."

The coffee maker crackled as the liquid dripped into the carafe, wafting a delightful aroma into the room.

"Can I help?"

"No, you stay there." Brett eyed the broom. "Listen, I'm sorry about last night. I owe you an explanation."

She raised her hands. "No, it's okay. You don't. I shouldn't have pried."

"Gideon died at the age of twelve, and it was my fault." Brett lifted a frying pan from a wall hook.

Keeley's jaw dropped. "I somehow doubt it's

your fault. Tell me what happened." She fiddled with her housecoat belt. "Only if you want to."

"I was fifteen and had some friends over, playing video games. Mom was on one of her trips, and Dad was on shift." Brett added bacon to the pan and turned on the burner. "Gideon kept interrupting us and I got annoyed, so we went to the local park and shot some hoops. I told him not to come. He was twelve and old enough to stay alone."

Keeley placed her hand on his back. "What happened?"

He startled as he failed to hear her approach. He turned.

Her softened eyes revealed her concern. "Tell me."

"A member of one gang Dad put away threw Molotov cocktails into the window. The place caught fire, and my brother died." He rubbed his heavy chest as if that would relieve his guilt. "I can't forgive myself for leaving him alone."

She caressed his arm. "You didn't cause the fire. It's not your fault, Brett."

"My father said the same thing. Why can't I put it behind me?" He added another frying pan to the stove. "Your mother robbed you of knowing you had a sister. I robbed myself of my brother."

"Don't do that to yourself. You need to let it go. Stop beating—"

"Mama!" MJ screamed from the bedroom.

"Oh dear. He woke up and doesn't know where we are. I'll be back." Keeley headed to the bedroom and, moments later, reemerged with MJ in tow. "See, we're at Mr. Brett's cabin. Isn't this a neat place?"

Brett smiled at his son's open mouth as the boy studied the rustic setting.

"Cool." He ran to a cabinet near the window and pointed. "What's in here?"

Brett turned off the burner and moved to where MJ stood. "That's our game cabinet." He opened the front doors. "Check it out."

Multiple board games, movies and books lined the shelves. Gideon used to refer to it as their toy cabinet. Once again, sadness washed over Brett, but he suppressed the sudden memories of his brother. He had to focus on getting to know his son.

MJ's eyes widened, and he brought out a checkerboard, placing it on the table. "I love checkers. Can we play?"

Brett chuckled. Gideon and Brett had spent

hours playing the game when they were younger. "Of course, but how about some breakfast first?"

MJ bounced on his tippy-toes. "Yes!"

Keeley held her hand out. "Let's go wash up, slugger."

Two and a half hours later, after breakfast, a game of checkers, and a hike to the lake and back, MJ sat in front of the television watching cartoons.

Brett had reached out to Nancy using one of the sat phones. She reported no change in his father's condition.

Keeley nursed another cup of coffee as she viewed her emails. Thankfully the internet was working today. For now. It kicked in and out at his father's cabin.

Keeley took a sip and set her mug down. "Oh my. Come and look at this picture Layke sent."

Brett positioned himself behind her chair and leaned over her shoulder.

A photo of an unlinked barbed-wire tattoo was displayed on her screen.

She pointed. "This is the same one as my attacker's."

"Does Layke say anything else? Did they identify who the tattoo belongs to?"

"He said he'd call—"

The sat phone rang in Brett's hand. "That's gotta be him." He pressed the appropriate buttons and used the hands-free option. "Brett here."

"It's Layke. Did you guys get the picture?"

"Yes, we're looking at it now. You found this fast. What can you tell us about it?"

"Constable Antoine visited a few shops and got a hit. We found the tattoo artist. He operates a shady business and doesn't keep records, but he remembers the man. Said his name was Davey, and he bragged about getting a big score, so he thought the tattoo would make him look tough."

"Davey was my attacker. It has to be the same person. When did he say this?"

"Says he was in approximately fourteen months ago."

Keeley's gaze popped to Brett's, her eyes widening. "Wait—isn't that around the same time the hikers went missing? Could there be a connection?"

"Possibly. But I have something else."

Brett held his breath in anticipation of the constable's news.

"No prints on the knife, but it was definitely

the one used to kill Cameron and stab Hopkins. The coroner confirmed that the unique markings on Cameron's body matched the blade. Hopkins is recovering nicely but said he didn't see his attacker because the perp surprised him from behind. He remembers seeing two hunters before he passed out." Shuffling papers sounded over the phone. "However, we got DNA from the hair, and we're checking all databases to see if there's a match. That might take a while."

Brett whistled. "That was quick."

"Yeah, the mayor has put the pressure on us to find his daughter's killer. Not that I blame him," Jackson said. "Just wanted to keep you apprised. I'm praying this is a step in solving both the cold case and the attacks on you."

"I hope so." Brett checked to ensure MJ hadn't been listening.

His eyes were still fixated on the television. Good.

A thought entered Brett's mind. "Wait, Keels. I just remembered something you said back at the Diglos' cabin. You said Eddie looked familiar. Do you remember from where?"

She snapped her fingers. "I forgot about that." She twisted a chunk of her red hair as if that would help her thinking process. "No, I can't remember. So frustrating."

Brett placed his hand on her shoulder. "It's okay. It will come to you."

She huffed. "Hopefully."

"If it does, contact me right away. We have cruisers patrolling your area around the clock. I'll let you know if we spot anything suspicious. We're in close contact with each officer out there." The constable cleared his throat. "I'm praying for you both. God's got you."

Brett bristled. Could he believe that when a malicious gang was out there targeting his family?

Keeley studied Brett's pained face as he paced the living room area after the constable's call. Was it talk of the Diglo brothers that worried Brett or the fact that Layke had mentioned God? *Lord, I sense a battle raging in Brett's heart. Can You calm his doubts and show him You're there? He needs You.*

I need You, too. Father, I'm struggling on why we're going through this hardship. I—

A ding on her laptop halted her prayers. She clicked her email program and found a message from Beth requesting Keeley call her right away at the lab. It was important.

"I gotta make a call." Not trusting her cell phone's reception, Keeley snatched the sat and punched in the lab's number.

"Beth Bower speaking."

"Beth, it's Keeley." Keeley walked to the window and peered at the sky. Dark clouds had moved in again. Great. That was all they needed. A storm in the middle of nowhere.

"Oh, hey. I wasn't sure it was you, as the number's blocked. Where are you calling from?"

Beth's question jolted Keeley back to her conversation. "Sat phone. Poor reception here. What's going on?"

"Just got a call from someone looking for you."

Why did that warrant the urgent message to call? People telephoned her lab all the time. "Who was it?"

"Someone named Davey. Said he was a good friend of yours who needed to get in touch with you right away. He wanted to know where to reach you."

Keeley caught Brett's attention. "What did you tell him?"

Brett raised a brow.

"That I didn't know, because I don't. I wouldn't have told him anyway. I realize there are creeps after you, and this guy sounded—I don't know—antsy." A pause. "I was scared it was one of those Diglo brothers."

Wait. Keeley tensed. She'd never mentioned the Diglo brothers to Beth. Had she? Suspicion turned Keeley's breakfast into lead. First Audrey and now Beth. Did she know her coworkers as well as she thought? Was Beth feeding them information all this time, and this was a ruse to give up their location?

"Did you hear me, boss?"

Keeley gripped the phone tighter. "Sorry, what did you ask?"

"Can you tell me where you are? I just need to know you're safe."

No one can know where we are.

Brett's words filtered through Keeley's mind. At this point, she didn't know who to trust. Not even her assistant. "I can't tell you, but I'm safe."

"But what if I need to get in touch with you? In case this Davey calls again?"

Keeley massaged her lower back. "Email me. Is there anything else?"

"I wish you'd tell me." Her voice faltered.

"Beth, I can't." How much clearer did she have to get?

"Fine. Be that way." *Click.*

Wow. What had warranted Beth's shift in disposition? She normally was a fun-loving woman.

"What was that all about?"

Keeley set the phone on the table. "Beth telling me Davey called looking for me, but she acted strangely."

"In what way?"

"Well, she mentioned the Diglo brothers, and I'm pretty sure I never gave her their name. Plus, she got mad at me when I wouldn't tell her where I was." Keeley rubbed her left palm with her right thumb. "She's never gotten upset with me before. Something isn't right."

"Let's not jump to conclusions. Beth was probably having a bad day and missing you. But we should mention it to Layke. Just in case." Brett raised his index finger. "Wait—that reminds me. Tina acted strange the other day, too."

Keeley twirled her hair, then dropped it as if it had scorched her fingers. "Do you think the leader of this group could be someone close to us?"

"Right now, I don't trust anyone. Perhaps Layke can do a deep dive into all of their backgrounds."

Keeley bit her lip. She hated spying on friends. "Sure." A tear formed and fell before she could stop it.

Brett flew to her side, bringing her into a hug. "It's gonna be okay."

She melted into his arms. *I want to stay here forever. It feels like home.* "I just want all of this to be over."

"I understand. Me too." He squeezed tighter.

"Hug time!" MJ plowed into their legs and wrapped his little arms around them. "Mr. Brett, I love you."

Brett stiffened in her arms.

Keeley pulled back from his embrace and stared into his eyes, asking him a silent question on her mind. *Are you staying?*

He looked away, but not before she caught his wrenched expression.

He *was* leaving.

Keeley dug her fingernails into her palms, curbing her frustration. She couldn't let MJ see her disappointment.

Brett tousled MJ's curls. "You too. How about some lunch, sport?"

"Yes. Then more checkers?" MJ clapped.

Brett folded his arms, tapping his index finger on his upper arm. "You just want to beat me again, don't you?"

MJ giggled.

Keeley suppressed a sigh and returned to her laptop. *He can't commit, so close that crack in your heart you let open up.*

Had she misread him? She thought they were getting closer and their spark had reignited.

How could I have been so wrong?

Keeley wiggled her mouse to bring her laptop back to life.

She sucked in an audible ragged breath.

Her black screen held a message in bold red letters.

We will find you. You can't hide forever.

Had Beth sent this message? The timing couldn't be a coincidence.

Or had the Diglos hacked her computer?

Chapter Fifteen

Brett snapped a picture of Keeley's screen seconds before it pixelated and changed to a skull and crossbones, then disappeared. His pulse elevated. This proved someone connected to the Diglos had serious hacking skills. Or it was one of the brothers. Brett quickly tapped on his cell phone, sending the picture and details to Constable Jackson.

Keeley stumbled backward, gasping for breath. "Can't breathe."

"Mama?" MJ ran to his mother's side, his eyes widening with each of Keeley's sharp intakes.

She was hyperventilating.

Brett darted to the kitchen and snatched a paper grocery bag. "Keels, breathe into this." He scrunched the top to create a small passageway and handed it to her. "Slow, deep breaths."

He yanked out a chair. "Sit."

She sat and lifted it to her mouth, breathing

in. Out. In. Out. After a minute, her rhythm slowed, and she removed the bag from her mouth. "Thanks."

MJ tugged at her arm. "Mama, you okay?"

"I'm good, slugger. Sorry for scaring you. Go grab a book, and we'll read before lunch."

He smiled and skipped to the toy cabinet.

"Thanks, Brett." Keeley set the bag on the table.

"Do you hyperventilate often?"

"Not normally, and I almost did in the forest when the brothers attacked. But this time they got into my computer, and it shocked me. They're getting closer." She inhaled another deep breath.

Brett sat. He must calm her. Her pale face told him she still struggled. He rubbed her arm. "It's gonna be okay." He glanced at her laptop. Something niggled at the back of his brain. "Keels, do you really think the Diglo brothers are capable of hacking systems?"

She shook her head. "Honestly? No."

"Why do you say that?"

"Just a hunch. Their odd dialect makes me feel like they may not have finished school." She held her hands out, palms up. "Not judging or anything, but they just don't seem the computer types."

"Who could be the hacker, then? This Mama they referred to?"

"Possibly."

MJ squealed and shot to his mother's side, interrupting their conversation. "Can we read this one?"

"Good choice, slugger." Keeley got up and nudged him toward the couch.

"I'll start lunch." Brett watched the two snuggle together, and a picture formed in his mind.

The three of them sitting together with MJ in the center as they read a book in front of a Christmas tree.

Would that happen?

Could he trust that the woman before him wouldn't betray him like all the others?

She'd certainly never given him any sign of that, but she'd pulled away from him more than once lately. Just when he thought they were getting closer.

She doesn't want you around, Brett.

And that broke his heart.

Later that night, MJ yawned as the coals in the fireplace held his focus. Brett had wanted to keep them toasty, so he had built a fire earlier. They had taken a walk in the afternoon, staying close to the cabin. MJ had made Brett promise to take him fishing sometime soon.

If only.

"I think it's bedtime," Brett whispered.

"Agree." Keeley uncurled her legs and moved to get up.

Brett eased her back down. "Let me do it. How about you make us some tea? I promise not to break my mug this time." He smiled and scooped up MJ, taking him into the bedroom.

He placed him on the bed, covering him with the quilted bear-and-moose comforter. Brett tucked it in all around MJ's little body— something his father used to do with Brett and Gideon. He'd said they were snug as a bug and could sleep better.

Brett smiled at the memory and kissed MJ's forehead. "Night, my sweet son," he whispered.

He squared his shoulders. Time to ask Keeley the question he'd been waiting to ask. First a tea to calm them both. Brett slipped out of the room, easing the door shut. He walked to the kitchen, where she'd been boiling water. Brett placed a lavender tea bag in a mug. "Are you feeling better?"

She poured the water into both cups. "Much,

thanks. I just want to relax for a bit before turning in. Hoping for a better sleep tonight."

"Sounds good."

They took their teas and sat together on the couch.

Brett fished out his cell phone from his back pocket and placed it on the log coffee table in front of them.

"Brett, I've been wondering something." Keeley paused. "Why did you leave policing? Wasn't that your passion?"

He slumped against the couch. Could he own up to the mistake he'd made? If he wanted her to trust him, he had to give something in return. Right?

Brett took a sip of his tea as if that would give him courage. "It was once. Until a mistake I made cost my partner's life."

Her mouth dropped. "What?"

He shut his eyes, trying to erase the picture in his head from that day. The picture etched in his mind. *Time to face the past, Brett.*

Brett opened his eyes. "My partner and I, along with other constables, were tasked with protecting a key witness in a huge case, so we were patrolling outside the safe house. The witness had gone to bed, and the place was secured.

We were rechecking the perimeter when we heard an explosion." He clenched his jaw. "We rushed around to the back only to find our cruiser in flames. We had hidden it behind the house on a side street to conceal our presence."

"Oh no. What happened?"

Brett set his cup down and got up, moving to the window. He brushed the drapes aside and checked to ensure they were still alone. *Humph. Old habits.* He turned back to face Keeley. "We called it in, but the perp used it as a diversion and hacked into the system. They somehow gained entry using the code. The witness screamed, and we ran inside." The scene flashed again.

Blood. So much blood.

"There were two of them. One stood in between the bodies of our constable and the witness. He turned his gun on me, and I dodged behind a counter. The other perp caught my partner by surprise and held her at knifepoint. Said we had to pay for interfering. He stabbed her before I could even react. Then the pair fled." Brett bit his lip to ward off pending tears. "I didn't save her."

He slumped back onto the couch and held his head in his hands.

Keeley wrapped her arm around him. "But, Brett, how can you say you made a mistake?"

He lifted his head. "Because I didn't properly enter the house. I should have seen the second man."

"It's still not your fault." She rubbed his back. "So that's why you switched to becoming a paramedic?"

"Yes. I didn't have the right tools to save her and never wanted to be in that situation again." He grimaced. "I hated to tell my cop father, but he took it well. Said he was proud of me."

"You're an amazing man, Brett Ryerson, and don't you forget that."

"Thank you. I decided when I came back to the Yukon to also train with Search and Rescue. I looked into it, and they were happy about the possibility because they wanted to add a paramedic to their team."

"That's awesome. Seems we're both furthering ourselves. I've been taking a self-defense class."

What? "Why? Did something happen?"

"No. Just wanted a break from single parenting and work for one night a week."

"Good idea." He gazed into her beautiful

hazel eyes. *I could get lost there.* "Keels, can I ask you a question?"

"Sure."

"Can we tell MJ I'm his dad now?"

His cell phone buzzed, and a message appeared on the screen.

Need your decision. Are you coming back?

Brett noted Keeley's hardened eyes. She'd seen the text.

"You're leaving, aren't you?" The disdain in her voice revealed her disappointment.

He didn't want to. *Ask me to stay.* He gnawed on his lower lip. "No, I'm not."

She bolted upright. "You hesitated. Not sure I believe you. So, until you're sure, we don't tell MJ." She scrambled out of the room, slamming her bedroom door behind her.

Once again, Brett buried his head in his hands.

Convince her you're staying.

Keeley woke to laughing coming from the living room. She groaned and checked her smartwatch: 8:00 a.m. She popped into an upright seated position. How had she slept that long? Then she remembered... She'd had a hard time getting to sleep after seeing the text from Brett's leader in Ontario. His response to her question didn't convince her. *He's leaving.*

And her heart was broken.

She had cried herself to sleep. He had worked his way back into her heart so quickly. Not that she was surprised. Their previous connection had been strong.

MJ's giggle coming from the living room stuck in the imaginary knife, deepening her wound.

Oh, Brett, how could you?

Keeley had watched her son get closer and closer to his father without even knowing his true identity.

A squeal sounded, followed by thudding steps.

Brett must be chasing MJ.

Keeley fell back onto her pillow and rubbed her eyes, feeling a bulge. *Ugh!* How could she face them with puffy eyes? *They'll know.*

MJ will know.

Preston's face entered her mind, and she sat up.

Get it together, Keeley. You've done this before. You can do it again.

For MJ's sake.

She just wished she didn't have to.

Keeley squared her shoulders and rolled out of bed. *Time to face the music, as they say.*

After dressing in jeans and a green sweatshirt, she proceeded into the hall, tiptoeing into the bathroom. She splashed multiple handfuls of cold water onto her face, hoping to shrink the puffs. However, it didn't help.

So be it.

She inhaled deeply and plastered on a smile before thrusting open the door. "Morning, boys. What's going on out here? All this noise is gonna wake the animals outside."

"No, it won't, Mama. Don't be silly." MJ threw himself into her arms. "You're a sleepyhead."

Keeley stole a peek at Brett, but he had moved into the kitchen and turned his back to her, obviously distancing himself. She kissed her son's head. "Morning, slugger. Did you sleep okay?"

"Yup. Guess what?" He returned to Brett's side.

"What?"

"Mr. Brett is making us pancakes this morning. My favorite."

She laughed. "Everything is your favorite."

DARLENE L. TURNER 263

"No. I don't like broccoli." He scrunched his nose. "Ewww."

"That's true. You spit it out whenever Gramma tries to hide it in her veggie lasagna." Keeley meandered into the kitchen.

MJ pushed a stool next to the counter and climbed up, sticking his finger in the pancake batter.

Brett play-slapped his hand away. "Hey now. None of that." He met Keeley's gaze. "Trust me. You don't want your mother mad at you."

She ignored the implication and brought out plastic plates from a cupboard. "Slugger, help me set the table."

"Yes, Mama." He hopped down from the stool and extended his arms. "I'm a good helper."

"You are. Now hold tight." Keeley set the plates in his hands.

He trudged toward the dining area, taking baby steps. "What are we doing today? Can we go fishing, Mr. Brett?"

"We can if it's okay with your mom. It's supposed to be warmer."

After a day of catering to MJ's every whim, Keeley tucked her son into bed. They said their nightly prayers, and she kissed his forehead. "Sleep well."

"I will, Mama. I had fun with Mr. Brett today. Can you marry him so he can live with us forever?"

Keeley recoiled as if her son had punched her in the stomach. How could she tell him Brett was leaving?

She pushed a red curl from his eyes. "I don't think that will happen, but you can be friends with Mr. Brett."

His lip quivered. "I want him to be my dad."

So do I.

Once again, she kissed his forehead. "Time for sleep. Love you."

He rolled over and faced the opposite side without another word.

Like father, like son.

Keeley sighed and opened the door, then startled.

Brett stumbled backward, looking down. "Sorry. I didn't mean to eavesdrop. Listen, I need to tell you—"

The sat phone rang, ending their awkward conversation.

One Keeley didn't need right now.

Brett scooped up the phone. "Brett here." A pause. "I'll put you on speaker." He turned to Keeley. "Layke has news."

She nodded and sat.

"Go ahead, Layke."

"Okay, we got a hit off the DNA from the hair. Davey Hawkins. He was in the foster care system. We found a picture of him as a boy and had Scarlet, a renowned forensic artist, do an age progression sketch. She lives in British Columbia now, but she's good—and fast. Sending it to your cell phones. Hopefully you have good reception."

Keeley fished out her cell phone just as it dinged. "Got it." She stared at Davey's evil eyes, a shiver paralyzing her muscles. Scarlet even included the tattoo Keeley had described. Impressive.

Brett whistled. "You said he was in the foster care system. What family?"

"We're still checking into that, as it appears he bounced around for a few years."

Brett tapped his thumb on the table. "So, his last name is Hawkins. Does he have any priors?"

"That's the odd part," Layke said. "No records at all. It's like he doesn't exist. What happened at your mother's and the fact they got into your laptop tells us someone connected with the Diglos is a black-hat hacker."

Keeley tensed. "We came to that conclusion

as well. I don't think it's any of the Diglos, though. From the time I spent with them, they just don't seem that smart. I realize I sound judgmental. I don't mean it that way. Just an impression I got." She told him her concerns about Beth.

"Brett mentioned her, and I did a deep dive. That's another bit of news I have. Did you know the police arrested her in her early twenties for assaulting her college roommate?"

Keeley shot upright. "What? How did she get that by me? I did a thorough reference check."

"She was never officially charged. The female dropped her claim. Said she lied."

Keeley strode to the window, twirling her hair. She scanned the area. They still had daylight later in the evenings during this time of year in the Yukon.

"Wait. Antoine is giving me an update." A muffled conversation filtered through the sat phone.

The wrinkles on Brett's forehead revealed his worry.

"Guys, Davey was just spotted near your location."

Brett charged out of his chair. "Where, Layke?"

"About five kilometers. We're sending units

to check it out. Stay indoors and alert. I'll reach out when I get further updates." He clicked off.

"Keels, get away from the window." Brett raced to a tall locked cabinet and pressed in a code. He opened the door, revealing a gun collection.

Keeley closed the window drapes and hustled to the center of the room. "What are you doing?"

"Arming myself for the possibility of an intruder." He lifted out a rifle and loaded it. "I need to protect my family."

Keeley sucked in a breath.

The Diglo brothers had found them again. The question was—how?

Chapter Sixteen

Brett's pulse thundered in his ears, elevating his guard to keep his family safe. And Keeley and MJ were his family. Even if she didn't want him there. She had distanced herself ever since he got the text from his supervisor. He was about to convince her he wasn't taking the job when Constable Jackson called. Right now, he had to secure the perimeter. He wouldn't let past mistakes cloud his judgment.

Brett removed a Glock from the cabinet and passed it to her. "Keels, do you know how to use one of these?"

Her expression contorted. "I've taken lessons. What are you going to do?"

"I need to make sure there's no one out there." He gathered his jacket from the hook and put it on, securing the rifle over his shoulder.

"Layke said to stay inside, Brett." Her shaky words revealed her worry.

He rubbed her arm. "You're safe. I just have to make sure Davey isn't out there." He moved to the entrance. "I'll only be gone five minutes. Bolt the door after I leave and don't let anyone in other than myself or the constables."

She nodded, biting her lip.

Lord, hear me. Please protect Keels and my son.

Brett stepped onto the veranda, senses on high alert.

The lock clicked into place behind him. *Good girl, Keels.*

He raised the rifle and inspected the forest around the cabin. Five minutes later, he knocked on the cabin door. "Keels, it's me."

She unlocked and opened the door.

He bounded inside and locked them in. "No suspicious sightings. All okay here?"

"Yes." Keeley handed the Glock to him. "Can we lock these back up? I don't want them out with MJ here."

Brett took the weapons and went to the cabinet, entering the code. He tucked the guns away. "Keels, the code is 02161212. My birth date and Gideon's. If you need to get back into the cabinet in case something happens to me."

She threw her arms around him. "Don't say that. Nothing is going to happen to you."

He held her tightly, chin resting on the top of her head. *She fits perfectly in my arms.*

They stayed in the same position for a few minutes. Then he leaned back. Their gazes locked, and his eyes shifted to her lips.

He inched closer, wanting to press his lips on hers.

She tilted her chin upward.

Did she want him to kiss her?

He caressed her cheek and—

The sat phone shrilled, severing the moment.

He broke their embrace and snatched the phone from its docking station. "Brett here."

"We got him," Layke said. "Taking him inside the station now."

Brett turned to Keeley. "They got him." He pressed the speaker button. "You mean Davey?"

"Yes. He was lurking at a store down the road from your location. There are still two brothers at large, so stay put. I left a constable near the entrance to the cabin." A slamming door sounded through the phone.

"Can we listen in? I just want to be sure it's him. I'll recognize his voice." Keeley's twisted expression revealed her apprehension.

"That's not normal, but okay. Keep the line open and wait a sec. We're going to see what we

can get out of him. Moving him into an interrogation room now. We won't tell him you're
on the line."

Brett pulled out a chair at the table. "Keels,
sit," he whispered.

She obeyed.

He sat beside her and placed the phone in the
middle of them. Brett motioned for Keeley to
remain silent.

A minute later, voices sailed through the
phone. Jackson telling the brother to sit, followed by the sound of handcuffs clicking in
place.

"Okay, let's begin," Jackson said. "We know
you're Davey Hawkins. Tell us what you were
doing at that hardware store."

The man swore. "Whatcha think? Shoppin'.
You had no right to arrest me. I wants a lawyer."

"Are you part of the Diglo gang? Where are
your brothers?"

"I ain't tellin' you squat." His wicked tone
shot through the airwaves.

Keeley gripped the sides of the table.

"Did you attack Dr. Ash in her home?" Jackson asked.

A chair scraping sounded. "I did nothin' of
the kind. Did Keeley tattle on me?"

"How did you know her name?"

"I—I— She's…" His stammering proved his nervousness.

Keeley grabbed Brett's arm and mouthed, "It's him."

Brett extracted his cell phone from his pocket and texted Jackson, confirming the voice identification. He prayed it would go through. Thankfully, the reception had been good today.

A pause in the conversation sounded before Brett's phone dinged. Jackson.

Okay. Stay on the line for a minute.

"Tell us about this business you have helping fugitives." Jackson continued the interrogation. "Where is your hideout?"

"Not sure what yous talking about."

"What are the names of your brothers? Is it Diglo? We know the youngest was Eddie. Who's Mama? Roy?" Jackson fired question after question.

"Diglo was our dog." Davey snickered. "You'll never find 'em."

"Mama!" MJ appeared at the entrance.

"Who's there?" Davey asked.

Their son just announced their presence.

"Is that the brat? Keeley, we's comin' for ya.

You can't hide forever." Once again, evil bull-rushed through the phone.

MJ whimpered.

Brett hit the button to end the call. He'd forgotten to put them on mute. *Stupid, Brett. Stupid.*

He scurried over to MJ and lifted him. "It's okay, sport. You're okay." He held him tight, praying for protection.

Once again, Brett's cell phone dinged. He returned to the table and examined the text. Nancy.

Your dad doesn't have long. You need to come home. Now!

"No!" Brett sank into a chair with his son in his arms. How had his father's condition changed again so rapidly?

He was dying, and the wicked Diglo brothers were coming for Brett's family.

How could he choose?

Keeley noted Brett's haunted expression, and she followed his line of sight to his phone. She turned it toward her and read the message. Her jaw dropped, and she stood, reaching for MJ. "Let me take him back to bed."

He nodded and handed him to her.

"Let's go, slugger. Everything is okay." Keeley took him back to his bed, tucking him in tightly. "There. You're all nice and snuggly."

"Was that the bad man, Mama?"

She brushed his bangs to the side. "You never mind about him. You're safe here." *Lord, make it so.*

"Will you sing to me, Mama?"

"What song?" She smiled. Leave it to her son to lighten the load.

"'Jesus Loves Me.'"

Keeley cleared her throat and sang her son's favorite song.

He was asleep before she finished.

She kissed his forehead before backing out of the room.

"You have a lovely voice."

She jumped. "You scared me." Heat flushed her cheeks. "Thanks. I'm so sorry to hear about your father. What are you going to do?"

His jaw tightened. "I can't leave you and MJ."

She took his hands in hers. "You'll regret not saying goodbye. Get the patrolling constable to park in the cabin's driveway. Just in case." She pointed to the gun cabinet. "I know the code, remember, so I can arm myself."

Brett bit his lip, revealing the trepidation she guessed plagued his body.

Lord, give him strength. "Brett, you have to go."

He snatched the second sat phone. "Okay, I'll call Layke and take this phone with me. Each number is programmed into the other. I want to be able to reach you at all times."

"Understood."

A wave of worry locked every muscle in her body, but she refused to show him. Or he'd never leave.

She wouldn't let that happen. He'd regret not being with his father as he passed.

Keeley studied him as he spoke to Layke, requesting a constable at the cabin.

Brett paced as he raked his hand through his hair. A habit she remembered from years ago.

He stopped at the window, peeking out. "Okay, thanks." He clicked off and turned. "Constable Antoine is on his way."

Keeley picked up Brett's jacket and handed it to him. "Go. Before it's too late."

He blanketed her in his arms. "I have to tell you something."

She pulled back. "What?"

"I'm not taking the job. I'm staying in the Yukon with you and MJ."

Keeley inhaled a sharp breath. "When did you make that decision?"

"As soon as I realized MJ was my son, I knew I couldn't leave. I just haven't been able to tell my former supervisor." A smile danced on his lips. "We've been a tad busy."

He's staying. However, a question remained lodged in Keeley's mind. Did he want a relationship with *her*? Preston had made promises, too. Promises he broke.

Plus, Brett wasn't a believer.

She retreated.

Sadness wrenched his handsome face.

She'd disappointed him again.

A pounding knock sounded.

"Guys, it's me. Constable Antoine. Let me in."

Brett grabbed his car keys and the phone. "I'll call you. Stay safe." He opened the door and spoke in hushed tones with Len before turning back to her. Brett waved and raced toward his vehicle.

Keeley watched his Jeep drive down the long driveway, out of her reach. *Lord, comfort him and protect him. Most of all, bring him to You.*

Len cleared his throat. "You okay?"

"I'll be fine. Come in. I'll make us some tea."

"Actually, if you have leaded coffee, I'll take one instead. I think it's gonna be a long night." He locked the door.

Keeley moved into the kitchen and loaded the coffee machine. "Did you get anything else from Davey? Did he reveal who the woman is in their organization?" Thoughts of Beth, Tina and Audrey entered her mind.

"No. Says he's not snitching on his kin." Len plunked down at the table, facing the door. "We're searching for records to determine the home he'd been placed in."

Keeley took some mugs from the cupboard. "Hopefully, you find out soon. I'm tired of running."

"Understood. We're close to—"

Thudding footsteps coming up the stairs silenced his words. Len shot upright, unleashing his weapon.

Pounding sounded on the door. "Keeley, it's Mom. Let me in."

"What's she doing here?" Len holstered his gun, then unlocked and opened the door. "Judge, you're supposed to be staying put. Where's Terry?"

"I ditched him." She stepped inside. "I got Keeley's text to get here right away."

Keeley dropped her mug on the counter. "Text? What text?"

Her mother strode into the kitchen and held out her phone. "This one."

Keeley inched closer.

Mom, need you at the cabin right away. Here are the directions. Come quickly. Alone. My safety depends on it.

Keeley's jaw dropped. "Mom, I didn't send you a text."

Her mother staggered backward. "Then who did?"

Once again, Len unholstered his weapon. "Brett told me you have access to guns. Get one. I'm going to call it in and secure the perimeter. Lock the door and don't let anyone else in." He raised his gun and opened the door, rushing outside.

"Mom, stay low and get on the couch." Keeley bolted the door, hurried to the cabinet, punched in the code and withdrew the Glock.

"Keeley, who's doing this to our family?" Her mother's hushed words revealed her alarm.

"I wish I knew." Keeley straightened. "Wait. If they were able to hack into your phone, make it look like I texted you, then they could do the same to Brett."

"Where is he?"

"He got a text telling him to come to his father's house because he was dying." Tears welled. "I have to call him before—"

The door crashed open, splintering the wood. Keeley pivoted, raising her weapon.

And stared down the end of a double-barreled shotgun. Terror coursed through her body, icing her veins.

"You're not going anywhere," the mocking voice said. "Drop it, Keeley, or your mama dies." The woman shifted her aim to Olivia Ash.

The Glock slipped from Keeley's hands when she realized the mama of the Diglo brothers had been under her nose the entire time.

Keeley stumbled forward. "You."

Chapter Seventeen

Silence greeted Brett as he entered his father's foyer. Hospital smells wafted in the area, and he suppressed the sadness overtaking his emotions. *Put on a brave face, Brett. For Dad.*

Brett dashed toward his father's room and eased open the door. Stillness permeated the area.

Nancy was nowhere to be seen.

Odd. Wouldn't she stay close to his dad's side in his hour of need?

He moved to the chair beside his father's bed, taking his hand. "I'm here, Dad."

His frail cop father fluttered his eyes open. "Hey, son."

Tears welled at his father's whispered greeting. Brett swallowed the lump forming in his throat. *Keep it together.* "How are you feeling?"

His father turned his head, and a tiny smile

formed on his face. "Better now that you're here. How's my grandson?"

"As spunky as ever. I heard him say he wants me to marry Keeley so we can all live together."

"Well, are you?" Brett's father squeezed his hand. "I would be ecstatic to know you've found love before I leave this world."

"Dad, Keeley hasn't forgiven me for leaving. At least, that's what I sense. She keeps pulling back."

"Do you admit MJ is your son?"

"I do. Even without a DNA test." Brett checked his father's pulse. Fairly strong.

Odd.

Wouldn't it be weaker in his last hours?

"That's good, son. Then what are you waiting for? Tell her how you feel."

Brett stood and placed his hand on his dad's forehead. No temp. "How can I when I don't know myself?"

"It's written all over your face. You've fallen for her and your son. Time to form a family."

Was that true?

His father coughed.

Brett lifted the glass on the nightstand and tipped the straw to the man's lips. "Drink."

His father obeyed. "Son, sit. We need to talk."

Brett plunked back in the chair. "About what?"

"Have you thought any more about what I said to you regarding promising to come back to God?"

Brett huffed and slumped back. "Dad, don't—"

"Listen to me carefully. God uses our tough circumstances to shape and grow us." He retook Brett's hand. "But the question remains—will you let Him? It's time. You've been holding on to the past for too long." His father squeezed tightly.

While the question gnawed at Brett, his father's strong hold perplexed him.

Nancy shuffled into the room, carrying clean towels. "Oh, hey, Brett. What are you doing here?"

Brett froze. "Didn't you text me to come?"

"I did no such thing." She placed the towels on a shelf by the window. "Why would you think that?"

Brett flew to his feet. "You said Dad only had a short time left and to get home."

"Son, I'm stronger than I was last week. God is giving me more time to spend with you, Keeley and my sweet grandson."

If Nancy hadn't texted him, then who had?

Images of crossbones on Keeley's laptop flashed through his mind.

No! The Diglo brothers had gotten to them.

He kissed his dad's forehead. "Dad, pray. Keeley and MJ are in danger. I need to go. Love you."

"You too."

Brett brought out the sat phone and dialed the other sat's number. He ran through the house and out to his Jeep as he waited.

And waited.

No answer.

He dialed Antoine. "Pick up. Pick up."

"Constable Antoine."

"Len! What's going on? Where's Keeley?" Brett started the engine.

"She's with her mother in the cabin."

"Olivia is there?" Brett backed out of the driveway and onto the street, squealing his tires. "How did she know where we were?"

"Not sure. Listen, I've secured the perimeter and I'm on my way back to them. We just got a hit on who the foster brothers were adopted by."

"Who?"

"The names are Donald and—"

A commotion cut off his words.

"Len! What's going on?"

For the third time tonight, silence greeted Brett. And he hated silence. He accelerated and turned onto the highway back toward the cabin.

Lord, protect my family.

Keeley's pulse hammered as she fought to keep her breathing under control. *You can't hyperventilate. Not now.* She breathed in, exhaling in extended breaths. She clung to her weeping mother, who crumpled at the sight of the head of the Diglo brothers.

Audrey Todd.

"How could you, Audrey?" It all came into plain view for Keeley. The woman knew plants and would know how poisons worked. Plus, Keeley now remembered why Eddie had seemed so familiar when she'd seen his face at the hunter's cabin. A picture of him had fallen out of Audrey's bag, and she'd scooped it up quickly, but Keeley had caught a glimpse of it.

Stupid, Keeley. You should have remembered that before. Now it's too late.

Audrey's sneer transformed into an evil expression. The normally kind woman vanished.

Had it all been an act?

Audrey raised the shotgun higher. "Yous

should have left well enough alone. My Eddie is gone, and now Davey is with the coppers."

Keeley noted her switch of dialect. She obviously put on a front while at college but now returned to her backcountry way of speech. Like her sons.

"You killed my sister and kidnapped my son." Fire burned in Keeley's gut. "How could a mother do that?"

"Easy. Them hikers should have stayed buried. You were too close to pinning their deaths on my boys. I had to get you to back off. Tried to steal your evidence, but you were too smart." She advanced farther into the cabin. "I gave yous your boy back, but what did you do? You kept digging."

"That case had to be solved. Anyone with a conscience would realize that. How did you find us here?"

Audrey pointed to Keeley's purse on a nearby chair. "Easy. I put Bluetooth tags in your purse when you weren't looking. We've just been waiting for the perfect opportunity to strike. Now's that time."

A wave of angst threatened to immobilize Keeley. *Keep it together.* She squeezed her mother tighter. "Why did you lure my mother here? She has nothing to do with this."

"I had to. I couldn't let a judge go free after I kill her daughter." She snickered. "But don't worry. We's not gonna kill MJ. Me and my kin are gonna raise him in the backcountry."

"You will not have my son!" Keeley pulled her mother to a standing position.

"You took mine. I'm taking yours." She turned her head. "Ivan! Get in here."

A burly man dressed in a hunter's jacket sauntered through the entrance. "Yes, Mama?"

"Find the kid." Audrey pointed to the bedrooms.

Ivan moved toward the closed doors.

"No! Don't you touch my grandson." Keeley's mother flew at Ivan.

Audrey fired, hitting Olivia in the shoulder. She dropped.

"Mom!" Keeley rushed to her side and squatted, wrapping her arms around her mother. "Stay with me." She snatched a blanket from the couch and pressed it on her mother's wound.

Audrey scoffed. "She's okay. For now."

Keeley must save her family. *Think, Keels. Think.* Where were the constables? She prayed Len had contacted his fellow officers. She needed to give them time to get here. "Tell me, are your sons foster kids?"

She chuckled. "I guess you can tell they don't look like their mama, huh? All my boys were gifts from God to Donald and I. We took 'em in and raised 'em to live off God's creations. Taught 'em to shoot, archery, axe throwin'. You name it, Donald taught them."

Her mother moaned.

"Which one of them is your hacker?" Keeley pressed harder on her mother's wound.

"*Pfft.* That was me. Them boys barely know how to operate a cell phone."

"Where did you learn to do all that?"

Audrey took one hand off the shotgun and blew on her nails, wiping them on her shirt. "Taught myself. Well, had some help from my video-gaming buddies."

"I'm impressed. Not everyone can hack into someone's computer." Keeley would play up the woman's strength. Try to get on her good side. "Did you also form this fugitive-hiding business?"

Ivan walked to the next room after he'd searched Brett's room.

Nausea attacked Keeley. *Lord, protect my boy!*

"Sure did. I put word out on the dark web

that if anyone was lookin' for refuge and a way to flee the country, they just had to pay me. I's had the means to give 'em a new identity." She tapped her temple. "Told ya. Smart mama. You see, I had to provide for my sons, and my teaching career wasn't cutting it, especially since my beloved passed two years ago and left us with nothin'." She placed her hand on her heart. "God rest his soul."

Footsteps thudded on the cabin's front steps, and another man entered. "Mama, we's ready. Bombs is set."

Bombs? Plural?

Keeley's jaw dropped. "What are you talking about?"

Audrey gestured toward the man. "This here's the brainchild, Roy. Say hi, Roy."

He waved. "Mama, can I go get him now?"

Get who?

Audrey patted the top of Roy's head. "Good boy. Yes, go claim your reward."

The bearded Roy with the messy hair knelt in front of Keeley and caressed her face.

Keeley shuddered. "Stay away from me."

"Eddie was right about you. Yous are purdy." He lifted a wad of her hair and sniffed, dragging her closer before planting a rough kiss on her lips.

She fought the urge to cry, but squared her shoulders. She would not give this man the satisfaction.

Roy pushed himself back to his feet. "Now I'm going to kill your boyfriend. It was Mama who texted him. We had to separate you. By now, he's probably figured it out and is on his way back. At least, that's what I'm counting on." He withdrew a nine millimeter. "I'm gonna be waiting in the trees." He charged out of the cabin.

"No! Leave Brett alone. Take me."

Audrey guffawed. "Don't bother. He's out for revenge. You all will pay. And to answer your question, we know where all the evidence is, including the boots you took from Eddie. We're bombing everything. Your lab. Coroner's lab. I also sent a virus to your systems since I failed to destroy it the first time. And if anyone dies?" She shrugged. "So be it."

"But why now? Why didn't you do that days ago?"

She removed a rag from her back pocket and rubbed her shotgun. "Isn't this guy a beaut? I like to make it shine. Gave it to Donald on his last birthday." Her voice quivered. She cleared her throat. "Anyway, been kind of busy with them fugitives. You know the sayin'—'If you're gonna do something, do it right.' I needed time to get ready." She stuffed the rag away and raised the weapon. "Now's the time."

"You're sick. I can't believe you fooled me all this time."

Ivan returned, holding a sleeping MJ. "Mama, this little guy is a sound sleeper. Didn't hear me. I like him."

Keeley blasted to her feet. "Give me my son!"

Audrey backhanded Keeley across the face.

She stumbled backward, her hand flying to her cheek to soothe the sting.

Come on, Len. Where are you?

Keep her talking. "Where did you get the privet to poison me?"

"Where do you think? Imported it, then planted it on my property."

"And where is that?"

Ivan carried MJ from the cabin.

"Not far from here. We hid it well." She aimed the shotgun in her direction. "Hand over your cell phone. We can't have them tracking you now, can we?"

Keeley hauled her sleeve farther down her

wrist to hide her smartwatch, then extracted her phone from her back pocket and held it out.

Audrey threw it on the couch. "Now, get your mother. We're leaving. You don't want to be here to see my Roy kill your love."

Keeley stuffed the laces of her hiking boots inside and fumbled to put them on as a thought shot through her mind.

They were out of time.

And no help had arrived to save them.

Brett parked on the side of the cabin's driveway to hide his approach. He had to enter by stealth mode. He wouldn't risk giving away his presence...for Keeley and MJ's sake. Brett had gotten in touch with Constable Jackson and requested assistance, but Jackson informed him they were responding to a suspected bomb threat in Carimoose Bay. However, he'd leave another officer in charge and be there as soon as he could. *Hurry!*

Fishing out the flashlight from his glove box to use as a weapon, Brett silently chastised himself for not bringing his rifle along. He had to get to his father's gun collection. He stepped out of his Jeep and inched toward the cabin, moving from tree to tree to keep himself concealed.

Lord, I know I haven't trusted You, but I need Your guidance and help in saving my family. I love them and can't lose them now...just when I found them.

He peeked out from the tree in front of his father's cabin, searching for any movement. Their daylight was diminishing quickly, and soon darkness would be upon them.

Stillness blanketed the area, including the cabin. *Lord, help them to just be hiding.* However, his gut was telling him something was wrong.

Terribly wrong.

Once Brett ensured he was alone, he dashed to the veranda and bounded up the steps. It was then he noticed the demolished door. *No!* "Keels! Where are you?" His hushed cry amplified in the small area.

Silence greeted him.

Again.

Creak.

He pivoted.

A bearded hunter stood on the step with his gun aimed at Brett's heart. "Welcome home. I's been waiting for your return. I'm Roy, and you're about to die for killing my baby brother."

Brett's heartbeat jackhammered, sending terror to every part of his body.

Give me strength, Lord.

"Where is my family?" He took a step toward the hunter. "If you've done anything to hurt them, I'll—"

Roy lifted his nine millimeter higher. "You'll what?"

Brett gripped the flashlight tighter, contemplating a takedown scenario. He observed the open gun cabinet. Could he outrun a bullet?

Hardly.

"You'll never make it. If you want to see them, drop the flashlight." Roy shot up the rest of the steps. "Now!"

Brett didn't have a choice. He let his only weapon slip from his fingers.

Roy grabbed Brett by the arm and pushed him off the veranda. "Get moving."

"Where are we going?"

"To sleep." Roy hit him on the head.

Brett's legs buckled, and he felt himself falling. A thought arose as the darkness called out to him.

The man hadn't worn a mask.

That only meant one thing.

They wouldn't leave anyone alive.

Chapter Eighteen

"Get out of the vehicle!"

Keeley shuddered at Audrey's sharp command. "Where's my son?"

"Don't worry—he's right behind us. You'll see him soon. Now get out."

Keeley opened the truck door and exited the vehicle before helping her mother.

Her mother winced at the movement.

Lord, she's losing blood. Please send help. "Mom, press on your wound."

"I'm so tired." Judge Ash's weakened voice conveyed her condition.

"I've got you." Keeley wrapped her arm around her mother's waist and surveyed her surroundings. But only trees were in her path. "Where are we?"

Audrey raised her shotgun. "See that cluster of trees? Go."

Keeley and her mother hobbled through the

opening until they came to a clearing. Keeley stopped short.

They had multiple small structures built into different rock formations. Camouflaged trees hung over each building. Some cliffs were in the distance.

No wonder they'd stayed hidden from the world.

She spun around to face Audrey. "You live underground?"

"Best place to be." She waved her gun toward a patch of low-lying bushes. "That way."

Keeley examined the area Audrey had referred to and almost missed it. Vegetation hid a latch. "What's in there?"

"Our tornado shelter, or as I like to put it, your grave. Open it."

Goose bumps slithered up Keeley's neck, and she forced herself to move. She reached between the plants and pulled on the handle. The lid opened, and she pushed it forward, exposing steep rock steps leading into a black hole.

There was no way her mother could make it down them. "My mom is too feeble."

A vehicle sounded, and then a door slammed.

Audrey tipped her head and sneered. "Well then, help her. You don't have a choice, or I will shoot your son, who just arrived. Go or watch him die."

"No. Don't hurt him." Keeley gently nudged her mother's arm. "Mom, I'll go first and help you take one step at a time. Okay?"

She nodded.

It took them a few minutes to reach the bottom, guided only by a small beam of light coming from somewhere deep in the ground.

Keeley clung to her mother and moved forward. "Where to, Audrey?"

The woman yanked on a string, flooding the shelter with bright light.

Keeley blinked to allow time for her eyes to adjust. A small room stocked with shelves containing jars of food, flashlights, batteries and other preservation supplies came into view.

"Welcome to your dungeon. Don't worry, *Keels*. You won't be here long." Audrey gestured toward her mother. "But she will die here."

Keeley gasped. "Don't do this. We won't tell anyone. I'll help you destroy the evidence." Could she really uphold that promise?

"Sit." Audrey pointed to the round table and chairs next to the shelves.

Keeley helped her mother into one of the chairs.

"Mama!" Her son's scream sent shivers throughout Keeley's body.

"MJ!"

Ivan appeared around the corner, holding MJ. He squirmed in the man's arms, kicking and screaming. Ivan charged forward and practically threw MJ into Keeley's arms. "You take the brat." He turned to his mother. "Mama, I'm not so sure we's should keep him. He's feisty."

Keeley hugged a crying MJ tightly and dropped into the chair. "Shhh, it's okay, slugger. I've got you, and God's got us."

Audrey slapped the back of Ivan's head. "Simmer down and get ahold of yourself. We need to go prepare."

Prepare for what?

Audrey marched into Keeley's personal space and poked her in the arm. "You keep MJ quiet. We'll be back."

"Where are you going?"

"None of your business, and don't try screaming. There's no one around these parts. Just my kin and I. Oh…and a few wanted fugitives. They ain't gonna help ya." She addressed Ivan. "Let's go."

They headed up the steps, and seconds later,

the latch door slammed shut, followed by a dead bolt.

They were locked in with nowhere to run.

Brett stirred. His head pounded. He forced his eyes open and stared into pitch blackness. He touched the bump where Roy had smashed his gun into and winced. Panic pummeled him. He had to escape, but where was he? How long had he been out?

Brett ignored the questions and placed his hands on the damp, broken floor. Cement. He pushed himself into a seated position and rubbed his eyes to clear his vision. It didn't help. The darkness blanketed him, sending another wave of panic surging throughout his body. A steady drip of water sounded nearby. Musk assaulted his nose.

Great. Roy took him to a similar place Brett had never wanted to be again.

Somewhere underground. Brett flashed back to being a five-year-old boy when he'd gotten locked in his grandparents' root cellar for hours. It was where his fear of confinement began.

God uses our tough circumstances to shape and grow us. Will you let Him?

His father's words once again filtered through

Brett's brain. It was time to allow God to change him.

Brett drew his knees to his chest and rested his head. *God is the only one who can help me now. God, I should have come to You years ago. How could I have been so blind? You've been right beside me, haven't You?*

Brett sighed. *You've taken me into the wilderness to make me a better man, and I've failed You. I'm sorry. Please forgive me. Create in me a clean heart. A new heart.*

I surrender whatever is left of my life to You.

Show me how to save Keels and my son. I love them.

Tears flowed freely, cleansing Brett of his past. His failures. His guilt over Gideon's death. His anger at losing his mother. Of his father's sickness.

Everything.

Peace washed over him in only one way he knew was possible.

Through God.

Adrenaline powered his body, sending strength into his muscles and a thought racing into his mind. *Find a way out.*

He stood and felt his way around the damp walls, his feet crunching on pieces of broken cement floor. Finally, he reached a wooden door. He glided his hands over the exit, looking for any flaws. His fingers stopped at the top hinge. The pin was exposed from the barrel. If he forced it out, along with the others, he'd be able to escape. But what could he use?

The darkness prevented him from seeing anything.

Brett dropped to his knees and ran his hands along the cement floor, crawling around the room as he prayed.

He struck a hard object.

A chunk of broken concrete.

Lord, help it to work.

He gripped the tool and fumbled his way back to the door. *Help them not to hear me.* Brett held his breath and placed the cement under the pin's lip, thrusting upward again and again until it loosened enough for Brett to pry it out.

He did the same to the others, then heaved the door open from the hinge side.

A dim light greeted him, and he blinked, allowing his eyes to adjust before moving forward.

He examined his surroundings and spotted cement steps going upward. Brett inched along the wall, concealing his approach and listening for his attackers. He stopped at the bottom of the stairs and peeked around the corner.

Empty.

He took one step at a time to silence his hiking boots. When he reached the top, he tried the doorknob. Unlocked.

He guessed they figured he was in a locked room and that would keep him contained. However—

God provided a way.

Brett eased the door open and slipped outside.

Darkness had descended.

He let his eyes focus, then looked around and surveyed his surroundings.

Brett was deep in the forest.

But where?

He glanced upward. Even the clouds hid the moon, blocking its light.

And any hope of guiding him through a maze of trees to find his family.

Keeley rocked MJ until he stilled. She had to stay quiet to keep him calm. She rested her chin on the top of his head. *Lord, show us a way out of this mess. Save us. Save Brett.* She observed her mother. Her ashen face told Keeley her mother's weakened state would make it impossible for the group to act quickly if the need arose. "Mom, you okay?"

"Tired. And ashamed."

"Why?"

"I've been a fool, Keeley." She reached out and grabbed Keeley's hand. "I've failed you and have been a terrible mother. I see that now. I'm just sorry it took tragedy to open my eyes."

How could Keeley stay mad at her mother at a time like this? After all, God forgave Keeley for all her mistakes. It was time for Keeley to do the same.

"Mom—"

"Let me finish. I should have told you about Zoe. I should have kept Zoe. My pride and desire for fame blinded me into not doing what God wanted me to." She squeezed Keeley's hand harder. "That's why I tried so hard to make it up to Zoe. I shut you out and gave her my love. I robbed you of a sister's love. For that, I wouldn't blame you if you never forgive me."

Keeley let her mother's apology sink in.

"Honey, I'm so sorry. Sorry for a lot of things." Her mother bit her lip. "Most of all, I'm sorry for not telling you how proud I am of you. Of the woman and mother you've become. Of the work you do. I love you and MJ to the moon and back." She inhaled. "I just wish I'd have told you sooner and not at such a precarious time as this."

A tear slipped down Keeley's cheek.

These were words she had longed to hear for years.

Keeley leaned forward and wrapped her free arm around her mother. "I forgive you, Mom, and I love you, too."

Tears flowed from the eyes of a powerful Supreme Court judge.

Her mother.

"I'm proud of you, too, Mom."

Clapping erupted from behind them. "Aw, ain't that sweet. Making up for lost time?"

They both startled.

Audrey removed a nine millimeter from her waistline. "I'm afraid your time is up. Keeley, you're coming with me. Stand."

Keeley hesitated. *Lord, help!*

MJ jolted awake and screamed.

Audrey thrust the gun's barrel into her mother's temple. "Give MJ to your mother or I'll blow 'er brains out right in front of your son."

"Okay, okay." Keeley kissed her son's forehead and stood. "Mama's gotta go, MJ, but you'll be okay here with Gramma."

"No, Mama!"

Keeley forced her tears back and handed her son to her mother. "It will be okay. I promise."

Audrey wrenched Keeley's arm and leaned in. "Don't make promises you can't keep. Now go! And, Judge Ash, don't try anything. Ivan is guarding the entrance. You won't escape him. His papa taught him well."

Keeley blew her son and mother kisses. "Love you guys."

More tears from both of them tore at Keeley's heart as she forced her legs to move up the rock steps and into the darkness.

Rain pelted the region. Keeley lifted her face and let the drops soothe her skin. Peace washed over her.

She knew its source.

Her Father. Her life was in His hands.

"Ivan, kill them if they try to escape. I'll be back." Audrey pushed Keeley. "March."

She stumbled but caught her footing. "Where are we going?"

"Straight ahead." Audrey flicked on a flashlight, powering a beam toward the cliffs in the distance.

Horror gripped Keeley by the throat, smothering her air. The woman was leading her to her death. "You don't have to do this."

"Yes, I do." She poked Keeley in the back with her gun.

Keeley walked, listening to her son's screams lessen as she moved farther from the shelter. She stopped at the edge and turned to face her accuser, a plan forming in her mind. Her only ray of hope. Something she'd learned in a self-defense class.

"You won't get away with this. You—" Keeley doubled over, pretending to be in pain.

"What's wrong with—"

Keeley thrust her body forward, bulldozing herself into Audrey.

They both fell to the ground as Audrey's gun fired into the air.

Keeley yanked on the woman's hair.

"You brat!" Audrey clawed Keeley's face.

Keeley rolled away and scrambled to her feet as one hiking boot slipped off.

Audrey bolted upright and lunged.

Keeley sidestepped out of her path, but not far enough.

Audrey clutched Keeley's ankle as she plummeted over the cliff's edge, taking Keeley with her.

Their combined screams pierced the night. Audrey let go of Keeley and plunged down the rocky incline.

Free of Audrey's grip, Keeley fumbled to grab anything to break her fall. *Lord, help!*

Her wrist slammed against the rocks, and dirt peppered her face moments before she felt a tree root. She latched on to the lifeline tightly and dug the toe of her left boot into the cliff's edge, slowing her descent.

Her feet landed on a narrow ledge, breaking her fall. She clung to the root and cowered against the cliff's side.

The rain had ended but had soaked her clothing.

She shivered and tapped her smartwatch to send out an SOS to emergency services.

And prayed.

Brett sprinted toward the gunshot that had echoed through the forest a few minutes ago. *Lord, help Keels and MJ to be okay.* Thankfully, the rain had subsided. For now. He stumbled through a wooded area and stopped at the sound of a loud male voice. He hid behind a large tree.

"Roy, what do you mean, kill the kid?" the voice asked. "I know he's a brat, but I thought Mama wanted to keep him."

Brett drew in an uneven breath. MJ! *Lord,*

no! Show me where my son is. He poked his head out but kept himself concealed.

A slim, bearded man stood beside a cluster of low-lying bushes, waving a flashlight beam in different directions. "Fine. I'll do it. Where's Mama? I's heard a shot earlier." A pause. "Me neither. She took that redhead to get rid of her."

What? No! Brett blinked back the tears forming. Had he found the love of his life only to lose her?

"Yup, the mother and kid are still here in the bunker." He swore. "Stop telling me what to do, Roy. Yous better get here to help me bury the bodies." He clicked off the call, leaned down and opened a door hidden among the bushes. He unleashed a gun and disappeared into an underground hole.

Brett's pulse skipped a beat. He had to save his son and Olivia. *Lord, give me strength to overpower this brother.* He zipped toward the opening and searched for any type of weapon. He spied a large branch and scooped it up, praying as he descended the rock steps. Thankfully, a dim light coming from below lit his way.

"Leave him alone!" Olivia yelled in the distance.

Brett inched along the corridor, staying

as quiet as he could with both hands tightly wound around the stick.

MJ whimpered.

Brett stole a peek.

The brother stood with his back to Brett, pointing a gun at MJ.

He had to act now or lose his son.

Brett tiptoed closer. He raised his makeshift weapon, mustered strength and thrust the branch down hard on the man's head.

The brother dropped.

"Brett!" Olivia pushed herself upright. "Thank the Lord."

Brett dropped the stick and lifted MJ. "You okay, sport?"

The boy responded by burying his head in Brett's chest.

Olivia wrapped her arms around Brett. "Thank you. Find Keeley. Audrey took her."

"Audrey Todd? She's Mama?"

"Yes." Olivia rubbed her shoulder and winced.

The hunter stirred.

Brett set MJ down, then scooped up the man's sat phone and gun. "Hurry, let's get out of here and lock him in. Can you walk?"

She nodded. "The bleeding has lessened. I'll be okay. God will give me strength."

The trio trudged up the stairs, and Brett slammed the door shut, locking the Diglo brother inside.

"Not so fast, Mr. Paramedic," a menacing voice said behind them.

Brett spun around and raised the gun, moving in front of his family.

"You're smarter than I thought you was." Roy had a shotgun aimed at the trio. "Give it up. There's no escapin' my kin and me."

"Leave us alone. I used to be a cop and have impeccable aim." Brett widened his stance in protective mode.

"Well then, we's got us a good ole-fashioned shoot-out here." Roy snickered. "Who will win? The hunter or the ex-copper-turned-paramedic? Yous still a good shot?"

"I killed your brother, didn't I?" Brett hated to antagonize him, but perhaps the man's anger would catch him off guard.

"Why, you…" Roy lifted his gun higher and charged toward him.

Brett fired, hitting Roy in the shoulder.

Shouts sounded in the woods.

Lights bouncing through the trees lit up the forest like fireflies on the East Coast.

Jackson and multiple constables charged

through the tree line, weapons raised. "Police! Stand down."

Brett placed his weapon on the ground. "Layke, Roy is armed, but I shot him in the shoulder."

Jackson rushed forward and scooped the shotgun up, pointing his gun at the moaning brother. "Move again and you'll be sorry." He turned to another constable. "Get him in cuffs and take him away."

"Is Antoine okay?" Brett wiped his forehead with the back of his hand.

"Yes. We found him passed out in the trees by your cabin. Paramedics are on their way here."

"How did you find us?"

Jackson raised a device. "Keeley's SOS from her smartwatch." He pointed behind Brett. "In that direction."

Fear coursed through Brett's body, depleting his energy. *Stay strong. For Keels and your son.* "Olivia, can you and MJ stay with the constables?"

She nodded.

Brett addressed Jackson. "I'm coming with you, Layke. Let's go."

The duo dashed through the trees and to the cliff's edge.

Jackson pointed. "The reading is coming from down there."

Brett followed the direction where Jackson had indicated.

A single hiking boot sat on its side at the cliff's edge.

"No!" Brett grabbed Jackson's light and shone it over the side.

Keeley sat cowered on a narrow ledge.

She was alive.

Thank You, Lord. "Keels!"

"Brett." She lifted her face in their direction, her eyes widening in the light's beam. "You're alive!"

Jackson spoke into his radio, requesting Search and Rescue. "What do you mean? That's too long, and another storm is predicted to hit soon. We need them now." A pause. "Fine." He hung up and turned to Brett. "They're on their way but can't be here for six hours."

"But we have to get to her. Now!" Brett hated his forceful words, but he had to rescue the woman he loved.

Jackson squeezed Brett's shoulder. "We will."

He glanced over the side. "Good—she's not too far down. The ledge saved her life."

Once again, Brett peered over, shining the light on the cliff's wall. Roots and tree branches poked out. They must have stopped her descent. "Keels, are you okay?"

"Head hurts. Soaked. Freezing. Help." Her broken words revealed a weakened condition.

"Help is on the way. We'll get to you as quick as we can!" Jackson shouted back. "Hold tight."

"Where's Audrey?" Brett asked.

Keeley pointed downward.

The mama of the Diglo brothers had fallen to her death.

Brett tugged Jackson away from the edge. "Listen, do you have spotlights and climbing gear of any kind in your cruiser?"

"Yes. What are you thinking?"

"I've been training with SAR, as they want a paramedic on their team. I can get to her."

"It's too dangerous, and you're still in training. We have to wait for daylight and the team."

Brett pointed to the edge. "Would you wait if it was Hannah down there?"

Even in the darkness, Brett didn't miss the constable's softened eyes. "No. You love her, don't you?"

"I do. I can do this. Get the gear here now."

"It's risky, Brett."

Brett let out a hissed sigh. "I know, but it's *my* risk."

Jackson hit his radio button and spoke to his team, requesting any spotlights and gear they had in their cruisers. "Okay, now we wait."

"Thank you." Brett returned to the edge. "Keels, I'm coming to get you."

Two hours later, Brett guided Keeley out of Olivia's hospital room to a lounge across the hall. Brett had rappelled down the side of the cliff and gotten her to safety with the help of spotlights, a harness and an axe they'd found on the Diglos' property. Paramedics had checked her for injuries before she reunited with Olivia and MJ. Right now, MJ slept, cuddled on a chair by his gramma's hospital bed—safe and sound. Doctors had examined Keeley and confirmed she just had bumps and bruises. No concussion.

Police had arrested the other brother, so all Diglos were in custody. SAR would look for Audrey's body at daybreak.

"Keels, I need to tell you something." Brett gestured to vacant seats in the room's corner.

They sat.

He took her hands in his. "I'm so glad you're okay. I thought I lost you. Again." His voice shook, exposing his emotions.

"What are you saying, Brett?"

"I need to tell you why I wouldn't believe you about MJ." He inhaled deeply, gathering his thoughts. "I once had a woman lie to me, claiming I had fathered her child when I knew I hadn't. It was after I changed my wayward life."

Keeley's eyes widened. "That's why you wouldn't believe me? I get it, but that's not me. I wouldn't lie to you about something like that or anything."

"I realize that now, and I know MJ is mine." He chuckled. "I don't need a DNA test, as he's exactly like me."

Keeley smiled. "Right?"

"I also wanted to tell you that I've surrendered my heart to God. I've been a fool for doubting Him."

"I'm so glad."

Brett hesitated in asking the question he dreaded. She had distanced herself from him over the past few days. Did she want him in her life?

"What is it, Brett?" She rubbed his hand with her thumb.

Their gazes locked, and he tucked a wiry curl behind her ear. "I'm not going anywhere, and I want you back in my life. But my question is, do you want me in yours?"

She looked away.

Brett held his breath.

Keeley turned back to him, a smile dancing on her lips. "I've waited so long to hear you say that. It's my turn to tell you something. Besides being scared you were leaving, I've had a hard time opening up to you because another man, Preston, made promises to both me and MJ, but he left and broke our hearts."

Brett leaned in. "Keels, I'm not Preston. I'm not going anywhere." He leaned closer, staring into her eyes. "I love you."

She let out a soft cry. "Me too."

He placed his hand behind her head, pulling her toward him. Their lips met in a tender kiss.

Brett released her. "I can't wait to tell MJ I'm his father and we're going to be a family."

The pitter-patter of feet filled the room.

They turned.

MJ ran toward them. "You're my papa? For reals?"

Brett stood and lifted him, twirling MJ. "I am, son."

"Yippee!"

Brett chuckled and stopped twirling, bringing Keeley closer. "We're a family."

Words from his father reentered Brett's mind.

God brings His people into the wilderness to shape them.

Brett now believed the truth in those words. Not only had God shaped him, but He eliminated his doubts and welcomed Brett back into His family.

And it was the only place Brett wanted to be.

Epilogue

Seven months later

Keeley hummed the carol playing on the stereo and placed the last ornament on the Christmas tree at Harold Ryerson's cabin. She inspected her work and smiled before glancing out the window. Snow floated like feathers, bringing holiday cheer one week before the official date when Christians rejoiced in Jesus's birth. MJ insisted they spend Christmas Day at the cabin, and Brett agreed. Much had happened in the past seven months, and they had lots to celebrate.

SAR had found Audrey's body the morning after the attack. Keeley struggled with the woman's death, even though she'd been the source of all their troubles. Keeley counted her older colleague as a friend. Beth had apologized to her for her abruptness but confessed how her

worry for their safety got the better of her. The
Diglos were devastated at their mother's death
and tried to blame everything on Keeley. They
still denied their involvement in any criminal
activity and killing the mayor's daughter—
Keeley's half sister. However, after studying
the vegetation around the Diglos' hidden underground structures, Keeley linked seeds on
their boots and clothing to the poisonous privet
growing in a concealed greenhouse on their
property. They'd imported the seeds, which
was their downfall. The plant couldn't be found
anywhere else in the Yukon. Plus, Davey, the
younger of the brothers left, finally tattled on
the others, explaining how Eddie Bishop—the
brother Brett had killed—had stumbled upon
Zoe and her boyfriend too close to their hidden property. They had agreed the couple had
to die, rather than taking the risk of them exposing their organization to the police. The
hikers had simply been in the wrong place at
the wrong time.

Police also found three wanted criminals hidden on the Diglos' property. The fugitives had
revealed everything they knew about the un-

derground organization, clinching the evidence stacked against them.

Keeley's mother had healed from her shotgun wound and welcomed Brett into the family with open arms.

Doctors had also surprised them all by stating Brett's father had gone into remission, so the group indeed had lots to be thankful for.

Brett and Layke had quickly become best friends after the ordeal. Layke had called to tell them Hannah had a baby girl, and they'd named her Hope because they were thankful God blessed them against all odds. Kind of like Sarah and Abraham.

Keeley studied the cabin. After they'd shared the news with MJ that Brett was his father, MJ had requested they spend lots of time here. Brett and Harold, along with Keeley's mother, had planned an expansion. They added more bedrooms and a sunroom to the back of the building.

Enough room for everyone.

"You forgot an ornament."

Keeley jumped. "Brett, you scared me." She pointed to the empty box. "No, I didn't. They're all on the tree."

"Are you sure?" Brett snickered.

MJ stepped out from behind his father, holding a plastic marshmallow snowman sitting on a slab of chocolate and graham cracker. "Look close, Mama. There's a surprise for you."

Brett tousled his son's hair. "Sport, you weren't supposed to say anything."

Keeley inched closer for a better look. She gasped and covered her mouth.

An engagement ring hung from the snowman's stick arm.

"I love you with all my heart." Brett knelt, removed the diamond ring and held it out. "Keels, will you marry me?"

She dropped to her knees and flung her arms around him. "Yes! I love you, too."

"Gramma and Grampa, she said yes!"

Keeley pulled out of their embrace as Harold and her mother entered the room.

Her mother clapped. "Praise the Lord!"

"Well, put it on her, son." Harold beamed.

Keeley held out her hand.

Brett slipped the ring on her finger before reaching in and kissing her on the lips.

"Ewww. That's gross." MJ wormed his way in between them.

Laughter filled the cabin as "Joy to the World" played softly in the background.

Yes, indeed. Joy filtered into their world, and Keeley praised God for bringing them through the tough wilderness of life.

He was in every detail, and for that, she was grateful.

★ ★ ★ ★ ★

Hidden In The Canyon
Jodie Bailey

MILLS & BOON

Jodie Bailey writes novels about freedom and the heroes who fight for it. Her novel *Crossfire* won a 2015 RT Reviewers' Choice Best Book Award. She is convinced a camping trip to the beach with her family, a good cup of coffee and a great book can cure all ills. Jodie lives in North Carolina with her husband, her daughter and two dogs.

He shall not be afraid of evil tidings:
his heart is fixed, trusting in the Lord.
—*Psalms* 112:7

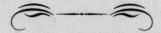

DEDICATION

To Emily

Thank you for believing in this Army wife's stories

Chapter One

At least the protestors seemed to have taken the night off.

Angie Garcia slowed to a stop at the gate to her family's ranch near the south rim of the Grand Canyon and allowed herself one small sigh of relief. At nearly three in the morning, after a four-hour drive and a night that had gone entirely sideways, she was in no mood to engage with a group of people who wanted her gone.

The signs of their presence remained, though.

Literal signs, propped along the fence.

The Canyon Belongs to Everyone!

No More Tourists!

And her personal favorite: *Stop Destroying the Land!*

That was the exact opposite of what she was working to do on Fairweather Ranch. As a meteorologist, she'd studied how weather and the environment worked together, how man could protect or ravage the environment they held dear. The *environment* included the land itself. Her goal was to preserve, not to destroy. To educate, not to harm. The protestors would understand if they'd talk to her instead of making assumptions and spreading rumors.

For three weeks they'd dogged her gate, making her the unexpected target of their misdirected outrage.

She punched the remote in her car to open the electric gate and drove through, making sure it closed behind her. There had been two instances of vandalism on the property in the previous week, perpetrated by a couple of the protestors. The last thing she needed was a repeat.

Navigating the road through stands of trees on the edge of the Kaibab National Forest, it was too easy to imagine eyes were on her. People lurking in the darkness… Protestors in the shadows waiting…watching.

This shouldn't be how she had to live, looking over her shoulder, wondering if someone was going to do more damage to the ranch she loved. Her family had been gracious and kind to the people who wanted them to return their pocket of privately owned land to the federal government for conservation. The escalation to trespassing and vandalism in the previous weeks had been jarring.

Angie shuddered and gripped the wheel tighter. Paranoia was not her friend, and it was likely the result of high-running emotions and lack of sleep. What she needed was her bed and sleep to forget her name hadn't been called tonight in Vegas for the half-million-dollar Celeste Hyacinthe scientific research grant.

No, it hadn't been her name broadcast through the microphone to nearly a thousand of her peers. Instead, she'd been slapped by the name of the one person she'd never wanted to lose to. Had been forced to clap for his success… and her very public failure.

Surely the reason she felt like she was being watched in the dark isolation near her home was because she was certain every eye had been on her as Owen Matthews took the stage to accept the money on behalf of his environmental research foundation, Crucial Causes.

She forced herself to breathe and to focus on reality. There were no prying eyes on her property, and she was safe. One of the protestors, Monica Huerta, had been a high-school classmate. Though they'd lost touch over the past decade and a half, Monica had promised Angie at church the previous Sunday that the group had rooted out the vandals and would keep things from escalating further.

At the moment, she was too emotionally wrung out to put coherent thoughts into place. She needed sleep. Quiet. A few minutes to ask God what in the world He was thinking. He knew what she needed to run the research center that was her dream. Why hadn't He provided?

She slowed to make the turn into the drive to the house, but her foot shifted to the brake.

The hairs on the back of her neck stood up.

The night felt different. Strange.

In the distance, about a mile away, the glow from the scattered buildings at the ranch's research center softened the edges of the darkness. Ellis West was the only one there tonight, taking care of the horses in the large ranch barn and preparing to ride out to move their small herd of cattle. Her manager, Rosa Boyd, had gone to visit her mother, who was recovering from a stroke, while two of the other ranch hands were also visiting family. The researchers who were staying on the property were all on an excursion into the canyon.

To her right, the exterior lights on her brother's cabin shone from half a mile away, even though he wasn't home.

Nothing was wrong, yet something felt different.

She let the SUV coast toward her home. The light above the garage offered a welcoming circle of warmth. The floodlights on the small horse barn behind the house lit the paddock. The barn was empty at the moment. Her horse, Flynn, and her brother's horse, Shiloh, were being temporarily stabled at the large barn at the main ranch with the working horses to make it easier for the hands to care for them during her absence.

Rolling to a stop close to the house, she scanned the area, still feeling as though someone was watching her.

Automatically, her hand moved to her phone to call her brother, but Jacob was on the other side of the Atlantic with his wife and young daughter, celebrating their two-year anniversary as a family.

She tapped the phone, staring at the pattern of her headlights on the white garage door as tinges of unease prickled along her spine. She still had Lincoln Tucker's number saved, though she'd hovered over the delete button more than once. Because he was Jacob's closest friend and his team leader with the National Park Service Investigative Services Branch, she'd kept it in case of emergency.

Well, a shudder down her spine was definitely not grounds for making a call into the past. She pulled her hand from the phone. She'd been drained by her past enough for one night.

There was nothing odd going on, other than exhaustion, paranoia and humiliation.

Gathering her things, she pulled her keys from her purse and headed for the front door, using starlight and instinct to guide her along the flagstone-and-white-rock path her father had laid years before.

Nights like this, she missed him more than usual. She'd have talked to him all the way home. He'd have comforted her. Told her she was still a rock star and Owen Matthews had nothing on her.

If only she could hear Dad's voice one more time…

She walked up the porch steps and aimed her keys at the door.

Something crunched on the gravel path behind her. An animal?

A person?

Fear flashed fire to her fingertips. Angie reflexively gripped her keys as she whipped around to face what was likely a protestor who hadn't listened to the warnings the sheriff had doled out. She let the shot of adrenaline fuel her anger. "This is trespassing and I *will* call law enforcement. Leave now."

But the words died as she caught sight of a man at the foot of her porch stairs, not six feet away.

Angie's jaw tightened.

It was tough to make out more than a vague shape in the black night. The man was wearing jeans and a dark hooded sweatshirt zipped to his neck. Something covered the lower half of his face, and his hood was pulled down nearly to his eyes.

He was formless. Shapeless. A living monster.

Angie couldn't move. Couldn't breathe.

This wasn't happening. Regular people didn't find themselves in situations like this. It was the stuff of horror movies.

The man's head tilted, and he regarded her as he walked slowly to the porch, blocking her exit down the stairs. He seemed to size her up, then made his way up the steps methodically, one menacing inch at a time, obviously aware she had nowhere to run, no time to enter the house and bolt herself inside.

No one close enough to hear if she screamed.

Not that she could make a sound. A shriek stuck in her throat, and leaked out as a pathetic whimper. The breath seemed to freeze in her lungs.

Her phone slipped from her fingers and clattered to the wooden porch.

Lights danced in her vision. She might pass out before he reached her. *Jesus, help.* There was no one else. Nothing else. No other salvation.

The figure planted a booted foot on the top step and lifted his hands toward her, seeming to hesitate as though he might be taking pleasure in her fear.

The pause kicked her flight response into gear.

Driven by instinct, Angie charged, shoving all of her weight against the man's chest.

He stumbled backward. His foot hit the edge of the porch at an awkward angle and he hurtled to the ground, landing hard on his hip. He grunted and cursed as he scrambled up.

Angie didn't wait to see what he did next. She lunged for the door, blindly aiming her keys for the lock.

The porch shook as the man thundered toward her. The key slid into the lock and she turned it.

Strong arms wrapped around her waist and jerked her backward, dragging her away from the door.

A guttural scream escaped her throat and echoed off the trees.

She tried to fight, but he was too strong. He held her too tightly against him.

She couldn't escape.

He dragged her down the stairs, away from her home. Away from safety.

And into a nightmare.

The headlights of National Park Service Investigator Lincoln Tucker's pickup truck swept the front of the two-story white farmhouse at Fairweather Ranch...

And his heart nearly stopped.

At the foot of the steps to the wraparound porch, a man was dragging Angie Garcia toward the side of the house.

As the lights washed over him, the man

looked up. A mask covered the lower half of his face. A hood shadowed his eyes. He tightened his grip on Angie.

This was not about to happen. Not on Linc's watch. Not to Angie.

After drawing his sidearm, Linc shoved the door open and jumped out of the truck, holding the pistol low as he stepped forward. "Stop! Federal agent!"

The dark figure froze.

With a fierce scream, Angie drove her foot back and swept the man's leg from under him.

They tumbled to the ground in a heap.

Angie rolled to the side and scrambled to her feet, standing over the figure as though she was going to fight for her life.

"Angie! Back away!" The closer she was to her assailant, the more she risked injury.

Angie eased toward the porch.

When he was about fifteen feet away, Linc stopped and raised his SIG toward the man's center mass as he lay on his back. "Federal agent. Get on your stomach and lace your fingers behind your head."

For a second, the scene froze as though someone had hit the pause button. The only sound was Linc's breathing, short and quick. The next few seconds could change all of their lives. Everything hinged on what the dark stranger did next.

Slowly, the man rolled onto his side, seeming to comply. At the last instant, he jumped to his feet and ran for the corner of the house.

Linc bit back anger and holstered his SIG. Keeping his hand on the grip, he chased the assailant around the corner but stuttered to a halt.

The inky night offered no light. As his eyes adjusted, he could make out trees to his left and the horizon straight ahead, where starry sky met dark ground. On the far side of the narrow stand of trees, an engine started, then a vehicle roared away.

He puffed out his frustration and dragged his hand through his hair, ignoring the way his upper back protested the motion. In a perfect world, he'd call for backup, but by the time they made it to the remote part of the canyon near the Garcia ranch, the suspect would be gone.

"I'm behind you." Angie's voice drifted from the front of the house. Smart of her to warn him she was approaching, especially given the way adrenaline was pumping through his system.

No way would he acknowledge that the

sound of her voice gave his heart a different kind of jolt entirely.

When he turned, she was standing about six feet away, highlighted by the glow of his truck's headlights. She was wearing a dressy gray pantsuit, but her feet were bare. Likely she'd lost her shoes in the struggle. Her dark blond hair straggled out of a low bun, evidence of the ordeal she'd been through.

Despite everything, she stood tall, as though someone had rammed a steel rod into her spine.

He tried to read her expression in the shadow across her face. "Are you hurt?" If she was, he'd race after that vehicle himself. On foot. In spite of the pain between his shoulders.

She sniffed and ran her fingers along the hem of her jacket. "He's gone?"

"I heard a vehicle take off, so, yeah, he got away." Saying it made his neck burn with the shame of his weakness and failure. Linc didn't lose his man.

Angie tipped her head and exhaled through pursed lips. "I don't know where he came from. I don't know how he snuck up on me. I don't—"

"It's okay." Linc stepped toward her, recognizing she was rattled and trying to hold it together.

The best thing she could do was fall apart. He'd watched her too many times when Jacob was recovering from the life-altering injuries he'd sustained in combat. Angie had a habit of burying her emotions, tending to the task at hand without letting the pain and fear touch her.

That led to trouble. The kind that made snap decisions.

The kind that ruined friendships and lives.

She held up both hands, building a barrier between them. "I'm fine. I'm not injured. I'm..." She backed away as though Linc was the threat. "I'm fine."

So it was going to be like that. He'd saved her life, and she was going to act as though he was somehow the villain in her story.

Not that he could blame her. He'd been the one to walk out when she needed him the most, because he couldn't handle—

"Why are you here?" The question was quiet, holding a slight sense of wonder, probably because he'd arrived at the exact right moment. Given that he rarely came to the ranch, his presence there at oh-dark-thirty justified the question. It also kept him from diving too deep into his thoughts about their past.

But before he could answer, he needed to get her somewhere safer than out in the open. If someone genuinely wanted to harm her, a pair of night-vision goggles and a rifle would do the trick. "Let's go inside. We can talk there."

"I…" She turned and walked to the front of the house as though the words had fallen apart before they made it into the air.

Linc trailed her. Yeah, she was definitely working hard to hold it together. It was tough to say if she was succeeding.

On the porch, she scooped up her phone and stared at the door as though she wasn't sure how it worked.

He gathered her shoes from the bottom of the stairs and stepped beside her. "Want me to open it?"

"Do you think it's safe?"

Chances were good. If her assailant had access to the house, he would have waited for her behind closed doors instead of coming at her on the porch. "I'll clear the rooms as soon as we get in. You can wait by the door and get it locked."

"If you're sure."

He nodded. "I'm sure. I'll clear the house, then turn off my truck and we'll talk."

She stepped aside and let him open the door to enter the house first.

He made quick work of checking all of the rooms, then shut off his truck, made a call to the county sheriff and headed inside.

Angie had turned on all of the lights and was standing in the kitchen on the far side of the island.

No doubt, it was a physical barrier between them, similar to the emotional one he'd built years ago to prevent them from getting too close to one another.

She crossed her arms. "I guess I should thank you."

"No need. I'm glad I was here." He strode across the living room and planted his hands on the island. "You can't do this, Ang."

She straightened and narrowed her eyes. "Do what, Linc?" She hit his name hard, and she loaded it with sarcasm.

The message was clear. He shouldn't have used the familiar nickname her brother used. The one he himself had once affectionately called her.

Too late to retreat now, though. "You can't act like nothing happened, like you're not upset or scared or—"

"Don't tell me how to feel." The walls she'd built were tall. He was quite familiar with them. They resembled his own. "How did you know to be here?"

"Jacob called me."

Her hands fell to her sides with a smack that resounded in the quiet. "How did Jacob know something was wrong? He's in London."

"He tried to call you several times to see how your award thing went, and when you didn't answer, he looked to see where you were." Like a lot of families, Jacob and his wife had linked their devices with Angie's, and they could all see one another's location.

He'd never really understood that.

Of course, he had no one to share information with anyway, so who was he to judge?

"I had my phone on 'do not disturb' for the ceremony and forgot to switch it." Angie's expression softened. "When Jacob saw I was on the road in the middle of the night—"

"He asked me to check on you. He figured it didn't go well and wanted to make sure you made it home safely. He also gave me strict instructions to tell you to take your phone off DND."

She grabbed the device and thumbed the

screen. "Yeah, he called a few times." Glancing up as she set the phone on the counter, she caught his eye. "So did you."

"It's a long drive from Vegas in the middle of the night. I wanted to make sure you were okay." Despite what she thought, he did care about her safety. "And seriously, reactivate your notifications. The sheriff is on the way and he'll need you to open the gate."

"You called the sheriff?" When he nodded, she grabbed the phone, flicked the screen, then slipped it into her pocket. "I'd offer you coffee, but it's so late…"

"I'm good." He slid onto one of the barstools, trying not to wince in pain. He needed to act as though this was just a conversation, but he wanted to get to the bottom of what had happened out there. The quicker they caught the guy, the safer she'd be and the better he'd feel. "Let's talk about what happened."

He glanced around the room. He hadn't been in the main house since Jacob's recovery several years earlier. Any visits he made had been to the cabin Jacob shared with his wife and young daughter about half a mile away. With all of the lights blazing, it was clear three years had changed nothing in the cozy house that bore Angie's touch everywhere he looked.

He shifted on the stool. A detour through the past would get him nowhere in the present.

"I don't want to."

"You need to."

Angie chewed her lower lip and stared at the counter. "What do you think he wanted?"

There was no way to know, but he hoped the light of day would bring answers. Otherwise, the only theory he had was the man had wanted Angie…and it was clear from the boldness of the attack that he would go to any lengths to have her.

Chapter Two

Angie poured two cups of coffee and slid one across the counter to her ranch manager, Rosa Boyd. Thankfully, Rosa had returned that morning, so she'd no longer be alone on the ranch.

She tightened her grip on the coffeepot. She wasn't a fan of the way her hand shook as she settled the carafe onto the burner.

"That's a nice tremor you've got." Naturally, Rosa noticed. Not much got by her. It was one of the reasons Angie had hired her nearly four years earlier. Rosa saw things others missed, whether in people or in the two dozen head of cattle that ranged the land.

When Angie turned, Rosa was watching over the rim of her mug as she took a sip of black coffee.

Plain coffee was something Angie had never

understood. She doctored her brew with creamer while she decided how to respond.

"Stalling?"

"No." Sometimes, Rosa was too intuitive. "I got one hour of sleep. My brain isn't firing on all cylinders."

"And the sheriff is outside collecting evidence from your assault."

"Please don't use that word." It made her insides quake. She wasn't ignorant, but she didn't need to keep hearing about it.

She'd gotten her fill from the detective the night before. *Victim. Assault. Attack.* If she never heard those words again, it would be too soon.

Loaded words made it hard to stay in the logical part of her mind. If she was going to get through this, she couldn't let emotions take the reins. The meteorologist in her was trained in scientific facts and data.

Fear had no place in facts.

Rosa flipped her long, dark braid over her shoulder and said nothing.

No way was Angie falling for that trick. She wasn't filling the silence with words. Instead, she defiantly sipped her coffee. Rosa had been raised on a Colorado ranch and had spent her life outdoors. Though she was only a couple of years older than Angie's thirty-three, her dark skin bore the evidence of wind and sun. She had a ready smile and was incredibly organized. While Angie ran the research center, Rosa had charge of the ranch and the three hands who worked there.

Rosa broke the silence. "I saw Lincoln Tucker when I came in."

Guess even she couldn't stay quiet forever, but it would have been nice if she'd landed on a different topic.

"Jacob sent him to check on me."

"Good thing."

That was the other fact Angie hadn't wanted to acknowledge. If Lincoln hadn't pulled into the driveway when he did...

Her stomach turned in on itself. She shoved aside her coffee, the brew suddenly acidic.

"So this *does* bother you." Deep furrows creased Rosa's forehead. "You can't do the thing where you act like nothing's wrong."

"I already got a speech from Linc. And I'm fine."

"Then why did you turn so pale?" Rosa snapped her fingers. "That fast. When I mentioned Linc."

"Stop." Angie dumped her coffee in the sink,

then opened the fridge. Yogurt would make her stomach feel less like it was practicing gymnastics, wouldn't it? After snagging a container of peach, she shut the door. "Fill me in on the ranch." Regardless of what had happened the night before, they had a business to run. Their morning meetings were meant to be a rundown of the day, not an airing of personal business.

With a sigh, Rosa pulled her phone from her hip pocket and flicked the screen. "Wiley and Danny are back from their nights off and will inspect the fence line today. Ellis rode out yesterday morning with the cattle. He'll be back this evening. We have a couple of head in the barn waiting on a scheduled vet check this afternoon. Also, Carter Holbert called. There was an issue with his renovation at the Desert View Watchtower, so he may not get here today to finish the demo on the old cabins where we're building the second dormitory."

"Just as well. There's too much happening here anyway." She also needed to find the money now that she'd lost the grant she'd been counting on. She could dig into savings, but the thought of losing her cushion made her stomach quake.

She shoved her spoon into her half-eaten yogurt and set it aside.

"Let's talk about Carter, since he needs to be paid." Naturally, Rosa followed her thoughts. "How did the award go last night?"

"It didn't."

Rosa's expression dropped. "I was sure you were a slam dunk."

Same. Angie stared past Rosa at the front window as Detective Kari Blankenship passed, studying the wide porch boards.

Between the loss and the…incident, it was no wonder food wasn't Angie's friend this morning.

"Who won?"

"I'd rather not say."

"Not Crucial Causes."

"Don't make it sound like we wanted another group to lose." Although if *she* had to lose, why did it have to be to the organization Owen Matthews chaired?

"That's why you came back last night instead of staying for the rest of the conference."

Rosa was one of the few who knew the whole story about her history with Owen, the man she was supposed to marry. The one she'd dated junior and senior years in college. The one who'd made her so many promises that she'd lost count.

The one who'd eloped with his old high-school girlfriend over spring break, two months before graduation.

The betrayal had shattered Angie's trust and reset her future. The moment her roommate had shown her the social-media post of Owen's last-minute Vegas wedding, Angie had denied it, then grown angry... Then had been intent on not letting him see he'd wrecked her.

She'd set aside her pain and thrown herself into finals, refusing to hear apologies or excuses. They'd both been in the running for the Johnson–Markly Scholarship to fund their graduate studies in meteorology, and she'd been determined to win.

She had.

She'd been equally determined to succeed at everything she'd attempted since, to prove to Owen that he hadn't beaten her down. Grant after grant, award after award, she'd outpaced him.

Until last night, when she'd sat across from him for the first time since college at a ceremony for the largest grant she'd ever pursued. Half a million dollars would have funded the new dormitory and research center she wanted to add to the existing buildings on the property.

She'd lost to Owen. Publicly. In front of hundreds of their colleagues.

Her research facility was in jeopardy, and her pride had taken an intense blow.

Adding insult to injury, Lincoln was outside her front door, another reminder of her horrible past judgment. *God, did You really have to bring every humiliation at once?*

"Let me guess." Rosa stood and reached for her hat, which she'd laid on a barstool. "You don't want to talk about the grant, either?"

"Not especially."

"Let's circle back to Lincoln."

Definitely not. That part of her history was the one thing Rosa didn't know.

No one did. Not even Jacob knew what had happened to wreck their friendship. "I do not want to talk about Lincoln."

The front door opened and the man himself stepped through, holding a small paper bag. "Did I hear my name?"

Rosa planted her brown Stetson on her head and turned her back to Linc, dropping a wink at Angie. "Not that I heard." With a wave, she headed for the side door. "I have to get to the ranch. I'll check on the researchers and tell them you'll be over later."

"Thanks." There were currently four re-searchers-in-residence on the property. Two meteorologists and two archaeologists were studying the effects of weather on artifacts in the canyon in an effort to develop better pres-ervation techniques.

When the door closed behind Rosa, Lincoln stepped into the living room. Shadows under his blue eyes told of his sleepless night aiding the sheriff's department in their investigation. His light brown hair looked as though he'd run his hands through it, a nervous habit Angie recog-nized. He'd slid the top back until it was nearly flat, though the short sides remained styled. His close-shaven beard needed a trim. In dark cargo pants and a gray polo, he looked the part of a federal agent.

An *exhausted* federal agent.

No matter how uncomfortable their relation-ship was, she owed him her life. The least she could do was offer him breakfast. "You hun-gry?"

"That's why I came in." He strode across the room as though he lived there and settled the bag on the counter. "I had one of the guys on the team bring breakfast burritos from Misty's."

Misty's was a tiny lunch counter in the back of a gas station/general store only locals really knew about. Misty made some of the best eats in Arizona.

Suddenly, her stomach felt like it could handle food.

Linc opened the bag but paused to glance at his phone. He frowned.

"Do you need to get that?"

"No." He pocketed the device and passed a paper-wrapped bundle across the counter. "I'll trade you for coffee."

"Deal." Angie poured the cup and handed it over, then bit into the flour tortilla wrapped around the burrito. Spicy sausage and fiery homemade salsa were tempered by egg and melted cheese.

It was exactly what she needed.

Linc chased a healthy bite with coffee. "I remembered how much you liked them from when…" He set his cup on the table. Uncertainty hazed his normally confident demeanor. "I remembered you liked them."

Without looking at him, Angie bit into her own burrito, although she'd lost her appetite again. He remembered from their time tag-teaming during Jacob's recovery, helping him through the mental, physical and emotional issues he'd wrestled with when an IED had scrambled his insides and nearly killed him.

When her own emotions had overflowed in the trauma and had sought an outlet...

As had Lincoln's.

Then, she'd been a different person. Scared. Angry. Lost.

She'd been—

Her phone trilled with three quick rings that indicated a call from Rosa. She'd take anything to derail her train of thought. She pulled the phone to her ear. "Hey, what's—"

"You need to get down here with the sheriff." Rosa was breathless. "We were hit by vandals again."

He probably ought to be thankful the phone had rung when it had. They'd been two seconds from a conversation he wasn't ready to have. The night he'd walked out of this house had been tough on both of them. The more time that passed, the more awkward it was to discuss.

Even so, news about more trouble on the ranch wasn't the distraction he'd have chosen.

Neither was that call from his doctor. He was supposed to be at the hospital right now, getting the MRI that might clear him to return to full duty. The fall he'd taken a couple of weeks earlier in training had sidelined him, and today was the day he was supposed to find out how soon he'd get his life back. Hopefully, they'd skip surgery and go the route of pain meds and physical therapy, but he'd put in the work no matter what they said.

Right now, though, he had more pressing things to deal with.

Given the way Angie was working the hem of her sweatshirt through her fingers as he started the pickup, she was feeling the effects of everything coming at her. What had happened to Angie was a traumatic event, and she needed to process the ramifications.

Knowing her, though, she was wielding a heavy-duty shovel and trying to bury it, which was the worst thing she could do.

"Linc?" Her voice was small, which was unlike her. Not even two minutes earlier, she'd demanded to ride along, not giving him any room to say no.

That was Angie. She tended to charge in and take control. She handled what needed to be handled, sometimes to her detriment. She was competitive and driven to win.

Hearing her quiet tone twisted his gut.

Especially since he knew part of her problem was this guy, right here, behind the steering wheel. "Yeah?"

"Did you guys get any clues to who was at the house last night?"

"Not a thing." He hated telling her. All he'd wanted was to find some condemning piece of evidence that would point them straight to her attacker.

Instead, they had nothing. Not even a usable shoe print. Even the clearing beyond the woods, where the assailant had escaped, hadn't yielded any clues, just indistinguishable tire tracks on the pine needles heading toward the canyon and the back entrance to the ranch.

Angie looked straight out the front window. She was diving into her head, and he needed to pull her into the present. When she withdrew, she tended to stay locked away from her emotions for days, weeks…or longer.

He sifted through a few thoughts, then hit upon the one least likely to spark an uncomfortable conversation. "Hey, can you clarify a few things? I want the facts straight in my head so I don't overlook something important."

"I guess. Yeah." It wasn't the most enthusiastic response, but it was something.

Linc pulled out of the drive and aimed the truck for the ranch, taking the old asphalt road at a slower pace than usual to give Angie time to talk.

"Let's think about the protestors, since they've caused some trouble on the property recently. I heard you tell Detective Blankenship you're friends with some of them?" If he was going to guess, he'd say the trouble started with the group that had been gathering outside the gate for several weeks.

"One of them. Monica Huerta and I went to school together and now we go to church together, but we're more acquaintances than friends."

"When's the last time you two spoke?"

"Nearly two weeks ago at church, the Sunday before I headed to Vegas. She told me they'd figured out who vandalized a couple of the old cabins last week, the ones we'd slated to tear down. Detective Blankenship told me this morning the names of the trespassers had been turned over to the county, and I have the option to prosecute."

He was certain the county would check alibis for the whereabouts of those two for the previous night, but he'd ask to be sure. "So will you press charges?" It would send a message to anyone else thinking of causing trouble for her.

"I don't know. They broke a couple of windows and spray-painted on the walls. They really didn't hurt anything."

"They trespassed. That's a way bigger issue." If the protestors felt they had a right to be on Angie's property, then they might be emboldened to try far worse crimes than tagging a couple of old structures.

Crimes like assault...or kidnapping.

"If you're thinking that's who came at me, I doubt it. No one has even so much as raised their voice at me or anyone else as we've passed the gate."

Trespassing and vandalism were a far cry from "raised voices," but it seemed Angie was determined to stay in denial. "Why do the protestors want to shut you down?"

She turned from the window to give him a withering look. "Jacob's your best friend. You're not ignorant about what I want to do here."

At least she was feeling some emotion, although he'd prefer it wasn't animosity toward him. There was still something ugly sitting between them. A couple of years ago, when he'd been helping Jacob protect the woman who was now his wife, Ivy, and their daughter, Wren, Linc had spent a little bit of time with Angie as they kept the kid out of harm's way. It had been an uneasy, short-lived truce, but she'd filled him in on some of her plans for her family's property. Still, having her tell him again would ground him in the story and might help him discover a clue. It would also keep her from holding everything in. "Humor me."

With a heavy sigh, she stared out the front windshield. "In the 1850s, my several-times-over great-grandfather purchased this land and built the cabin where Jacob lives. This was before the National Park Service was a thing. He brought in cattle and started ranching. When the government started creating Grand Canyon National Park in the early 1900s, the family opted not to sell."

Their situation wasn't unusual. The country's national parks were dotted with private land, "inholdings" that had been in families for generations. Most of the time they went unnoticed, but there were instances when frustrations about private land in public parks boiled over. "So the protestors want you to, what? Walk away?"

"They want me to cease constructing and running the research center and to hand the land over to the government. They see what I'm doing as development and not as conservation or research. Somehow, they've gotten the idea all of this will operate as a resort."

"When that's the furthest thing from what you're intending."

"Right. I want to preserve what's here and to make sure the canyon is cared for long after we're gone. A private research facility will help. If I walk away, I can't control what happens, and I want to know the land is being used for the best purposes. Initially, this was about meteorological research, but I realized we could do more good if I modeled us after the North Rim ranches, which are working ranches with small herds, research facilities and conservation areas. There are scientists coming in to study everything from climate to plants and animals to the land itself. I'm providing a place for them to work and live while they're here. The plan is to offer an inexpensive alternative to researchers who can't get the grants they need." She bit off the words at the end, almost bitterly.

Interesting, but no time to chase that rabbit down the trail now. "So you're actually doing what they want, but they can't see that because you're not doing it their way."

"Maybe? I think they believe the government can do a better job. Maybe they can. But there are bigger things I want to do. We're just beginning. We'll be a dedicated space that isn't funded by tax dollars." She waved a hand in the air. "I know it's what I'm supposed to do, if that makes sense."

Like he knew he belonged in the canyon and not sitting behind a desk. "And the cultural part?"

"So much has happened with the eleven tribes who have lived here for longer than we've been a country. Weather affects them. Tourism affects them. Government policies affect them. There are ways to get permission to dig in the park to maintain and preserve artifacts. Rosa and I started thinking… What if we provided a place to act as home base for the tribes and those working with them, so they can further preserve their history and culture? It goes along with what I'm already doing, and it's really my passion project. More than the weather side of it, which shocked me since that's what my degree is in."

"I get it." The tribes around the canyon had long struggled, and that was part of the reason he was passionate about his own job.

Linc would have said more, but they were approaching the ranch. As he turned to make his way across the cattle guard in the road, he scanned the area. Beyond the massive horse barn that the ranch horses were housed in, construction equipment waited to be used. It was clear that work hadn't started for the day and had possibly been halted due to the presence of law enforcement. Several debris piles stood nearby. "Is that what's left of the vandalized cabins?"

Angie followed his gaze. "Yeah."

"What did they paint on the buildings?"

She puffed out a breath. "Same as the signs out by the gate. 'Stop destroying the land' and 'no more tourists.' Oh, and 'the Canyon belongs to everyone.' As if one person could own it. We don't even back up to the canyon. There are several miles between us and the rim. The sheriff thinks the vandals got in by cutting across public land and coming through one of our back gates."

It was also the likely ingress and egress point for her attacker. "You should have cameras on those."

"Or the ranch workers and I should start coming in that way so the protestors don't know when we're here."

Hiding wasn't like Angie. His heart hurt for her. It couldn't be easy to be the target of a group who misunderstood and opposed you. "How long has this been going on?"

"They started camping out here when I pulled the permits to build a bunkhouse and a second research facility about three weeks ago. I guess the idea of two new buildings was more than someone could bear."

Possibly. But that man hadn't been simply trying to stop her—he'd been trying to take her, and maybe worse.

Linc feared it *was* worse, and the issue with her land was something they hadn't considered. Something someone out there was willing to kill for.

Chapter Three

As Linc slowed to a stop behind two sheriff's SUVs near the cabins, Angie tapped her knee, wishing she could be anywhere else. Had her week gone the way she'd planned, she'd have awakened in Vegas this morning, hit an enormous breakfast buffet and would have been sitting in on group discussions about weather and the environment.

Instead, she was stuck in a pickup truck with the only man aside from Owen who'd ever left scars on her heart. The one man whose presence reminded her of her weakest moment, one he'd had to deflect and one she could never forget. Shame burned far too often.

It was no wonder Linc had essentially avoided her since.

Which begged the question... "Linc, why are you here?" He could have left. Her case was for the sheriff's department, not for the level of

Linc's federal investigative team. As far as any obligation to her was concerned, he was finished once the deputies arrived.

"I'm here because Jacob asked me to be."

Of course. The two of them were as close as brothers, although the tension between Linc and Angie meant she rarely saw them together. Jacob could be overprotective, but how many guys could say the love of their lives had been targeted by a hired killer? Still, her brother had other friends he could have called.

"But why you specifically?" Linc was happier scaling canyon walls and hiking isolated areas. He thrived on seeking evidence in the toughest, most remote places in the park.

While he claimed this was about Jacob, there had to be more. Why was he cooling his heels on her ranch?

Something Jacob had mentioned recently tweaked at a memory, but it didn't hold. He rarely talked to her about Lincoln, although they had been battle buddies in the army, until Linc decided to become an investigator for the National Park Service. After Jacob suffered massive internal injuries overseas, Linc had convinced him to make a career with the NPS.

That move had probably saved her brother's life.

"He asked me because I'm available." His voice was husky, heavy with a timbre that could make a girl's stomach quake.

If she was that kind of girl. And if he wasn't Lincoln Tucker. Linc wasn't a guy who wanted commitment. He'd made that abundantly clear the night she'd destroyed their friendship.

It had happened at the end of a grueling thirty-six hours during Jacob's recovery, and they'd both been up all day, all night and through another day, walking him through the pain. Exhausted, all of her filters had worn away. In the fog of fatigue and emotion, she'd essentially thrown herself at Lincoln.

He'd nearly caught her.

While she was grateful he'd set the brake, her humiliation had built a wall between them. Their friendship had fallen apart. He'd no longer been by her side in nursing Jacob. Instead, he'd switched off duties with her, taking the nights so she could sleep, then disappearing during the days. Clearly, he'd been wary of being alone with her.

Things hadn't been easy between them since. He was uneasy around her. She was angry and hurt by his rejection, then ultimately embarrassed by her behavior. The more time that passed, the harder it was to address the moment.

And the more time they spent apart, the harder it was to be in his presence.

It hadn't been long after when Rosa had come to the house and witnessed a rare emotional breakdown. When Rosa had prayed her through it, Angie had realized what it meant that Jesus loved her. Everything changed…

Except the gulf between Lincoln and herself. Some days, she missed their friendship. Others, he reminded her of her own weaknesses, of the road she'd nearly traveled in a search for acceptance and love.

She cleared her throat of rising shame. "You're a team leader. Doesn't your team need you?"

Lincoln's grip on the wheel tightened. "Angie, listen. There are a lot of things at play." He killed the engine and turned his entire body to face her. It wasn't the first time he'd moved as though his neck and shoulders were fused. "The best thing we can do is keep this professional. I'm here because Jacob asked me to be here. Anything else is…" Abruptly, he pushed open the door and stared toward the nearest cabin, where Detective Blankenship was speaking with Rosa and a man she didn't recognize. "Anything else is something we'll discuss on any day other than this one." The truck rocked when he got out and slammed the door.

Big talk from a guy who'd been all up in her business a few minutes earlier.

Still, he was right. There was no need for a personal discussion. Ever. They'd done fine keeping their distance, and it was best to maintain the status quo.

Her heart couldn't handle any other option.

She'd tuck him away in the logical lockbox where she'd kept his memory for three years. No emotion was allowed there.

Stepping out of the truck, she slid on sunglasses against the early morning sun. This day had been too long already, and it was only a few minutes after nine.

Ignoring the official vehicles, she scanned the area. On the edge of the Kaibab National Forest, patches of trees dotted the red landscape that stretched to the canyon's rim several miles away. To the right of the five employee cabins, where they'd parked, a fence outlined a corral by a large barn that housed the ranch horses. Beyond, a dormitory provided space for six guest researchers.

To the left of the wide main path, a larger cabin housed the ranch's office and Rosa's living quarters.

Beside it stood the building that made her chest swell with professional pride. Built to blend with the older cabins, the research center was four thousand square feet of office and laboratory space. Half a dozen researchers worked in the center at a time, but they'd recently broken ground on the second dormitory and a research facility behind the barn.

Her dream wavered in her stomach. For a few hours, the previous night's grant loss had been overshadowed by the fear she'd been wrestling down. Now burning humiliation rose. She'd been counting on the grant to carry her through construction. Without it, the expansion would take all of her savings, and the thought of operating without a safety net paralyzed her.

Not only had she lost to Owen, but protestors also wanted her to fail.

And someone might be willing to harm her in order to put an end to her dream.

A wave of nausea made the horizon seem as if it was wobbling. She pressed her hand against the warm hood of Linc's truck and waited for the wave to crest. When she closed her eyes, her mind played the movie of that man, creeping up the steps...

With a gasp, she opened her eyes. *Deep breaths. Clean air.*

She forced the image away. The man was gone. She was safe.

Maybe.

Forcing herself into the present, she followed Linc as he approached the small group of people standing in front of Ellis West's cabin. The two side windows were broken, but there was none of the graffiti she'd expected.

When another wave of anxiety threatened, she willed her brain into thoughts over feelings. *One crisis at a time. Handle what you can fix.* This was a time for action, not for emotion.

Rosa broke away from her conversation with Detective Blankenship and the stranger who was wearing a deputy's uniform, perhaps Blankenship's partner.

The site of Rosa's familiar braid and cowboy hat calmed Angie's nerves. They'd gotten through a lot while working together, and they'd get through this as well.

The law-enforcement officers ended their discussion, and the man stepped forward, extending his hand. "I'm Detective Blankenship's partner, Duane Majenty." His dark hair was cropped short, and his brown eyes scanned her face. "How are you doing, Ms. Garcia?"

Behind him, Linc watched the proceedings, but he said nothing.

Angie kept her attention on the younger detective. "I'm fine. What happened?" If she focused on one thing at a time, she might get through this day.

Before he could respond, Detective Blankenship stepped beside him. "Ms. Garcia, I need your permission to enter the cabin."

Angie looked over the other woman's shoulder at Rosa. "Didn't Ellis take the satellite phone? Call him. He can give you permission." While she owned the property, she wasn't comfortable allowing someone into Ellis's space without his consent.

"I haven't been able to reach him." Rosa eased to the side so she could speak around Blankenship. "I've tried several times but it doesn't connect."

The ranch maintained a small herd, largely to study the effects of sustainable livestock practices on land overgrazed in the past. When the hands were out with the cattle, they kept in contact by satellite phone. It wasn't unusual for them to be unreachable for brief periods due to sunspots, weather or terrain.

The day was clear, however, and the area where Ellis was working was wide open.

"I'd prefer not to wait," Detective Blankenship said. "As the owner of the property, you can give us permission."

"I thought this was vandalism. It's the exterior that's the problem." Her eyes went to Linc in silent question.

"On initial thought, yes, but..." He puffed air out, then turned her gently toward the broken windows. "Look again."

Angie tried to see what Lincoln saw. The lack of graffiti. The busted windows. The glass on the ground glinting in the—

The glass. If someone had vandalized Ellis's cabin by breaking the windows, the glass would largely be inside the structure.

She grabbed Linc's forearm.

Whoever had broken those windows had done the damage from the inside.

This wasn't vandalism.

It was something much worse.

★ ★ ★

Linc took a wide berth around the side of the cabin, making sure not to step on any glass. He stopped and studied the window. Because the cabin was raised to allow air to flow underneath, the windows were high enough he couldn't see inside.

He scanned the broken panes and the glass on the ground, searching for evidence of blood but finding none. At least he could partially rule out someone being shoved through the window. Still, the observation left him with more questions than answers.

Answers they'd only find inside the silent structure.

Beside him, Detective Majenty had kneeled to photograph the glass. He looked to the front of the building, where Angie was with Blankenship and the ranch manager, then stood so he was shoulder to shoulder with Linc. "What do you think we're going to find inside?" He kept his voice low, probably to keep Angie from hearing.

Good call. She'd been through enough. The way she was tugging at the sleeves on her shirt spoke to the stress she was trying to tamp down. If he hadn't been so self-focused years ago, he might be able to offer her some comfort now. Instead, she'd reject him if he tried. Rightly so.

He kneaded the dull pain in his neck, ignoring the way his fingers tingled. He'd have to call the doc when he had a minute and reschedule that MRI. It was the only shot he had of getting cleared to go back out.

Of being useful again.

"Agent Tucker?" The detective was waiting for an answer.

"Yeah. Right. I'm not sure, but it's possible there'll be signs of a struggle. I doubt anyone would *intentionally* break a window from the inside for no reason." Linc motioned for Majenty to follow him to the rear of the building. "You guys check the perimeter yet?"

"No. We saw the damage to the window, knew it was from the interior and called you. Blankenship has decided, this close to the park, she wants to keep you looped in. The protestors make her squirrelly. She's put in a request for you to act as a liaison between your agency and the sheriff's department."

At the corner of the cabin, Linc stopped and looked at the detective. "Sounds like a plan. Until the official word comes through, I'm here as an advisor."

"Appreciate it."

He stopped to tug on his gloves as Majenty did the same. "The main thing I want to know once we've determined what happened is how this links to the attack at the main house. There's no way this is a coincidence."

There were so many other questions as well. If Ellis was out on the ranch land, who had been in his cabin? Was Ellis truly out of sat-phone range, or had something terrible happened?

Only one way to find out. "Let's do this." Linc rounded the corner and headed for the back door, but he stopped with his foot on the bottom step of the stoop.

Using a key Rosa had provided, Linc unlocked the door and eased it open. He stepped into a small entry that held a stacked washer and dryer and a wooden bench. He paused to listen as Majenty stepped into the space behind him. Only the low hum of the refrigerator in the kitchen marred the silence.

From Rosa's description, he knew the small kitchen came next, with a bedroom and connecting bathroom to the right. On the other side of the kitchen would be an open living area.

That's where the busted windows were. He

stepped into the kitchen and aimed at the bedroom with two fingers, directing Majenty to clear the room.

The kitchen was spotless, but several clods of red dirt, likely from the treads of a shoe, lay in a path along the floor to the living area.

He sniffed the air, praying it wouldn't reveal the metallic scent of blood.

It didn't. Just the vague smell of bacon.

He stepped into the living area and scanned it. No closets. No place to hide. The room was empty. "Clear." Holstering his weapon, he surveyed the space.

Majenty echoed him and entered the kitchen. "Bedroom's clear also. Not a sign of anything out of place."

"I wish I could say the same." He motioned Majenty forward.

It was obvious there had been a struggle. An oval coffee table was turned on its side and had been shoved against the wood-framed couch. A barstool from the counter that divided living room from kitchen was splintered near the window, possibly the weapon that had shattered the glass. Blood was smeared along several of the stool's wooden shards and had spattered across the floor.

Linc kneeled and studied the trail. It wasn't enough blood for someone to bleed out, but it was enough to indicate an injury, almost as though the victim had taken a blow to the nose or mouth. "Definitely was a fight in here. How did no one hear the struggle or the glass breaking?"

Majenty paused in photographing the space. "Rosa was gone last night, and she said the ranch hands on both sides were away as well. The one immediately next door went to visit his family for a birthday party and didn't get back until late. The other went to visit his girlfriend, but he stays two cabins away. Both rode out before dawn this morning to check perimeter fences. The other two cabins are empty in preparation for renovation."

Whoever did this had to know there was little possibility they'd be heard, which indicated they'd either been watching the cabins, or they knew the movements of the workers and guests.

"Let's try to get DNA from the blood, see if it belongs to Ellis or to someone else." Hopefully, they'd get a hit in a database.

Linc walked to the kitchen counter, where a stack of mail rested. "I'm not liking how this looks. If Ellis is out with the cattle, who was here?"

"Maybe he came back to meet someone? That doesn't track, either, though. Rosa said his horse isn't in the barn, so he's likely still out."

It simply didn't make sense. Linc filtered through the stack of opened envelopes, but it offered no clues. A generic postcard of the canyon with no message, just signed with a heart by someone named Nica, a campaign ad and a credit-card statement that revealed nothing out of the ordinary.

He set down the mail, then walked to the front door and pulled it open. Stepping onto the small porch, he avoided looking at Angie, who hesitated at the foot of the stairs.

He couldn't face her, not when he had no answers to the storm brewing around her. Instead, he turned to Rosa. "Do me a favor. Call Ellis's sat phone again."

"Is he…?" Angie widened her stance as though she expected a blow. "Is he in there?"

Linc shook his head. No need to give her the details of what they'd found, especially given it made no sense.

Rosa dialed and listened, then shook her head and pocketed her cell. "Nothing."

"Okay, here's another question." Linc jerked his thumb over his shoulder. "Did you happen to walk by the cabin yesterday? Are you sure the window wasn't broken before last night?" Maybe something had happened to Ellis before he was supposed to ride out. Their timeline could be flawed.

Rosa scanned the sky as though searching for something, then slowly shook her head. "No, it wasn't broken before. I was at Danny's next door yesterday, talking to him before he left. I'd have noticed the glass."

"There's a geolocator on Ellis's sat phone, so we need to look into that." If the device was getting even a weak signal, they could ping it and figure out if he was actually out on the ranch, where he was supposed to be. "And you're sure he left?"

"I'm certain. I helped him gear up yesterday morning. Some of our guys ride ATVs, but Ellis is old-school. He might be young, but he likes being out on his horse. Chance is not in the stable. I fed the horses about an hour ago and he's the only one gone." Rosa backed a few steps toward her cabin. "I have a program on the office computer that can ping the phone."

Detective Blankenship looked up from her cell. "I'll go with her."

When Angie didn't move, Linc jerked his head toward the women. "You go, too."

"Not until you tell me what's in the cabin. I own the place. I have a right to know."

Ah, there she was. This was the Angie he was used to. Stubborn. Defiant. Bossy to her own detriment.

He nearly smiled, but the situation weighed too heavily. "Nothing. Looks like a fight went down in there. Not sure what to make of it. And, no, you can't come in. It's a crime scene." He texted Thomas Canady, who was acting as team leader while Linc healed. Do what it takes to get us assigned to an assault and a possible missing person on Fairweather Ranch. Send a crime-scene unit to my location.

The reply was immediate. I'll get the necessary permissions. Shouldn't be hard since it's an inholding within the park. Might take time. Hearing rumors of another case coming our way. Will update you later. Need anything else?

No. Coconino County was capable of investigating, but he wanted the added power behind his own team. The sheriff's department didn't have all of the resources his federal team did.

But what else would his team be investigating that he hadn't heard about? His fingers itched to ask for details, but he needed to focus on what was happening in front of him.

He walked down the stairs to Angie. "I want to get you to the house. We'll let these guys do their job and—"

"Agent Tucker!" Detective Blankenship burst out the door to the office at a full run, headed for the stables. "We got a hit on the sat phone."

Linc glanced at Angie. "Stay here." He jogged after the detective, who stopped at the back of the barn and started scanning the ground.

She pointed toward the corner of the building, her expression grim. "There."

Half-hidden in a bale of hay, a phone was barely visible.

Someone had clearly shoved it there, likely in an attempt to hide it in a hurry.

Lincoln balled his fists and stared toward the horizon. Ellis West wasn't out on the ranch with the cattle. He'd come back, likely the night before. Was he responsible for what had happened to Angie? "Let's wait until—"

A gunshot cracked.

Linc whirled toward the sound as the firearm's echo mingled with Angie's scream.

Chapter Four

Angie bit back another scream as Detective Majenty shoved her toward the porch steps of Ellis's cabin.

He dragged Rosa along beside him and moved her in front of him, urging her to follow Angie. "Get inside. Go to the left. Stay low." The detective drew his pistol as he pushed her onto the porch, staring in the direction of the gunshot's echo.

Another crack sounded across the distance, and wood splintered on the corner of Rosa's cabin.

The two women scrambled through the front door and dropped into the corner beneath the window on the left, then huddled together in the small space.

Angie struggled to catch her breath. The world was moving too fast, seeming to spin triple-time on its axis. Surely she was living in a horrible dream or in the rising action of a horror movie. The world seemed unreal—exactly the same as it had the night before, when that man approached her.

"What in the world?" Rosa's voice was hot, blazing with anger. She shifted as though she planned to stand and charge outside. "If I had my rifle—"

"You'd stay right here." Angie grabbed her friend's arm and dragged her to the floor beside her. Both of them needed to get their minds into gear. Rosa needed to withdraw from action mode. Angie needed to settle into it. She couldn't afford to devolve into a puddled mess of fear any more than Rosa could afford to charge out into the unknown with literal and metaphorical guns blazing. "We need to let the authorities handle this."

Rosa made a face and settled against the wall, her expression tight. It was killing her to sit still when she could be helping.

Well, it might kill her to step into the fray.

Angie closed her eyes and counted to ten, inhaling the faint smell of bacon that permeated Ellis's cabin, grounding herself in the moment. Everything had fallen silent outside, and the only sound was Rosa's breathing and the light hum of something in the cabin. She focused on scents and sounds, trying to shove aside how someone had fired two shots at them.

Someone had tried to kill them.

She gasped, then struggled to wrestle her breathing into rhythm. She would not panic. Could not panic. This was her ranch. She was in charge. Falling apart in a moment of weakness would serve no one.

Falling apart in a moment of weakness always led to trouble. Always.

Beside her, Rosa shifted. "You okay?"

Angie took three more deep breaths, then nodded. "We're safe in here. The walls in these cabins are old, heavy timber. It would take a tank to blast through one of them." Hopefully, there were none of those rolling toward them.

"You saying that to convince me or to convince yourself?"

Angie shot her what she hoped was a cutting look. "Don't."

"Don't what?"

"Don't pick a fight with me so you don't have to think about what's happening outside." She tilted her head, listening. Someone was on the porch, likely Detective Majenty keeping an eye on the front door.

There was a back door to the cabin as well. Who was guarding that?

She shook off the thought. No need to invent imaginary monsters at the gate when there were very real ones already stalking the ranch. Angie fought a shudder and focused on the tension radiating off Rosa.

"Oh, don't pick a fight with you? How about you don't sit over there and force your brain into a place where nothing is wrong so you don't have to deal with reality?" Rosa pivoted to face her. "Fear is a real emotion, you know. And an understandable one."

Angie dug her teeth into her bottom lip to keep from saying something she'd regret later. "Back at you." The words were ground out in frustration and anger and, yes, fear.

Rosa smirked. "I'm not denying I'm terrified. I'm masking it with rage."

Outside, a female voice rang between the cabins. "All clear!" It sounded like Detective Blankenship.

From the rear of the cabin, Linc's voice answered. "Clear here!"

Angie sank against the wall and closed her eyes again. They were safe, for now. Linc was safe for now. She hadn't let herself acknowledge he was out there in the open with whoever was shooting at them, but she couldn't deny the weakness of relief at the sound of his voice.

Beside her, Rosa mimicked her posture, bending her knees and propping her elbows on them. "Neither of us handles being out of control well, I guess."

Angie leaned her shoulder against Rosa's. "Never have."

"We've been through a lot together, but being shot at is a new one."

Angie opened her eyes and stared into the kitchen. She'd rather forget it had happened. Talking solidified the threat in her brain. Made it real. The last thing she wanted was for this moment to sear itself into her memory. She had enough trouble forgetting what had happened the night before. If she could get through the next few minutes, she could survive it and put it into the past.

Unlike last night. A man's hands pulling her away, tugging her toward—

She stood and shook her hands at her sides. "They said it's clear. We need to get moving."

Rosa reached up and grabbed her hand, her head cocked to one side and her ever-present cowboy hat askew. "Ang, seriously. Please don't. It's okay to be—"

"I'm fine. It's over." She pulled her hand from her friend's grasp. Rosa didn't understand. Emotions swamped her. They clouded her judgment. They made her miss the truth about people who could hurt her, and they made her do things she shouldn't. "There's too much happening to deal with this now."

Rosa stood, staring her in the eye. "This *is* now. This *is* happening. If you keep burying the bad, eventually even the good is going to escape you."

"I'm fine." She pulled her gaze away from Rosa's and stared over her friend's shoulder. Her eyes widened. "Rosa…"

What she was seeing couldn't be real. Linc was right. There had been a fight in the cabin. Furniture was broken. The window was shattered. And the floor was smeared with—

"Angie? Rosa?" Linc's voice came from the rear of the house, dragging Angie's gaze from the renewed horror she was viewing. He strode in from the kitchen. "Are you two okay?"

The question skimmed Rosa and landed straight on Angie. His eyes scanned her from head to toe, as though he wanted reassurance that she hadn't been hit.

She turned her gaze to the refrigerator, ignoring the gentle heat his concern created in her stomach. It was taking all of her strength to hold fear at bay. She didn't need whatever this was to come in and crack the dam holding all of her emotions in check.

Rosa responded when it became clear Angie wouldn't. "We're good. Detective Majenty got us inside quickly. Is everyone outside okay?"

"We're all good." Linc came all the way into the living area, holstering his pistol as he did. "Whoever it was took two shots then fled. We heard the vehicle leave. They were in a stand of trees on the far side of the paddock."

"I'm headed out, then. I want to call Danny and Wiley in, let them know what's going on. They don't need to be out there on ATVs if someone's taking potshots at us."

"Good idea. Keep everyone close. It may be time to consider getting your guests off the ranch until this blows over."

At the suggestion, Angie's head jerked, a sizzle of panic running along her nerves. "No." If the researchers left, then refunds were in order. They couldn't afford to let money go now.

Immediately, guilt cooled her concern. Money could be replaced. Lives couldn't. Linc was right. For the safety of all involved, they needed to clear the researchers from the property. She turned to Rosa. "Go ahead. Let them know what's going on. Tell them we'll hold their spots and keep an eye on what they leave behind if they want to go."

Rosa nodded and headed toward the door.

"Wait." A horrible thought shuddered through her. "Chance. Ellis's horse. Can we get someone looking for him? If he's not in the barn, he's out there somewhere."

Rosa's expression darkened. "I'll make sure Danny and Wiley get out to search immediately."

"I want to talk to them first." Linc looked between the two women. "It's standard procedure. We'll need to check alibis and ask them a few questions."

"Really?" Angie couldn't imagine either Danny or Wiley harming Ellis. The men were like brothers.

Rosa closed her arms, her posture rigid. "You'll want mine, too?"

"Like I said, standard procedure."

With a curt nod, Rosa walked out the door,

her head held high as though they hadn't been targets a few minutes earlier.

Linc waited for her to leave before he spoke. "I doubt your people had anything to do with it, but we have to check all of the boxes, so, please, don't fuss at me."

Angie swallowed her next words. Her brother was on Linc's team. She well knew how an investigation worked, even if the thought of her crew being temporary suspects made her squirrelly. She let his comment slide and surveyed him from head to toe. "You weren't hurt?"

"No. Whoever was firing seemed to be aiming at the buildings, not at any of us. Based on several things, Blankenship and I think this was more scare tactic than attempted murder."

The unspoken words hung in the air. *If he'd wanted us dead, then we'd be dead.*

Who was to say that whoever was targeting her wouldn't shift from fear to murder in order to get what he wanted?

And who even knew what he wanted?

"You don't need to come back from your vacation, Jacob." Angie pressed the phone tighter against her ear and walked to her bedroom window on the second floor of the main house.

From this vantage point, she could see across the land behind the barn to the canyon in the distance. The summer sun wouldn't set for a few hours, but dark cumulonimbus clouds built in the western sky, lightning chasing between them as they rushed closer.

It was normally a sight she loved, but today it couldn't keep her from staring toward the ranch. Multiple law-enforcement vehicles had passed on the road in front of the house in the past few minutes, indicating they were probably done collecting evidence. It had been hours since Lincoln had banished her to the house with a female deputy.

One who'd stared at Linc with the kind of adoring big brown eyes usually reserved for TV romance movies.

Linc hadn't seemed to notice.

That shouldn't have given her a sense of triumph.

The deputy was downstairs now, keeping an eye on her from a distance. For most of the afternoon, the younger woman had tried to distract Angie with conversation, but not much had worked. When Jacob had called, Angie had fled to her room, craving some time to herself. She was jealous of Rosa, who was alone in her office finding off-site lodging for the researchers.

Once she got her brother off the line, Angie might get some alone time as well. For now, he was saying his piece. "Ang, this is too big for you to handle alone."

"I'm not alone. Half of the sheriff's department is here. Rosa, Danny and Wiley are at the ranch." She squinted as a man walked around the corner of the house, headed toward the small barn at the rear of the property. His familiar gait would be recognizable anywhere, although there was a hitch in his step she hadn't noticed before. "And Linc has arrived."

Where was he going? He had his phone to his ear, and he disappeared around the side of the barn, likely looking for somewhere private for his phone call.

To whom?

Angie let the curtain fall. It wasn't her business, but wondering about his actions kept her from thinking about worse things.

This land had always been her safe place. But now? She shuddered.

From a hotel room in London, her brother exhaled heavily. It was late in the evening there, and he and his little family ought to be settling in to rest after tea or some other very British activity. Instead, he was talking to her, the brother in him unable to stop worrying while the investigator in him couldn't stop asking questions.

The selfish part of her wanted him to chuck his vacation and come home.

But the sister in her couldn't let him sacrifice a trip he and Ivy had been dreaming about. "I'm fine."

"Look, you stepped up to the plate a couple of years ago when Ivy was in trouble. You were there when I was hurt. I can't—"

"Jacob, I have no proof this is about me. When Ivy was in trouble, someone was actively hunting her. When you were hurt, it was my job to help you get better." She dug her teeth into her lower lip. It had been her job, but with Linc's help.

She cleared her throat. "I'm guessing someone had a beef with Ellis, though I can't imagine what." Ellis West had worked at the ranch for a little over six months, and he'd spent most of his time with the cattle. While his father had worked at the ranch years ago, before he died in a car accident, she didn't know Ellis well. His job fell under Rosa's supervision, not hers.

"Someone came at you last night, Ang."

"You think I forgot?" The terror would live in her memory forever, although she was trying to squash it. "Maybe they thought I saw something. But he tipped his hand today with that sniper act. Now law enforcement is on high alert. Trying again would be foolish."

That's what she told herself, anyway. But as the day raced toward night and the law-enforcement officers left the property, she was growing less confident.

"I'd feel better if you went somewhere else for tonight, at least."

"I'll be fine." *Hopefully.* "Besides, I hear the protestors are at the gate again. That ought to scare potential bad guys away."

"Not funny, especially since they're probably involved."

"The deputies spoke to them today, and they're checking alibis. You taught me how to defend myself. There's nothing to worry about." *I hope.*

Besides, she didn't want company. She wanted time to process. The events of the past twenty-four hours threatened to swamp her if she didn't find a journal and write them out in bullet points, praying over each one. She needed time with God that didn't involve scattered, angry prayers like the ones she'd spouted as she navigated the roads from Vegas. She didn't need the threat of someone walking in on her outpouring of emotion.

A series of attacks. A dying dream. A burning humiliation.

While some issues were bigger than others, all of them blended into a toxic stew that needed to be filtered.

"I'll set the alarm. I'll call for help if I need to. You enjoy your week and keep my niece safe. If something is going on, then we want Wren as far away as possible." That precious little girl had been through enough.

Across the ocean, Jacob muttered something that sounded like resignation.

Angie almost smiled. Appealing to his feelings for his wife and daughter was a sure way to sway him.

She refused to let that make her jealous. Her brother had something she'd never been able to find. Something she'd never be able to trust in, even if she did manage to locate it in this mess of a world.

"Fine." Jacob clipped out the word, probably to make sure she knew he wasn't happy. "But if anything else happens, I want to know."

"Fine."

"Also, I want Linc to stay tonight."

"Absolutely not." Linc had been on the property all day, and she'd been keenly aware of every move he'd made. She didn't need the distraction.

"It's the only way I'm staying in Europe."

He had her backed into a corner. "Fine." She ground out the word. She'd do anything to make her family happy, including, she supposed, allowing Lincoln Tucker to sleep in the storage room connected to the barn.

He certainly wasn't staying in her house.

After goodbyes and a promise to give Wren a hug, Jacob disconnected the call.

The deputy's voice floated from downstairs. "Ms. Garcia?"

Pocketing her phone, Angie went to the door, unwilling to head down for more empty conversation, no matter how well-meaning the young deputy was. "I'm here."

"I'm heading out. Agent Tucker is on his way in as soon as he finishes taking a phone call. Do you need anything?"

Angie sagged against the doorframe. Maybe she'd be able to find five minutes of quiet. "I'm good. Be safe."

"You, too." The downstairs floor creaked slightly, then the alarm chimed to indicate a door had been opened. At the front of the house, a car started.

Exhaling slowly, Angie walked to the window. If she could get even two minutes to herself, it would be something. She pulled back the corner of the curtain.

Linc was nowhere to be seen. She'd have heard him come into the house because the door chime on the alarm would have indicated he'd opened the door. With a storm coming in fast, he should get inside.

Movement at the fence along a ravine beyond the barn kept her from dropping the curtain into place. Surely Linc wasn't all the way out there.

Angie squinted into the fading light as dark clouds drew closer. Was that…?

A horse. The animal was saddled and facing the fence, shaking his head as though he was caught on something. As the brown horse tossed his head, he turned slightly, revealing a large white patch along his hindquarters.

Chance.

Ellis West's horse.

The animal hadn't been there ten minutes earlier. Where had he come from?

She bolted down the stairs and out the front door, hoping to catch the deputy before she left, but a puff of orange dirt along the driveway indicated it was too late.

In the distance, thunder rumbled, rolling from the canyon.

She couldn't leave the horse in the brewing storm. Judging by the height of the cloud tops, it promised to be a raging one.

Linc was somewhere around the barn, and the fence where Chance was caught was a few hundred yards beyond. He'd be able to hear her, maybe even see her if she ran into any trouble.

Another roll of thunder, followed by a gust that rattled the windows, made up her mind. Linc might have told her to stay inside, but she couldn't leave a helpless animal in a storm.

She raced across the downstairs, then passed through the mudroom, snagging her raincoat on the way, and headed out the side door.

The world had changed in the moments she'd been making her decision. Dark clouds roiled overhead. The scent of rain and dust blew on the stiff breeze that whipped across the open land from the direction of the canyon. Lightning crisscrossed the sky, too close for comfort.

She was definitely within the ten-mile strike zone. She needed to move quickly.

Running past the barn, she called for Linc, but her voice was carried away by the wind.

Surely he'd know where she went. If she could see Chance from the house, Linc should be able to see him from the barn.

As she neared the horse, he stopped moving and watched her with wide eyes. She'd helped train him when he came to the ranch a few years earlier, so he knew her. Hopefully that would be enough to calm him.

Angie held her hands out toward the massive creature, eyeing him from nose to tail. He didn't appear to be injured, but his reins were tangled in the top fence rail, pinning him close to the rough wood. "It's okay, buddy. I'm going to get you into the barn, where it's safe."

She stepped closer, and Chance eyed her warily. He tried to move away, but he was tethered too tightly to the fence.

She halted her forward progress, not wanting to spook him into hurting himself. "You know me, buddy. It's okay."

As the wind gusted again, she studied the reins and eased closer to the fence, facing the horse with her back to the trees.

Something about those reins didn't look right.

Angie leaned closer. They weren't snagged. They were looped around and knotted.

She jumped, and Chance jerked his head, whinnying loudly.

This wasn't an accident. Chance hadn't gotten caught in the fence. He'd been tied there by someone who'd known she wouldn't be able to resist rescuing the animal.

Heart rising into her throat, Angie turned as the rain unleashed. "Linc!" she yelled toward the barn, hoping he'd hear and praying she was wrong.

But she was right.

A shadowy figure leaped from the woods and grabbed her by the arm. A gloved hand covered her mouth as the man pulled her against his chest and lifted her feet from the ground, hefting her into the trees where a gray truck waited with the doors open, ready to steal her.

Forever.

Chapter Five

Tucking his phone into his pocket, Linc stared at the angry sky as a wind gust nearly shoved him backward. The next available MRI appointment wasn't for two weeks.

Two weeks until he'd know the extent of his injuries and whether he could return to full duty, be the man he was supposed to be.

Lord...please. Pleading made him feel weak, as though he was taking from God instead of offering anything of value.

He'd never felt more worthless.

The sky unleashed a furious deluge. He ducked around the corner under the lean-to at the rear of the barn, where the Garcias kept their father's old farm trucks. He needed to get to the house, to make sure—

"Linc!" The wind screamed his name.

Or was that Angie?

She couldn't have left the house. He'd have seen her.

Except he'd been walking along the side of the barn with the house out of sight.

Linc and the sheriff had been clear she was safer inside, but Angie was headstrong.

Ignoring the rain, Linc walked to the edge of the overhang. Maybe he was hearing things.

Lightning struck on the far side of the ravine, beyond the fence. Thunder crashed.

A horse's frantic squeal followed.

Linc squinted against the storm.

There. Against the fence, a horse pulled at his reins, which were tangled in the rails. Had Angie come outside to—

Movement to the left jerked his attention from the animal.

A man, dressed in dark clothing with a hood over his head, was dragging Angie into the trees. She kicked, but her fight was useless.

Linc bolted forward, his hand on his weapon. The quick motion shot pain down his spine. Adrenaline rattled through him. "Federal agent! Let her go!"

Raging wind threw the words against the barn.

The man hesitated.

It was a nightmarish repeat of the previous night.

The rain fell harder, whipping between them as Linc edged closer and the man tried to drag Angie farther. His movements were slowed by her struggling.

Why didn't he let her go? There was no way he could escape with Angie hindering his speed and maneuverability.

Linc maintained his steady approach, moving as quickly as he dared with his vision hampered by the rain. Maybe the man had an accomplice waiting in the woods, or he planned to kill Angie rather than kidnap her.

The thought chilled him more than the slashing rain. "Let her go!" The last thing he wanted was a physical altercation, the very thing he'd been warned by the doctors to avoid, but hesitation could sign Angie's death warrant.

The man pulled Angie tighter against him with one hand as he reached behind his back with the other.

It was likely he had a weapon tucked in his waistband.

Time had run out.

As Linc rushed forward, Angie seemed to grasp what was happening. She went limp, then straightened, driving her elbows into her assailant's ribs.

It was an awkward blow, but it was enough to cause the man to stumble.

Linc dove into the fray, and the three of them tumbled to the ground in a heap.

Angie gasped.

The man cursed.

Linc landed hard, one shoulder driving into the man's chest and the other colliding with Angie's shoulder. White heat shot dancing lights and dark spots into his vision.

Had they been struck by lightning?

No. This bolt was from inside. It turned his muscles and mind to mush.

Angie's assailant shoved Lincoln to the side, then scrambled to his feet.

Linc tried to stand, but he got to one knee before a wave of dizziness pinned him to the ground. If the guy doubled back and dealt another blow, there would be nothing Linc could do to stop him.

But the dark figure ran into the trees. Over the pounding rain, an engine roared, then he could hear a vehicle race away.

Dropping his chin to his chest, Lincoln gulped air and waited for the pain to subside.

Please, Lord. It had to stop. This couldn't be the fatal blow.

The world wobbled. Black haze crowded in as his ears rang. He was helpless. Useless.

Angie dropped to her knees and rested a hand on his shoulder. "Linc, look at me." Gently, she tilted his chin, the simple gesture ripping pain down his spine.

He struggled to bring the world into focus as rain ran down his face.

Her green eyes locked on to his, wide with terror. "We have to go."

He could do this. He *had* to do this.

And he'd do it without her lifting him like a flopping rag doll. It took all of his strength to rise. "I need to call this in." The horizon was rocking back and forth, but he stayed on his feet.

"The horse." Angie stood with him, keeping one hand on his arm as she stretched the other toward the animal, who jerked at his reins. "I can't leave Chance."

She'd never let an animal suffer in this weather, and neither would he. Linc drew his pistol and faced the woods, wrestling the pain. "Get the horse."

Before he knew it, she was leading the animal toward him. Quickly, with Linc watching the woods and Angie leading the skittish horse, they made their way toward the barn.

Each step caused a jolt of fresh pain. He took them one at a time, fighting to keep the darkness at bay. If these were the last steps he ever took…

He shoved aside the thought. Getting Angie to safety was vital. He had no choice but to soldier on.

Linc shut the barn doors against the deluge, grateful for the rollers that made the massive door slide easily along the concrete floor. The pain between his shoulders felt like a creature was gnawing on his spinal cord, but the more he moved, the less he felt like he was falling into an abyss. His vision came into focus as the pain receded.

As Angie led Chance into a stall, Linc glanced around the barn. Three stalls lined each side of the wide center aisle, where the family's horses, Flynn and Shiloh, typically sheltered. The wood ceiling was high, providing for storage above. At the far end of the space, a closed door separated the office and storage from the rest of the building.

The smell of horses and hay hovered in the air.

There was something comforting about the familiar scents that made him feel almost normal.

Rain pounded the metal roof and lashed the sides of the barn, making it difficult to hear anything outside. There were no windows. They were boxed in.

He didn't like it.

Angie was talking quietly to the skittish horse as she removed his tack.

Gently pulling his head to one side, hoping to stretch away the pain, Linc took out his phone.

No service.

Cell signal was weak on a normal day. During a storm like this one, they didn't have a chance. He was on his own.

He pocketed the device and walked slowly to the stall to keep from spooking Chance, who had finally calmed. He studied the animal as Angie brushed him. "I don't recognize this guy."

"He's Ellis's horse." She slowly moved around the animal, scratching his nose before she took a position on his opposite side, facing Linc.

Why was Ellis's saddled horse roaming Fairweather? They'd seen no sign of Ellis all day.

Thunder cracked nearby, and Chance jumped.

Angie shushed him, humming a wordless song as she brushed his coat.

It was tough to tell if Angie was soothing the horse or herself. "How are you doing?"

"I'd rather not talk about it while I'm dealing with a skittish horse."

As though he understood, Chance jerked his head like he was about to buck.

With a pointed look at Linc, Angie steadied the horse. "I'll deal with my feelings later."

There she went, focusing on the task and not on what was happening inside of her. It was her worst habit.

"I'd rather talk about you." She let her eyes follow the path of the brush as she worked. "What happened out there?"

Linc's shoulders stiffened, zinging pain through him. He schooled his expression.

When the horse tensed, Linc stepped away from the stall and shoved his hands into his pockets. "Got the wind knocked out of me."

"Hmm." Angie's gaze flicked to him, then to Chance. "You move like a robot, and you're completely pale. What's the deal?" Rounding the horse, she scratched Chance's nose, then grabbed a bucket and eased out of the stall, closing the door behind her. She stopped in front of Lincoln. "How bad are you hurt?"

The fact that he'd foundered enough for her to notice was humiliating. If he'd lost consciousness or had been unable to get off the ground, she could have died.

He'd failed her. So, no, he didn't want to discuss it.

"Linc…" She walked over to a faucet a few feet from the floor and filled the bucket. The rush of water drowned out every other sound.

He watched, feeling helpless. Even the weight of a five-gallon bucket was too much for him at the moment.

Angie didn't speak until she'd settled the bucket in front of Chance and stepped into the aisle, latching the stall behind her. She faced Lincoln. "Tell the truth, then I'll tell you how I'm really feeling."

Lincoln leaned against a stall door and crossed his arms over his chest. It was a rare offer, and it might be the only way to get her to speak truthfully.

Was he willing to make the sacrifice?

Across the aisle, Angie mimicked his posture, her gaze holding a challenge.

Rain lashed the roof harder, filling the space

with noise. The roar outside and the silence inside made him feel as though he'd stepped outside of time, as though anything that happened in the barn could be left there when the storm ended.

With a loud exhale, he made his decision. "A few weeks ago, we were practicing a rappelling drill. I was about twelve feet up when…" He pursed his lips, not quite ready to admit he'd gotten cocky. Maybe he'd been showing off. Maybe he'd been careless. "Long story short, I landed flat on my back, staring at the sky."

"Linc." Angie's hands thumped against the stall door.

Chance looked up, then went back to drinking water.

Angie winced. "How bad?" A shadow crossed her features. Likely his story brought memories of Jacob's pain.

He might as well tell all, or she'd invent an injury far worse than the one he suffered. "I ruptured a disc in my cervical spine. The MRI showed it putting pressure on my spinal cord. Made my arms numb. Brought on some epic headaches." The pounding pain that pulsed in his eyeballs had been the worst. He'd refused stronger painkillers, having seen in the military how quickly opioid addiction could take hold.

"That's why you're available here instead of being active on the team."

Pain arced up Linc's neck as he nodded. Available? More like useless.

Except... There was no way anyone could watch Angie 24/7. Resources were stretched too thin. If he wasn't injured, she'd probably be here without protection.

For a few minutes, the only sound was the squall outside and Chance's huffing as he made himself comfortable.

Right when he thought the conversation was over, Angie broke the silence. "What's your prognosis?"

That was the part he had never spoken aloud, barely acknowledging it when Dr. Collins had studied her tablet for an eternity before handing over her thoughts.

But here, in this isolated moment, the pressure squeezed his chest until words found their way out. "Surgery is risky. Could leave me paralyzed from the neck down. I can do physical therapy, but the doc thinks..."

He closed his eyes. The doc thought the worst. That he'd lost his job and himself...forever.

★ ★ ★

Linc was quiet so long, Angie wondered if he would ever speak again.

His expression was nearly the same as when Jacob had first been moved from Brooke Army Medical Center in Houston to the VA center in Las Vegas. That had been the first time Linc had been able to visit her brother and to see the extent of his injuries. They'd been unsure if he'd recover enough to lead a normal life, let alone serve his country again.

She'd found Linc in a small waiting room at the end of the hall, staring out a window, struggling to hold himself together. Jacob's injuries had been extensive after an IED blast in Afghanistan, and his rehabilitation had been grueling. Linc had never wanted her brother to see the effect the initial sight of Jacob's pain had inflicted on him.

That day, he'd become more than Jacob's battle buddy and best friend, at least to her. Without even considering whether he'd want her to or not, she'd rested her hand on his back and her head on his shoulder. She'd understood his pain. Had felt the way they shared the struggle in a way that bonded them immediately.

When he'd pulled her free hand to his chest

and held on tight, they'd simply stood with one another and grieved what had happened and sought strength for what was to come. They had solidified a friendship, a partnership forged in working together to make sure Jacob got well as they shielded her mother from the worst of his pain.

Angie had kept on a brave, smiling face at the hospital, at the rehab center and at the house…

Until the night she hadn't.

Now she'd gone too far, asking personal questions when everything between them had begun to settle into cordiality.

She needed a distraction. Needed to not think about the pain in her ribs where that man's arm had dug so deep she likely had a bruise. Needed to not think about what would have happened if Linc hadn't rescued her.

Again.

Right now, she could be…

A shudder ran through her. She could be anywhere. The victim of anything.

Chance snorted, probably sensing her unease.

She forced even breaths to keep from riling the horse and so Lincoln wouldn't recognize her fear.

Leaning on him was not an option. Not after what had happened the last time.

There was also no way she could close the space between them to hug him or extend comfort.

Because the last time she'd reached out to him that way, she'd kissed him. She'd kissed him and then pushed for more in an effort to cover her roiling, out-of-control grief and fear.

Although she wasn't that person any longer, Linc would likely rebuff any touch she offered.

So she stood as the rain pelted the roof and the wind rattled the doors and Chance slurped water from his bucket.

Stood…and waited for whatever came next.

With a huff, Linc spoke. "The chances of me returning to what I love are slim. Likely, once we're all the way through this, I can live what most people would call a normal life. Drive, eat, sleep, work a job somewhere…all without fear and with minimal pain." He finally faced her, but his gaze landed at her feet. "Climbing? Strenuous hiking? Wrestling with the occasional bad guy? Anything that relates to the job I love?" His hand sliced the air. "Out of the question."

At his declaration, even the storm outside

seemed to still. The rain pounded the roof with less ferocity, and the wind eased. It was as though the whole world heard the weight of grief in Linc's voice and had responded in kind.

"I'm sorry." What else could she say? How did someone comfort a man who'd been told he might lose everything he held dear?

Linc's life was his job. He'd said so the night he told her he respected her too much to use her. He'd tacked on a speech about how he didn't want a relationship. Never planned to get married. All he wanted to do was exactly what he was doing with the National Park Service.

Every word had made her feel smaller. More rejected. Until it became not about the physical line she'd tried to cross, but about her personally. Never good enough. Never worthy of love. Never worthy of a man who stayed.

Even now, all these years later, her cheeks and neck burned at the memory of her behavior and of his rejection.

No way would she let him see her discomfort. She turned, opened the stall and grabbed the half-full bucket Chance had been drinking from. She crossed to the faucet, then refilled it and set it into place before she felt as though she could speak in a normal voice.

"You know… They told Jacob he'd never be the same again. That he'd be in pain the rest of his life. And now he's out working with you, doing all of the things the experts told him he'd never be able to do." The external forces from the blast in Afghanistan had scrambled her brother's insides and left him in intense pain. His recovery had been grueling, but he'd overcome. He'd—

"Don't act like his life is all sunshine. He can do everything except the one thing he wanted most." Linc's words were bitter.

Angie dug her teeth into her lower lip. Linc was right, to an extent. Her brother's internal injuries had ensured he would never have another child of his own.

Through a twist no one saw coming, he'd learned a couple of years after the IED explosion that he'd previously fathered a child with his ex-fiancée, who was now his wife. Wren was a joy to the entire family.

Still, Jacob would never have another.

"Some things can't be fixed. Some things can. And do you know what? I plan to be one of the ones who beats this." Linc knocked twice on the stall behind him and straightened. "It sounds like the rain is letting up. Will Chance be okay out here by himself?" He glanced at his phone, made a face, then pocketed it again. "I don't have service yet. You?"

Well, sharing time was over. Angie hesitated. There was so much more to say. He'd spilled his pain onto the concrete and she'd left it there, unable to help him. It felt wrong. There must be something she could do. A Linc who couldn't roam the canyon freely in service to others simply wasn't Linc.

"Angie? Cell service?" He said the words in a clipped tone, impatience rising.

Probably because he believed he'd said too much. Rather than argue, she pulled the phone from her jacket pocket. "No bars. Sorry. The rain's going to have to ease more before you get any bars. That's why I have a landline. Sometimes out here, cell signal is worthless."

"I don't like that, especially now." He glanced at his phone again. "I'm glad you have a landline, but if you're out on the ranch like you were today, how are you going to communicate when the weather wrecks your signal?" His chin rose and he pinned her gaze. "You're no longer dealing with a skittish horse, so I'm going to ask again. Are you okay? You said if I talked, you'd talk. So talk."

She'd known the conversation would eventually return to her. She'd kind of hoped he'd forgotten her promise. As much as she'd rather pretend nothing had happened, she'd have to hand him something or he'd hound her until she cracked.

There would be no more cracking in front of Lincoln Tucker.

Besides, she had Jesus now. He could get her through anything.

"I'm a little bit sore, but—"

"Sore?" Lincoln crossed the wide aisle in two long steps and stopped in front of her. His blue eyes were dark. "How so? Did he hurt you?" His hand hovered between them as though he planned to touch her.

Angie stepped aside. "I'm not hurt. He had on a watch or something. It pressed into my ribs. I'm certain nothing is broken. At the worst, I'll have a bruise." *And a few nightmares.*

No need to pass that along. She could deal with it herself. Linc didn't need a shivering victim on his plate, not with all he was already dealing with.

Thunder rolled across the space, a distant wave that indicated the storm had passed over them and was moving on. The rain on the roof had slackened to a gentle shower. "I think the weather's about spent itself, and Chance is calm enough for some hay. I'll feed him, then we can get to the house and you can use the land-line to call out." She backed another step away from him, toward the door to the storage area and the stairs to the haymow. "I'll have to toss a bale down from upstairs. Later I'll call Rosa to let her know Chance is here." She was bab-bling. Too many random words were pouring out, but she couldn't stop them.

It was nerves. Or Linc. Or fear. Or a thou-sand other things she never wanted to admit lived inside of her.

Linc matched her step for step as she backed toward the door. "You stay down here. I'll go up. I'd rather clear the building before I let you go anywhere by yourself."

Her foot dragged on the concrete and she stumbled to a stop. Her eyes went to the hay-mow above them. "You think someone's up there?"

"I think someone is everywhere. Especially now."

That statement was way too ominous for her taste. It sounded too much like paranoia. Fear. Things that held her back. Turning, she strode for the door. "Nobody is up there. If they were, they'd have already made themselves known."

She was nearly to the door when Linc's strong arms grabbed her from behind and dragged her against the wall of his chest. "Angie, stop."

A flash of terror raced through her at the memory of arms that intended to harm her. Of a faceless figure dragging her into the woods.

If Linc hadn't arrived when he—

"Angie, listen." Gently, he pulled her away from the door. "Don't touch anything. I'm going to let you go, but don't touch anything."

"What are you—" She scanned the area. What had he seen? A gun? A bomb? Some sort of device that—

Her eyes caught on the door and she froze. Near the handle, smeared fingerprints marred the metal. Something that looked like dark paint had dripped on the pristine concrete floor.

Her heart pounded harder. Those fingerprints… Those drops… They weren't paint.

They were blood.

Chapter Six

"Back away, Angie. Now." With one hand, Linc turned Angie around and aimed her toward the opposite end of the barn. He reached for his phone with the other, praying the rain had eased enough to give him a signal. One bar showed on the screen. It had better be enough. Detective Blankenship needed to get to the barn immediately. So did his team's crime-scene unit.

He had a horrible feeling that Ellis West's whereabouts weren't going to be a mystery for much longer.

"Linc…" Angie hesitated, her voice shaking as she said his name.

She hadn't asked him for help since…

Well, since Jacob had been injured and they'd been caring for him together. Before her grief drove her into his arms and he'd had to tell her no, not only because he couldn't exploit her vulnerability, but also because he couldn't be the kind of man she deserved to have in her life.

For the first time, he saw open fear in her expression. She was struggling to bury it, and she was failing. He needed to stop being an investigator for half a second. Take a deep breath. Focus on her.

As soon as he called the detective.

His heart breaking for Angie, wrestling the line between duty and compassion, he guided her toward the barn door, then pulled her close, wrapping his arm around her waist and holding her against his side. He thumbed his phone with his free hand until he found Blankenship's number.

When she answered, he kept it brief. "It's Tucker. Bring the team to the horse barn behind the main house. I think I know where West is. And…" How to say this without upsetting Angie? "Bring Ortiz." Blankenship would know the name. The coroner would need to be on-site, he had no doubt.

As soon as she'd confirmed, Linc killed the call, pocketed his phone and turned so Angie's back was to the door. He held her to his chest and simply let her rest there, her face pressed against his shoulder. It wasn't advisable for him to have her in his arms, but he also wasn't going to send her away to battle her fears and grief alone.

She shook, her breathing ragged. "What's happening?"

Linc stared over her head at the door, which still looked new after the rebuild of the barn following an arsonist's attempt to destroy it a couple of years prior. The metal door was pristine except for the smears of blood around the handle. Too much blood to have come from a mere cut. Had he walked to the door sooner, he'd have seen the evidence long before Angie had come close to touching it.

"Linc? Answer me." Angie tried to pull away, but he tightened his grip. She didn't need to see any more than she already had. There were enough horrible imagined images already swirling in her brain, he was sure. There was no need to cement them with reality.

In the aftermath of the wind and rain, the barn was eerily quiet, adding to the surreal feeling of the moment. Linc wished he could make all of the horror go away. "I don't know exactly what's going on, but you need to trust me. As much as you think you want to know the details, believe me, you don't." Too many nightmarish scenes lived in his head. Too many murders. Too many fallen hikers. Too many victims. Every one of them resided in his memory. Every one of them awoke him at night, sometimes in a cold sweat that wouldn't let him fall into the peaceful darkness of sleep.

He'd spare Angie that, at least. Sometimes, imagination was worse than reality. Other times, it wasn't. Because if his suspicions were right, Ellis West was about to join that never-ending line of horrifying images that he could never forget.

He needed to get her into the house, but he also needed to keep his eye on her and on what he now recognized as a crime scene. They should have checked the barn earlier in the day, but the detectives had been focused on the scene of her assault and the site at the ranch, assuming the two scenes were connected.

Well, they'd officially passed making assumptions. It was now almost a certainty that Ellis's disappearance and Angie's confrontation were part of the same heinous crime.

He had no idea how long they stood silently with her warm against his chest before Angie's phone chimed. She eased away from him and pressed the screen. "It's the deputies. They're at the gate. I let them in."

Within moments, several cars approached from the direction of the main gate. His time to comfort Angie was over. Now he needed to shift into work mode. Gently, he eased her away from him. "I need you to go to the house, okay?" He spoke to her in much the same way Angie had spoken to the skittish Chance earlier. With their history and the tension of her situation, she could easily buck.

He guided her to the entrance as he spoke, then tugged the door open, working hard to ignore the fresh pain in his back.

A female deputy entered the corral and walked closer. She gave Lincoln a terse nod as she rested a hand on Angie's back. "Hey, Ang. Let's go inside while these guys work."

When Angie saw the woman, her face registered recognition and she seemed to relax slightly. She pulled away from Lincoln, following the auburn-haired deputy without a word and, thankfully, without looking back.

She'd be in good hands.

He watched her walk away until Detective Blankenship approached with her department's crime-scene investigators, who were already gearing up and heading into the barn.

They were pulling out all of the stops on this one. *Good.*

Blankenship hung back with him in the corral as the crew entered the barn and immediately started taking photos. "What are you thinking?"

He shot her a look. No need to answer. There was no doubt that their suspicions matched perfectly.

She sighed. "I was hoping for a different outcome." Looking over her shoulder toward the house, she frowned. "You think our bad guy believes Angie saw something last night when she arrived home?"

"Most likely. It would explain the attacks last night and this afternoon, as well as the shooting at the cabins. When she pulled up, they could have been here in the barn. She might have spooked them into thinking they had a witness on their hands. They could have decided..." No need to finish that sentence. He didn't need that kind of potential horror living rent-free with the other terrible images in his head.

One of the techs appeared in the doorway and waved them over.

Blankenship passed him a set of gloves. "Ready for a new nightmare?"

He took the gloves, although he had his own, but didn't respond.

Blankenship led the way through the barn that had been a refuge moments earlier.

From his stall, Chance watched the proceedings with interest, though he seemed calm.

If only Linc felt that kind of peace.

At the door, he and Blankenship both stopped, scanning the scene inside. A wide hallway led straight through to the back of the barn. To the left, the office door was open. To the right, the door that led to a storage space and the stairs to the loft was closed.

In the center of the aisle, a man was pitched forward in a wooden chair. His hands were tied behind him, and his ankles were bound to the chair's legs. He wasn't wearing a shirt, and blood pooled beneath him on the concrete. The way his body slumped, it was clear he was past saving.

Training kept Linc from backing away. From the amount of blood and the marks on his face, arms and bare chest, the man had been beaten until his body succumbed to the brutality.

Linc swallowed the revulsion that rose at the

evidence of such brutal cruelty. It never seemed to dim, no matter how long he was on the job.

He cleared his throat. "This is Ellis West?"

It took a moment for Blankenship to answer. "His face is so swollen I can't make a totally positive identification but that would be my assumption." She walked a wide berth around the man and studied his back. "It's him. West had a distinct tribal tattoo down his spine. It's damaged but still visible."

Linc searched for footprints, but there was nothing but blood and clumps of mud on the concrete, likely from the killer's boots. There was nothing to identify the attacker, but the crime-scene unit would dust for prints and gather evidence. "We don't have much to go on."

"No, but we do have Ellis. I doubt our killer planned to leave him here like this. Chances are high he was forced to flee when Angie came home, and then, with our presence on the property, he wasn't able to return and clean his mess."

Linc pursed his lips and turned away from the body. He walked to the door and stared into the outside world, where the sun was beginning to set. "Why basically torture the guy? What did someone want from him?" It was possible this wasn't about Angie at all. Someone had a clear beef with Ellis, and they'd taken their time causing him pain. Whatever it was about, it was either deeply personal, or it was the work of an incredibly depraved mind.

"We'll take a deeper dive into his background, but off the top, I have no idea. I looked at his file at the ranch. They ran thorough background checks before they hired him, and he came out with a spotless record outside of a couple of speeding tickets when he was a teenager. That's not to say everything is spotless in his world, though. He could have been running with the wrong people and never got caught. Could have seen something somebody didn't want him to see. Could have crossed the wrong person."

"What about his family?" There could be a vendetta there.

"Mom is a nurse at a local clinic. Dad was killed in a car accident about ten years ago. Sister is married to a warehouse manager and stays at home with two kids."

Nothing raised alarm bells there. "Why bring Ellis here if this started at his cabin? Rosa was with her mother. The other two hands were away. The researchers are out in the canyon. No one was there. Somebody injured the guy in his quarters, loaded him into a vehicle and brought him here. Then they either hid his horse or stumbled upon the animal and brought him here to bait Angie. That's a lot of chances to be seen and a lot of evidence to risk leaving behind."

"Maybe the killer didn't realize everyone else was gone? Whoever brought West here may have known Angie was in Vegas and assumed they wouldn't be interrupted. Probably thought they'd have time to do whatever they'd planned, then clean up behind themselves."

"But Angie came home early."

"And they wound up with a bigger problem."

Linc walked up the barn's aisle to the door and looked at the house.

From the dining-room window, Angie was watching the barn.

He turned to the detective. "If they knew her movements, then it's possible it's someone close to her. Someone who has access. Angie is still in danger."

"You cannot tell Jacob about this." Angie shook her hands by her sides as she walked across the living room. So much nervous energy and terror coursed through her that she was tempted to do something she never did.

She was six seconds from strapping on running shoes. If only she could push herself until she dropped and not think of anything else. Until all of this energy poured out of her in sweat and tears. Forget that it was past midnight and the crime-scene unit had just left her property. Again. That someone had been murdered mere feet from her home. That someone had tried to kill her three times. All she wanted was to escape. Maybe if she ran far enough, she'd wake up and this would all be a terrible nightmare.

She stopped in front of the couch and turned toward the kitchen.

It had to be a dream, because Lincoln Tucker was in her home in the dark of night, and that hadn't happened since Jacob's recovery.

There was another vision she didn't need.

Linc stood in the middle of the kitchen, watching her pace. He was so calm she wanted to scream to see if he could be rattled.

How could he be so undisturbed? They'd found a murdered man in her barn. A man who worked for her. This was escalating so fast her head was spinning from the altitude change.

She ripped a hair band from her wrist and pulled her hair into a ponytail, seeking any sort of normal constructive behavior, no matter how minor. "Linc, seriously. You can't tell Jacob."

"He's going to find out."

"He'll come home, and I can't let him. You're here. You're handling it. Right?"

"I'm trying my best." There was something bitter in his tone.

Frowning, Angie sank onto the edge of the oversize chair by the huge stone fireplace. *Right.* Linc was injured. He might even be worse after defending her this afternoon.

Yet here she was worried about her brother's vacation.

This was not her rational self. This was her emotional self. Stomping around the living room. Making demands. Feeling as though her skeleton might crawl out of her skin. She hadn't been this out of control since—

Since the night everything had fallen apart. When the dam holding her fear and anger and pain over her brother's injury had burst under the weight of exhaustion. That night, she'd ranted and raged like this...and the outlet she'd sought had been Lincoln's arms. That night, she'd asked him for everything, and he'd politely extricated himself from her embrace, packed his things in the guest room and left.

The long nights sitting at the kitchen table together had ended. The friendship that had morphed into something more through the trial of Jacob's recovery had died.

He'd simply...vanished. Afterward, Linc helped when he could, but his full-time presence was gone.

She'd resented him at first. Had wanted to hate him. But after she'd come to her senses and later handed over her life to Jesus, she'd realized what she'd asked of the man. How much she'd demanded they both compromise.

All of her frustration and anger had morphed into a burning humiliation over her own actions, one that made her uncomfortable around the man she'd once opened her heart to.

The one who'd rejected her. After all, he could have told her no and stepped away. But no. He'd packed and left. She hadn't been worth staying for.

It was a different kind of leaving than what Owen had done to her, but it was leaving nonetheless. She'd been too much to handle. She'd been too needy and emotional. She'd let him see a vulnerability she hadn't shown to anyone since Owen's betrayal.

Well, that mistake wouldn't happen again.

This was why she focused on what she could do. This was why she made sure there was a job in front of her at all times. Like a shark, if she kept moving from one task to the next, she wouldn't drown.

"Okay." Angie stood and balled her fists, refusing to fidget any longer. It made her look overly emotional and weak. "What do we do now?" She needed a goal. Something to focus on.

Linc didn't leave his spot in the center of the kitchen, but he rested his hands on the island. "Now? You sleep. You have to get some rest. How long has it been?"

She'd fallen asleep sitting on the couch in the dark hours of the previous morning, when the sheriff had been gathering evidence on the porch. It probably hadn't been enough.

But the thought of going upstairs to her room and closing her eyes terrified her more than she wanted to admit. If she turned out the lights and tried to lie still, she might not be able to get the day out of her head. Her brain would construct pictures of the scene in the barn, the one

Lincoln hadn't let her see. She'd think too much about the gunshots and mayhem and death in her own backyard, and she might lose herself completely.

Besides, Linc had no room to talk. "You've had less sleep than me." She planted her feet, not willing to step closer to him but needing to stand her ground. Leaning forward slightly, she crossed her arms and studied his face. Dark circles under his blue eyes spoke of his fatigue. Lines furrowing his forehead told the story of his pain. "You don't look so good."

He puffed his cheeks and blew out a slow breath, almost as though he was leaking out frustration that threatened to explode without a pressure release.

Good. Maybe she needed to get under his skin.

"Angie, I know what this is about." He leveled his gaze at her and seemed to stare straight into her brain.

There was no doubt what he was referring to.

She felt her nostrils flare, but she wasn't sure if the response was anger or shock. Surely he wasn't going to bring up their past. Not now. Not with the coroner still en route from her ranch to the medical examiner's office. Not with crime-scene tape around her barn. Not with fresh bruises on her body and soul.

Linc took a deep breath and stared at the beams in the ceiling. "I'm sorry."

The soft words slammed into her chest and rocked her off her feet. It wasn't at all what she'd expected. She sat hard in the chair. "Sorry?" She hadn't wanted to engage in this discussion, so why was she egging him on?

Because she needed to know what had happened. And because talking about their past was preferable to wondering if she had a future.

"I left you alone to care for Jacob on your own, at least part of the time. I can't explain why. It's… I didn't handle your hurts very well." He shook his head, the pain in his face deepening. "I'm sorry, and I feel like if I'm going to be staying here for a few days you need to know."

He was apologizing to her? Yeah, he'd trashed her heart and definitely needed to address that, so she was grateful, but… "I started it."

"There was a lot going on then. You were dealing with too many things." Linc's shoulders tightened as though he was gripping the edge of the counter with all of his strength. "You're dealing with a lot now. I need you to know I'm here for you until this is resolved. I'm not going anywhere. I've made sure to be assigned as the liaison between the sheriff and the park service."

I'm here for you. The words fell like gentle rain on dry ground. Tears she hadn't known were waiting at the gate pressed against her eyes.

Her father had died. Owen had decimated her heart. Linc had left her.

Yet, it was as though God was whispering to her heart through Lincoln's words. *I'm here for you.*

"Thank you." Maybe she was talking to Linc. Maybe she was praying out loud. She wasn't really sure, but the sense of peace that overtook her stilled the restlessness in her body and spirit.

Still, she couldn't bring herself to address her own actions on the night he'd walked out of the house. Who she'd been then was so much different than who she was now. She needed some time to adjust before she could make her own apologies.

She settled in and crossed her legs, watching Lincoln, needing to say something. Needing, despite the peace inside of her heart, to do something. "What comes next? I can't stay in the house forever, hiding from whoever is after me." The thought of herself as a target still sent a shudder through her.

Linc hesitated, then rounded the counter and sat on the end of the couch farthest from her. "I want to talk to the protestors. Detectives Blankenship and Majenty spoke to them before we found—" He cleared his throat. "I want to talk to them myself. I'd like for you to come with me."

"Why?"

"To see if you recognize anyone. To look at build, at eyes, to listen to voices, to—"

"He never said anything." Other than the muttered curses whenever Linc had intervened, her attacker had been silent both times.

A trait that made him twice as terrifying.

"I think the answer lies with the protestors. They've escalated from vandalism. Maybe someone thinks, with you out of the way, they'll get what they want."

"But what about Ellis?" Why not kill her, if they wanted her gone? Lincoln's theory held water, but there were leaks in the bucket.

"Ellis could be unrelated. Look, I could be totally barking up the wrong tree, but we need to at least eliminate the possibility someone outside of your gate has decided to move outside of the law."

Not only outside of the law, but also squarely into murder.

Chapter Seven

A soft scraping sound reached into Lincoln's subconscious and jerked him awake. He sat straight, dragging numb fingers down his face as he tried to orient himself. His upper back and neck throbbed pain straight into the top of his skull, probably from the way he'd dropped off with his head awkwardly positioned on the sofa.

How had he fallen asleep? Sure, the house alarm was on, so the door chimes would alert him if someone entered, but he'd never fully trusted technology to do the job a vigilant and trained human should do. He'd only sat down for a minute to talk to Angie, then—

The sound came again, softly.

Linc bit back a chuckle and settled in the sofa, as another soft snore drifted from Angie's chair.

It seemed she'd succumbed to sleep as well, her head resting on the back of the oversize chair. He ought to wake her so she wouldn't have a serious pain in her neck, but it was probably too late.

It was definitely too late for him. Gently, he stretched his neck from one side to the other, hoping to alleviate some of the pain.

Who was he kidding? It never really went away. After his run-in with Angie's attacker the day before, there was no way he'd find relief anytime soon. He hated weakness. Hated himself for the momentary lapse in attention that had led to his downfall. If he could have that moment back...

He glanced at Angie, then away. If he could have a lot of moments back, he'd do them so differently.

The windows glowed with morning light, indicating he'd slept for several hours. Sure enough, a glance at his watch showed it was nearly six in the morning.

Across the room, Angie shifted and breathed more quietly, but she didn't wake. It was no surprise. She had to be exhausted after all she'd endured since arriving home from Las Vegas. Losing the grant would have been enough to deal with. But two attacks, a shooting, a murder... No one was superhuman enough to overcome all of that stress quickly, no matter how much Angie wanted to pretend she was okay.

It was no wonder she'd come close to cracking the night before. As she'd paced and shaken her hands, Linc had been taken back several years to the night she'd finally fallen apart during Jacob's recovery. There were times in that season when he'd wondered how much emotion she could hold in before she exploded, and it had taken longer than he'd have ever imagined. The night she'd succumbed to grief and exhaustion, the same caged-animal behavior she'd exhibited last night had risen to the surface, as though the energy pent up inside of her would destroy her if it didn't find release.

Angie didn't like to cry in front of anyone. She didn't like to show weakness. She valued control.

That was something Linc could appreciate.

Still, her behavior the previous night had been more than he could bear. The first time he'd witnessed it, that restless need to move had driven her into his arms, seeking an outlet that wouldn't have been good for either one of them.

Frankly, it had driven him into hers. He could have easily let her lead the way in taking things too far. If he was being totally honest, he had wanted to allow it more than anything in the world.

The alarm bells in his brain had stopped him. The force of his own emotions had shocked him into backing away from her, maybe too abruptly.

For him, that moment hadn't been a simple need to connect in any way that would cover the pain. Something around his heart had snapped and a totally new thing had rushed in through the gaps.

No, he'd realized their late-night talks and their teaming up to help her brother through physical therapy and long, painful days and nights had created a bond between them, one like he'd never felt with another person, not with his army buddies and certainly not with any other woman he'd ever met.

What he'd felt for Angie had been completely different. Whatever had happened between them in those long weeks had made him want something with her that he'd never wanted with another person.

He had realized with a mind-shattering clarity he was falling in love with her.

Not only would his respect for her never let them push across physical boundaries, but his sense of self-preservation also wouldn't let him cross the emotional line.

Overwhelmed by the strain of caring for Jacob and with his heart's new realizations, he'd practically bolted from her embrace, from where he was right now, on this couch.

He could almost see himself standing in the center of this very room, dragging his hands through his hair where her fingers had been, stuttering and stumbling over his words in an effort to explain his actions without explaining himself.

In the end, he'd simply walked away, knowing if he stayed, he'd find himself leading the way down a path they didn't need to follow. He'd packed his bags and fled the house like she was chasing him with a knife.

Maybe she had been, metaphorically, because the next few months had left him feeling as though someone had sliced open his chest and left him to bleed out. He couldn't be alone with her. Couldn't bear to be in the same room with her. Every time he was, he wanted to say things he shouldn't—not to his best friend's sister. Not when their lives were upside down.

He'd taken the coward's way out and offered to "help" by only coming by during the night, when Angie rested. When her mother had arrived, he'd only visited when Angie wasn't home.

Once Jacob was well and was working with him at the NPS, he'd stopped visiting the ranch at all.

It was too much.

He'd missed everything about Angie, and it had taken months for him to convince his heart she'd be better off with someone who wanted a family and a future. He liked his job and his bachelor life, with no one else to worry about, no matter what his heart had tried to tell him.

Now, as she slept, the worry lines that had etched her forehead the day before relaxed. He hadn't realized how deeply they were ingrained until this moment of peace.

Linc looked away. He shouldn't be noticing anything. Not her serenity. Not the way her dark blond hair had straggled out of the ponytail she'd nervously pulled the night before. Not the way everything about her reminded him of what might have been if he hadn't been a coward.

Now he was no longer a coward. He was a broken man. Even his team was moving on without him, possibly catching a case he still knew nothing about. The last thing he wanted was to burden someone, and he was headed that way at breakneck speed. With this injury—

Linc jerked his head to one side as if he could throw off the thoughts, but it drove home the fact that every little movement led to pain.

He stood quietly and walked into the kitchen. This day needed to begin. He needed to be alert if he was going to watch out for Angie.

In the kitchen, he slipped the carafe from the coffee maker and let the water run slowly to avoid waking Angie. Out the window over the sink, the sky was lightening rapidly, a riot of pinks and oranges fading into a blue washed by the previous day's rain.

If only he could wash away the memory of Ellis West's battered body.

He shook his head again, trying to clear it.

A soft sound from the living area told him he hadn't been successful in his attempts at silence. "What time is it?"

When he turned away from the sink, he saw Angie standing at the bar. She'd pulled the band from her hair so it flowed past her shoulders in chaotic, sleep-tossed waves. An air of restful sleep seemed to cling to her.

He turned away. "Where's your coffee?" The

words were gruff and clipped. He really didn't need to see her newly awake. It made him start thinking of what it might be like if this was their normal kind of morning, if they shared coffee and conversation on a regular basis as they started their days together.

Angie walked into the kitchen, securing her ponytail, and grabbed a canister from the counter near the coffee maker. She handed it to him then went to sit at the island, seeming content to let him work. "Did you sleep?"

"I did." Linc measured out the coffee, careful not to look at her.

"Good. You needed it more than I did. How's your back?" She sounded genuinely concerned.

"Fine." He clipped that word, too. The sooner he got food into him, the sooner he could down some ibuprofen and hopefully make that true. In the army, he used to choke down those things dry, on an empty stomach. Age and stomach pain had cured him of that habit.

There was a long stretch of silence, broken by what sounded like Angie drumming her fingers on the counter. Finally, she sniffed. "What happens now?"

"With?" He capped the canister and slid it

across the counter, then went to the fridge. There was zero desire in him to talk about what came next with his injury, especially since he didn't have any answers. He pulled open the fridge and grabbed the eggs. "Hungry?"

"Not really, but I'll eat whatever you make. There's bacon in the deli drawer if you want some." The light tapping sound continued. "What happens now with the—the…" The words trailed into nothing.

Bumping the fridge door to close it, Linc turned and looked at her. She was staring in the direction of the barn. *The murder.*

He needed to get out of his own stupid head. His little rebound into past feelings was trivial compared to what Angie was dealing with. *This is not about you, Tucker.*

"How much detail do you want?" He set the bacon and eggs on the counter with some cheese from the deli drawer. Was she asking for details about how the coroner would proceed with autopsies? About interviews and testing and all of the minutiae that went with a homicide investigation?

"I mostly want to know what's next for me. You can handle the stuff I don't want to know about." She shredded the edge of a receipt he'd noticed on the counter earlier.

She needed a plan, some direction. That much, he could give her. "Like I said, I want to talk to the protestors, and I'd like you to go with me. Maybe you—"

Her phone vibrated on the counter and she reached for it, frowning at the screen. "It's the contractor. He's on his way over."

"Why?"

"Because he has a job to do." The snap in her words betrayed her anxiety.

"Not today. Have him come straight to the house so you can talk to him, and I'll see if I can get him cleared to work tomorrow. I think the crime-scene unit is finished there."

Unless this continued to escalate.

He couldn't allow that, because if this went any further, then Angie might be the next victim of a killer.

She was tired of being bossed around. Tired of being told what she could do and where she could go on her own property. In the wake of Ellis's death, it was necessary, she understood. Still, the restrictions served to drive the horror of the situation deeper into her mind when all she wanted to do was make it all stop. If she didn't move forward, fear and grief would destroy her.

She texted Carter, then headed for the door to meet him when he pulled in.

Lincoln followed. "You're not meeting anyone alone."

With a huff, she stopped in the middle of the living room. This used to be her safe place, but now Linc was everywhere she looked. With everything else happening, having him in the house felt like the most dangerous threat of all. "It's my contractor, not the Big Bad Wolf."

"Wolves wear sheep's clothing."

She blew out another puff of frustration. "I've met with him alone dozens of times. He and his crew have been working on the property for weeks. They built the original dorm and lab a couple of years ago. I'm pretty sure if he wanted to drag me away, he'd have done it already. He's had more than his share of chances."

Linc followed her onto the porch and stood to the side as Carter Holbert pulled up in his white pickup with *Holbert Construction* splashed across the side in shades of red and orange. Dressed in jeans and a white button-down with the company logo over the right pocket, he was already talking when he stepped out of the truck. Despite the salt-and-pepper in his hair, Carter looked younger than his sixty-plus years. "I figured you'd want to meet down at the ranch." Slamming the truck door behind him, he squinted toward the porch steps, where Angie waited. "Sorry about yesterday. Half of my crew is out with the flu and without Isla…" He cleared his throat, looking pained. "We'd planned to get out here bright and early to get some excavating done, but the park service called. Had an inspector at the Desert View Watchtower yesterday who wasn't a fan of the fencing we put up to keep the public out of the construction zone."

"I had to take care of some things here." She really didn't want to go into detail about her woes. "Has there been any news about Isla?"

The lines in Carter's forehead deepened. "No. I talked to some detectives right after she disappeared, but I haven't heard anything since." Isla had worked for Carter for years, keeping his office running in top condition. She'd always been friendly, though she'd seemed distracted in the weeks leading to her disappearance.

It clearly pained Carter to talk about her, so Angie moved on. "I'm sure restoring a historic structure comes with its own set of headaches." Built in the 1930s, and now housing a gift shop on the ground floor, the tower was a landmark on the South Rim. Conservationists had been working floor-by-floor to preserve the structure. Carter's company had been called in to restore the exterior. The entire site was closed to tourists, and Carter had been under pressure to finish quickly. It had caused multiple delays to the work on the ranch, but now that she was dealing with a money crunch, the delays didn't make her quite so antsy.

Carter walked to the porch and rested one foot on the bottom step. He glanced over at Lincoln. "Carter Holbert." He squinted. "Have we met before?"

"No. I'm a friend of the Garcia family. Lincoln Tucker."

Carter nodded slowly. "Good to meet you." He turned to Angie. "I can get my crew out this afternoon. I need to bring in a few big machines to dig a couple of feet down. You've got enough topsoil here before you hit rock that we can do a crawl space instead of elevating the structure on piers like some of the cabins were built. That'll give you easier access to the plumbing and electrical and give you flexibility for future expansion."

From the quotes, it would also cost more. It was time to swallow her pride and face the facts. "We might need to press Pause for a bit." Not because of Ellis's murder, either.

"Why? I know you're ready to get moving on this next phase." Carter had done all of her renovations and new construction. He knew what the project meant to her. He'd also gone to school with her father. They'd played football together and had been friends until her father's death from cancer while Angie was in college. Ellis's father, Javi, had been killed in a car accident a short time later.

The idea of going into details made her stomach squeeze, so she took the easy route. "We've had a few incidents on the property." Linc hadn't told her how much she could say, so she kept it to a minimum. "Coconino County is investigating and they want some space while they look for evidence."

"They've shut down the job site?"

Linc spoke from behind her. "The construction site isn't involved, but we'd still like to keep traffic to a minimum."

Carter nodded slowly. "I'll hold my crew

until you say the word, but is it okay if I head over and look around? I told Mac I'd help dig the trenches for his plumbing. His crew's got the same flu bug that's decimated mine."

"Tomorrow." Linc walked up beside Angie and looked down at Carter. "I'm sure they'll be cleared out by then."

One eyebrow arched, Carter lifted a half smile. There was no telling what he thought was going on between Linc and Angie. "Gotcha. I'll head over to the tower, tell my guys to keep on keepin' on there. With the crew reduced, it'll help not to split them." He dipped his chin and headed for the truck. "Call me when you're ready."

Angie chewed her lower lip. She should be honest about her financial situation, but she didn't want to do it in front of Linc. She looked over at him. "Stay here."

She jogged down the steps and caught up with Carter. "Hey." She kept her voice low and prayed he'd understand her plight.

Carter looked over her shoulder toward the house, then lowered his voice. "You okay? You look a little stressed. Is it…him? You need help?"

The man had no idea, but it wasn't whatever Carter suspected. "No. It's money." Carter would probably drop the project, which meant she'd have to start over getting bids and signing contracts. They were already behind schedule, and with the ranch in the center of a criminal investigation, this could be the end of her dream. She charged ahead. "I lost out on a grant I was counting on. I need to move some things around before I can pay you."

"I see." Carter nodded. He scrubbed his hand along his chin and stared toward the canyon. "Angie, we'll get this done, okay? You've always been good with paying, and I'll work with what your deposit covered until I run out. We'll excavate the site, even if I have to do the digging myself."

His kindness might be what broke her. "Thanks, Carter." He gave her hand a quick squeeze. He stared toward the ranch for a long time, then turned his face toward the sky as though he was reading something in the cirrus clouds that wisped the big blue. "I believe in what you're doing here. My great-grandmother was Hopi, and I want to see that heritage taken care of."

"I know. I can dig into my savings and pay you, which is likely what I'll do, but it leaves me nothing for a rainy day. I was counting on that grant." She'd been so certain.

Carter chuckled softly. "Got a little cocky, did ya?"

Her head jerked back and she looked over her shoulder to see if Linc was listening. He was texting on his phone, pretending not to watch. "I... What?"

"I'm sorry," Carter said quickly, as though speed could erase his original thought. "We've worked together and I knew your dad and all, but not well enough to say that to you." He cleared his throat as he winced. "Sorry."

She'd ignore his mild criticism, though it gnawed at something at the back of her neck. "It's okay."

"What if...? What if I bought the ranch from you?" Before the shock fully registered, he hurried on. "I'll keep you on as a manager, and Rosa, too. And I'll only buy the ranch land, not the land around the house. I've got some saved. Business has been good, and it'll be a tax write-off, if—"

She gasped. "Carter." The pressure from too many decisions and the voices of too many people saying she needed to give up her home exploded in her chest. "The ranch isn't for sale.

Not to you. Not to the government. Not to the protestors outside my gate. Not. For. Sale."

He nodded slowly, his expression sympathetic. "I'm sorry. That was a big jump. A lot of what I've said today has been out of line."

"It's okay. I shouldn't have snapped. There's too much going on here."

"Oh. Yeah. I... I wasn't going to say anything, but I ran into the sheriff when I was getting coffee at Misty's. He said they found Ellis West. I'm sorry to hear that."

"Me, too."

"Listen, Angie, you be safe. There's a lot of weird things going on around the area lately. I've heard rumblings about a serial killer or something and—"

"A what?" Angie straightened. A serial killer? Had that been who killed Ellis?

Who was after her?

Was Linc hiding something? "Carter, I have to get moving. Come by anytime after tomorrow morning to work. You've got a gate code— just give me a heads-up." She walked him to the truck and watched as he drove away.

Behind her, the door closed. She stood a long time, staring at the land her family had owned for over a century. Why did everyone suddenly want her to give it up? *God, are You telling everyone else something and not me?*

The response was silence. She went inside to what might be another uncomfortable encounter. Life was full of discomfort and danger.

It was easier to focus on discomfort.

When she walked into the house, Linc was setting plates on the island, but even his bacon, egg and cheese sandwiches couldn't distract her. "A serial killer? There's a *serial killer* out there?"

He froze, holding a plate an inch from the counter. "Where did you hear that?" There was genuine shock on his face. "Is that what the rumor mill has spun up?"

She related Carter's comments, leaving out his offer to buy the ranch. She still hadn't decided if she was shocked, angry or confused.

The plate settled onto the granite counter with a thunk as Linc shook his head. "Not that I know of, but I'll make some calls. It's possible my team knows something and they haven't told…" His expression hardened, and he turned toward the fridge. "Juice?"

Her agitation dropped a few levels. Linc should be with his team, not babysitting her and making her breakfast. If they were truly keeping something from him, that would wound him more than she could imagine.

Angie was grateful for his protective presence, but her gratitude was tinged with guilt. There was nothing she could say to help ease his hurt and frustration. She opted for gratitude. "Thanks for breakfast."

"Yep." He didn't turn as he poured juice. "Eat. We have some protestors to talk to."

His unspoken words hung in the air. *And a killer to find.*

Chapter Eight

That case Thomas had mentioned in passing... If rumors of a serial killer were flying, then there had to be more to it than Thomas had hinted at.

Linc lifted his foot from the gas pedal and let his truck slow as he neared the gate. Was his team purposely keeping things from him? Or had they simply moved forward without his unnecessary weight?

Not needed. Not wanted. Useless.

He gripped the wheel tighter, dragging his focus to the present. Half a dozen protestors had arrived already. He needed to shove aside his little pity party. Angie's life might depend on it.

Another vehicle approached, probably more people planning to make their desires for Angie's land known.

What did this crew do for a living? Who had time to sit all day long, even for something they believed in? He couldn't remember being still for a moment in his life, at least not after elementary school. He'd worked from the time he was old enough to get a job, had signed up for the army at eighteen and had moved straight from there to the National Park Service. If he wasn't working, what good was he? The only time off he'd ever taken had been to help Jacob recover.

Look where that had landed him.

He hardly dared to look at Angie. *Focus*.

She'd come into the house with fire in her eyes, and it wasn't about the idea of a serial killer on the loose. Whatever Carter had said had upset her, and she wasn't inclined to talk about it.

Interesting.

Linc shifted the truck into Park and killed the engine as the protestors grabbed signs and moved to the sides of the road, preparing for him to drive through their miniature gauntlet.

Surprise, folks. He was staying firmly on his side of the gate.

He studied the crowd. "Didn't you give me a woman's name the other day?" There were no women in the group, just men who appeared to be in their twenties.

"Monica Huerta. She works part-time as a manager at an apartment complex, so she's only here some of the time."

"You're pretty familiar with the protestors?"

Angie shrugged, seeming distracted by the small knot of people. It had to be disconcerting to be the object of an organized campaign bent on misunderstanding her motives. "I know Monica and maybe one or two others by sight. Most are from out of town. They rotate through on a schedule, it seems."

So there were a lot of strangers involved, people unknown to local law enforcement. He'd see about gathering names and running a few federal checks. With the violence on the ranch and the rumors of a killer on the loose, the idea of out-of-towners bent on causing trouble made him antsy.

Reaching for the door handle, Linc watched Angie. "Anybody look familiar?"

Angie chewed her lower lip, a sure sign she was stressed, probably at the idea her attacker could be staring through the truck windows even now. Finally, she shook her head. "No, but he was wearing heavier clothes both times. It all moved so fast…" Her hand fluttered then dropped into her lap. "It could have been anybody."

"I want you to stay in the truck, okay?" Before she could protest, he charged on. "Watch these guys unless I wave you over. I want to see how they react to your presence. See if anybody acts strange when I start talking, or if anyone is overly interested in you and not paying attention to me. Body language says a lot, and you can be my eyes while I'm speaking with individuals." When he was actively working with the team, this was a routine he and Jacob had pulled off naturally. Given Jacob was out of the country, and Linc was currently separated from his team, he would have to improvise.

He shook it off. There were bigger things at play than what his guys were doing without him.

The group of men eyed Linc warily as he approached, but they didn't retreat. Three of them stood quietly along both sides of the road.

When he reached the gate, the approaching car parked by two others in the shade near a stand of trees. Three more men got out, and with curious glances at Linc, they joined the rest of the group, taking signs that were handed to them. All of them watched silently, letting their placards speak for them.

Stop Destroying the Land!

The Canyon Belongs to Everyone!
No More Tourists!

He bit back a sardonic smile. That last one was ironic, given what Angie had said about several of the protestors being from out of state.

The driver of the car exited the vehicle and watched Linc closely, his posture rigid.

Linc kept a careful eye on him.

The guy knew he was under scrutiny. He seemed to deliberately relax as he shut the car door and approached, tossing his keys repeatedly. He walked past the other men, saying hi and smiling as though this was a soiree at the country club. He stopped at the center of the gate and extended his hand toward Linc, who was a few feet away. "Hi. Riley Jeffries."

This guy was slimy. Everything about his demeanor said he believed he ran the show. This was his club and he was the consummate host. *Disgusting.*

Linc ignored the extended hand as he eyed Riley, from his artfully mussed dark hair to his hiking boots. He was wearing gray cargo pants and a green athletic shirt, as though he was about to go hiking in the canyon. Given the extreme differences between Riley's outfit and the clothing of the man who had attacked

Angie, there was no way to tell if they were one and the same. The build was similar, but the hooded sweatshirt had distorted true height and weight.

Linc tapped the badge hanging around his neck. "Special Agent Lincoln Tucker, National Park Service Investigative Services."

"Is that an actual thing?" The veiled derision in Riley's voice was acidic.

Lincoln responded, not with fake sugar, but with the law-enforcement equivalent. Humor. "Yeah, we're hoping for our own television show any day now."

The flicker on Riley's face said he wasn't sure whether Linc was being sincere or sarcastic.

Good—this guy needed to be off balance.

He recovered quickly. "Well, man, how can I help you?"

It took a lot of training to stay calm in the face of overwhelming arrogance. Personal feelings couldn't affect Linc's investigative instincts, no matter how much this guy rubbed him the wrong way. "I know the deputies talked to you yesterday, but I wanted to get some clarification, talk to you guys myself." He propped an elbow on the fence and leaned as though they were two guys chatting about the weather. It was taking everything he had not to pull the tough-cop card and put this guy in his place, but that would wound Riley's pride and shut him down. "How late were you all out here yesterday?"

Riley studied the sky as if he could calculate time and date by the position of the sun. More likely, he was buying time. "Not sure what time it was, but when the storm started blowing, we booked. Definitely don't want anyone getting struck by lightning for the cause."

"And what's the cause?"

"You don't know?" Riley arched an eyebrow, and he gestured toward the men behind him, who'd dispersed to the camping chairs in the shade of trees near the cars. "We don't believe in legacy inholdings in the national parks, and we particularly don't agree with continued development on those lands. Angie Garcia and Fairweather Ranch are planning to expand the tourist trade here. Her family has a history of overgrazing the land and running a dude ranch that brought in way too many careless tourists. All of that leads to erosion and endangers the canyon. We want to keep the canyon pristine for future generations and open for everyone to enjoy. No one should own part of our country's natural heritage."

Despite his best efforts, Linc's jaw tightened. Aside from the opinions on inholdings, everything Riley said he wanted fit with what Angie was doing. These guys really were clueless.

Either Riley wasn't being entirely forthcoming, or somebody else was pulling the strings of this protest. They had to know the truth about Angie's plans. She'd publicized everything, had held public fundraisers, and her grant nomination had made the local news.

Yet Riley seemed ignorant.

"I'm with you on keeping public land public." And with returning native lands to tribes, but not taking private land from its owners. Seeming to agree with Riley might open the guy up. "So how did you learn about the new development on the Garcia ranch?"

For a split second, Riley froze, almost as though he'd entered suspended animation. As quick as it happened, his arrogance settled around him again. "It's not like she's kept it a secret. Everyone around town knows."

So he *had* seen the news about what Angie was doing. Riley was either lying about how he'd found out, or he was lying about his understanding of what Angie was working to build.

Linc was pretty sure he was never going to be a fan of Riley Jeffries.

"Anything else?" Riley glanced over his shoulder at his group. "We're due a quick meeting. Want to go over the rules. With the recent happenings on the ranch, I want to make sure our people know trespassing won't be tolerated. And before you ask, I assured the sheriff's detectives the two protestors who did the previous damage have been handled. We turned their names over to the sheriff, and they're no longer welcome with us."

The words weren't spoken with any sort of compassion for Angie. In fact, the speech had the air of a rehearsal.

When Linc had a few minutes, he'd call Detective Blankenship and see if she'd gotten the same verbiage. It was likely she had. "I'm going to need those names."

"You can't ask the sheriff?"

"You're right here in front of me. Lot easier for you to tell me." Riley offered two names, and Linc jotted them down, then jerked his chin toward the men in the chairs. "I want to talk to the rest of the group."

With a bored sigh, Riley shook his head. "I told you. We're about to—"

Linc whistled shrilly. This was getting old and going nowhere. He held up his badge for the protestors to see and waved them closer.

Riley's face was a thundercloud. Gone was the arrogance and condescension. Linc had usurped his authority, and he wasn't happy about it.

Yeah, Riley Jeffries was one to keep an eye on. On the surface, he didn't seem the type to kidnap a woman or beat a man to death, but evil came in all shapes and sizes.

The small group of men gathered around the gate, close enough for Angie to see. None of them paid any attention to the truck, even after Linc turned and made a point of looking in her direction. He asked a few generic questions, then let them go. He could get the rest of what he needed from the sheriff's office, and he wanted to maintain some goodwill in case he had more to ask these guys later.

As he walked to the truck, he replayed the conversation in his head, searching for answers.

That conversation had brought him no closer to finding Ellis West's killer or Angie's attacker, but it had made one thing very clear... The danger to Angie came from multiple angles, and he'd have to be vigilant if he wanted to keep her safe.

He was missing something. The conversation with Riley Jeffries had left him feeling like he was juggling and was about to drop all of the balls. The attacks, the shooting, the protestors, the murder, the mysterious mention of a case but no word from his team...

While Angie talked with Rosa in the house for their morning meeting, Linc had headed for the barn, promising to feed and water Chance while he was there. He needed some time alone to put his thoughts in order, and he certainly thought more clearly when Angie wasn't in the room.

The horse had been reluctant to trust Linc at first, standing at the back corner of the stall when Linc entered. Chance wasn't combative or afraid, just wary. After realizing Linc was the key to food and fresh water, though, the horse warmed up considerably.

When Linc set the bucket of water on the floor, a warm weight rested on his shoulder. A slightly damp puff blew across his ear.

So Chance was a snuggler? He hadn't seen that coming.

Linc allowed himself a smile as he scratched the horse's muzzle. "You lonely out here, buddy?"

Chance huffed as though he recognized that Linc understood.

"Yeah, you're used to a barn full of other horses who work like you do." Though other things had taken precedence, they should probably move him back to the main ranch barn. The horse likely also missed his rider. While Chance belonged to Fairweather Ranch, Ellis had been the one he'd bonded with, according to Rosa and one of the other ranch hands Linc had spoken to the day before. It was an accepted fact around the property that Chance and Ellis were buddies.

Given how he'd been found saddled and tied to the fence, there was no telling where he'd been between the time of Ellis's disappearance and the attack on Angie. Chance's reappearance near the barn brought up more questions.

Ducking his shoulder slightly, Linc turned and faced the horse, scratching his neck as he searched the animal's eyes. "What did you see out there? Where were you for an entire day?

And who tied you to the fence?" If only the horse could answer. Had the attacker simply stumbled upon Chance on the property and seen an opportunity to draw out Angie? Or had he taken the horse at the same time as Ellis and held him somewhere, hoping to use the animal to get to Angie?

Yeah, if this animal could talk, they could probably apprehend their killer and close this case by nightfall. "Too bad you never learned English, huh?"

Linc's phone buzzed in his pocket.

Chance tossed his head and backed away at the slight sound, then nudged Linc out of the way and started slurping water.

Guess that conversation was over.

With one more pat to the horse's neck, Linc left the stall and latched it, then checked the screen before answering. "Thomas." He walked across the aisle and leaned against the same stall door he'd used to hold himself up the day before. At least now his pain level had dropped to a three so he could function. "Thanks for calling me so quickly." He'd texted a few minutes earlier, knowing Thomas would call when he was free.

"I'm headed to a possible crime scene, and

thought I'd give you an update while I'm on the road."

Linc's eyes shut tight. If he wasn't sidelined now, he'd be headed out, too, tracking down evidence and searching for answers with his team by his side. "What's happening?" His throat was tight, and the words squeezed out with a measure of pain.

"Remains in the woods near Widforss Trail."

"New or old?" Deadly things happened in the canyon. As peaceful and beautiful as it was, danger lurked, both from the natural world and from men plotting evil. Nature often revealed the dead who'd passed centuries earlier alongside the ones who'd passed on more recently. If his team had been called in, the probability was high it was a recent death.

"I won't know how recent until I get there." The click of a turn signal filled the brief silence. "You can't be calling about that because I just hit the road. You need to brainstorm about the West homicide?"

That wasn't his original intention, but bouncing things off Thomas might help untangle the spaghetti in his head. "It's the horse."

"Tell me the horse isn't hurt." Thomas's voice

took on an edge he reserved for people who harmed animals and children.

While death and pain were always tragic, when it came to animals and kids, hearts were especially soft. "Chance is fine, but he's missing his rider." He ran down his brief set of questions, hoping Thomas would see something he didn't.

Silence rode the line as Thomas drove. The man was quieter than Linc and Jacob—friendly, but fond of his personal space and protective of his time off-duty with his wife and toddler daughter. He thought deeply and tended to see angles Linc's overthinking and Jacob's rush to action missed.

Finally, Thomas spoke. "If he was still saddled, I'm inclined to believe the bad guy found him wandering and took a chance. I saw you sent his tack in for printing and DNA testing, so maybe something will come from that."

"I'm not sure the horse was wandering. He's lived on Fairweather for years and has only been stabled in the ranch barn."

"So why was he by the house instead of heading for his own stall?" Thomas sighed. "And where was he all day? Better yet…you found West's phone near the barn, correct?"

Thomas's train of thought barreled right

through Linc's suspicions. "If Ellis had returned to the ranch, he'd have either stabled his horse or tied him near the cabin. Chance was in neither place."

"You've got an odd one on your hands."

Linc dragged his hand down his face. He needed a whiteboard or a giant piece of paper to start connecting all of his thoughts. "Keep thinking. Maybe something will trigger in that brain of yours."

"Or yours."

True. It was wild how often his subconscious worked through things when he wasn't even trying.

"So was that the only reason you called?" The question was weighted with something hard to read.

Guilt? Linc didn't want to sound like he was whining, but he did want to know what was going on with his team. "You mentioned a case yesterday. I was following up. And then, yeah, I had another question."

"What's your question and then I'll tell you about the case. Yours is probably shorter than mine."

"Doubtful." Still, Linc quickly outlined who Carter was and what he'd said.

"Where would he get the idea there's a serial killer out there? Is that something we're tracking?" Even though Linc wasn't in the field, he was still the team leader, even if Thomas was acting in his place. He should be read in on everything. That he wasn't was painful.

"Interesting."

Linc switched the phone to his left ear. What was Thomas putting down that he wasn't picking up?

"The FBI reached out to us early yesterday. Seems a woman went missing a couple of weeks ago, and she works for Carter Holbert."

So that was what Angie had been asking about when she mentioned a woman's name. "Isla or something?"

"Isla Blake."

"When were you planning to tell me?" There was a kicked-dog bite to the words. His team was shutting him out, realizing his powerlessness to do anything of value for them. Gripping the phone tighter, he tried to ignore the pain of tension piercing his back.

"Hold your literal horses, Tucker." The low hum over the line died away. Thomas had likely reached his destination and shut off the engine of his park-service SUV. "I don't know yet if anything is going on, and the FBI just reached out. They're concerned a serial killer has gone active again."

"Which one?" Arizona had been home to several serial killers, as had multiple national parks across the nation. Unsolved murders and missing persons were plentiful around the Grand Canyon, but none had come across the wire to him lately.

"About a decade ago, there was a rash of seven disappearances around this area. No bodies were found, but it's highly likely, and assumed, that the women are dead."

"I remember that. Seven women vanished, no linking characteristics to them, ranging in ages from seventeen to forty-eight. Differing heights, hair colors, body types, locations—"

"Yep. The only connecting factor was they were all talking to a man online, though he could never be traced because he used the browser on a different burner phone with each of them in order to talk to them online. All drew money from their bank accounts at ATMs, and cameras showed them under some duress as they did, though no one was seen with them. They disappeared with any papers that could identify them, from birth certificates to social-security cards. One woman, Claire Foley, even took hers out of a safe-deposit box a couple of days before she disappeared."

"I remember. About a week after they vanished, their families received their driver's licenses sealed in plastic bags and covered in their blood."

Thomas exhaled loudly. "Yep."

"The FBI thinks Isla Blake was taken by this guy who hasn't made a move in a decade?"

"Isla Blake didn't show up for work after going on a date with a guy she met online. Last sign of movement from her was the use of her ATM card around midnight, at an isolated convenience store outside Williams. FBI is working on getting the footage. Two days ago, her driver's license showed up at the house, covered in her blood. It was slow to get there because the zip code was obscured. Mohave County recognized the MO and contacted the FBI, who had Isla's sister check her files at home. Both her birth certificate and her social-security card are gone."

Linc closed his eyes and exhaled slowly. "Wow."

"It gets worse. The FBI got a call yesterday from the police chief in Williams. A little over a week ago, a twenty-nine-year-old woman disappeared after meeting a guy online—ATM, missing papers and all."

"That's too specific to be coincidence." So a decade later, a killer had returned? What if he'd come after Angie?

But no, nothing about the attacks on Angie or about Ellis West's murder fit the profile.

"These remains we're checking out with the FBI could be one of those two women. We also have a couple of recent missing hikers, so I don't know what to add until I get there."

"I assume Carter Holbert was questioned and cleared?"

"He was. He had an alibi for his missing office manager, and nothing points to him."

At least he had a little bit of good news. "Who's the other missing woman?" His phone buzzed, and he glanced at the screen. While the number wasn't one saved in his phone, he recognized it from earlier in the day. Now was the worst possible time, but he couldn't leave the call unanswered. "Hang on. I have to take another call, but keep me posted."

"You, too. Let me know if you need anything. We'll do what we can."

He was sure they'd help where they could, but his team was moving forward without him.

And it was all because of phone calls like the one he was about to take—the one that could change his life forever.

Chapter Nine

She'd never felt so exposed in her life.

Angie glanced around the radiology waiting room at Flagstaff Medical Center and tried not to shrink.

She was not a person who shrank.

They'd called Linc back for his MRI nearly an hour earlier, after a whirlwind rush to make the ninety-minute drive to Flagstaff. He'd received the call about a cancellation and had rushed into the house like a tornado, scaring her half to death before she figured out why he was in such an agitated state.

The last thing she'd wanted to do was leave the ranch to make the trip to Flagstaff. She'd argued.

He'd countered.

She'd finally given in. No amount of reminding him she knew how to protect herself, or that Rosa and two other ranch hands were nearby, could dissuade him. *Look what's happened already with everyone around. You think it's going to get better?*

Clearly, he didn't believe it would. He'd been hypervigilant the entire drive, fidgety even for Linc.

Well, she was fidgety, too. No matter what games she played or books she opened on her phone, she couldn't escape the feeling someone was watching her.

She scanned the room, but no one seemed to be paying her any undue attention. A handful of people were waiting in the small space, and most were absorbed in their phones or in quiet conversations with companions.

Well, she couldn't sit still any longer.

Angie stood and walked to the entrance of the waiting room, then stepped into the hall, running her hands down the seams of her jeans. The gesture made her look as antsy as she felt, but she couldn't stop herself.

Medical facilities set her teeth on edge. The smells. The sounds. Even though Jacob's treatment had largely been at the VA hospital in Las Vegas after he was transferred from Texas, all hospitals were cut from the same cloth.

Being here brought back the intensity of her

fear and stress in those long days and weeks of her brother's recovery. It was bad enough Linc had been beside her pretty much twenty-four hours a day since she'd been attacked, but dumping a hospital visit into her lap on top of it? Even for a simple MRI?

Leaning against the wall, she turned her eyes toward the ceiling and squeezed them shut. *Really, God? It's not enough I lose the grant to Owen. It's not enough I have protestors at my door and masked men trying to take me, and a murdered employee. And Linc. Now this?*

Why was He bringing back every single worst moment of her life? *If this is some kind of test, I'll give You the answers You're looking for. Just make it stop.*

"It's tough going through the hard stuff, huh?"

Angie's eyes popped open, and she jerked her head toward the sound, using all of her restraint not to take a defensive swing at the male voice.

"Sorry." A young man, probably college age, stepped back and held up his hand. "I didn't mean to scare you. You looked…" He balled his fists, tensed his shoulders and scrunched his face, then relaxed and smiled. "You looked kind of like that."

She could have taken offense at the characterization, but he wasn't wrong. The tension in her shoulders and jaw spoke to the truth. "It's okay. I could use the distraction."

"We all could." He leaned against the wall about a foot away and shoved his hands into his pockets. Studying his canvas shoes, he twisted his mouth to one side. "One thing I can pretty much promise you is none of us want to be here." He glanced at her. "Family or friend? Or yourself?"

How would she characterize Linc? He wasn't her family. Three days ago, she wouldn't have called him a friend. But the way they'd talked over the past twenty-four hours… The way she was sweating his test results as much as she was her own safety… The way he'd started taking over her thoughts…

That might be a bridge too far. "A friend. You?"

"My mom. She finished chemo and radiation, and this is her first set of scans after, to see how it worked. The waiting is the worst."

"It really is." At least Linc wasn't waiting to hear if he was going to live or die.

Or was he? For Linc, the job was everything.

If he couldn't be a hard-charging federal agent any longer, he'd see it as a kind of death.

Like her and the ranch. If she didn't get things moving soon…

But there were bigger things at play in this moment than her dreams. "Tell you what, I'll pray she gets good news."

"Thanks." The young man offered a smile that seemed to come from somewhere deep inside. "And I'll pray for good news for you, too. Although my mom has said all along she doesn't call the shots here. God does. She keeps texting me that verse in the Bible about how what we suffer here doesn't compare to what God's got for us once we get to Heaven. I'm trying to remember. It's hard, but I'm trying."

Angie turned away to look up the hall. The words landed hard against her heart. Was she thinking of this in God terms? Or in human terms?

"I'll be honest." The young man straightened and stepped into the middle of the hall. "Another thing." He balled his fists and scrunched his face. "Holding it all? Trying to make it go away? It's not good for you. Eventually, you explode. I learned the hard way. You've got to take things as they come, let the feelings rock you before they settle. Otherwise… Boom." He threw his hands into the air to mimic a bomb.

How well she knew. The night hers had volcanically erupted, feelings had cost her a friend and her peace of mind. She frowned. But had she learned?

"I see you're thinking, so my work here is done." The man smiled as he backed up the hall. "It was good talking to you. I've got to grab a coffee so it'll be nice and hot when Mom gets out. It's her reward for dealing with an MRI. She hates them." He waved, pivoted on one heel and strode up the hall as though he was familiar with the journey.

He probably was, if his mother had already walked the road of diagnosis and treatment.

Life could turn so quickly. All of the plans in the world could fall to pieces in an instant. Jacob had nearly been killed by an IED. Her father had died of cancer. Instant change.

But cancer… It sort of made the chaos around her feel a little less urgent.

Not much less, but a little.

Angie said a quick prayer for the young man's mother and vowed to pray whenever the woman and her son came to mind.

She stared at the wall across from her, letting

his words sink in. Was she repeating the mistakes of her past?

Gnawing her bottom lip, she considered her midnight drive from Vegas, how she'd spewed anger but not allowed disappointment to touch her. How she'd pressed her spine into the wall when bullets flew and forced her fear into a dark closet, focusing on what she could do over what she felt. How she'd turned her energy into caring for Chance rather than falling apart in terror in front of Linc.

The truth crashed against her. She was hiding. Burying her emotions. Taking one step, then another, then another, in an effort to outrun them. Focusing on action over feeling.

The practice had made her numb. When was the last time she'd felt joy?

Her eyes slipped closed and she leaned heavily against the wall. She couldn't remember. In burying the fear and the anger, she'd buried the good as well.

The last time she'd squashed her emotions, they'd destroyed what might have been with Linc. Tucking away the negatives also meant she'd hidden anything good she might be feeling toward him.

Things her heart said she was starting to feel again. Things that might never have gone away.

Something in her heart shifted, as though a crack had opened, ushering in a sliver of light. If she allowed herself to feel the fear she'd been burying, was it possible she'd also feel lo—

"Hey."

Her hand flew to her chest as she whipped toward the voice, heart racing.

Linc stood outside the entrance, an eyebrow arched in question. "You were deep in thought."

Something warm and heady rushed from her heart to her fingertips at the sight of him, tall and strong and… And Linc. For a heartbeat, she considered rushing to him, throwing her arms around him and…

And what?

That had happened once before, and he'd pushed her away. There was no way to explain how this was different. If she reached for him again, it would be because he was Linc, not because she was lost and afraid.

"Ang?" He tilted his head. "You okay?"

Exhaling through pursed lips, she wrestled her heart into submission and found her voice. "Good thing we're in a hospital. You nearly gave me a heart attack." She wasn't ready to talk about the thoughts running through her mind. They were too raw, too fragile to expose to the air. "Are you finished already?"

"Already?" He stepped into the hall and motioned for her to walk beside him. They headed for the main entrance. "I was in that metal tube for approximately eight days." He offered an overexaggerated shudder. "Never been a fan of small spaces. I recited every Bible verse I knew and sang every top-forty song since the year 2000."

Angie laughed as they stepped into the sunlight, shoving her feelings into the closet, where they belonged. She couldn't think of them now. "You put on quite a show, huh?" She could sympathize. A knee injury had sidelined her college-basketball career. The worst moments had come in the MRI. It wasn't an experience she wanted to repeat.

Linc tapped his temple. "All in my head, but it was an amazing display of talent."

"I'm sure. Did they tell you anything?"

"No." When the parking lots had been full, they'd parked on top of the parking garage, both seeming to prefer the open space to the enclosed structure. Once they stepped into the shadows, Linc opened the door to the stairs and ushered her in. "They'll send the results to my doctor. She's booked me an appointment for late this afternoon."

Angie stopped on the second landing and faced him one step below her, putting them eye-to-eye. "You took me to the hospital this morning with you, so I'm assuming I'll be along for this visit as well?" Linc shouldn't be alone to face news he might not want to receive.

Some of the tension around his mouth eased. His gaze locked on to hers, shifting as though he was trying to read her thoughts through her eyes.

Angie let him. Whatever he needed…

Suddenly, time raced backward to before she'd nearly driven them a step too far. Before everything had been awkward and strained between them. When their easy friendship had been shifting into something more.

Into something she'd desperately wanted.

Could they…? Should they…?

Above them, a door crashed closed.

Linc's head snapped toward the sound, breaking the connection. He gripped the handrail tighter, then shook his head.

Angie fought to keep from melting in humiliation. She'd nearly done it again. Had led him down a path they shouldn't have gone down, one he clearly had no interest in walking.

Before she could speak, another door slammed below them.

Linc stepped beside her, drawing her to his side.

A zip of fear ran through her.

From above and below, footsteps approached.

They were caught in the middle, with nowhere to run.

Linc eased Angie closer to the wall. He stepped in front of her, trying to watch the stairs below and above at the same time.

It was probably nothing, but in their current situation, taking chances was out of the question.

He wanted to bang his head against the wall. A wise man would have taken the elevator and avoided being trapped in a stairwell, but he'd had enough of enclosed spaces for one day. He'd made a rookie mistake.

There was no time for self-recrimination now, though.

Reflexively, his hand went to his hip, but his sidearm wasn't there. He had secured it in the vehicle because he had no way to lock it up in the hospital while he was getting his MRI.

He stepped to the side, prepared to shield Angie against whatever came. Likely it was two other people avoiding the elevator.

He prayed that was so. Otherwise, they were about to go to war.

This is what he got for letting her steal his attention. The care in her voice as she'd looked him in the eye and offered to stand beside him... He hadn't realized how much he'd craved connection with her. It was like being lost in the canyon in blistering heat and getting a cool drink of water. Her concern had washed over his soul in a way he couldn't put into words except to say he'd missed her.

He'd been oblivious to everything else in the world, wanting nothing more than to close the two-inch gap between them and—

The footsteps drew closer in both directions. Any second now, people would appear.

If they were bad actors, the only way out was to fight.

The person coming down the stairs appeared first. Running shoes. Black leggings with a bright pink stripe. A T-shirt above the waist. A blond ponytail bopping in time with whatever was playing in the earbuds in the young woman's ears. She appeared to be a college-age kid.

But appearances could be deceiving. She was slightly out of place in the parking garage, seeming to belong more in the gym or on a track. And she was approximately the same age as the protestors who'd been hounding the ranch.

Lincoln tensed, preparing for a confrontation, but the young woman barely seemed to notice them as she passed on the landing, her nose buried in her phone.

He didn't allow himself to relax.

She hardly stepped aside as she passed a man coming up the stairs. His head appeared first, dark hair peppered with gray. A dress shirt and tie. Pressed slacks. A hospital ID hung around his neck.

Lincoln fought the urge to relax. An identification badge meant nothing. It could have been stolen.

The man's gaze caught Linc's as he approached, and he saw Angie tucked into the corner. The man slowed and stopped halfway up the stairs, concern knitting his eyebrows together. "Is everything okay?" He tried to see around Linc to Angie, pale blue eyes seeming to be concerned for her welfare.

Here was the catch... Did Linc continue to stand wary guard against the possible threat, even though he looked like a predator who'd cornered his prey? Or did he defend himself against the idea he was somehow the bad guy? If this guy was innocent and he called Security, they could have big problems. But if Linc let down his guard and this guy was on the hunt, it could sign Angie's death warrant.

"I'm fine." Angie's voice came over his shoulder, though she didn't move from behind him. "I hate elevators, but I'm also creeped out by stairwells. Too many true-crime podcasts." Her chuckle actually sounded authentic.

The man nodded slowly, his gaze roaming the two of them. He hesitated when he saw Linc's badge, which was clipped to his belt. Pausing, the guy nodded slowly, his expression clearing. "Understandable." Keeping to the side of the landing farthest from Angie and Linc, he passed and headed up the stairs. "Be safe." His feet retreated toward the next landing, and Linc nearly sagged against the wall.

Well, against Angie, who was still behind him. Given that his awareness of how close he'd come to kissing her was still zipping through his veins despite the scare, he really didn't need to touch her right now.

"Can't say that wasn't an aerobic workout." Angie eased from behind him and put some distance between them. "My heart's definitely run through a good cardio session. Is it safe to go up now?"

Everything about her was false, from the stilted words to the high-pitched tone they were spoken in. Either she'd been rattled by the threat…

Or she'd been as affected by the emotion between them as he had.

Dare he hope? Or did he assume she'd read his thoughts about kissing her and was shoving him away?

He huffed out his exasperation. Once again, he was distracted by her. His main job was to get her to the ranch safely, then to discover who had killed Ellis and was out to harm her. Everything else needed to stay locked away.

"Let's go." Ushering her to walk beside him, he headed up the stairs as she matched him step for step. "I'm not a fan of being in this space for much longer. I want to get you home." The sooner she was in a secure location, the better he'd feel.

It had been a mistake to bring her with him. He should have left her with Rosa and the ranch hands, but the thought of having her out of sight for too long had left him uneasy. Later, he'd have to address the deep-seated belief that no one else could protect her as well as he could.

Arrogance like that got people killed.

Especially since, the way his neck and back were throbbing with the tension of the morning and the odd position he'd had to lie down in for the scans, he wasn't so certain he could protect her, either.

They stepped through the metal door into the bright, midday Arizona sunlight. He squinted against the brilliance and paused to acclimate, blinded as his eyes adjusted.

A shadow moved to the right.

Angie screamed.

A blow to the back of his knees rocked him forward and dropped him hard to the concrete.

Chapter Ten

"Linc!" Angie's throat ached as his name ripped out in a hoarse shout. Linc dropped hard onto his knees and pitched forward, catching himself before his head hit the concrete.

A man wielding a tire iron spun toward Angie. His face was covered with a bright orange mask. A blue knit cap hid his hair. Dark brown eyes glared a malevolent threat.

A red sedan waited feet away, the driver's-side door hanging open and the engine running.

Not again. Not this again.

She should run, but she couldn't leave Linc, who was struggling to his feet. If the man swung that tire iron at his back, it could paralyze him.

She had to protect him, even if it cost her everything.

At the sound of Linc's movement, the man hesitated, turning away from her. He raised the tire iron, prepared to deal what could be a horrific injury to Linc's upper back.

How did he know where to strike to deal the worst injury to Linc? Or was it simply the most strategic spot to land a blow?

She could not stand by and watch this man destroy him. Without considering the possible consequences, Angie dove. She tucked her shoulder and ran straight into the assailant's side, tumbling them sideways against the door to the stairs. The door held, and the man grunted but managed to stay on his feet.

He dropped the tire iron, wrapped his arms around Angie and steadied himself. Using the door for leverage he shoved her toward the waiting car, obviously determined to push her into the vehicle and make his escape.

Linc rolled to his side and rose as Angie kicked and flailed. This was not happening. Not on her front porch in the dark of night and not on the roof of a parking garage in broad daylight.

Planting her foot against the car's rear door, Angie shoved backward, spinning them sideways as Linc lunged forward and grabbed her attacker's jacket, jerking him off his feet.

As Angie wrenched away from him and stumbled to safety, a siren suddenly screeched.

A police car accelerated toward them across the open roof, lights whirling as the siren screamed.

The man turned one way and then the other, seeming to judge if he had a way of escape. Finally, he lifted his hands. "I surrender. I'm not armed."

Just like that, he morphed from a horrifying assailant to a quaking coward.

He kneeled and laced his fingers behind his head as the police car came to a stop beside them. "I know how this works. I'm unarmed. I swear."

Mouth hanging open in shock, Linc stared down at their attacker.

Angie backed against the stairwell door. This had to be a trick. The man who'd come at her at the house hadn't shown any signs of backing down. Maybe he knew he was cornered? Could this be over so easily?

A police officer exited his vehicle, hand on his pistol. "What's going on here?"

Linc raised both hands, but he aimed one finger toward his waist. "I'm a federal agent."

Reflexively, Angie raised her arms as well.

Her heart pounded against her chest, as though it had remembered how to beat after being frightened into submission.

The officer glanced at Linc and nodded, motioning for him to lower his hands, then looked down at the kneeling suspect. He kept his hand on his pistol as he glanced at Angie. "You okay? We got a call from one of the docs about a man possibly assaulting a woman in the stairwell. I was headed over when I saw your altercation. Figured the siren would put a quick end to things."

Angie said a silent prayer of thanks for the fast-thinking officer and for the suspicious doctor in the stairwell who was the reason for their salvation. If she could find him, she'd thank him repeatedly for being paranoid. She'd even bake him a cake. "I'm fine. That was us. Special Agent Tucker was protecting me. This guy, though?" Angie lowered her hands and pointed at the masked assailant. "I have no idea who he is."

"But he definitely assaulted me and tried to kidnap her." Linc addressed the police officer while keeping one eye on the bad guy.

The officer moved swiftly to cuff the man and to haul him to his feet, then he nodded to

Lincoln. "Want to do the honors of unmasking him?"

As Lincoln stepped forward, hysterical laughter bubbled in Angie. She swallowed it, and it went down in a painful lump. Somehow, this felt like the ending of a Scooby-Doo episode, as though they were going to reveal the masked man was her long-lost great-uncle, or Carter the Contractor, or Rosa the Ranch Foreman.

But it was none of them.

Linc stepped back, the mask dangling from his fingers, his glare ice-cold as he stared at the protestor who'd seemed to be in charge earlier. Linc's jaw was tight, and he clenched his fists as though it was all he could do to hold in his anger. He looked at the police officer. "This man, supposedly, is Riley Jeffries. He organized a protest outside of the ranch Ms. Garcia owns."

"I wasn't going to hurt her." Riley's eyes darted from the police officer to Linc. Gone was the swagger he'd displayed earlier in the day. A scared little boy remained in his place, shaking in the face of authority. "I really wasn't."

"No?" Linc widened his stance and crossed his arms, leveling a hard gaze on the younger man. "You hit me with a tire iron."

Riley's head shook back and forth in denial.

"No. I mean, yes. But in the back of the knee, not where it would actually injure you. I just wanted to knock you down."

"And then hit him in the back?" The words raced out before Angie could stop herself.

For the first time, Riley looked at her. "No. I wouldn't have hit him again. Not hard."

"Kidnapping is a serious offense." Linc exhaled loudly and motioned his head toward the officer's patrol car. "Get him out of my sight, please. We'll come by the station and make a statement." He reached into Riley's car and shut off the engine, then passed the keys to the officer.

"Really." Riley jerked and the officer's grip on him tightened. "I was just trying to scare her. We know from the sheriff's questions what happened at the ranch and we thought..." His shoulders sagged. "We wanted to scare you into selling. That's all."

That's all? Angie startled. Terrifying her into believing her life was in danger was a *that's all*? And Ellis... Had they killed Ellis in some failed attempt to frighten her? Her stomach roiled. "You beat a man to death."

"No!" Riley's head shook again. "No. We had nothing to do with anything on the ranch.

Today's the first time any of us have laid a hand on you. What happened to that man, we weren't involved. I swear."

"We'll see." Linc handed Riley's mask and cap to the police officer, then hesitated, cocking his head to one side. "You keep saying *we*. *We* followed. *We* didn't do anything. You have an accomplice here today." He looked over his shoulder at the stairway door. "The woman in the workout gear. She was with you. She let you know it was us headed up the stairs and there was someone walking ahead of us. She was texting you when she passed, wasn't she?" He gave the officer a description of the woman. "There may be more. Don't trust this guy. He looks innocent, but this is the fourth attack on Ms. Garcia in a few days, and there was a man murdered on her property. I'm not buying it wasn't him."

Riley nearly whimpered as the officer tugged him toward the car. He protested his innocence the whole way, claiming an alibi. He was yelling frantically when the officer shut the door and walked back, then handed Linc and Angie business cards. "I'll take him straight in and you two can follow. We'll take care of having his car impounded, too." He pointed toward the corner of the roof. "I'll have our guys pull camera footage to seal the deal on this guy."

"Thanks." Linc glanced at the card then pocketed it. "We'll be right behind you."

After the officer pulled away, Angie sagged against the door. With the threat removed, her hands were shaking and her knees had lost their strength. Her heart might never return to a normal rhythm. "I don't understand. This was all done by the protestors? Why would they kill Ellis? It doesn't make any sense."

"No, it doesn't." He reached for her hand and drew her to him, pulling her into a too-brief hug before releasing her. He grabbed her hand to tug her to the car. "That's why we have to get out of here."

Angie forced herself to follow, although she wanted to curl into a ball on the concrete and make herself as small as possible. Or she wanted to beg Linc to hold her until the terror passed. He was moving her too quickly across the parking deck for her to do either. It was all she could do to keep from tripping over her feet. "This isn't over, is it?"

Linc's expression was grim. "Not by a long shot."

★ ★ ★

There were no protestors at the gate when they returned to the ranch.

Linc punched in a code Angie gave him and they drove through. He watched the gate close behind them. "I'm guessing, now that Riley is talking, we won't see them again."

It hadn't taken long for the police to get Riley to open up, especially when he learned they'd also picked up his girlfriend, Skyler Cliff, waiting in her car in the parking garage for Riley to text her their next move.

For all of his swagger at the gate earlier, Riley had collapsed like a kite in a thunderstorm. While the protestors were a mix of out-of-towners and locals, the catalyst had come from something entirely different.

An anonymous user had posted on a message thread on an environmental website that they'd pay a group to protest the "development" at Fairweather Ranch, so his suspicion had been right. Someone else was pulling the strings.

Following the money might lead to who was coming after Angie. At the very least, it would lead to an interesting conversation with the backer. His team was already on the hunt, tracking the finances and the IP addresses of the person who'd made the offer. It could take hours or days, but at least it was a lead.

Angie shifted in her seat, but she didn't turn her head. She'd been staring out the passenger window for the past half hour, watching the sun sink lower. The way the clouds were streaming in from the west, the sky would be a riot of oranges and reds when the sun set in a little over an hour, lighting fire to the burnished landscape. It was his favorite time of day.

Or it had been. Now he dreaded the darkness that followed.

Approximately twenty-four hours earlier, they'd found Ellis West's body. Five hours earlier, he'd thought it possible they'd found the man's killer.

Three hours earlier, he'd been convinced they hadn't. As much as he wanted this to be over, the uncertainty and the danger dragged on. Their lead wouldn't save Angie if her assailant struck again before they could find answers.

This had to be wearing on her, because it was chewing him up. The day had been far too long, and he'd had to push back his doctor's appointment to the next morning. Answers would have to wait. Angie's safety came first. "What are you thinking over there?"

She shrugged. "Wondering why someone would pay a bunch of college kids from Rhode Island to protest my ranch." She dragged her finger along the window ledge. "Why is this happening to me?" She chuckled, but the sound held no joy. "I'm having a pity party, to be honest."

"Well, if anyone deserves one, it's you. I'll even buy you the cake and candles."

This time, her laugh was genuine. "Thanks. At least you didn't offer me cheese with my 'whine.'"

He smiled, then turned his gaze to the road. As much as she'd had to endure over the past couple of days, she deserved some time to ask the *why* question.

"Hey." Angie leaned forward as they neared the house, squinting toward the ranch out of sight beyond several stands of trees. "Would you mind if we run over to the ranch? Carter said he was going to do some excavating today, and I'd a lot rather go see how that looks than hole up in the house. The sunset will be pretty epic from there, too."

He lifted his foot from the gas as he neared

the turn-off for the house. The ranch was fairly wide open, so he'd see if anyone was coming after them. He could keep her shielded from any potential sniper, and they'd be safely in the house before dark settled.

Although the hands were out with the cattle, Rosa was there, so they'd have some form of backup. As much as he hated having Angie in the open, the request made sense. She was bound to feel caged, and it wasn't like she'd asked to gallop off to the canyon alone or something.

He moved his foot to the gas pedal. "We can do that." It would give him another chance to see if they'd missed anything that might relate to Ellis's murder. Then, when they returned to the house, he'd call Thomas. There had been a couple of missed calls from him earlier, when they were at the police station, but Linc was reluctant to talk to him about a possible serial killer in front of Angie until he had more details.

When they parked near Ellis's cabin, Linc held his arm out in front of Angie. "Wait here. Let me scout around to be sure we're clear."

She sat back with a huff. Tough to say if it was frustration, fear or exhaustion.

He could sympathize.

Linc made a quick check of the area, keeping one eye on the truck. He let up on his surveillance when Rosa stepped out of her cabin and walked to the vehicle. The ranch manager carried a pistol at her hip, likely to ward off snakes, but it was wise with all that was happening.

She tossed a wave in his direction, then spoke to Angie through the passenger window.

When he was satisfied the area was as safe as it could be, he motioned for Angie to join him on the far side of the cabin. Behind the crew cabins, a large rectangular pit had been dug, a little over a foot deep. It looked as though Carter was planning to put a crawl space beneath the dormitory to provide for easier access to ductwork and pipes instead of raising the structure off the ground like some of the others on the property.

Rosa and Angie joined him, and Angie studied the excavation. She looked over her shoulder at Rosa. "He got a lot done today."

"Yep. Said once his crew is healthy, he'll get them out here full-time."

Angie frowned. She was probably wondering how she'd pay for the work without dipping into her savings.

Rosa leaned her shoulder against Angie's.

"He said he'd work out funding with you, but he believes in what's happening here. His great-grandmother was Hopi. Let him help you out. You've run this place on donors for years. If he wants to be one of them…"

Angie's smile was tight. There was something else going on, but Linc couldn't read what it was.

He paced the perimeter, eyeing the work. A number of smaller trenches ran off from the main site, several feet in every direction. "What are these? Do you know, Rosa?"

Angie joined him. "I might know. Carter was helping one of the subcontractors by digging where they're going to run pipes and drains."

Made sense.

"He took the dirt from the excavation over to that spot behind the barn and evened out the ground so we can enclose a paddock later. Said to consider it a favor."

"That was nice." Angie jumped into the hole, which came to below her knees, and Rosa joined her. They wandered the space, pacing off rooms and discussing their vision.

Planting her boot heel, Angie dragged a line down the center of the excavation. "If the hall-way is here, then—" She stumbled, and Rosa reached out to steady her. Rotating her ankle, Angie inspected the heel of her boot. "Rock."

Linc jumped in and headed toward her, eyeing the ground. "You okay?" While the topsoil was a bit deeper here at the edge of the forest than it was in other areas of the canyon, it still didn't take much digging to get down to solid rock.

"Yeah. I caught my heel on…" Angie trailed off, then kneeled, swiping gently at something in the dirt. "It's not rock. Something's buried here."

Linc and Rosa dropped to their knees beside her. Fossils were sometimes uncovered in the area, as were artifacts left behind by the first peoples to inhabit the canyon. If that was the case, construction would stop until the area could be properly assessed and excavated.

That was time Angie didn't have.

But as Linc helped brush away the soil, it became evident what was buried was neither natural nor ancient. The side of a five-gallon plastic bucket emerged from the dirt. There was a cap on the top, sealed around the edges with a rubbery adhesive, likely designed to keep water out…

Or to keep whatever the bucket contained in.

Linc rocked on his heels and motioned for Rosa and Angie to back away.

Angie mimicked his posture. "What's wrong?"

He shook his head, thinking. It was possible the bucket had been discarded on the ranch some time ago. It was evident the thing had been in the ground for a while. But given how deep it was buried, it hadn't been covered naturally.

No, it had been purposely buried. Sealed, then buried. Almost like a time capsule.

He frowned. "Did you and Jacob ever bury a time capsule you planned to come back for in fifty years?" It was a long shot, but one he had to take.

Angie shook her head slowly. "No. Why?" She stiffened, her expression growing tense. "This is bad, isn't it?"

"I don't know." He pulled his phone from his pocket and dialed Thomas. Normally, he'd dig up the thing himself, but given that it was sealed, it could contain anything from hazardous waste to parts of human remains. He'd hate to disturb a crime scene.

What was the probability they'd find evidence of yet another crime on Angie's property?

Given the way things were going, the probability was astronomical. His gut said Angie's land was about to be the center of something much worse than they'd already imagined.

Chapter Eleven

The crime-scene unit had put a temporary open-sided tent over the area around the bucket and had set up spotlights to combat the coming nightfall. Linc and Thomas waited by a folding table for Erin Navarro to finish unearthing the bucket.

He'd sent Rosa and Angie to Rosa's cabin with Patricia Cassidy, the junior member of their team. While this could be an innocent discarded bucket, his gut said it was more. The seal led him to believe either someone had dumped industrial waste, or buried crucial evidence. "What's the likelihood this closes at least one of the cold cases we've had on the books for years?"

Thomas exhaled and crossed his arms over his chest, watching the crime-scene techs work. "The way you've told me things have been going out here the past couple of days, I'd say really good." He chewed his lower lip, studying the scene. "We may break several cases all at once if we can link ones we've been investigating to what's happening here."

He really didn't want to think about that until he needed to. "So you guys have been busy while I've been gone."

"No doubt." Dropping his arms, Thomas shoved his hands into his pockets. "We're waiting on cause of death for the hiker, though based on location and initial investigation, it looks like she fell. As always, we want to rule out homicide, though." Identification and a cell phone found on the remains the team had investigated earlier had named the woman as a missing hiker who was unaffiliated with the serial-killer case.

"At least you can rule out the serial killer."

"True. But we've still got two missing women."

"Isla Blake and…?" In the hubbub the day before, he'd never gotten a name for the second potential victim.

"Monica Huerta."

Linc's head came up. Why was that name familiar?

Thomas arched an eyebrow. "You know her?"

"No, but…" *Monica Huerta*. He'd heard it

recently. He tried to cycle through the conversations he'd had over the past few days. So many names, places, faces... A lot had happened since Jacob had asked him to check on Angie a couple of nights earlier. Too many facts were flopping around his head like clothes in a dryer. Exhaustion, coupled with stress about his unanswered medical questions, made everything worse. When he got to the house, he'd flip through his notes and see if he'd written anything down. Could be it was one of the protestors who'd—

A flash of conversation. *Monica Huerta and I went to school together and now we go to church together, but we're more acquaintances than friends.*

"Monica Huerta is one of the protestors. Angie knows her."

Thomas turned toward Linc. "Wait. Not only is she missing in a way eerily similar to Isla Blake and seven women from a decade ago, but she's linked to the protests? And she's friends with Angie?"

"More of an acquaintance, I think, but yes." The web was tangling more than ever.

"Do you know when Angie last spoke to her?"

"I think she said it was before she went to

Vegas, maybe two weeks ago? Monica reassured her they'd figured out who'd vandalized the ranch and had dealt with the problem, had turned the names over to the sheriff." He tried to remember more. "I think she might have said Monica was one of the organizers, but I'm not sure."

"I need to talk to Angie." Thomas's voice was grim.

Linc's heart sank with his teammate's tone. Interviewing Angie about Monica would pile onto an already heavy load. It would tell Angie someone she knew might be in danger. It might even drive home the truth a serial killer seemed to be hunting in the area.

He prayed not.

"If the serial killer is back, he's not after Angie." Thomas was studying Linc as though he could read his thoughts. "This guy approaches women online first, then somehow controls them enough to get them to hand over as much cash as they can easily access, along with enough info for him to steal their identities as well."

"Which is odd." Most of the women didn't have a lot of money, and what they got from ATM withdrawals didn't amount to much. It also risked putting them on camera, although that could be his way of taunting the authorities.

What made less sense was the identification. Why go to the trouble of forcing women to hand over their documents? "Unless he's got a lucrative side business going on, selling birth certificates and such on the black market."

"Risky business, giving someone the name of a dead woman, though."

"True." Thomas nodded toward the small group in protective gear as they cleared the bucket. "Frankly, all of this is convoluted and confusing. It's like Fairweather Ranch is suddenly the hub of criminal activity for the canyon."

Angie's attacks, the missing women, Ellis West's death… They all could be linked.

He stared at the group working around the bucket, and they seemed to be wrapping up. "Looks like we're about to take over here." And none too soon. This conversation was getting too personal.

Sure enough, Erin Navarro approached with the bucket and set it on the table between Linc and Thomas. "It's clear. No remains. No chemicals." She shrugged, her expression unreadable.

"I'll take photos and document while you guys check it out."

Evidence discovery always kicked Linc's heart up a notch, but this time it felt as though his pulse might rocket to the stars beginning to twinkle in the night sky. Whatever was in the innocuous white five-gallon bucket was going to affect Angie—he had no doubt.

He hoped it wouldn't wreck her.

He tugged on gloves.

Thomas did the same, then motioned for Linc to do the honors.

With Erin documenting every step of the process, Linc removed the loosened lid and peered inside, leaving room for Thomas to look as well.

An oversize plastic zip-top bag rested in the bucket with a large brown mailing envelope sealed inside. Whatever it contained was thin. Duct tape further sealed the package. The person who had put it there clearly wanted to protect it from the elements.

Thomas watched closely as Lincoln slid the bag onto the table for Erin to photograph. "Think we're dealing with a treasure map?"

Lincoln actually chuckled. It would be a relief to discover someone had concocted a wild-goose chase for fake treasure rather than the host of more sinister things that could be at play.

Erin smiled. "Dibs on the map. We can keep a secret, right?"

"Sure." Thomas curled his lip. "You do realize every single bit of anything hypothetically hidden out there would go to the government. No 'finders keepers' for us."

"Yeah. Big sigh. Wreck my wild wishes with your boring truth." Erin snapped another photo. "My dad has a ton of those buckets in his garage from when he redid the bathroom when I was in high school. That was twelve years ago, so that bucket's probably not very old."

Twelve years. Linc glanced at Thomas. While the likelihood of this being linked to a serial killer from ten years earlier was slim, it felt too coincidental given everything else happening at the ranch.

"Let's see what we've got." Linc carefully cut away the duct tape, and Thomas bagged it. It was possible the conditions in the bucket had preserved fingerprints. He slid out the envelope and opened it, then tipped it to slide the contents onto the table.

A birth certificate. A social-security card. A passport. Several bank statements. And...

Linc picked up the paper and scanned it. A DD 214, a copy of a service record when someone separated from the military. He scanned the name on the top and passed it to Thomas.

His teammate grimly read the paper. "Janis Nichols." Dropping the document in line with the others, he stared at the row of horrifying evidence.

There was no reason for any of them to speak. The minute they'd seen the documents, they'd all known.

He couldn't look away from the table, couldn't stop himself from noting the only form of identification missing was the driver's license, which had been mailed to Janis Nichols's family ten years earlier, covered in her blood.

Thomas looked grim. "Well, we know our bad guy's not selling the identities. It looks like he's keeping trophies."

"I don't know." Erin eyed the documents spread out on the table. "Don't killers usually keep their trophies close or easily accessible? Why bury them in the middle of the Garcias' ranch?"

"Because he or she had a connection to the place." This was the exact thing Lincoln had hoped wouldn't happen. Angie didn't need more trouble. Ellis's death had already—

"Wait. Erin's right." Killers liked to keep their prizes where they could see them, touch them, bring back the thrill of the kill. "These aren't trophies. These are preserved." Lines were drawing in Lincoln's mind, connecting ideas that had been random thoughts before. "Whoever buried these was keeping them safe."

"But why?" Thomas didn't look convinced. "To sell later?"

"I've got a wild thought." Really wild. First, he needed to confirm something. "Erin, you took photos of the West cabin. There was mail on his counter. Do you still have those on your camera?"

"Sure do." She started clicking as she watched the screen. "I uploaded them to our database, but I haven't wiped the memory card yet. What are you looking for?"

"A postcard." Something was tweaking his memory. "Thomas, the women went missing over a decade ago, right? And then it all stopped?"

"Yeah."

"Before or after Ellis West's father was killed in a car accident?"

Thomas tapped on his phone as Erin passed her camera across the table to Linc.

Linc studied the photo of the postcard. The front showed a glorious sunrise over the canyon. He clicked to the next image. Ellis's address was on one side along with a postmark from Houston two days before Ellis died. There was no return address or message, just a heart and the name *Nica*. He stared at the signature. "It would be odd to send a postcard of the canyon to someone who lived at the canyon, right?"

"A little," Erin said.

Thomas nodded. "Not out of the realm of possibility, but odd. And the disappearances ended about five weeks before Javi West and Angie's father died." He looked up, pocketing his phone. "What are you thinking, Tucker?"

"That there's never been a single body found for any of these missing women. The only evidence that they were killed or injured is their blood on their IDs." He looked up at Erin. "I want someone to go through Ellis's things and see if there's another postcard similar to this one. I also want to know of any reports of domestic violence around any of the missing women." He held up the camera so Thomas could see and maybe follow along with his train of thought. "Nica could be short for—"

"Monica." Thomas's eyes widened as he caught on. "That would be… You think…?"

"I *suspect*," Linc clarified as he handed the camera back to Erin. "What if the identification and money were taken as insurance? And buried out here for safekeeping? What if Ellis West's father and possibly Angie's father were helping these women escape something? And what if Ellis was following in his father's footsteps?"

"And what if that postcard was a way to communicate a safe arrival in a new location?" Thomas already had his phone out again. "I'm getting on those records now. Because if you're right…"

If he was right, those women were still alive and hiding from something horrible.

Without concrete evidence, they still had to investigate as though the women had been kidnapped and murdered, but this was definitely a trail to follow, and it might provide a motive for Ellis West's murder.

Because the best way to save someone's life was to make it look like they were already dead.

★ ★ ★

"Wait." Angie sank onto the couch that sat squarely in front of the stone fireplace in Rosa's living room. The way the space had seemed to tilt when Linc's teammate Thomas spoke, she didn't trust herself to remain standing. "Repeat that. Please." *But say something totally different than what I heard the first time.*

Sending a pointed look toward Thomas, Lincoln sat beside her and faced her, resting a hand on her knee. "Where do you need me to start?"

Forget starting. She wanted this to be finished. No more surprises.

But that was impossible unless this was a nightmare.

It wasn't. The last time she'd checked, she'd definitely been awake.

Might as well begin with the worst. "So Carter was right and there really is a serial killer?"

Linc stared at her for a long time before he finally spoke. "We've found evidence that might link some women who disappeared in the past to two women who disappeared recently." Linc's voice was low and gentle, as though he was trying to calm a skittish horse.

That creeped her out way more than if he'd spoken in normal tones. "Talk to me like I'm me, Linc, not like I'm a kindergartner who doesn't understand math."

His teeth dug into his lower lip. Surely he wasn't biting back a smile at a time like this? "That bucket contained identification documents belonging to a woman who vanished a decade ago when several women were taken by someone the federal authorities believe was a serial killer."

"Are they trophies?" Her voice pitched to an octave that might have shattered eardrums. "You found a serial killer's trophies on my property?"

"Angie, I—"

She threw up a hand, nearly smacking Linc in the face. *No.* More words weren't going to fix this. "I need a second." Her thoughts spun. Ten years ago, someone had murdered women. Someone who'd likely been connected to the ranch. Sure, back then the property had been in its last years as a dude ranch, so anyone could have buried that bucket. But to place it so close to the main cabins?

Her stomach dipped and twisted. No one would dare to hide something in that spot unless they had unfettered access. "A decade ago, a killer probably lived on my family's ranch." She had been away at school. So had Jacob, but there had been ranch hands, visitors... Pressing her fingers to her lips, she looked across the room at Rosa, whose expression was as stricken as her own had to be. While Rosa hadn't worked for the ranch then, this was too close to home for both of them.

Rosa drew in a shuddering breath. "I'll get you the employee records from then." Her words were soft, almost resigned. The idea anyone connected with Fairweather could do such a thing was horrifying.

One more horror to add to a growing list. If only she could roll back the clock to Sunday night, when her biggest problem had been losing a grant to Owen. She'd thought that was the worst that could happen.

It certainly paled in comparison to everything that had occurred since. Attacks. Murder. Serial killers. "What next, Linc? When does this end?" *Are there bodies buried on my land?*

She couldn't bring herself to ask. The answer might be more than she could handle.

She'd sure picked the wrong day to start feeling her emotions.

"I hope it ends soon." Linc squeezed her hand and released it.

She studied his face, and he didn't look away.

He was leaving something out. As much as she wanted to demand to know more, rationality said she was better off letting Linc decide what might be too much for her to handle. After all, she'd passed being overwhelmed hours ago.

From where he stood near the fireplace, Thomas spoke. "We don't think you've been targeted by a serial killer." Thomas was tall and thin, more bull rider than federal investigator. His dark hair was short, and though she knew he and Linc were both in their early thirties, salt had already streaked through the brown. Unlike Linc, he wasn't a fidgeter. He stood extraordinarily still, as though disturbing the air in the room might upset some delicate balance. Despite his rigid stance, his brown eyes were compassionate. "I wish we had more answers."

So did she.

Linc withdrew his hand from her knee and pivoted so he sat straight on the couch, no longer facing her. Instead, he stared at the coffee table, which was strewn with files and papers. Contracts were scattered over the top of the mess, and a yellow legal pad filled with numbers sat in the middle of it all. Rosa had been working through their financial mess, trying to figure out how to cover costs with the grant gone and their current group of scientists off-site due to the investigation.

Angie stared at her fingers, clasped between her knees. Her brain didn't want to consider all of the options in front of her. Or, more realistically, the *lack* of options in front of her.

"We also don't think the protestors have been directly involved in the attacks on you the past few days, outside of the one at the hospital. Given what Riley has said, the working theory is that whoever paid them is behind that." With a heavy sigh, Thomas sat on the other side of the coffee table and leaned forward, mimicking her posture with his hands clasped between his knees. "We do have some questions about the protestors, though."

"Okay." But if the protestors weren't directly involved, why did it matter?

"You told Linc you knew one of the local organizers."

"Sort of. We went to school together. We attend the same church, but we have a large congregation so we don't cross paths a lot."

Thomas jotted something in a notebook he pulled from his pocket. Like Linc, he seemed to prefer pen and paper. "What's her name?"

"Monica Huerta." Surely they didn't think… "Monica wouldn't hurt me. She's always been friendly. She even apologized for any trouble the protestors caused. She's the one who told me they'd turned over the vandals to the sheriff."

Looking up, Thomas studied her with one eyebrow raised. "Why would she help organize a protest if she's sorry for doing it?"

"You'd have to ask her to be sure, but Monica has ancestral ties to the Havasupai. She's proud of her heritage. If she somehow came to believe, like the protestors seem to, that I was going to hurt the land, then I can understand her being upset. The fact it's me, someone she knows, wouldn't change her convictions. I just wish she'd talk to me about what I'm truly doing. She might understand I want to help preserve history and heritage by providing a place for research and preservation. I want to be part of the solution."

Again, Thomas wrote in his notebook. He flipped a few pages and read something.

The silence grew long. Even Rosa, who was

normally steady, shifted as though she couldn't get comfortable. She fired a grim look at Angie.

Lincoln stood and walked to the window, looking out as though he felt caged.

She could appreciate that. Every ounce of her longed for a wild run on her horse, but not to the canyon. Now she wanted to ride headlong deep into the forest, where she wouldn't feel so exposed.

"When did you last speak to Monica?" Thomas didn't look up.

"At church a couple of weeks ago. That's when she told me about the sheriff." There were too many questions about Monica. This had to be what Linc wasn't talking about. Angie stood and faced him. "Linc, what are you hiding? Did Monica do something?"

When Linc turned from the window, it was to carry on a silent conversation with Thomas. The look they exchanged spoke of a discussion already completed, a plan already in place.

When Linc walked closer, Angie backed away. "What?" There was a wild extra beat to her heart. The news wasn't going to be good.

"Monica's missing." Linc's voice was quiet but firm, leaving no room for her to argue with the facts.

"That's impossible." She'd argue whether he liked it or not. "I saw her before I went to the conference."

The room was heavy with silence that crashed her protests to the hardwood. No one would look at her. Even Rosa stared at the fireplace, seeming stricken by paralysis.

"Do they think…?" If they were talking about serial killers, then they thought Monica was a victim.

"I'm sorry." Thomas closed his notebook, keeping his finger tucked into the spot where he'd been writing. "I know this is a lot, but can you tell me about your last conversation? Remember anything else she might have said? Anything unusual about her behavior?"

Thoughts swirled. There was too much information assaulting her. She closed her eyes and tried to picture the large sanctuary and how Monica had looked.

Nothing stood out. It had been a brief conversation, and Monica had simply squeezed her shoulder in a quick side hug before she left. "I'm sorry. I've got nothing."

"She hasn't mentioned talking to anyone online?"

"We weren't close enough to talk like that."

If only she could remember more. "It was a quick conversation. She was on her way to get her sister from children's church."

Linc leaned forward. "How old is her sister?"

"Sasha is much younger. I think seven or eight?"

Linc turned to Thomas. "Has anyone from our team interviewed the family yet?"

"No." Thomas slipped his notebook into the leg pocket of his uniform. "I'm supposed to do that tomorrow morning."

"I'll go." Linc looked down at Angie. "We'll both go."

Thomas moved as though he was going to say more, but he seemed to think better of it and simply nodded. "Call me when you're done."

Angie stared at Linc. He was up to something. She had no idea what, but she was along for the ride, whether she liked it or not.

Chapter Twelve

Lincoln locked the dead bolt and punched the alarm code Angie had given him to arm the system. By the time he turned around, Angie was halfway up the stairs, her shoulders slumped as though the weight on her shoulders was more than she could bear.

It most assuredly was.

The last thing Angie needed was to be alone. She might think she needed quiet, but he'd been around long enough to know how deep she could dive into her own head. With all she had going on, she needed to talk it out, maybe get a notebook and write it out, but she certainly didn't need to let everything simply sit.

He'd taken one step toward the stairs and was about to call her name when his phone buzzed. A glance at the notification on his watch told him he dare not ignore this one.

It was his doctor's office, likely calling to confirm his appointment.

He winced. If he went to interview Monica Huerta's family in the morning, he would have to push back receiving his results.

Again.

He pressed the answer button and held the phone to his ear, waiting for the recording to tell him which number to push to reschedule.

Instead, there was silence.

His forehead creased. "This is Lincoln Tucker."

"Special Agent Tucker." The voice was familiar. "It's Dr. Collins."

His doctor. She wasn't waiting until morning to tell him the results to his face.

Suddenly his knees didn't want to hold him. The next few seconds would determine the course of his future. He would continue to live the life he loved, or he would lose everything.

He sank to the arm of the sofa. Shifting the phone to his other ear, he cleared his throat as emotion tried to clog it. "Can I return to full duty?" Why bother with formalities? He knew why she was calling. She knew what he wanted to hear.

She was the kind of no-nonsense doc who understood. She'd been a surgeon in the army and now worked with veterans and the National Park Service. She understood the language. Pass on the news, get in and get out, keep moving at all costs.

"I know from speaking to the clinic's receptionist you're working a case, so I thought I'd call rather than have you pulled out of the field to come in." The words were kind, but they were also brusque.

The tone…

Lincoln had never felt his heart sink before, but he was pretty sure it landed somewhere around his feet.

She didn't need to say more.

His eyes slipped shut. His entire body tensed, pushing a deep ache from his spine into his head. He'd known all along. No matter how much he'd tried to fool himself, the pain always told him otherwise.

Silence reigned for several heartbeats, then the doc exhaled. "I'm sorry, Agent Tucker. I even got a second and a third opinion before I called you, and you have access to your scans so you can get a fourth, but given the current state of your injury and the rate at which it's healing, I can't clear you to return to full duty."

"Now or ever?" Man, he hated the way the words cracked.

"I didn't necessarily say that. We'll revisit this in a few months, but…"

His arm threatened to go limp, but he pressed the phone tighter to his ear. "Surgery is still out of the question?"

"Too risky, as we've discussed in the past. The chances of permanent paralysis are high. Once you go through physical therapy and this initial pain subsides, you'll be free to live a normal life, but you'll have to curb some of your riskier activities, to include climbing and rappelling." She hesitated. "I know this is a lot, and I'm sorry to tell you over the phone. Schedule an appointment when you're done with your current case, and we'll go over your options, okay?" Her voice softened, clearly affected by his pain. "This may not be forever."

Well, he didn't want the pity. "Yeah." He killed the call without saying goodbye then stared at the phone, clenched in his white-knuckle grip. What he wanted was to throw it across the room and watch it smash against the wall. It took everything he had to behave like an adult.

No climbing. No rappelling. That likely

meant no backcountry hiking, possibly no horseback riding. The doc might as well lock him in a closet. Bury pieces of him in that bucket they'd unearthed. If he couldn't do those things, he was useless to his team.

Nothing else mattered.

"Hey." A touch on his shoulder nearly sent him through the ceiling.

He whirled toward the voice.

Angie withdrew her hand but didn't back away, the way he would have in her position. Instead, she studied him with concern. "That call didn't sound good."

He stared down at her, trying to pull his mind into reality. He'd forgotten where he was and that she was in the house. The way his brain spun, her presence wasn't computing, and for the quickest moment, he couldn't separate past from present.

With one brief shake of his head, he paced to the breakfast bar between the kitchen and the living area, then to the dining-room table. He couldn't force himself to stand still. His future had disintegrated while his past stood in front of him.

He wanted to run.

There was nowhere to go.

Had it only been a few hours since he'd watched Angie pace this same route around the living room, frustrated and frightened? Now here he was, wearing the same groove in the floor.

He stopped in front of a large china cabinet filled with knickknacks her mother had left behind when she moved in with her sister. Photos, seashells and art were nestled behind the glass doors.

His own mother had never been one to keep "treasures."

How was he going to explain to his family the job he'd committed his life to was gone? They'd have plenty to say. He'd failed and had nothing to show for—

Angie's hand rested at the center of his back, below the damaged place in his spine, warm and… And tender. "I'm sorry."

"You didn't do anything." Somehow the words came out at half volume. In the glass front of the cabinet, he could make out the shape of her reflection.

She was watching him in the glass. "I know how much your job means to you. I know you wanted a different answer. I know right now everything feels broken."

His chin dropped to his chest, tugging at the pain. At this moment, he didn't want anyone to understand. He wanted to be angry and hurt. To punch a wall or run until his legs gave out. He didn't want sympathy.

Yet, he couldn't move away from her touch.

Silently, Angie turned and rested her forehead on his shoulder. It wasn't a gesture that spoke of pity. It was a gesture that offered strength.

She didn't feel sorry for him. She wanted to help him stand against the winds of this storm.

After their friendship died, he'd never expected to partner with her in anything again. Had never imagined the two of them could be there for one another in trying times.

Yet here they were. He was walking her through a nightmare. She was supporting him in a hurricane.

How was that kind of grace possible?

Soft warmth flowed from his brain to his heart, then rushed out to his fingertips.

This was right. This was what the two of them were meant to be, what he'd slaughtered with his awkward self-centeredness years before.

She needed him, and he needed her. There had been a gaping hole inside of him ever since he'd walked out the door that day. He'd missed her laugh and her smile, her honesty and her vulnerability. Most of all, he'd missed her friendship. Her presence.

With an exhale he'd been holding for years, he slid his arm around her waist and gently pulled her against his chest. Resting his chin on the top of her head, he simply held on.

Her back stiffened. For a moment, she didn't breathe, and he thought she might pull away. Then her arms slipped around his waist and she pressed her cheek against his chest. She was bound to be able to hear the effect she had on his heart rate.

She didn't let go. She simply held on as though she could keep him from flying apart.

Maybe she could. Or, better yet, maybe God could, through her. The one thing he'd learned over the years was God mattered most. Somehow, God had given him the gift of Angie's presence to help him through.

Even more, God had given him the gift of helping Angie through. He wasn't useless. Pointless. Helpless. She needed him, and he was available because of the careless mistake that might have cost him his career.

The anger faded, though he knew it would

return to fight another day. In this moment, his shattered dreams weren't as important as protecting Angie.

He was where he needed to be.

His head dipped, and his cheek brushed hers. Her breath was warm against his ear, and it hitched in a way that said she felt the same rush that ran through him. Warm emotion flowed through his veins, bringing the vision of a new future, a dream he'd only considered one other time. A dream he'd kept under lock and key.

One that now saw daylight as his former dreams fell to pieces.

If Angie turned her head…

If he turned his…

This moment could go very differently. He could pour into her everything he was feeling. This gratitude. This new awareness of what she meant to him. He could say it all without words. Could promise her something new, something neither of them had ever dared to hope for.

Her head tipped ever so slightly.

Lincoln backed away, wanting to see her expression, to measure her emotions. He let his gaze roam her eyes, her face, her lips. With his entire being, he wanted to close the gap and pour everything into a kiss that would change their worlds all over again.

But he couldn't.

It took all of the strength he held in reserve to back away from her, to let his hands fall to his sides and to deny himself what he wanted most.

Because kissing her here, now, when they were both emotionally exhausted and pushed to their mental limits, would be too much like the last time he'd kissed her, when they'd nearly thrown everything over a cliff's edge.

He couldn't layer that moment over this one. Couldn't let their past mistakes color a precious heartbeat that might lead to a different future.

No, he wanted to start at the beginning. To treat her with the care and tenderness she deserved.

Cupping her cheeks in his palms, he pressed a kiss to her forehead. Then he pulled her into a hug he hoped would convey all of the things he couldn't say.

What was happening to her life?

Angie pulled the seat belt from her chest and let it thread through her fingers as it slipped into place. Through the plate glass window of Misty's eclectic gas station/gift shop/lunch counter, Linc kept one eye on Angie in the truck and one eye on the conversation he was having with Misty, who nodded before she disappeared through a door in the back of the store.

Angie eyed the gravel parking lot, empty in the gap between breakfast and lunch. Linc had insisted they stop on the way to talk to Monica's family, giving her no explanation for this detour.

Just like he hadn't given her an explanation for his behavior the night before.

She leaned her head against the window and stared at him, unsure if he could see her through the sunlight reflecting off the truck's windshield. Their silent conversation had touched something deep inside her, unraveling years of pain that had formed the night her grief had pushed him one step too far.

The memory heated her cheeks, the shame still stinging.

Somehow, last night had provided a salve that made the burn less raw.

When she'd walked down the stairs and heard Lincoln's clipped phone conversation, she'd sensed his loss as clearly as if he'd broadcast the words with a skywriter. The doctor's news had thrown his future off a ledge. He'd been seconds from dashing his hopes on the rocks at the bottom.

His slumped shoulders, pained expression and white-knuckle grip on his phone had made her pain fade. Letting him know he was seen had become the most important thing.

No words would have done that, so she'd held him and let him hold her.

And in the process...

Well, in the process everything had changed.

She could still feel the way he'd clung to her. For a moment she'd nearly bolted, horrified by the fact that she'd drawn them into that space where they'd nearly made an irreversible misstep years ago.

This time was different.

This time, that broken wounded mess they'd both been had somehow knit itself together. It wasn't about feeling alive or hiding from the horror of a brother's brokenness and pain.

This time, it had been about sharing one another's hurts. Understanding one another's feelings. The last time they'd approached each other, it had been all about her, about escaping the emotion and exhaustion.

This time, all she'd wanted was to help him hold it together. To let him know he wasn't alone.

The change inside of her was monumental. The shift in her thinking and the crack straight down the middle of her heart indicated she was no longer the same person.

She'd accepted God's forgiveness long ago, but the barrier between Linc and herself had seemed insurmountable. That had all changed when Linc pressed a kiss to her forehead, then held her as though she was fragile, although he was, too.

In that moment, she forgave him.

In that moment, she forgave herself.

Now, sitting in Linc's truck, still fearing for her safety, her heart was raw and the tears were close. Her past mistakes no longer defined her, not with Linc and not with anyone else. For the first time, she truly understood what it meant to be made new.

As Linc walked out the door of Misty's carrying a huge box, she studied him. While she knew this shift had changed her relationship with Jesus, had made it more real and much deeper, she had no idea what it meant for her relationship with Linc.

Was there a future?

Did she want one?

He stashed the box in the bed of his pickup, then slid behind the wheel without looking at her. He'd been quiet all morning. Given the news he'd received, he was probably wrestling with reality.

She let a few miles go by, trying not to think about everything happening in and around her. It would probably be easier on them both if she could start a conversation, but the silence felt too heavy.

So heavy she had to break it. "It's going to storm later." The pressure was dropping, and although it was only midmorning, cumulonimbus clouds were already building. It was a volatile time of year around the canyon. Hopefully, they'd avoid flooding rains.

"Really? We're going to talk about the weather?" It was tough to tell if that was sarcasm or amusement in his voice.

She opted to believe it was amusement and pushed toward something slightly more personal. "What's in the box?"

He kept his eyes on the road as they approached the outskirts of Williams. "You said Monica has a younger sister."

"Sasha. She's not in that box, though."

He arched an eyebrow, an indication her attempt at humor had fallen flat. "No, but with her sister missing, there's a lot of turmoil around her. I figured with the variety of stuff Misty sells, I might find something to help the kid out." He slowed and made a turn onto a narrow street, studying house numbers.

The homes here were small and packed tightly together. It was a neighborhood in transition, an eclectic mix of aging original and newly remodeled, of well-kept lawns and overgrown yards.

He parked in front of a small house with a brick facade and an older sedan in the driveway. Large windows dominated the front of the structure, though the curtains were drawn.

Linc looked at her for the first time since he'd returned to the vehicle. "I'm going to talk with Monica's parents and likely ask some hard questions. You're here to make me less intimidating."

Under normal circumstances, that blunt declaration would have made her laugh. The truth removed all humor from the situation. "I'm here because you didn't want to leave me at the ranch."

"That, too. Look, I—" Linc shook his head,

as though gnats were buzzing around him, then abruptly shoved the door open. "I need to focus on this right now." He left the truck and slammed the door behind him.

Okay, then. Angie slipped out of the vehicle and followed Linc and his mysterious box to the front door.

It opened before they reached it, and a middle-aged man stepped out. He was shorter than Linc and thin, his skin darkened and lined by the sun. "Can I help you?" Wary exhaustion weighted the words.

Linc set the box on the low brick porch wall and lifted his badge where it hung on a chain around his neck. "I'm Special Agent Lincoln Tucker with the National Park Service Investigative Services. We're helping to search for Monica. I spoke to her mother earlier."

The man's posture relaxed and he stepped aside, holding the door open. "I'm her father, Martin. Her mother's inside."

Linc let Angie walk in ahead of him, and she stepped from bright midmorning sunlight into oppressive darkness. The curtains were closed. The lights were off. The air felt heavy and still. As her eyes adjusted, she took in a crowded living room stuffed with mismatched furniture.

A counter with overhanging cabinets separated the living area from the kitchen.

A familiar woman about Angie's height walked out of the kitchen carrying a coffee cup. At her heels was Monica's sister, Sasha, carefully pulling the paper from a muffin.

Mrs. Huerta stopped abruptly when she saw Angie. "Oh. I'm sorry." She looked past Angie to Linc. "I forgot you were coming." Her head tilted as she returned her gaze to Angie. "You go to church with us."

How did someone forget that law enforcement was coming to help search for their missing daughter? It took a second to comprehend the second part of Mrs. Huerta's statement. "Oh. Monica and I went to school together, and yes, I go to Daybridge with you, Mrs. Huerta."

"Call me Celia."

"Celia. I'm so sorry about—"

"Sit. Please." Mrs. Huerta motioned to the couch near the front window as Mr. Huerta shut the door and sat in a recliner. "Coffee?"

"I'm fine." Everything felt odd, stilted. Maybe that was normal. She'd never been around a family whose daughter might have been taken by a serial killer, so who was she to judge their behavior?

As Angie sat, Linc settled the box in the middle of the floor. "I brought something for Sasha. Is that okay?"

The little girl peered from behind her mother, then looked up for permission to approach.

Mrs. Huerta nodded.

Sasha shoved the muffin into her mother's hand and lunged for the box. She ripped open the flaps then dove inside to retrieve the contents.

Angie bit back a laugh as Sasha squealed in delight at the massive stuffed animal. Taller than the little girl, the unicorn was a riot of pastel colors and featured a squishy gold lamé horn. Sasha dove on top of the toy and sprawled like it was a bed, her smile radiant. "Thank you!"

Linc offered a smile as he kneeled beside her. He tapped the gold horn. "I figured now would be a good time for a new best friend."

Sasha threw her arms around the plush unicorn's neck and held on tight. "I love it!" As fast as only a small child could move, she leaped at Linc and wrapped her arms around his neck. "Thank you, Mr. Policeman. I love you, too."

Linc winced, then his eyes closed and he hugged the little girl tight before she squirmed away and turned to her mother. "Can I take it to my room?"

"Sure."

Sasha hugged Linc again, admiration and maybe the beginnings of a little-girl crush in her expression. He'd brought joy into her rocky world, had considered her feelings when she'd probably been shoved to the side by circumstances.

Angie looked away, her heart squeezing in her chest with feelings she was only beginning to acknowledge.

I can relate, Sasha. I can relate.

Chapter Thirteen

Some moments reminded him there was still good in the world.

Linc was reluctant to let this one go.

Sasha shouted another thank-you and dragged her prize down the narrow hallway out of sight, taking some of the sparkle from the room and reminding him why he was really here. Not to brighten the day of a little girl whose world had been turned upside down, but to talk to the parents of a woman who had vanished, either on her own or at the hands of a serial killer.

He rose, trying not to wince at the pain being tackled by a seven-year-old had inflicted. Glancing around the room, he chose a seat in a side chair instead of taking a spot on the couch by Angie.

Being near her messed with his senses. The entire ride to Williams, he'd been distracted by her instead of working through the questions he needed to ask the Huertas. She'd unlocked something in him the previous evening, and he had no idea what to do with it. This was different than the last time they'd walked through trials together. There was no desperate sense of need. This was quiet. Deeper. It bordered on lo—

He drew a deep breath. He needed to focus, not only to help locate Monica Huerta, but also to uncover any clues that might point to who had killed Ellis and attacked Angie.

From where she stood by the kitchen entrance, Mrs. Huerta offered a tight smile. "Thank you, Agent Tucker. She's been a bit out of sorts with everything that's happened. Since Monica has been living on her own for a while now, Sasha hasn't processed the day-to-day of Monica's being gone, but she has certainly picked up on our tension. That present was a bright spot for her." She walked over and sat on the opposite end of the couch from Angie. "Are you sure I can't offer you anything?"

"I'm fine. Thank you." He pulled his notebook from his thigh pocket and glanced around the room, trying to appear casual.

In his peripherals, he watched the Huertas.

Martin sat rigid, his gaze on his wife as though she was in control of what happened next.

Celia held her coffee cup lightly, seeming to be calm. It was clearly an act. Her posture was stiff, and her words were measured and carefully chosen. While people for whom English was a second language often spoke formally due to their lack of idioms or contractions, he knew from reading the case notes that Celia had been raised in an English-speaking home.

Something else was going on. There was a practiced air to her movements. He'd seen families react oddly under stress, but this?

The vibe was off in the Huerta household, and it made him wonder if the theory he'd shared with Thomas actually held water.

He stared at a blank page in his notebook, pretending to study words that weren't there. He'd have to be careful how he presented himself, or they'd shut him out.

When he finally looked up, Martin was still watching his wife, and Celia sat with her coffee mug resting on her bent knees, her straight posture and crossed ankles reminding him of photos of the British royal family.

The most truthful answers would likely come from the father. He angled toward Martin. "Sir,

I know this is difficult. You've answered a thousand questions for the local police, but my team is working with the FBI and I have some follow-up questions." He guarded his words, not wanting to guide the Huertas' answers.

"I don't understand why the FBI is involved." Martin stared at work-worn hands, balling his fists as though he was holding in emotion. Fear? Anger? Whatever it was, it was volatile. His body language betrayed his calm words.

"It's standard when someone disappears under these sorts of circumstances. You're going to hear me repeat a lot of questions, so I apologize in advance."

Martin's gaze flicked to his wife, a hard look that seemed like a challenge. He worked his mouth from side to side, then met Linc's gaze with what was almost a look of defiance. "Whatever you need. I just want to know my daughter is safe." He shot a hard look to his wife before staring at the floor.

The nagging feeling that something was off grew stronger. "We'll do everything we can, sir." He ran down a few basic questions about the last time they'd seen Monica and whether they knew anything about the man she'd been chatting with online. Their answers were consistent with the intel Thomas had already given him. "Where did Monica work? It was after she failed to show up for a shift that you noticed something was wrong, correct?"

Celia nodded, turning her coffee cup in her hands. "Yes. Her boss called. She worked as a plumber's apprentice and missed several appointments she'd been assigned."

Angie leaned forward, her forehead creased. Clearly, that had surprised her.

Martin's head jerked up, his eyes wide, but he quickly looked away from his wife toward the hallway where his daughter had disappeared.

Everything about this was weird, including that answer. Angie and Thomas had both told him Monica worked as a manager at an apartment complex. "She was a plumber's apprentice?"

"Part-time." When Celia looked at him, the fire in her eyes was totally out of place given the circumstances. "She used to talk to the plumber who did work for the complex, and he told her she could make more money hands-on than she could behind a desk. So she worked in the mornings as his apprentice and at the apartments in the afternoon and evenings."

"Who was this plumber?" *Was the FBI aware of this?*

"A man named Mac."

Angie seemed to jump, almost as though the name had jerked her into the room from somewhere else. "Mac Dwyer?"

Martin stood suddenly.

Linc eyed him, ready to intervene if necessary. The man moved like a caged animal. "Is everything okay, Mr. Huerta?"

"We're done talking. If you need anything, I'm sure the FBI can provide it. My family has been through enough." Martin walked to the door and pulled it open. "If you'd like to come back in a few days, maybe we can arrange something."

He'd learn nothing more today. Nodding slowly, Linc rose and waited for Angie to join him. He flipped his notebook closed and shoved it in his pocket. "I understand. This is a trying time, and I'm sure it's difficult to keep repeating your story." He pulled a business card from his pocket and laid it on the arm of the couch. "If you need me or you think of something that might help us find your daughter—"

Find your daughter. Like a key in a lock, his

nagging thoughts clicked into place. He knew what was wrong.

He glanced around the room, attempting to make eye contact, but neither parent looked his way. "Please, don't hesitate to call." Motioning to Angie, he walked out the door, holding himself together until he got into the truck and started the engine. He needed to call Thomas, ASAP.

Angie snapped her seat belt. "You learned something, didn't you?"

Staring at the closed front door, Linc shook his head then backed out of the driveway. The Huertas were probably watching. Once he was out of the neighborhood and onto State Route 64 heading north, he felt like he'd sorted through the details enough to speak. "Something's not right."

"Their daughter is missing. There's a lot that's not right."

"No." He kneaded the steering wheel, forming his words carefully. Things often stood out to him that others missed. It was part training, part instinct. But this? This had been obvious. How much should he reveal to Angie? "Did you notice how they talked about Monica's disappearance? 'We want to know our daughter is safe.' Stuff like that?"

"Seems natural to me."

"I've worked dozens of missing-persons cases. Parents, spouses...they all inevitably say 'find my daughter' or 'bring my child home.' They bargain. They beg. They'll do anything, offer anything. But the Huertas?"

Angie sank into her seat and stared out the front windshield. "None of that happened. It was all—"

"Controlled. Like they had something to hide." It was as though they were reading from a script. But who had written their lines?

He reined in his thoughts and tried to think through all of the angles, not just the ones that matched his theory. People reacted to trauma in different ways. It was best to gather evidence with an impartial eye, but he still wanted to run all of this by Thomas soon.

Besides, he had more questions. "How did you know the plumber's name?"

Angie hesitated. "He subcontracts with Carter and did all of the plumbing work when we built the dorm and the lab."

Linc turned to her, then had to jerk his attention to the two-lane road. "What?" There had definitely been some weirdness in the air when Mac's name came up. He was connected directly to Monica, and as a subcontractor, he was connected through Carter to Isla Blake.

Due to the construction, Mac also had access to Angie's property.

They might not have reached two plus two equals four yet, but they were getting close.

Angie gripped the edge of her seat. "Whatever you're thinking, no. Mac is… He's pushing seventy. He plays Santa at church every Christmas and buys gifts for kids who wouldn't get gifts otherwise. He's constantly giving money or food or clothing to people who need it. He's practically everybody's grandfather. Mac was good friends with my dad and with Javi West, Ellis's father. He even recommended… He…" She exhaled something that sounded like word salad.

When he pulled his eyes from the road, she was staring past him, her mouth slightly open. "Angie? What do you remember?"

"Ellis West used to work for Mac. We hired him as a ranch hand on Mac's recommendation."

Linc pressed the Bluetooth button on his steering wheel. He was calling Thomas right now. He wanted Mac Dwyer brought in and questioned immediately.

Either that man had helped those women disappear…or he was guilty of murder.

Angie had been right earlier. Another storm was rolling in.

As a gust whipped the tape around the excavation site, Linc stood beside Thomas and watched the crime-scene units from the FBI and the National Park Service stow tents before rising wind could rip them away.

Thomas looked grim. "They've been out here since daybreak, and they've found nothing." He shoved his hands into his pockets and watched the activity. "Maybe the other evidence either doesn't exist, or it's buried somewhere else."

Linc let his gaze sweep the surrounding area. Stands of trees dotted the landscape at the edge of the Kaibab National Forest. Nearer the canyon, very little marred the space between horizon and sky.

The Garcias owned over a thousand acres, nearly two square miles of land. Beyond their inholding, two miles of government-owned land ran to the canyon, which was nearly two thousand largely untouched square miles. The Garcias' land ran several hundred feet into the national forest, which contained over a million pristine acres. Each held secrets they'd kept for thousands of years. There was no way to dig up every square inch of the land. Even ground-penetrating radar wouldn't help. It would be like mowing millions of square acres and hoping for a hit.

He watched storm clouds roil over the canyon in the distance. "I don't know. It's all too coincidental not to mean something. Ellis is murdered after two women disappear for the first time in a decade. The original disappearances stopped when Ellis's father died. Mac Dwyer knew Monica and has a connection to Isla plus access to this place."

"Where Ellis and his father both lived."

"And then there's that postcard…" That was the one thing that seemed to tie everything together. The most crucial piece of evidence was often the one thing that didn't make sense. That postcard stood out like a scream in the silence.

Thomas shook his head. "This is as close as you're ever going to get to a literal needle in a haystack."

He was right. They could search for decades

and never find another clue. It was like playing *Battleship* on an infinite grid. One inch to the left and they'd miss the prize entirely.

"And, Tucker? If you're right and those women faked their own deaths, then they ran away from something. A couple of them had domestic calls to their houses. One had escaped trafficking. They may not want us to find them."

That was likely true, but until they had proof the women weren't victims of a killer, they were obligated to keep searching. Lincoln swept his hands over his hair, trying to right what the wind had wronged. It was futile. "Any word on Mac Dwyer?" That's where the answers were. They'd been unable to locate him at work or at home and were waiting for search warrants before they could proceed.

"Nothing yet."

"So we still don't know anything?" Angie's voice was tense.

Linc turned.

As she approached, she swept her wind-whipped hair out of her face and held it against the top of her head. She frowned when she caught his eye. "Before you ask, I didn't recognize anything other than a couple of names from news stories when I was a kid."

She'd been with Rosa since they returned from Williams, poring over unclassified portions of the files about all of the missing women, attempting to see if anything rang a bell.

Because they were still technically searching for a serial killer until evidence proved otherwise, Rosa had handed over old employee records to Thomas, who'd passed them on to the team and the FBI. They had set up a remote office in the research facility and were busily cross-referencing with the missing women, searching for connections. So far, they'd come up short.

Thomas excused himself to take a call and walked around the corner of Ellis's cabin, probably to get out of the wind. The sun still shone overhead, but it made the clouds in the distance appear darker and more ominous.

It almost felt like a sign of things to come.

Angie stared at the incoming storm. "It's a volatile time of year. Aren't you worried about destroying evidence?"

"Whatever's out here has been here for years. Anything that could be destroyed is long gone." Linc kicked the dirt. There were places where the topsoil was too shallow to bury five-gallon buckets, so they could eliminate those areas, but that still left too much land to cover.

It was hopeless.

"Angie." Rosa walked out of her cabin, pocketing her phone as she hurried across the path. "I've got to go to my mother's."

Angie turned to her, hands outstretched. "What's wrong? Is she okay? Do you need me to come along?"

"No. She's…" Rosa's face was pinched. The lines around her mouth were white. "She's had another seizure and is refusing to go to the hospital. I may need to stay with her tonight."

"Go." Angie waved her hands toward Rosa's cabin. "We'll be fine here."

Hesitating, Rosa looked at the crime-scene tape that twisted in a frenzy with the rising wind. "I don't want to leave you alone."

"She's not alone." Linc stepped closer to the woman, who was clearly distraught. Given that her mother had refused medical treatment for seizures before, he could understand Rosa's concern.

The news about his own test results nagged. He never wanted to make someone feel responsible for him, nor did he want to saddle someone else with his pain.

His gaze went to Angie, then he turned toward where Thomas had disappeared.

He wanted more from her than friendship. The more he was with her, the more he wanted to be with her. He wanted to share life, good and bad.

He wanted forever.

The thrill ran through him so quickly, he half wondered if lightning had reached across the miles and hit him square in the spine. It sure felt like electricity. The ferocity of the emotion melded his feet to the ground.

He loved her.

He'd loved her since the moment she'd comforted him in that hospital waiting room years earlier. He'd walked away because he'd wanted what was best for her…

Because. He. Loved. Her.

Did he love her enough to walk away again, knowing his injury could leave her caring for him in the future? Did love mean he stayed, or did love mean he left?

"Linc?" Her light touch on his shoulder jolted him out of his thoughts.

Steeling himself for the sight of her, he turned.

"I'm going to hang out with Rosa while she packs. She wants to get out before the storm hits." She was already backing away. "With your team bunking in the dormitory tonight, I want to stay in her cabin so I can be available if they need anything."

Angie and Rosa had already planned to treat the NPS and FBI teams as though they were guests, providing food and lodging. Both agencies would pay a per diem, something Linc knew Angie desperately needed.

Well, if she was staying, so was he. She wasn't getting out of his sight, not when danger still lurked. They might suspect the serial killer was a cover for something else, but that still didn't explain who was after Angie. It wouldn't be the first time he'd bunked on a couch, and it wouldn't be the last.

But it might be the most uncomfortable. His neck still protested his snooze on Angie's sofa the night before.

He watched the door close behind her as the crime-scene units loaded the vans and shut the doors. They'd wait out the storm in the dormitory, then start again in the morning if the ground wasn't too saturated by the rain.

Thomas appeared at his side. He stood silently, watching the weather before he finally spoke. "That was Detective Majenty from Coconino County. He put me on a conference call with the head of the FBI team."

Oh, no. Those players on one call meant either something very good or something very bad. Judging by the tone of Thomas's voice, it wasn't going to be good.

He faced Thomas as the wind pushed against his back, bringing the damp smell of rain.

Thomas pocketed his phone. "Coconino County and the FBI team are headed to Mac Dwyer's house."

His heart sank to his stomach. "They found Monica Huerta." He'd hoped it wouldn't end this way. That she had disappeared on her own and—

"No." Thomas scanned his phone screen. "Mac Dwyer's neighbor found him in the workshop behind his house."

Hope and grief lay heavy in Linc's stomach. How much more violence could they all take? "He's dead, isn't he?"

"Nearly. They're taking him to the hospital, but it doesn't look good." Thomas's expression was grim. "Linc, you may be right about there not being a real killer. This doesn't look like a suicide attempt or a straightforward murder. Somebody wanted information out of Mac. Just like Ellis, Mac Dwyer was tortured."

Chapter Fourteen

Rolling onto her side, Angie punched the pillow and stared at the thin curtains over Rosa's window. Without a clock and with her phone charging on the dresser, she had no idea what time it was. Given the way the darkness softened around the edges, she'd guess it was somewhere in the vicinity of five in the morning.

She held her breath, listening, but heard nothing. Something had snapped her out of a doze, but she couldn't place what it was.

There was no sound from Linc, who'd slept in the living room despite her offering to take the couch so he could have the bed. His back had to be killing him.

Maybe he had stirred and that's what she'd heard, but there were no further sounds. Given how lightly she'd been sleeping, it could have been anything from the breeze that blew between the buildings or a member of the FBI or NPS moving with the beginnings of the day.

What she wouldn't give for blackout curtains right about now. Rosa tended to live life the old-school way, starting her day with the sunrise and ending it with the sunset. She didn't let a clock dictate the rhythm of her life. She rolled along with nature.

That made zero sense. Angie flopped on her back. If she had her way, she'd ignore the outside world and sleep until her body decided it couldn't be still any longer. Given that she'd lain awake for the vast majority of the night and had only succumbed to a couple of catnaps, that could take several days.

No, sleep had not been her friend the previous night. Dark thoughts had chased it away, leaving her desperate for a mind that would simply be quiet for a few hours. Instead, she'd been plagued by images of serial killers, dead bodies and the all-too-real memory of a masked figure trying to drag her into the darkness.

How did investigators like Linc and her brother and Detective Blankenship deal with what they saw every day? This was the dark side of humanity, the worst of the worst.

Yet somehow, they managed to sleep at night.

She assumed. Maybe exhaustion claimed them when they dropped their heads on their pillows. Rest wasn't always sweet. She knew for a fact Jacob sometimes suffered from nightmares, and the way Linc talked, he did as well.

Her career as a meteorologist—sitting in front of her computer running calculations, or being in the field taking measurements—hadn't prepared her for this, nor had it allowed her to consider what others actually went through.

Why was Linc so upset about being unable to return to that life? Maybe helping catch the bad guys gave him a sense of peace.

What she wouldn't give for that right now.

Well, sleep wasn't going to come anytime soon, so she might as well start the day. While Thomas had left last night to process another scene with part of the NPS team, the FBI's crime-scene unit had remained on the property, planning to rise at first light to search for more hidden buckets.

Since they were paying to stay on the ranch, she should give them the full experience. Normally, Rosa set out a continental breakfast in the dormitory kitchen. With her gone, Angie could certainly start the coffee and set out the food.

As soon as the sun fully rose, she'd check in with Rosa to see how her mother was doing. Angie had spent part of the night praying for the family and their ongoing concerns.

Dressing quickly, she grabbed Rosa's keys off the nightstand and clipped them to her belt loop, then stepped to the door and eased it open, wary of disturbing Linc if he'd managed to fall asleep.

He was leaned back in the recliner by the cold fireplace, covered in a quilt.

Angie stepped closer, keeping her footfalls silent on the throw rug. If he was asleep, he needed to stay that way. Rest had been in short supply for the man who had given tirelessly of himself, ignoring his own needs to protect her.

The slack muscles in his face indicated he was deep in slumber. Without pain lines around his mouth and along his forehead, he looked like a younger Linc, one who didn't have the chains of a thousand violent crimes threaded through his mind.

Until now, seeing him completely oblivious to the world, she hadn't considered how much stress he carried. Piling his own pain and loss on top of it all had to weigh on him.

Yet he'd set himself aside to care for her.

The urge to plant a kiss on his forehead was almost overwhelming. She stepped back and shoved her hands into the pockets of her jeans, unable to look away.

At some point in the past few days, the awkwardness between them had melted. They'd become a team again. Friends.

Maybe something more.

The feeling that had been welling in her chest since he'd received that awful telephone call burst into bloom.

He'd kicked down the walls her behavior had built between them years ago. Now, together, they were building something different, something that looked like a solid foundation. Each brick they laid shored up the sense of rightness inside her.

The way he'd sacrificed himself to shield her.

The way he'd apologized for wounding her when he'd walked out in an effort to protect her years ago.

The way he'd been so careful with her emotions, stepping lightly in any situation that might remind her of her past struggles and wounded heart.

Her eyes slipped closed, and she reveled in the vision of Linc kneeling on the floor beside a child whose world had been flipped upside down, presenting her with a stuffed unicorn that lived in every little girl's dreams.

The man constantly thought of other people ahead of himself, and somehow, she was blessed enough to be one of the people in his orbit.

She balled her fists in her pockets and opened her eyes, staring at him as the thought bubbled from her heart. Linc was so much more than a friend.

He was now, as he had been when Jacob was injured, the man she'd fallen in love with.

It was too much to think about. Too much to dream for. Turning, Angie headed for the door.

What she needed was to get outside into fresh, rain-washed air and shake loose these thoughts. Linc cared about everyone. He set aside his needs for everyone. That was one of the reasons she'd fallen for him the first time.

She was nothing special.

Was she?

Surely he didn't hold on to everyone the way he'd held on to her. Didn't watch every woman as though she somehow both enchanted and confused him. No, there was something about the way he looked at her that said she might be more to him. That she hadn't wrecked the something special between them all those years ago.

Shaking her head, she turned the lock and eased the door open. Let Linc sleep. She couldn't deal with looking him in the eye right now anyway. If she did, breakfast would never appear for the team because she'd stop everything to wake him up and ask him point-blank how he felt.

Nothing could be more dangerous.

As silently as she could, she shut the door and stepped onto the porch, bumping into a planter Rosa had set beside the steps. It scraped across the floor loud enough to wake the dead.

She froze, cocking her head to listen, but no sound came from the house. *Good.* Linc needed to rest.

No lights were on in the dormitory, so the teams were probably still asleep. She could have coffee ready for them before they got moving. She knew from experience with her brother that law enforcement ran on caffeine and adrenaline. Hopefully, caffeine would be all they got today.

Unclipping the keys from her belt loop, she headed down the steps to make the short walk to the dormitory. The ground was still wet from the previous evening's storm, marked with boot prints from the barn around the corner of the cabin where Rosa's window was.

Angie slowed, her heart picking up speed. Linc had come inside at the same time as she had the night before, and the rain had just started to fall. Given the downpour had lasted a large chunk of the night, water would have washed away any footprints they'd left behind.

Someone had been outside this morning, but no one should have been around the cabin. They definitely shouldn't have been sneaking beneath her window.

She turned to race up the steps, but an arm snaked around her throat from behind, dragging her backward and putting pressure on her neck. She struggled, the keys clattering to the dirt, but her attacker held her fast.

Her pulse pounded in her ears.

Her breaths couldn't reach her lungs.

The sky grew dark.

Everything turned black.

Linc sat bolt upright, his neck screaming. A sound seemed to echo in his head, but he couldn't figure out what it was. A scrape? A roar? His imagination in overdrive?

Easing the recliner upright, he tried to stretch gently, regretting his decision to sleep in his pants and polo instead of going to the main house for his sweats. He felt grungy and warm, and he ached all over. The faster he got some food and ibuprofen into his system, the better.

He glanced at his watch. Nearly five. Angie would probably be champing at the bit to get to the dormitory to take care of coffee and breakfast. The night before, she'd promised to be over there before six. Surprising that she hadn't shaken him awake yet. He'd knock on the door and rouse her as soon as he woke enough to settle the unease in his subconscious.

He planted his feet on the floor and listened. Maybe that noise had been a dream, but something told him it wasn't. There was a *knowing* he'd developed through training and intuition that told him something wasn't right. He scanned the room as he shoved his feet into his boots, stood and reached for the gun he'd left beside him on the coffee table.

The bedroom door was open.

Outside, near the barn, a vehicle engine started and the sound quickly moved away from him.

Okay, *now* he was awake.

Linc raced to the bedroom door. The room was empty. He spun around and scanned the living area. "Angie?" There was no sign of her.

His heart picked up speed. She could be anywhere. Had probably gone to the dormitory to start breakfast. That vehicle driving away could have been one of the FBI agents heading out to get supplies.

His gut told him different.

He parted the curtains and peered out the window by the door. Seeing nothing, he eased onto the porch, scanning the area in the milky predawn light. Nothing moved. The dormitory was dark and silent.

Flicking on his phone's flashlight, he searched the ground.

Footprints marred the recently dampened earth. One set was smaller—clearly Angie's, heading away from the cabin.

It was the second set that had him reaching for his phone. Men's boots. They circled the cabin and returned to the porch.

Since it had rained the night before, these

were fresh, and no one on the government teams had a reason to be near the cabin.

Ignoring the larger set of prints, he followed Angie's toward the dormitory then stopped, rooted to the spot. The mud was scuffed and gouged, as though someone had struggled before being lifted from the ground.

He turned. The boot prints moving away from where he stood were deeper, as though the wearer bore a heavy load. The trail headed for the barn.

The barn. Where he'd heard an engine moments earlier.

He stopped, feeling like a deer frozen in headlights. Race after that vehicle? Or alert the teams?

As much as he wanted to give chase down the bumpy road, backup came first. Pressing the phone screen to dial Thomas, he raced for the dormitory and banged his fist on the locked outer door.

The windows lit as he roused the agents, who'd probably open the door armed and ready to roll.

Thomas answered the phone before any of the agents appeared, and Linc didn't wait for formalities. "Someone has Angie. I'm gathering the teams. They took off in a vehicle headed toward the main gate. No description."

The sound of motion crossed the line and Thomas muttered something under his breath that Linc probably didn't want to decipher. "On the way. Get the teams and get moving."

The door eased open and two of the agents, Sloane and Mangum, pulled the door open wider and holstered their weapons when they realized it was Linc.

Before they could speak, he relayed the intel, then turned and ran for his truck, his heart pounding and his back protesting every step. Fear pulsed through him in a dangerous rhythm, adrenaline adding fuel to the frenzy.

Angie had to be okay. She had to be safe. She'd been right there, feet from him, and he'd lost her.

How?

He forced himself to breathe as he ran around the corner of the cabin, where he'd parked his truck. He couldn't let his emotions run the show, because that's how evidence was missed, mistakes were made and lives were lost.

Clicking the key fob, he glanced down and felt his world collapse.

The front driver's-side tire was flat. He ran up the path to the other vehicles and skidded to a halt, unable to comprehend what he was seeing.

Every vehicle had at least one useless tire.

There was no way to get to Angie.

Chapter Fifteen

Sheer panic rattled through Angie.

Consciousness returned in a rush, but her brain moved through a thick fog. Her body felt as though she was swimming in syrup.

She'd been dreaming about riding Chance through the trees, jostled by his gait. The colors were too bright. The sounds too loud. She'd jolted awake into darkness. The scent of grain overwhelmed her. The world had gone black. Her eyes were open, but there was nothing. Had she lost her vision? What was happening?

Her hands were wedged beneath her stomach, but she couldn't separate them. Her feet kicked, but they seemed to be bound. She tried to scream, but her body wouldn't cooperate. She was stuck inside something that covered her head, suffocating her. Stealing her thoughts. Controlling her emotions.

A low hum varied in intensity and pitch,

sometimes louder, sometimes softer, and her body seemed to flow with it, out of her control.

Cold sweat coated her body, although she was horribly warm. She was trapped. No way out. No way to breathe. No way to scream. And dizzy. So dizzy.

Focus. She needed focus. If ever there was a time to force down her emotions, it was now, but panic raced through her mind and forced her body to fight her bonds. She had to get out. Had to get free.

Pain cut into her wrists but she couldn't gain movement. Nothing she tried worked.

The lack of oxygen and wild thrashing exhausted her rapidly and she dropped her head, suddenly numb. Her heart raced, but her body lacked the strength to fight and her brain lacked the energy to process.

Her head bounced against something, and clarity kicked in. This sound was familiar. The hum revved again. Was it a vehicle's engine? She rolled, trying to feel anything with her shoulders. The space was confined. She ran through images in her mind. A box. A trunk.

The floorboard of a pickup truck. One riddle solved. Somehow, the knowledge felt like a small amount of power.

Forcing herself to breathe slowly through her nose, she tried to remember how she'd gotten here. She'd been walking to the dormitory, following the footprints on the ground, when—

Panic surged her racing heartbeat. Whoever had been hunting her had finally captured her.

She'd been so foolish.

Her eyes slipped closed. It was so hot. So humid. If she could free her head from the heaviness that covered it, she could breathe. Her entire being craved fresh, cool air.

She never should have left the cabin without Linc. If she'd have shaken him awake, they'd be at the dormitory now. Safe.

Linc.

Unbidden tears slipped down her cheeks. If she got out of this, she'd have to tell him the truths she'd realized this morning. Her heart was incomplete without him.

She'd tell him… *If* she got out of this.

Her chance for survival was probably slim. It seemed likely no one had realized she was gone.

This was all her fault.

The vehicle slowed and negotiated a turn, then came to a stop. The hum died. The world rocked as a door slammed, pounding against her rising headache.

She should fight.

The door opened, and rough hands grabbed her ankles, dragging her across the bumpy floor. Fear turned her muscles into spaghetti, and her plans for freedom died.

There was no fight left. Only terror, regret and the foggy sense that reality was six seconds ahead of her.

Her captor threw her over his shoulder in a fireman's carry.

Adrenaline surged, driving her to struggle, but with a muttered curse and a grunt, the man pulled tight on her knees and drew her closer, hindering her movement. With fear robbing her strength and a lack of oxygen leaving her light-headed, Angie surrendered.

More than anything, she wanted to say *please*, but whatever covered her head reduced the word to a mumble. She hated to beg. Hated to show weakness.

The man hesitated, seeming burdened by her weight or by guilt. Maybe he was reconsidering. Hope flashed through her, giving volume to her utterances. *Please, don't do this*. The words were a series of whimpers, like the cries of a newborn calf.

His step stuttered, but then his shoulders

straightened and he moved forward with re-newed purpose.

Desperation drove Angie's thoughts, insisting she plead for her life, that she promise this man whatever he wanted, from selling the ranch to leaving the country, as long as he let her sur-vive, but stubborn pride also rose, demanding she never give up.

She would not beg. She would not give her kidnapper the satisfaction.

She prayed as they seemed to be moving up a staircase. *Jesus, please. Please. Let Linc find me. Get me out of this.*

Her mind was fuzzy. Each step jarred against her diaphragm, making it harder to breathe in the already stifling, humid, recycled air.

Her breaths huffed faster. The air was too thick. Or she was panicking. Or dying. Or—

"Stop squirming before you throw me off balance and kill us both." The voice was a harsh hiss, barely above a whisper.

Either he was out of breath, or he was try-ing to disguise his voice. Still, something tick-led a memory. She'd heard him speak before, but where?

She whimpered, trying to indicate how dan-gerously low her air supply was. Between the covering over her head and the pressure of his shoulder on her chest, her oxygen was so depleted that her throat barely squeaked.

The man's steps leveled, and he slid her from his shoulder. Her feet touched the ground for a moment before he shoved her to the hard floor, her back against a rough wall.

She tilted her head, trying to get air from beneath whatever covered her head. It felt like a bag and smelled heavily of grain and animal.

It had to be one of the horse's feed bags, from the ranch barn. Meant to keep oats fresh, the heavy bags were airtight and waterproof. She'd suffocate soon if it wasn't lifted. Although blessed cooler air floated from underneath, it wasn't enough. It would never be enough.

She tossed her head, trying to indicate her distress as she slumped over her bent knees.

Footsteps stomped closer, and the bag jerked away. Beautiful fresh air, clean and cool, washed over her sweat-dampened face. She gulped in deep lungfuls. Nothing had ever felt sweeter to her mind or body.

Her hair hung in her face and over her eyes, sticking to her lashes and irritating her skin. She tried to swipe it away, but her movements were clumsy. She stared at the floor between her knees.

Heavy boots were nearly toe to toe with her running shoes. Who was this man, and what did he want from her?

Slowly, dread climbing her spine, Angie lifted her head and faced her captor.

The delay could have cost Angie her life.

Linc's truck, the park-service SUV and the FBI van all had tires speared with what looked to be a wide blade. Likely Angie's abductor had been in a hurry and hadn't wanted to take the time to cut more than one tire on each, thankfully. It had taken ten minutes to change to spares, but the delay had surely allowed the other vehicle to reach the main road, and who knew which direction he'd gone after that?

He prayed Thomas and Detective Blankenship had been able to rally in time to get on the road. With no vehicle description, though, they'd have to rely on random checkpoints. Setting those up would take more time than they had, especially if the kidnapper was a local and took the less-traveled back roads.

The FBI team was sweeping the property,

searching the barns and outbuildings, checking to see if the kidnapper had stayed close.

Linc prayed they had and Angie was found quickly. If not…

His brain didn't need to go there.

At the gate, he looked for protestors, hoping for witnesses, but no one was there. They hadn't returned after Riley's arrest.

While he'd disliked their presence before, he sure would love to see one of them now.

He rolled down his window to push the button on the keypad. As the gate swung open, he stared at the device.

Whoever had taken Angie had been driving a vehicle. The only way through the gate without Angie's remote was by punching in a code. He was fairly certain they'd exited through the main gate, but it was possible they'd entered that way as well.

Lord, let it be so.

If they'd entered through one of the padlocked back gates, then there was no way to know who it was. While no code was necessary to exit the main gate, maybe the camera had picked them up leaving. He'd heard the vehicle heading toward the main gate earlier, so perhaps they had a shot.

His heart surged and he uttered prayer after prayer. They might find Angie yet.

He roared through the gate with the federal teams behind him, punching the voice button on his steering wheel and practically shouting Rosa's name. Thankfully, he'd had the foresight to put her number into his phone the day before.

She answered on the third ring, sounding groggy. If she was caring for an ill parent, he might have interrupted her one shot at getting rest.

He winced, despite the urgency of the situation. "Rosa, I'm sorry to bother you, but I need help. Someone…" Should he tell her? In a rush, he exhaled. "Someone took Angie."

"What?" Her voice pitched higher, and the news had clearly startled her awake. "When? How?"

"No time to explain. I need to find out if anyone used a code to access the gate or if the camera caught footage of them leaving. Is that on your computer at the office?" If so, he'd have the FBI team access the data immediately. "Tell me how to—"

"I can check from my laptop to see everyone who's entered with a code. What time do you think they would have exited? That will help me isolate the video feed." As soon as he spoke an approximate time, the sound of fingers tapping on a keyboard clicked through the speakers, music to his ringing ears.

Linc gripped the steering wheel, kneading it with numb fingers. His back burned, and his shoulder throbbed. He was flying up the road toward the main highway, but he had no idea where he was headed.

All of his investigating had led him nowhere. No suspect. No motive. No idea who might have Angie or where they might have taken her. He could head to HQ, rally the troops, maybe—

"Linc?"

Hope rose at the sound of Rosa's voice. "Tell me you have something."

"No one has accessed the gate since you guys came in last night, although someone did leave less than half an hour ago. I can see that it opened, but there's no code required to exit."

"Is there a manual override to enter?" Maybe someone had managed to open it without the key code.

"No. It runs on solar, and if it does fail, it requires a key. Only Angie, Jacob and I have one.

I'm checking the cameras now." More key taps, then a slight gasp. "The camera went down over two hours ago."

Pounding his fist against the steering wheel, Linc winced at the pain that rocketed up his arm. This had all been planned. Whoever had grabbed Angie this morning had set themselves up for success and then waited for their opportunity. "Someone came in the back way, but they knew this place well enough to disable the main cameras in order to take the fastest route back to the main road."

"I shouldn't have left."

The regret in Rosa's voice nearly undid him. "Don't beat yourself up. You need to take care of your mother." He'd been present in the cabin, and he'd failed to protect Angie. He'd been so focused on his pain and disappointment that he'd botched Angie's investigation and left her in danger.

Now he had nothing. "Thanks, Rosa. I'll keep you posted." Pressing the end-call button, he stared at the road ahead of him, navigating a curve at breakneck speed.

Now what?

A phone call shattered the silence, and his eyes went to the screen on his radio. *Rosa.* Praying she'd had an epiphany and hadn't accidentally redialed, he punched the button to answer. "Tell me you have something."

"I might." There was a muffled sound as Rosa spoke to someone away from the phone. "I'm getting my mom's phone to make a call. Stay on the line and trust me."

This was killing him. "What are you doing?"

"If you come in one of the back gates, you take the back roads, right? We don't have cameras on those gates, but at the end of the dirt road that leads to the south side of the ranch, there's a widow who lives alone in an older cabin, Selena Raymond. After someone broke into her car, probably tourists, her son installed one of those video doorbells. She complained to me it takes video of every car that drives by on the road, but she's never changed it because she's nosy enough to enjoy the show. Maybe—"

"Maybe Selena Raymond spotted our kidnapper."

"Hang on." There was a muffled conversation. Sparse words came through as Rosa spoke to Selena. "Text me. Quickly, please. Thank you."

She had something. "Talk to me, Rosa." He was nearing the main road and had choices to make.

"She's texting a screenshot to me. It should be here—" A gasp cut her words. "Linc."

"There's something usable, isn't there?" Adrenaline shot through him. There had better be. This was his only chance at finding the woman he loved before it was too late.

"A truck passed just before four this morning, and the floodlights on her house illuminated it perfectly. But, Linc? I recognize the truck."

Chapter Sixteen

Angie shrank against the wall. Surely she wasn't processing what she saw. This had to be wrong. The way her world was spinning, her mind had to be playing tricks on her.

But as he stepped back and her vision focused, she knew.

She tried to swallow, but her mouth was dry. If the shock wasn't so profound, she'd cry out her *why*.

Carter Holbert stared down at her, anger and angst in his expression. He jammed his hands into his dark hair and walked away. "This wasn't how it was supposed to happen." Gripping his head with his hands, Carter paced like a caged animal. "You couldn't just leave. You had to mess everything up."

Nausea gripped her, and Angie tried to breathe in and out through her nose. Adrenaline and panic crashed in her system, derailing her body. She forced herself to breathe slowly and deeply, to focus on anything other than the whirling inside and her inability to run.

Her eyes darted around the room. Recognition washed through her, temporarily dampening the nausea. The room was circular, with a low wall surrounding an open space in the center. Murals in the style of Hopi paintings covered the whitewashed walls. Heavy plastic sheeting hung over the windows. Scaffolding lined one wall and surrounded part of the central opening. The ceiling opened to the floor above, through which she could see the painted roof of the Desert View Watchtower.

Hope bloomed. If they were at the watchtower, tourists would be near the popular attraction. The historic area was—

Was closed.

Her stomach plummeted as though it had been thrown over the railing. Renovations to the Desert View Watchtower Historic District had the place fenced off so that visitors couldn't get near.

Like a horror-movie tagline, there was literally no one to hear her scream.

She leaned her forehead to her knees, her stomach roiling. Lifting her head, she tried to pull herself together before something horrible happened. Angie gulped air, silently begging God not to let her embarrass herself on top of everything else. She regulated her breathing until the nausea passed and cold sweat sheened her skin.

The battle left her weak.

She sagged against the wall and stared at Carter as he walked around the low center wall. "Why?" If she had the strength, she'd spout off more words, but she needed time to recover, to gather her wits and devise a plan.

She started working her wrists and hands, testing how secure the duct tape was. Given the numbness in her fingers, it was tight, which could work to her advantage. After he'd gone to SERE school, where the army taught how to escape and evade assailants, Jacob had taught her some tricks, including how to break duct tape and zip-tie bonds.

It took strength, an opportunity and prayer.

Lord, please let Linc figure this out. Let Carter make a mistake. Anything. Please.

A continual plea wound through her mind as she flexed her wrists and hands against the restraints. Why would Carter do this? What was—

Realization dawned, and her movements slowed. Carter had been digging on the property. He was connected to both Isla and Monica. He'd been the first to mention a serial killer. "You murdered those women?" How? Carter had always been a friend of her family's. Yet all this time—

"What?" Carter whirled on her. Gone was the kind face she'd known. His forehead creased as his eyes narrowed. "I didn't kill those women. Ellis did. Him and his dad and Mac."

The words slapped against her ears, nearly toppling her. Shock shuddered through her. Ellis? Whom she'd hired to work on her ranch? His father, who'd been their first foreman and a cherished confidant of her father's? And Mac, the man who played Santa Claus?

"No." Her brain refused to assimilate the information. It was too far-fetched.

"They didn't actually kill anyone." Carter walked over and squatted before her, just out of reach. He studied her, seeming to weigh what he wanted to say.

Angie stared back, trying to read the truth behind familiar eyes. They were darker than she remembered, hard and cold.

Carter glanced away. "They made those women disappear."

Shaking her head, Angie bit her lower lip as the motion brought another wave of nausea. "They aren't kidnappers. You are."

"I am?" He spat the words, leaning closer, threatening her.

She wouldn't let him know he was terrifying. "I'm here, aren't I?" How could he not see what he'd done?

"And I'm willing to let you go free, if we cut a deal and you keep silent."

He had to know that would never happen.

"Ellis West's father, Javi, was some sort of bleeding-heart hero, I guess." Carter rocked back on his heels, settling in. "Those seven women who disappeared? Trouble, all of them. They were married to good men, or were working for good men. They didn't like to toe the line, so sometimes, they had to be set straight." He shrugged and stood, looking down at her with fire in his eyes.

"Set straight?" Angie's voice trembled, but she didn't falter, even though looking up at Carter made him more menacing. If he wanted, he could kill her with a swift kick.

It wasn't beyond the realm of possibility, not

the way he was talking. She moved her wrists, forcing herself to slowly work the tape. If she moved too quickly, he'd notice and—

Angie swallowed a wave of fear. That was something she didn't want to consider, because the way he talked, those women had been abused, and Carter was supportive of that disgusting behavior from a man. He'd have no problem "setting her straight" if she caused "trouble."

"Those girls went to Javi and Mac. They faked those women's deaths. Made it look like they'd met somebody online who lured them away and killed them, then got them out of town, away from men who took care of them. At the time, nobody knew, but I finally figured it out." He smirked the satisfied smile of someone who'd outsmarted an enemy. "Isla and I had been together for a while when I saw on her cell phone that she'd been talking to somebody else. I asked her who, but she wouldn't tell me, no matter how much I tried to convince her."

Angie didn't want to know what his *convincing* might have looked like. "You were dating Isla? You beat her, didn't you?"

Carter's eyes blazed, and he stalked closer. He hulked over her, his booted feet a mere inch from her hip. "Isla is my business to handle." His fists balled and he stared down at her as though he was debating using them.

Angie looked away. Let him think she'd backed down, and maybe he'd keep talking. The longer he talked, the more time Linc had to find her.

He had to be worried about her.

Her heart wrenched. She should have told him she'd forgiven him and she... She loved him. If he didn't find her or she didn't escape, he'd never know.

Angie started flexing her wrists again. The duct tape slid a bit, and the friction burned her wrists, but she didn't dare stop. "What happened to Ellis?" There was no doubt Carter had killed Ellis, but why?

"When we were doing preliminary excavating about a month ago, I unearthed a bucket. It had some papers in it, and I thought the name was familiar, but I threw it in the truck and forgot about it 'cause we were busy working on this place." He glanced around the tower then turned to her. "Then Isla went missing, and the FBI started asking me questions, throwing names at me. One of them rang a bell, and it all came together. That serial killer a while back.

The papers I found. They were from one of the missing women."

"But you didn't go to the police."

"I decided if I could figure out who'd buried that bucket, or maybe dig up some more of them, I could get some reward money out of the FBI. Couldn't hurt to wait a bit. Those women had been gone for years, so—"

"If you thought Isla was missing, that evidence could have saved her!"

Carter scowled. "It paid off, sort of." His expression darkened. "I looked around the property, but Rosa got suspicious, so I started to wonder… What if I could get you to sell me the ranch? I could search without questions, and once I got what I needed, I've got a developer on the hook who'd buy your place for a fortune. Wants to put up a resort. I'd profit pretty nicely."

Angie was going to be sick. Never had she imagined Carter could be so heinous.

"First I tipped off this little hippy nature organization and told them you wanted to build a resort. Thought they might scare you into selling, maybe be such a nuisance that you'd take off."

"I'm not leaving my family's land." He had to know that.

"It was worth a try. On the day you left for Vegas, Rosa was with her mother, I went to poke around a bit, and I saw Ellis with Monica Huerta. She'd been dating Syd O'Conner, and I thought she was maybe running around on him, but the next day, I saw she was on the news. It got me thinking."

"So you beat Ellis to death?"

He shot her a withering look. "Self-defense. With you gone for a week, I had time to figure out what I wanted to do. I gave it six days, then I called Ellis and told him to meet me at his cabin, that I was going to turn him in to the cops if he didn't talk to me. He had a postcard at the cabin that was in Isla's handwriting, and it was postmarked after she vanished. One I assume was from Monica, too. I guess that's how they let him know they'd gotten to wherever he'd sent them. I could have called the cops, but he'd helped Isla run away from me, and I wanted to know where she was. When it got…heated, I moved the chat over to your barn, since you were out of town and it was more private."

Angie clamped down on her tongue. Carter had killed Ellis while trying to find Isla.

"I can see you thinking." The haughty expression slipped, and fear skittered across Carter's face. "I never meant for Ellis to die, but he wouldn't give me the answers I wanted. By the time he did, the damage was done. He told me about his dad and Mac before he passed out."

"You mean before he died."

Carter shrugged. "I heard your car come back, and I thought...maybe I can scare her into selling. Turns out you don't scare easy." Carter stared at his hands, then shook his head as if to clear it. "Ellis told me that Mac and Javi had hidden the other girls' identification documents around the ranch in case they ever wanted to return to their lives. Mac had a map, but he wouldn't give it to me." Carter walked away and stood at a window as though he could see through the opaque plastic. Likely he was trying to erase the vision of what he'd done to Ellis and to his friend Mac.

While his back was turned, Angie twisted her hands, loosening the duct tape as her wrists burned and chafed. It was loose enough that maybe, if Carter remained distracted, she could slam her hands over her knee and rip the tape.

When Carter turned, she froze.

"I want to buy the ranch and find the rest of those documents. Might be some clues in there to lead those men to the women who did them wrong. If nothing else, it'd let them have proof they were done dirty. I bet they'll pay quite a bit to know their women are still alive." He looked down at her. "You have two choices." He squatted and grabbed her chin. "You can disappear and your ID can show up bloodied on your mama's doorstep. You start a new life, and I buy the ranch since your brother would never tackle trying to run it without you." He squeezed tighter, pinching her skin. "Or…"

There was no need to finish the sentence. Either she walked away from everything she knew…

Or Carter committed one final murder.

"Send someone to Carter Holbert's home and someone else to his business." As sunrise painted the sky in pink and orange streaks, Linc raced toward Tuba City nearly an hour away, where Carter lived and had an office. "Hopefully he's taken her there."

"It's a long shot, Tucker. There's a lot of places

he could be." Thomas was a realist, never one to offer false hope.

"It's all I've got. Coconino County is out searching, and the FBI team is scouring the ranch, but…"

"We'll find her. I know what she means to you. Always have. We won't let you down." Thomas ended the call before Linc could respond.

"Nobody knows what she means to me." He sped on, scanning side roads for evidence of recent activity. Carter Holbert could have driven any number of places on the rim of the canyon, could be deep in the forest…

And he had the woman Linc loved.

How had Thomas known when he hadn't even figured it out for himself until a few hours earlier? Likely because Linc had always loved her, and working with investigators who were both observant and intuitive made secrets tough to keep.

If he'd been intuitive about his own emotions sooner, maybe none of this would be happening now.

He pushed up the two-lane road toward the park exit, determined to reach Tuba City, and—

Wait.

His focus froze on a brown park-service sign illuminated in his headlights. He'd nearly passed it before the words registered, and he slammed on the brakes, the rear of the truck fishtailing before it stopped.

Desert View.

Linc stared at the sign. Desert View Watchtower was the next left.

Carter Holbert was a contractor working on the renovations to the tower. The historic area around the landmark was closed during the restoration. No tourists. No traffic.

But Carter had access.

It was the perfect place to hide.

Gunning the engine, Linc took the left turn and barreled up the road past the parking lot that led to the visitors' center, seeking the construction entrance.

There. What amounted to a small dirt road was flanked by signs that labeled the area a construction zone. The barriers that blocked the entrance had been moved aside, the drag marks evident in the mud.

Killing the engine, Lincoln studied the rough ground. Someone had pulled a vehicle onto the makeshift drive since the rain the previous night. This had to be the place.

He should notify Thomas.

No, he needed proof before he pulled anyone away from their assigned search area. If he was wrong, the detour would be a waste of valuable time.

As the sky brightened, Linc turned off the sound on his phone, shoved it into his pocket, checked his SIG and left his vehicle quietly. He crept toward the tower, keeping to the shadows. If Carter had Angie inside, he had the height advantage and a view of the entire surrounding area.

Linc slowed as the tower came into view. An impressive structure, it rose from the landscape at the edge of the canyon, as though it had been there since the dawn of time, created naturally from the rocks.

The canyon opened before him in a spectacular vista of light and shadow as the sun peeked over the horizon. The sky rioted with pink, orange and purple as night faded to day.

At any other time, the view would steal his breath.

But another sight entirely caught him in the chest. Carter's pickup was parked near the tower's entrance.

Linc ducked into the shadow of a small tree

and texted Thomas. *Found Carter's truck. Desert View Watchtower. Going dark.* Shoving his phone into his pocket, he studied the tower, searching for the best avenue of attack.

Built to look like an oversize Puebloan watchtower rising from rubble at the rim, the century-old structure afforded visitors spectacular views. It also gave Carter a vantage point to watch for their approach.

Construction equipment and supplies dotted the area, and the tower's windows appeared to be sealed off by plastic sheeting for protection during the renovation.

Thanks to that, he might be able to gain access without being seen, though he had no idea where Carter was holding Angie in the building. If they were on one of the upper levels, the open center of the tower would provide Carter a direct view down to the first floor. If Linc could get to the stairs, it would be possible to make his way up hidden by the half wall that lined the stairs as they twisted around the exterior walls of the building.

If only he could be invisible.

Linc crept to the truck and cleared the vehicle before moving cautiously toward the tower's heavy wooden door. A padlock was lying on the ground, useless to anyone on the inside.

SIG at the ready, Linc eased the door open inch by inch, braced for attack.

When no assault came, he slipped inside and pressed his back to the wall. The ground floor was empty, the gift shop sheeted in plastic to protect against the dust of construction.

"What's your decision?" A deep voice rumbled from above, close to the southwest wall.

Muscles pulsing with stress and pain, Linc eased toward the stairs. He crouched behind the low wall on the interior of the stairs, trying to gauge if Carter was the lone assailant and praying the question had been addressed to Angie.

Hunched low, Linc crept up, one slow, nightmarish step at a time.

"I won't let my family think I'm dead." Angie's voice, strong and defiant, wafted down from the opening in the floor.

Linc's muscles relaxed so quickly, they nearly puddled him to the stairs. She was alive.

For the moment.

"They can *think* you're dead, or you can actually *be* dead." Impatience laced Carter's words, as though Angie had been stalling for time.

Good job. She had to have known he'd come for her, that somehow he'd find her.

He had to move quickly if he was going to save her. Carter sounded as though he was done waiting.

Near the top of the stairs, Linc stopped, wary of exposing his position. He stretched his body out over the last three steps, his head nearly on the floor, and peered around the base of the wall that separated the stairs from the circular second floor.

In the center of the room, scaffolding stood on one side of the low retaining wall around the open center of the building. At the one-o'clock position, Angie sat on the floor, her face white with fear.

Linc drew back. Where was Carter?

He scanned the visible area, seeing nothing. He should wait for backup, but time wasn't on his side. If Angie died while he was within feet of her—

Linc forced himself to focus. That kind of thinking would only paralyze him. He shook it away, then eased to the top of the stairs and crouched, ready to round the corner and spring, although he was blind to Carter's whereabouts.

Weapon drawn, he rose, prepared to shout Carter's name.

The plastic sheeting rustled, and Carter leaped from the blind spot behind the scaffolding, driving Linc backward to the floor.

Chapter Seventeen

"Linc!"

Angie gasped as Carter slammed Linc to the floor. Linc's gun clattered to the ground and skittered beneath the scaffolding several feet away.

Carter raised a fist to pound Linc's head, but Linc rolled onto his shoulder.

Carter's knuckles slammed the ground. He roared in pain as Linc shoved him away and scrambled unsteadily to his feet, his face pale and his expression tight.

The fall had likely caused him further injury. How much more could his spine take? A fight like this was the very thing his doctor had warned him about.

She had to do something.

As Carter rose to one knee, Linc swung and caught him in the chin.

Carter dove for Linc's knees, forcing him onto his lower back.

She couldn't stand by any longer. Carter could paralyze Linc before her eyes.

Lifting her hands, Angie pulled her palms as far apart as the loosened duct tape would allow and slammed them over her bent knee.

Her first blow landed to one side, the impact firing pain into her left wrist.

Carter landed another punch and scrambled across the floor toward Linc's pistol as Linc appeared to shake off more pain. He grabbed Carter's ankle and pulled, bracing against the wall. "Angie! Get out!"

There was no way she was leaving him. She ignored the pain in her injured wrist and brought her hands down again. This time, her knee drove between her palms and ripped the duct tape. She twisted and pulled, her wrists burning, until the weakened bonds tore free. She moved quickly to unwrap her ankles.

Her left hand screamed with pain and the skin was already turning blue. Could she save Linc if she'd fractured her wrist trying to free herself?

Carter rolled and kicked upward, but Linc dodged and avoided a boot heel to the face.

He threw himself over Carter's legs and tried to stop the man from getting closer to the gun.

The last of the duct tape pulled free, and Angie leaped to her feet. She raced around the low central wall, away from the men, hoping to come around on the other side of the circular room to grab the pistol before Carter could reach it.

Carter struggled to his feet.

Linc rose with him, but he moved much slower.

It was the advantage Carter needed. He shoved Linc toward the thigh-high central wall.

Linc stumbled. The top of his body pitched over the wall.

"Carter!" Angie screamed the man's name, hoping to distract him. She reached the gun and scooped it from the ground, straightening as she raised the weapon.

It was too late.

As he fell, Linc flung his arm out and wrapped his elbow around the scaffolding. He hung on, dangling two stories above the ground.

A fall wouldn't kill him, but given his injuries, it could paralyze him.

Carter lunged forward to pry Linc from the scaffolding.

Angie steadied the pistol. "Back away, Carter, or I'll pull the trigger."

This time, Carter seemed to hear her. He froze, arms extended toward Linc as though suspended between a decision about finishing off his opponent or taking a bullet if he tried.

Linc's face was white with pain as he attempted to throw his leg over the wall.

The scaffolding shifted, off balance due to his added weight, and threatened to topple over the edge with him. He froze, and his gaze pierced Angie's. "Get out."

She shook her head. If she knew Linc, he hadn't rushed in here alone. He'd called for backup, and help was on the way. All she had to do was keep Carter at bay until they arrived.

Carter held his hands away from his sides, his expression neutral. "Angie, I know you. You wouldn't shoot me."

She ground her teeth together. "And I *thought* I knew you." Carter had already killed once and attempted to kill a second time. He had nothing to lose. She wasn't about to let him add Linc to the list.

"Angie, don't." Linc's voice was strained. He reached for the wall, but the scaffolding creaked and swayed.

Carter eased closer to Linc. "Put the gun down." His arm rose slightly, moving toward the metal frame. "Put it down or I shove the scaffolding and your boyfriend over the edge."

Angie refused to move. If she put the gun down, Carter would kill them both.

Quick as a striking snake, Carter lunged.

Angie fired.

Carter jerked. He stopped, stumbled toward her, then dropped to his knees, staring down at his right side. Blood seeped through his shirt in a quickly spreading stain. He lifted his gaze to hers, eyes wide with panic and disbelief.

She couldn't believe she'd pulled the trigger, either, but there wasn't time to consider her actions.

Shoving the pistol into her waistband, she ran the long way around to avoid Carter and grabbed the scaffolding, keeping one eye on Linc and one on Carter. "I'll hold the scaffolding. You get over the edge." She leaned back with all of her weight, counterbalancing his.

To her left, Carter stirred. If he charged, there would be nothing she could do. Letting go would plunge Linc to his death. Ignoring Carter could allow him to shove them both over the edge.

She held on tight.

Linc managed to pull himself closer to the circular balcony, then he threw his chest over the low wall.

Releasing the scaffolding, Angie helped him the rest of the way. When he was on solid ground, she turned to Carter.

He'd stood, one hand braced on the wall and the other pressed to his side over the wound. "You should have killed me."

He sprang before she could reach for the pistol.

"Stop! Federal agents!" Multiple voices rang out from the stairs.

Angie whirled.

Carter stumbled, then froze.

Thomas approached, followed up the stairs by several other agents.

Every ounce of breath left her.

It was over.

Angie dropped to her knees beside Lincoln, resting her forehead against his shoulder as men and women swarmed into the room.

Linc dropped his head against the wall, but he didn't reach for her.

Somehow, she'd assumed he'd pull her close or check to see if she was okay.

Instead, he was still and silent.

She backed away and took his cheeks in her hands. She'd promised herself if she saw him again, she'd tell him the truth about her feelings. It didn't matter the place was swarming with law enforcement. It didn't matter they were seconds removed from certain death.

All that mattered was they'd survived, and she wouldn't go another moment without saying what was in her heart before the chance was ripped away again. "Linc, I—"

"No." He looked past her. Grasping her wrists, he pulled her hands from his face. "Angie, please." His jaw was set. His eyes were cold. "Don't."

"I know we've been—"

"Don't." The word was jagged. As though his body was encased in concrete, Linc braced himself against the wall and stood. He met Thomas a few feet away, said something to him, then made his way to the stairs and slowly disappeared down them as Thomas approached her, his expression grim.

They'd been saved. She was safe. Lincoln should be relieved.

They should be celebrating one another.

Instead, he was walking away.

★ ★ ★

He was sick and tired of his stupid apartment in employee housing. His stupid physical therapy. His stupid everything.

Linc tossed a frozen meat-loaf dinner into the microwave and slammed the door. Since he'd started daily PT two weeks earlier, the exercises and the pain ate his energy and his will to do anything more than exist.

At least he seemed to be physically improving. They might even let him return to limited duty behind a desk eventually. The blow he'd taken in the watchtower, when Carter had knocked him onto his back, had done additional damage to his spine.

It had been the very thing his doc had warned him about.

It wasn't like he went toe-to-toe with bad guys every day, or even every year, but if it happened again—

The microwave beeped as someone knocked on his door.

Linc froze in the kitchenette. If he was super still, maybe they'd go away.

It could be Angie. She'd called him until he'd blocked her number. Had come to see him the first couple of days after his overnight stay in the hospital.

He hadn't acknowledged her knock then, but maybe she'd worked up the courage to try again.

Jacob had reached out when he returned from Europe, but Linc had ignored her brother as well. He wasn't ready to answer questions.

His visitor knocked louder. "Tucker, I know you're home. I heard the microwave. Open up, or I'll claim probable cause and bust in."

Thomas.

Linc made his way to the door, his back and neck throbbing a reminder that the damage might be permanent.

Pulling the door open, he blocked the entrance and glared at his teammate. "Make it quick, I'm about to eat."

Thomas smirked. "Aren't you just a brilliant burst of sunshine."

"What do you want?" If Thomas was looking for hospitality, he wasn't going to find it here. "You want happy people, go hang out with tourists."

"I brought you a wake-up call." Thomas stepped aside and someone moved in front of him.

Linc wanted to slam the door.

Jacob Garcia squeezed past him into the apartment, invading Lincoln's space. "I figured you weren't talking to anyone with the last name Garcia, so I had Thomas run interference." The words were hard, and his closest friend's face was a thundercloud.

Tough to determine if it was because Linc had been ignoring Jacob, or because he was ignoring Jacob's sister.

Thomas stepped in, shut the door behind him and made himself comfortable on the couch while Jacob stood in the center of the living room, arms folded over his chest. He looked ready for a fight.

Lincoln would give him one. He matched Jacob's posture, though crossing his arms caused him pain. "Whatever happens between me and your sister is between me and her." Although not talking to her was costing him everything. He thought about her all day and through the dark nights.

There was no denying he loved her, but love changed nothing. It was better for her future if he stayed away. Saddling her with a ticking time bomb of medical issues like himself wouldn't be fair. She deserved a whole man.

As Thomas watched from the couch like a spectator at a boxing match, Jacob tilted his head. "This is about you, *battle buddy*." He hit those last two words with heavy sarcasm. Jacob and Linc had trained together and been to war together, carrying one another through situations most people wouldn't see in their nightmares.

The term took the starch out of Linc's fight. He looked toward the microwave, where his meat loaf was likely congealing into a gelatinous blob.

Maybe Jacob had a point. Linc had been stewing in his pain, refusing to reach out for help. Bad things happened when a man got into his own head, when pride kept him isolated.

He'd lobbed that exact lecture like a grenade one night when Jacob had turned his face to the wall and declared his life was over, that he was a broken man who'd never fully live, who couldn't have a child and might as well put his dreams out to pasture.

Jacob exhaled loudly. "You're hearing your own words in your head right now, aren't you?"

"It's annoying when you think you can read my mind."

"We've been through enough together that I've earned the right."

Linc stared down the friend who was closer than a brother. For the first time in weeks, something besides self-pity and anger wound through him. Maybe it was friendship. Maybe it was hope.

Jacob leaned against the back of the couch. "I remember being in so much pain I couldn't remember my own name. Some nights I thought death would be preferable to the pain. I knew I was done with the army. I thought I'd never function again."

Linc couldn't look at him or at Thomas, who watched silently. "I remember." There had been moments he'd been afraid his friend would never recover. That no matter how much he and Angie tried to pour hope into Jacob, he'd wither away.

Today Jacob was nearly as strong as he'd been before the explosion. He worked on Linc's investigative team and, in a twist no one saw coming, was married with a child of his own.

"All of those things I'd assumed I'd lost, God restored." Jacob sniffed. "Not to be harsh, man, but you're not nearly as bad off as I was."

Lincoln winced. This was true.

"Dude, it's time to stop feeling sorry for yourself." Jacob leaned forward slightly. "And, yeah, it's time to stop torturing my sister."

He'd known this was coming. "You have no idea."

From the couch, Thomas finally spoke. "Clue us in."

Anger rose, but Linc swallowed it. The last thing he needed was an argument when he wanted understanding. "In the heat of battle, I couldn't save Angie. *She* had to rescue *me*."

"So your male ego is bruised?" Dropping his hands to his sides, Jacob straightened. "You're going to hurt Angie because your *pride* is wounded?"

"No." The word fired out like a bullet. "You don't understand. I could be an invalid someday. A car wreck or a fight with a suspect could paralyze me. No offense, Jacob, but I took care of you right beside Angie. It was tough, physically and emotionally. I won't put her through that."

"So unless you're perfect, you won't marry her?"

Linc's head jerked. Pain fired down his spine. "Who mentioned marriage?" Certainly not Angie. She didn't jump the gun that way.

"I did." Thomas stood. "You're in love with

her. She's in love with you. You two handle each other quite well."

"None of us are idiots." Jacob had the audacity to chuckle. "You've been in love with my sister for years."

"I—"

"Don't even start." Jacob shook his head, a half smile on his face. "Remember how you stood in my barn and told me the whole platoon knew I was in love with Ivy? They all felt like she was their little sister and took her side when I didn't fight for her?"

Yeah, he could vividly remember thinking Jacob was an idiot for not confessing his love to the woman he was clearly meant to be with. "How much of my advice are you going to throw in my face today?"

"All of it." Jacob arched an eyebrow and lowered his voice. "Because this time I really am the brother, and I really do take her side."

Emotion shoved at the back of Linc's throat. He loved Angie and had for nearly as long as he'd known her. "I don't want to hurt her." Great. He'd resorted to whining.

"Life can be painful, Tucker." Thomas fully joined the conversation. "Marriage isn't easy.

You stand in front of God and everybody, and promise to love each other no matter what. 'In sickness and in health' isn't something to be taken lightly, I get it, but any of us could go down anytime to anything. Car wreck. Heart attack. Gunshot. Life is risky. You take the risk and love someone you might lose. You take the risk they could lose you. *Or* you live alone and bitter in a government apartment, eating smelly frozen dinners and binge-watching car shows."

"You're a pain in the rear when you get like that." Jacob wasn't pulling punches. "You're not special. Love is a risk for everyone, not just for you and Angie. Maybe you'll work a desk job for the rest of your life. Maybe you'll get back into the canyon someday. Maybe a meteor will hit you in the head five minutes from now. Nobody knows, but you trust God and go for it. You promise to love no matter what. You make that promise *because* you don't know what's going to happen. If we knew what was going to happen, we wouldn't have to trust God."

That one hurt. Linc liked to think he was a

guy who put his faith in God, but he sure wasn't acting like it.

He looked from his microwave to his team-mates.

From his past to his future.

Maybe it was time to start.

Chapter Eighteen

The sky was streaked with feathery cirrus clouds that glowed like living fire as the sun sank toward the horizon. Sunset on the ranch felt sacred. The light was different here, where the land ran dotted with trees to the canyon's rim.

If only the peace here could heal her broken places.

Angie had opened up, let go of control and allowed herself to feel, and all she'd earned was pain.

Stepping down into the foundation of what would someday be a dormitory, she sat on the edge and braced her feet against the hard earth, staring at the hole where they'd found the original bucket. When Mac had awakened in the hospital, the FBI had been waiting with questions. While Angie hadn't been privileged to all of the information from that interview, he had clearly given them a list of coordinates for every bucket on the ranch. The agents had collected them without telling her anything, but she was smart enough to figure out that their actions confirmed what Carter had suspected. The women who were supposedly murdered by a serial killer had actually vanished of their own accord. Given that they'd left voluntarily, locating them would probably not be a priority.

It was likely that none of them wanted to be found anyway.

When news broke of Carter's arrest, Isla Blake came out of hiding in Texas. The rest of the women would probably stay where they were. Their abusers were still a threat.

It was heartbreaking to think a person could be so frightened of a loved one that they were willing to disappear, yet it had happened over and over.

With Carter in jail, Angie would have to restart the bidding process, which delayed the new research center. It might give her time to line up financing, though that had taken a turn as well.

Owen had called a few days earlier. Her ex had apologized and had offered to align his foundation with her research center, opening a world of new funding.

While the apology settled more easily than Angie had thought it would, the situation would take prayer. While she'd managed to forgive him, forgetting would be difficult. She'd asked him to give her time. Maybe she could work with him, maybe not. The answer was up to God.

So was her relationship with Lincoln.

The raw space in her heart had his name etched into it. Since he'd walked away in the tower, it was as though he'd vanished. Her calls went straight to voice mail. Her knocks on his door went unanswered.

They were both safe, yet he'd ghosted her. No updates. No explanations.

Yep, she'd opened her heart and it hurt worse than any pain Owen had ever inflicted.

Angie frowned. It wasn't fair, yet she was determined not to close herself off. God had built her to be a whole person, not one who denied her feelings and sabotaged her joy. As much as it hurt, she was going to let the feelings run their course.

"Is this a private sunset viewing or can anybody join?"

Angie jerked around and jumped to her feet, nearly stumbling backward into the excavated foundation.

Linc stood not six feet away, his hands in his pockets, his brown hair tousled by the breeze.

Her heart pumped sparks to her fingers and burned through her voice. Part of her had honestly started to believe she'd never see him again.

Now here he was.

All she could do was stare as emotion pulsed behind her eyes. Was she really going to cry?

Turning away from him, she faced the west, where the day was about to melt into night.

The next thing she knew, he was at her side, close enough to feel his warmth. He said nothing, merely watched the sun kiss the horizon as the sky roared with vibrant color.

After two weeks of silence, his presence was overwhelming. "Why are you here?" She looked at him from the corner of her eye, scared to fully face him for fear of igniting something in her heart she no longer wanted to feel if he was going to abandon her.

Linc inhaled slowly, as though his words needed oxygen to bring them to life. He watched her instead of the sky. "Honestly?"

"That would be nice."

He laid a hand on her shoulder and turned her toward him, pinning her gaze with his blue eyes. "I don't want to make the same mistake twice."

She was going to cry. There was no way around it. Her throat ached and her eyes burned. The breeze blew a wisp of hair across her face, but she couldn't swipe it away. She was scared to move, scared he'd spook like a wild horse. She was on the edge of having what her heart had always dreamed of, and she was terrified her instincts were wrong.

Linc's expression softened as his gaze roamed her face. "I walked away once because I was afraid I'd hurt you if I stayed, and I recently realized I'm doing the same thing again." He swept his index finger across her cheek, tucking the errant wisp of hair behind her ear. His eyes followed the motion as his fingers trailed lightly from her ear to the dip between her shoulder and her neck, making her skin tingle. "I was wrong both times."

Her eyes closed and she bit her bottom lip to keep the tears in check.

"Hey." He slipped his fingers to her chin and

tilted her head. "I want you looking at me when I say the next part."

Opening her eyes allowed the tears to gather, but they didn't fall. She watched, waiting for him to speak, praying the words would be what she wanted to hear.

He looked down at her with a kind of wonder. "I think we've proven we can get through anything together." His voice was husky. "I want to go through it all together, from here, right on until we both breathe our last. Looking out for each other. Loving each other." He tilted his head, and the conviction in his expression nearly undid her. "I do love you, and I don't know what's going to happen next, but I truly, more than anything I've ever wanted in my life, want to do forever with you."

He was killing her, but he was doing it in the best of ways. Her heart was going to wreck itself any second.

If she went out right now, at least she'd be with him. She swallowed, trying to will her voice into existence. "I really, truly, more than anything in my life, want to do forever with you, too."

He smiled in a way she hadn't seen in years. When she slipped her arms around his waist, he drew her closer, running his fingers into her hair, meeting her halfway in the kiss they should have shared the first time. One that gave instead of took. One that promised love and honor and more... Walking through the good and the bad together... Forever.

Romantic Suspense

Danger. Passion. Drama.

Available Next Month

A Colton Kidnapping Justine Davis
Hotshot's Dangerous Liaison Lisa Childs

Stalker In The Storm Carla Cassidy
Undercover Heist Rachel Astor

LOVE INSPIRED

Chasing Justice Valerie Hansen
Searching For Evidence Carol J. Post

Larger Print

LOVE INSPIRED

Shielding The Innocent Target Terri Reed
Kidnapped In Montana Sharon Dunn

Larger Print

LOVE INSPIRED

In Need Of Protection Jill Elizabeth Nelson
Hidden Mountain Secrets Kerry Johnson

Larger Print

brand new stories each month

Romantic **Suspense**

Danger. Passion. Drama.

MILLS & BOON

Keep reading for an excerpt of a new title
from the Intrigue series,
CONARD COUNTY: MURDEROUS INTENT
by Rachel Lee

Prologue

Krystal Metcalfe loved to sit on the porch of her small cabin in the mornings, especially when the weather was exceptionally pleasant. With a fresh cup of coffee and its delightful aroma mixing with those of the forest around, she found internal peace and calm here.

Across a bubbling creek that ran before her porch, her morning view included the old Healey house. Abandoned about twenty years ago, it had been steadily sinking into decline. The roof sagged, wood planks had been silvered by the years and there was little left that looked safe or even useful. Krystal had always anticipated the day when the forest would reclaim it.

Then came the morning when a motor home pulled up beside the crumbling house and a large man climbed out. He spent some time investigating the old structure, inside and out. Maybe hunting for anything he could reclaim? Would that be theft at this point?

She lingered, watching with mild curiosity but little concern. At some level she had always supposed that someone would express interest in the Healey land itself. It wasn't easy anymore to find private land on the edge of US Forest, and eventually the "grandfathering" that had left the Healey family their ownership would end because of lack of occupancy. Regardless, it wasn't exactly a large piece of land, unlikely to be useful to most, and the Forest Service would let it return to nature.

Less of that house meant more of the forest devouring the eyesore. And at least the bubbling of the creek passing through the canyon swallowed most of the sounds that might be coming from that direction now that the man was there. And it sure looked like he might be helping the destruction of that eyesore.

But then came another morning when she stepped out with her coffee and saw a group of people, maybe a dozen, camped around the ramshackle house. That's when things started to become noisy despite the sound baffling provided by the creek.

A truck full of lumber managed to make its way up the remaining ruined road on that side of the creek and dumped a load that caused Krystal to gasp. Rebuilding? Building bigger?

What kind of eyesore would she have to face? Her view from this porch was her favorite. Her other windows and doors didn't include the creek. And all those people buzzing around provided an annoying level of activity that would distract her.

Then came the ultimate insult: a generator fired up and drowned any peaceful sound that remained, the wind in the trees and the creek both.

That did it. Maybe these people were squatters who could be driven away. She certainly doubted she'd be able to write at all with that roaring generator. Her cabin was far from soundproofed.

After setting her coffee mug on the railing, she headed for the stepping stones that crossed the creek. For generations they'd been a path between two friendly families until the Healeys had departed. As Krystal crossed, she sensed people pulling back into the woods. Creepy. Maybe she ought to reconsider this trip across the creek. But her backbone stiffened. It usually did.

She walked around the house, now smelling of freshly cut wood, sure she'd have to find *someone*.

Then she found the man around the back corner. Since she was determined not to begin this encounter by yelling at the guy, she waited impatiently until he turned and saw her. He leaned over, turning the generator to a lower level, then simply looked at her.

He wore old jeans and a long-sleeved gray work shirt. A pair of safety goggles rode the top of his head. A dust mask hung around his neck. Workmanlike, which only made her uneasier.

Then she noticed more. God, he was gorgeous. Tall, large, broad-shouldered. A rugged, angular face with turquoise eyes that seemed to pierce the green shade of the trees. The forest's shadow hid the creek that still danced and sparkled in revealed sunlight behind her.

This area was a green cavern. One she quite liked.

Finally he spoke, clearly reluctant to do so. "Yes?"

"I'm Krystal Metcalfe. I live in the house across the creek."

One brief nod. His face remained like granite. Then slowly he said, "Josh Healey."

An alarm sounded in her mind. Then recognition made her heart hammer because this might be truly bad news. "This is Healey property, isn't it?" Of course it was. Not a bright question from her.

A short nod.

"Are you going to renovate this place?"

"Yes."

God, this was going to be like pulling teeth, she thought irritably. "I hope you're not planning to cut down many trees."

"No."

Stymied, as it became clear this man had no intention of beginning any conversation, even one as casual as talking about the weather, she glared. "Okay, then. Just take care of the forest."

She turned sharply on her heel without another word and made her way across the stepping stones to her own property. Maybe she should start drinking her morning coffee on the front porch of her house on the other side from the creek.

She was certainly going to have to go down to Conard City to buy a pair of ear protectors or go mad trying to do her own work when that generator once again revved up.

Gah!

JOSH HEALEY HAD watched Krystal Metcalfe coming round the corner of his new building. Trouble? She sure seemed to be looking for it.

She was cute, pretty, her blue eyes as bright as the summer sky overhead. But he didn't care about that.

What he cared about were his troops, men and women who were escaping a world that PTSD and war had ripped from them. People who needed to be left alone to find balance within themselves and with group therapy. Josh, a psychologist, had brought them here for that solitude.

Now he had that neighbor trying to poke her nose into his business. Not good. He knew how people reacted to the mere idea of vets with PTSD, their beliefs that these people were unpredictable and violent.

But he had more than a dozen soldiers to protect and he was determined to do so. If that woman became a problem, he'd find a way to shut her down.

It was *his* land after all.

Subscribe and fall in love with a Mills & Boon series today!

You'll be among the first to read stories delivered to your door monthly and enjoy great savings.

WE
SIMPLY
LOVE
ROMANCE

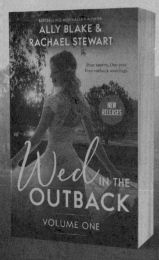 

MILLS & BOON